Joyce Holms was born an~~~~~~~~~~~~~~~~~~~~~~~~~. She has worked in a range of jobs, from teaching window-dressing and managing a hotel on the Island of Arran to working for an Edinburgh detective agency and running a B&B establishment in the Highlands. She lives in Edinburgh and Killin, and her interests include hillwalking and garden design. She is married with two grown-up children.

Joyce Holms's first crime novel, PAYMENT DEFERRED, is also available from Headline, and was warmly praised:

'Engaging and entertaining, it builds to a spectacular climax . . . Deft, daft and definitely delicious'
Val McDermid, *Manchester Evening News*

'Cleverly-plotted . . . the characters are well-drawn and the story moves along at an enjoyably brisk pace'
Susanna Yager, *Sunday Telegraph*

'A good story, light-hearted, full of fascinating characters, and it makes me look forward to more of the exploits of Fizz and Buchanan'   *Birmingham Post*

'A sparkling, sassy debut'   *Crime Time*

Also by Joyce Holms

Payment Deferred

Foreign Body

Joyce Holms

HEADLINE

First published in 1997
by HEADLINE BOOK PUBLISHING

First published in paperback in 1998
by HEADLINE BOOK PUBLISHING

10 9 8 7 6 5 4 3 2 1

ISBN 0 7472 5561 X

Typeset by
Letterpart Limited, Reigate, Surrey

Printed and bound in Great Britain by
Clays Ltd, St Ives plc

HEADLINE BOOK PUBLISHING
A division of Hodder Headline PLC
338 Euston Road
London NW1 3BH

Always for John

Thanks to Stirling Stewart, Private Investigators and the legal firm of Jardines, North Bridge, Edinburgh

Prologue

Get him out. Quick! Got to move fast. Not much blood. At the moment of death the heart stops pumping it out. Must have read that somewhere. Wrap something round his head in case it leaves a trail. Use his T-shirt. You can burn it later with the rest of his clothes. Right, come on, you bastard. Jesus, what a weight! You're never going to drag him all that way! No chance. A rope. Quick, get a rope round him ... over the chest and under the shoulders ... right ... right, now you can drag him. That's better. Quick. Quick now. Got to move fast. Got to move fast. Got to move move move. Damn you to hell, get out of that! You couldn't be more of a bloody hindrance if you were still alive! Come on, come ON! This isn't working. It's further than you thought. He's too heavy. Come ON, damn you! Keep going. Just to the gully. This'll have to do ... no. Too open. Too near the track. Anyone coming down off the ridge ... no. Got to keep going. Over there ... the scree slope. Climbers avoid that bit like the plague. Out of sight from the track ... plenty of loose gravel ... Couldn't get better. Come on, you bastard, move can't you! Dear God, help me now and I'll never ask you for anything again as long as I live. Keep going. Keep going. This is danger- ous ... your legs trembling like that ... one false step and ... Right, you bastard, you can lie there till I find a hole for you. What time is it? God! Get a move on. Get a move on. Behind

1

these rocks? No way. Might be spotted from up there. What's that? This'll do. Long enough. Could be deeper, but . . . Quick. Quick. Let's have you then. God, he's heavy. Clothes. Get them off. Hurry. Hurry. Damn, where did that button go? Can't leave anything . . . there, in the hole! Slow down, you're making mistakes. Think what you're doing. Keep your head. Got to hurry, though. Move fast: think slow. Everything wrapped up in the trousers. No jewellery. No birthmarks. Look again. Make sure. Right. In you go, sonny boy! God . . . dear God . . . those eyes! Don't look at his eyes. Got to get him covered over. Hurry! Rocks . . . no, bigger than that. This one. Can't . . . yes you can! Roll it. Get it to the edge. This one for his face. Oh God! That was bones smashing! Don't think about the noise. Get another. And another. And another. Hurry. Hurry. Smaller ones'll do now. Just get him covered. Get him covered. What's the time? Quick. You can still do it. Is he covered? Will that do? Can he be seen from above? Someone coming down the scree slope might just . . . no. Who'd come down there when the safe descent's so near? Leave it like that and get out of here. Get the clothes. Check the ground around the hole. Nothing. Footprint in that patch of snow. Scrape it away. Nothing else? Right, let's go. Got to calm down. Start to get a grip. Breathe deeply. Act normal. Put it behind you. Forget it ever happened. It never happened. It never happened. It . . . never . . . happened. Right.

The way Buchanan saw it, there were three options open to him when he got out of hospital: (1) he could spend his two weeks' mandatory rest and recuperation alone in his wee flat in Edinburgh; (2) he could retire to the parental home for a fortnight and suffer his mother's anxious cosseting twenty-four hours a day; or (3) he could fly somewhere hot, find a quiet hotel with a good chef, and pass the time by catching up on his reading.

2

Option one turned out to be a nonstarter. Within hours of arriving home he found himself pacing from lounge to bedroom and back again, unable to settle to anything. He felt perfectly fit but, with his surgeon's admonition to 'take things easy' still weighing on him like a ball and chain, he was acutely aware of the empty space in his guts where his gall bladder used to be. By four o'clock he had already scanned and spurned all the books he had been keeping for a rainy day so when the doorbell rang it was like music to his ears.

'Hi,' said Fizz, sparing him barely a glance as she marched past him into the lounge. 'You look like you've been recently exhumed.'

He shut the door and caught up with her as she collapsed on to the couch. 'Well, thank you, Fizz. You really know how to cheer a guy up, you know that?'

'It's a gift,' she said modestly. 'You've either got it or you haven't. Look what I brought you – black grapes.' She dropped a paper bag on the coffee table and helped herself to a large sprig. 'They're £1.65 a pound. I hope you appreciate what good friends you have.'

'Fizz, you're a saint. Have one yourself if you like.'

'Well, if you insist,' she said with her mouth full. 'So, how've you been?'

'Never better,' Buchanan told her. He could recognise a rhetorical question when he heard one and besides, if Fizz ever showed a genuine interest in his health it would be because she was planning on selling his liver on Harley Street. 'How are things at the office?'

'Just fine. Your daddy is having a wonderful time being monarch of all he surveys, Alan has been doing court work all week, and your indispensable Beatrice has been lighting candles to the patron saint of gall bladders for your speedy return to health.'

She unlaced her Docs and kicked them off, curling her legs up on the couch. A shaft of sunlight angled through the window behind her and lit her hair like a golden – and seriously misplaced – halo. There was something about her childish face and trusting eyes that reminded Buchanan of a Botticelli cherub. Except that a Botticelli cherub had never looked quite so innocent.

'So.' She chose another sprig of grapes. 'What are you planning to do with the next fortnight? You'll be stir-crazy in no time if you stay here on your own.'

'Oh, I don't know,' Buchanan said perversely. 'I expect a few of my pals will drop round in the evenings.'

'But, what will you find to keep you occupied through the day?'

He indicated the pile of books on the floor. 'I thought I'd get started on all the books I buy and never get time to read, but I just can't settle to them. To tell you the truth, reading during the day – I don't know why, but it just seems so decadent.'

'Live a little.' Fizz confined a smile to one corner of her mouth. 'It's not a sin as long as you don't enjoy it.'

'Then there's my mother. When I got back she was here waiting for me with a freezer load of egg custards and nourishing broths and she's been on the phone twice this afternoon to check if I'm still alive. If I turn my back on her for a second she'll be over here soothing my fevered brow and sitting up all night by my sickbed.'

'You have to get away before you start talking back to the television,' Fizz said, with a finality that brooked no further discussion on the matter. 'I don't know why you haven't fixed up something already.'

He sighed and looked out the window. The thought of making travel arrangements and queuing at airports was profoundly oppressive. 'I don't know. Maybe I'll see if I can get a last-minute flight to Marbella, or some place else with golf courses.'

'Not abroad, Buchanan, for heaven's sake!' She shook her head irritably and two wispy curls sprang loose from the elastic band at the back of her neck and dangled in front of her ear. 'What if your surgery scar starts to leak or you get some other sort of complication? You don't want to be too far away from your own doctor.'

Buchanan supposed not. There was also the possibility that his father, who had not taken sole charge of their law partnership for years, might need his opinion. Perhaps some place within a couple of hours' driving distance might be more practical. 'A nice quiet fishing inn maybe,' he mused aloud.

Fizz appeared to be counting the remaining grapes, which wouldn't have strained the mathematical capabilities of a five-year-old, but restricted herself, with an air of martyrdom, to a small loose one. 'All the good fishing inns will be booked up by this time and you'll get no peace at all in a crap one. Your bedroom will either be right above the lounge where you'll hear them laughing and swilling whisky half the night, or next door to the loo with the plumbing running along the wall behind your headboard.'

She appeared to give her mind to the problem for a moment, staring blankly at the kitchen door and picking at a scrap of grape skin that was stuck in her front teeth. Buchanan felt, vaguely, that he would prefer her not to interest herself in the matter but was too listless to dissuade her.

'What you want,' she decided, 'is self-catering accommodation where you can—'

'No, not self-catering—' Buchanan started to say but she waved an impatient hand at him.

'I know, I know. You want to be waited on hand and foot in

5

the manner to which you have become accustomed, but there are such things as restaurants, you know. There are some really nice places up in Perthshire, around Am Bealach where my grampa lives.'

Buchanan had heard her speak quite a lot recently about her grampa's farm and he had to admit that his interest had been stirred. There had been mention of salmon fishing, real ale, and first-rate golf courses, and of course the scenic beauty of Perthshire was legendary. If it weren't for all the hassle of locating the right sort of accommodation, he could see himself passing a couple of weeks there quite happily.

'I don't suppose you know of any suitable place offhand?' he said, being fairly sure that she wouldn't.

'No. I don't think so.' She wrinkled her brow in thought and absently ate a few more grapes. 'I haven't lived in Am Bealach for years, you know, and when I visit Grampa it's never for more than a couple of days at a time. I can think of a few nice hotels but none of them is what you need right now.'

'Oh well—' Buchanan started to say, preparatory to changing the subject, but she started to speak at the same instant.

'Actually,' she was saying apologetically, 'Grampa has a sweet little cottage on the farm which he lets in the summer, but it's certain to be taken already. Which, now that I think about it, is a complete bummer because it's exactly what you want. Auntie Duff – Grampa's second wife – is a fantastic cook and you could eat in the farmhouse. Of course, there's the inn at the end of the farm road, which is Egon Ronay recommended, but it's scarcely worthwhile walking up to it. And, with free salmon fishing right on the doorstep—' She pressed her lips together with visible annoyance. 'All of which is purely academic at this time of year. Shit. If only we'd thought of it sooner.'

Buchanan's disappointment was not undiluted because he

had a deep-rooted reluctance to getting too involved with Fizz. It was only seven months since she had last taken a close interest in his affairs and he was still a little traumatised. Admittedly, she wouldn't be around the place while he was there. She would be tied up here in Edinburgh for the next few weeks, not only because she had a part-time job in Buchanan's practice, but because her end-of-term Law exams were coming up and he knew she didn't dare miss a lecture.

'Well, maybe something else will crop up,' he said, but she wouldn't let it go.

'I'm just so annoyed with myself for not thinking to suggest it to you earlier.' She sat up and swung her feet to the floor. 'Well, I suppose there's no harm in phoning anyway. Not that there's a hope in hell.'

Before Buchanan knew what she was about she had grabbed the receiver and was tapping out the number with the rapidity of long familiarity. He watched her lethargically, wondering if he really wanted to bother going away.

'It's me, Auntie Duff. Uh-huh. Fine, how're you? Good, well what I wanted to . . . Really? That's nice. I'll see it next time I manage up . . . I don't know when. I've got a lot on right now. But listen, what I wanted to ask was – is the cottage let at the moment? Ah . . . I thought that might be the case. Too bad. No, it was for Buchanan. He . . . Saturday? Really? How long for?' She looked over her shoulder at Buchanan and her eyes widened in solemn amazement. 'That's fantastic! Yes, that'll suit him down to the ground . . . and he can eat with you and Grampa . . .'

Listening to her enthusiastic chattering, Buchanan began immediately to regret the whole business. What if he didn't like the place? What if the farm was a cesspit or Fizz's grandparents were congenital idiots? He could hardly insult all of them by cutting short his stay.

'All fixed up.' Fizz replaced the receiver with a self-satisfied flourish and set her hands on her hips. 'Isn't it a miracle? The cottage will be free on Saturday and you can have it for a fortnight.'

Buchanan tried to look delighted.

'You'll love it. Fresh air, good food, peace and quiet – and if you need company you can look up my old school chum Rowena, or walk up to the inn for a pint of real ale.' She glanced at the four remaining grapes, resisted them, and made for the door. 'Don't bother to thank me, muchacha, it's all in the day's work.'

'Just a minute.' Buchanan heaved himself to his feet and trailed her into the hallway. 'This is all very sudden. I'm not sure I—'

She paused and looked up at him, drawing her brows together in a minute frown. 'You want to stay here in your flat? In May? With the city full of tourists? When you have the chance of a fortnight's salmon fishing on Loch Tay? Has the anaesthetic affected your brain, Buchanan?'

Put like that, it did seem rather inane to quibble.

The flat seemed smaller and quieter than ever after she'd left it, but Buchanan decided he preferred it that way. He propped his feet on the coffee table and fell into an exhausted doze, after which he awoke feeling a trifle more optimistic.

The cottage couldn't be too austere or Fizz would never have suggested it. If the worst came to the worst he could always eat at the inn, and the fact that there were good golfing and fishing facilities close at hand could not be negated. Besides, it would be interesting to discover what sort of family had bred a girl like Fizz; what sort of environment she had turned her back on at the age of eighteen and scarcely visited for the next nine years. There were lots of things about Fizz that had made him curious and perhaps this was his chance to get some answers to the questions he had never dared put to her.

All things considered, he decided, it was as good a way of spending his convalescence as he, himself, could have devised.

He had been in Am Bealach only two hours before it dawned on him that Fizz had suckered him again.

Chapter One

It was about four in the afternoon when they found the hand.

Up till then Buchanan had had a lovely day. The sun had beamed down from a cloudless sky throughout the two-hour drive from Edinburgh, the little farm cottage that was to be his home for the next fortnight turned out to be quite charming, and even if Fizz had taken the opportunity to cadge a lift with him, he knew she wouldn't be around for more than a couple of days.

Am Bealach itself was all she had promised it would be: a tiny, isolated hamlet surrounded by mountains on three sides and Loch Tay on the fourth. The neat farm buildings, of which his rented cottage formed an integral part, were two miles off the main road, right down on the loch shore, and tucked into the elbow of one of the best salmon rivers in the area. Fizz's grandparents seemed nice people, and the lunch they had provided confirmed Buchanan in his decision to dine *en famille*.

He felt healthier straight away and when, after lunch, Fizz suggested a short walk 'to show him the lie of the land' he was happy to go along with the idea. Unfortunately, Fizz's idea of a short walk included a two-mile tramp up the farm track to the crossroads where the inn stood, and a further half-hour's climb up a forestry road to a viewpoint above the hamlet.

'Actually,' Buchanan was finally forced to say to Fizz's back, 'I'm not entirely sure that this sort of pastime was what my doctor had in mind when he prescribed rest and recuperation.'

'You're not tired already, are you?' she said, neither turning round nor pausing in her stride. 'Geez! You'd think you'd had your liver removed instead of a teeny wee gall bladder.'

'What do you mean "teeny wee"? You don't know what size my gall bladder was.'

He heard her snigger. 'No. But you know what they say about men with big ears.'

'It's all lies,' Buchanan panted. 'Besides I haven't got big ears.'

'Well, that's worse, actually. You know what they say about men with small ears.'

Buchanan was afraid to ask. He watched her yomping up the track ahead of him and marvelled at her energy. She was wearing a pair of sawn-off jeans and a fleece jacket, and she had manhandled her obstreperous hair – or, at least, most of it – into an old check cap of her grandfather's, so she looked more like a fourteen-year-old boy than a grown woman – give or take a few inches around the bum. Her thighs were lean and brown and her calves looked a lot more muscular than he remembered noticing.

'You're not planning on going right to the summit, I hope,' he said, pausing to gauge how far they'd climbed. Below them he could see the whole western half of Loch Tay with the Tarmachan Ridge and Ben Lawers on the north shore, directly opposite, and the village of Killin, two or three miles away, at the head of the loch.

Fizz halted and turned to face him, propping a fist on each hip and breathing only a smidgen faster than usual. The russet spaniel pup she had thought it necessary to bring with her from the farm circled them impatiently and then went off on his own to investigate a patch of bracken.

'We can cut through the woods just up there.' She gestured vaguely towards a firebreak a few paces up the track. 'The glen road passes by, just beyond that line of beeches, and runs right back down to the crossroads. We can be at the inn again in time to have a quiet pint before dinner, but first I want you to have an aerial view of Am Bealach. Come over here.'

Buchanan followed her across the heather to a shoulder of hillside where the ground sloped away sharply beneath them. There was a flat outcrop of rock at that point so he was able to take the weight off his feet while Fizz pointed out places of interest like a tour guide.

From this angle Buchanan could see that to classify Am Bealach even as a 'hamlet' was almost overstating the case. He could spot only five buildings, including the inn and the farm.

'That's the lot,' Fizz confirmed, when he commented on this. 'And only four out of the five are inhabited. Rowena, who was in my class at primary school, lives in Stronach Lodge with her husband, Lindsay, and her new baby.' She used the stalk of grass she'd been chewing to indicate the crow-stepped gable just visible behind a stand of Scots pines. 'The locals call it "the big house" but, in fact, the original big house stood further up the glen. It fell down years ago and Rowena's family moved into the shooting lodge. They only own a couple of hundred acres now, plus the gamekeeper's cottage at the end of the Lodge drive.'

She looked round for the dog, which had disappeared, and whistled long and loudly for him before he returned, tongue lolling and eyes bright with some mischief of his own.

'Luath! *Sit*, you wee devil! And *stay*!' Fizz pulled off her cap and her curly mane exploded about her head like a living thing that had been too long confined. 'Right. Where was I?'

'We have Rowena and co. in Stronach Lodge, and

13

presumably the gamekeeper in the keeper's cottage. Does he have a wife?'

'No, but he had a mother up till recently. Now he lives alone. Alistair Munroe. You can see his chimney just above the crossroads where the glen road comes out of the trees. And, in the inn we have Myra and—'

Neither she nor Buchanan had noticed Luath steal away but a loud rustling in the undergrowth behind them suddenly alerted them to the fact that he had returned, almost immediately, to whatever had been occupying him minutes earlier.

Fizz leaped to her feet, berating the pup in sulphurous terms and promising to nail his top lip to the back his head. She plunged into the rhododendron bushes and Buchanan followed, but at a distance, because she had a habit of bending branches out of her way and then letting them spring back in the face of anyone immediately behind her. It seemed a fitting metaphor for the way she lived her life but, in both cases, he was beginning to foresee the surprises.

He caught up with her in a small rock-strewn clearing a few paces into the thicket. She had halted in surprise at the sight of a one-man tent from which Luath was just emerging with a pleased look on his face and a bread roll in his mouth. A lightweight sleeping bag, which he had inadvertently caught up with his booty, trailed behind him. At Fizz's yell of rage, he dropped the roll, caught it up again and lunged for the security of the rhododendrons whence, after a minute, came the sound of happy crunching.

'God!' Fizz hesitated at the edge of the clearing, evidently in some consternation.

Buchanan, who was momentarily expecting the arrival of some large, muscular and very aggressive camper, watched her sidle forward, pick up the sleeping bag and edge towards the tent.

14

'Nobody home,' she breathed after a minute, bending down to peer through the open flap.

Buchanan moved up behind her to look over her shoulder. 'Shove the sleeping bag back in and let's get out of here before the owner comes back and sees us messing around with his gear.'

She got down on her knees and crawled halfway through the opening, pushing the bag in front of her.

The sudden, God-awful scream she let rip with turned Buchanan to stone. Before he could react she came barrelling backwards out of the tent, slamming into his knees and catapulting him sideways into a bed of nettles.

Adrenaline brought him instantly back to his feet but he could see her nowhere and it was only the faint keening noise she was making that gave away her position. She was flattened against a tall outcrop of rock about thirty feet away with her hands pressed to the sides of her head and an expression of absolute horror in her eyes, and the only reason that she wasn't still screaming was that her teeth were clamped shut over the noise.

'Christ Almighty, Fizz! What is it?'

He started to walk towards her but she removed a hand from her head and made pushing motions at him. She seemed to be indicating the tent. He looked unwillingly through the opening but could see nothing but some odds and ends of clothing. 'What is it?'

She took a few quick gasps of air and got her teeth apart. 'Hand . . . a woman's hand in there . . . *shee-iiiiite!*'

Buchanan felt quite ill. The awkward fall had wrenched the newly healed wound where his gall bladder used to be and it now appeared that his brow was bleeding into the bargain. He took a couple of deep breaths and, very unwillingly, crouched down in the tent doorway and stuck his head in.

It was quite gloomy inside but there was enough light to see a pile of clothes and a rucksack against the side wall. Packets of soup and tins of lager were scattered about, probably by Luath, all over the groundsheet. Among the gear there were bits of plastic cutlery, a brown paper package, what looked like a woman's shoulder-length blonde wig and a Sidney Sheldon paperback.

And the hand.

It was lying on its back at the rear of the tent, small, slim, with delicate upturned fingers and lacquered nails. From the wrist extended about an inch and a half of blood-rusted bone.

Buchanan's eyes ricocheted instantly away, refusing to focus properly. He withdrew rapidly and sat on the grass outside the tent flap, dabbing at his bleeding forehead with his hankie and wondering if he should get Fizz the hell out of here. His glimpse of the tent's interior had convinced him that it was currently untenanted, so there was little chance that the camper would turn up in the next few minutes, whereas Fizz looked as though she could use a breathing space.

She didn't look any better than he felt. Her eyes were huge and bruised-looking and she was regarding him with the vulnerable expression that always made him feel ridiculously protective, even though he was aware that she could apply it like lipstick when the need arose. This time it was probably genuine, but knowing that any sign of sympathy like, maybe, patting her shoulder, could result in the loss of at least two teeth, he said only, 'You OK?'

'Sure,' she snapped, hard as a twenty-minute egg. 'It's just that . . .' She paused in the way she did when she was searching for an alternative to the truth.

'Just that . . . what?'

She drew a long, reluctant breath. 'It's just that . . . well, I think I might know whose hand it is.'

Buchanan stared at her in disbelief. It was bizarre enough to find a severed hand halfway up a mountain in the middle of nowhere, but for Fizz to be acquainted with the owner was downright surreal. 'You know someone who has lost one?' he muttered.

'I know someone who disappeared over a month ago. Five weeks ago tomorrow.' She was grabbing handfuls of hair and twisting it back under her cap, destroying her earlier resemblance to Medusa on a bad hair day. 'An old lady called Bessie Anderson. She used to live in the wee white cottage on the Killin road.'

'When you say "an old lady",' Buchanan said, 'how old do you mean?'

'Bessie? Well, she went to school with Grampa so she must have been around eighty-one or eighty-two.'

'Mmm-hm. In that case, I suspect you could be wrong about the hand being hers. I didn't get a good look at it but the impression I received was that it wasn't an old person's hand.'

Fizz's eyes bored into his skull as she absorbed this information. 'You'd better take another look, then, hadn't you?' she said regally.

Buchanan's mind immediately flooded with arguments against that proposal but he knew she would scorn every one of them. He went over, hunkered down by the tent opening and moved the flap aside with one finger.

A smell of corruption, unnoticed on his first inspection, hit his nostrils, making him recoil, but he forced himself to take a closer look at the hand before he drew back. Yes, it was a young woman's hand, with rose-pink nails and unwrinkled skin. Very unwrinkled. Too unwrinkled. There was a faint gleam on the too smooth, too slim fingers. In fact, the whole hand, on closer examination, looked more like pottery than skin and bone.

As soon as his fingers touched it Buchanan knew what he

held. Relief bubbled up inside him and spilled out in helpless laughter.

'It's a fake, Fizz!' He backed out of the tent and carried the hand over to show her. 'Look, it's the hand of a window-dresser's dummy.'

She shied away from it, fending him off with a sweep of her arm. 'OK, OK. You don't have to shove the damn thing up my nose.'

Buchanan smothered a smile. He knew how she felt. Even now, there was something macabre about the way the steel peg stuck out of the wrist. 'Funny thing for a camper to be carrying, though, isn't it? I'll bet there isn't a shop window within miles of here.'

'Something like sixty miles, if you're talking about the sort of shop window that has models in it,' Fizz said, and took the hand from him as though to prove that she could. She looked it over carefully and then returned it and wiped her fingers on her jeans.

Buchanan said, 'If you thought it belonged to your missing neighbour no wonder it gave you a turn. How did she disappear?'

Fizz glanced away and shrugged. 'She went out for a walk one Sunday morning and was never seen again.'

It occurred to Buchanan that she was deliberately not meeting his eyes and instantly, in a dazzling flash of insight, he knew that he was here not because he wanted to be here, but because Fizz wanted him to track down this old woman.

'You don't say?' he growled. 'Well, well, well. Isn't that just—'

'Don't start, Buchanan! Just don't start, OK?'

'Why not? Why shouldn't I start?' he said coldly. 'Now that you've got me here you think I should just—'

'Don't get your boxers in a twist,' she interrupted, rolling up her eyes. 'I didn't "get" you here for any ulterior motive. In fact, I wouldn't even have mentioned old Bessie if we hadn't found the . . . the hand.'

'I bet you wouldn't,' Buchanan agreed. 'You'd have been quite content to let me find out in homeopathic doses from your grandparents or your chums. No doubt you have them all primed.'

'Well, I haven't, actually.' Her angelic-schoolgirl face was a picture of wounded virtue. 'You always have to think the worst of me, don't you, Buchanan? Who asked you to do anything? Nobody. You're not interested in finding out what happened to old Bessie? Forget it. I only thought that you might get bored here with nothing to occupy your mind and, since you were so hot at finding out who the murderer was in that business last year when I was helping you out at the Legal Advice Clinic . . .'

'Helping me out?' Buchanan had to smile. 'Well that's one way of putting it.'

She stuck her hands on her hips and jutted her chin at him. 'You're not going to start on about that again, are you? God, you're about as forgiving as Simon Wiesenthal, you know that, Buchanan? You know damn well you wanted to resign in any case, and as for that stick insect you were engaged to—' She saw his face and did a quick change of tack. 'Anyway, you didn't do *me* any favours, did you?'

'I let you live,' Buchanan muttered darkly.

'You even tried to dissuade your father from giving me a job!'

Buchanan hadn't realised she was aware of that little detail. He got to his feet and brushed most of the dirt off his trousers. 'The point is, Fizz, I don't like being manipulated. You could have been straight about it. You could have told me about Bessie Anderson right at the start.'

'Oh, sure. And you'd have been right up here like a shot, would you?'

19

'Maybe—'

'Bollocks.' She stooped to pluck a stalk of grass and stuck it aggressively between her teeth. 'You'd never have come anywhere near Am Bealach if you'd suspected I had a job for you. Admit it, anything that could conceivably be connected with criminality of any sort has you backing into a corner and sucking your thumb.'

'I do prefer not to get actively involved in matters—'

'Oh, stop it!' She flapped a hand at him, as though she were shooing a fly. 'You're such a fuddy-duddy, Buchanan. You know you're better off here than in your flat in Edinburgh and if you have something to occupy your mind it'll stop you from getting bored. I'm doing you a favour.'

Buchanan could have pointed out that if she ever did anyone a favour it would be a whole new experience for her, but he suspected there was a grain of truth in what she said. Boredom was likely to be a problem in this outpost of civilisation, especially if the weather took a turn for the worst.

'I'm going to be stuck in Edinburgh till after the end-of-term exams,' Fizz pointed out. 'There's no way round it. I've got lectures I can't miss, and I'm going to fail Company Law if I don't put in some work real fast. Otherwise I'd do my own detective work.'

Buchanan walked across and sat on the rocks beside her. Out of the corner of his eye he saw Luath slink out of the bushes, his belly close to the ground, and position himself, in an indolent attitude, just behind Fizz, as though he'd been there all the time.

'The question is, Fizz: is it any of my business – or of yours? Presumably the police have already looked into the matter?'

Fizz dismissed these minor details with a flick of her hand. 'Old Bessie wasn't just anybody. Almost all of us in Am Bealach had known her all our lives. She went to Killin school with Grampa and Auntie Duff, and with Malcolm Quinn, who owns the Clachan inn. Malcolm's daughter, Myra, was her godchild. Rowena and I used to make original works of art for her, out of toilet roll tubes and yoghurt cartons.'

'I get the picture. She was one of the family.'

'Right. And the thing is, I don't like the way Grampa is handling her disappearance. He's obviously still grieving but he won't speak about the business or let anyone else speak about it. It's as if he can't bring himself to believe she's dead – but, after five weeks, we're not going to find her alive and well and living off the land. It seems he's just refusing to face up to the facts.'

'Probably the lack of a body,' Buchanan opined. 'They say that can make it hard to come to terms with a bereavement.'

'Exactly.' Fizz rewarded this observation with a bright look, thickly larded with soft soap. 'That's what I thought and, I have to tell you, I don't like to see Grampa like that. It's the sort of thing that can make an old codger start to lose his grip on life.'

Buchanan winced. Logic told him that Fizz was probably exaggerating the matter. The 'old codger' he had met at lunch looked good for another ten years and had shown little sign of depression. But it was already perfectly clear to him – even without Fizz dangling the possibility in front of his nose like a matador's cape – that if she turned out to be telling the truth he'd have to live with the knowledge that he had refused to help. A rapid change of subject appeared to be the best temporary solution.

'We ought to be going.'

'You're right.' Fizz stood up and gave her bottom a brisk rub as though the rock had chilled it. 'Put the hand back and let's get the hell out of here.'

Buchanan complied, noting as he did so that the smell of corruption was coming from a tin that had once held corned

21

beef. All the food in the tent was well past its sell-by date. A pint carton of milk sounded pretty solid when he shook it and a half-used tin of tomatoes had grown a fluffy grey toupee. He showed it to Fizz.

'What do you think? Should we be worried about this?'

Fizz glanced at it and then fingered the sleeping bag. 'Down-filled. Probably cost well over a hundred pounds . . . and the tent's worth a fair amount as well. You don't walk away and leave this sort of gear lying around unattended, not even in a remote spot like this. Not for long enough to get mould on tinned tomatoes, you don't.'

'Maybe he fell off a mountain,' Buchanan muttered.

'More than likely. Happens all the time around here.' She gave the interior of the tent an unwilling inspection, barely sticking her nose through the opening. 'Men's clothes. A disposable razor. What's that? A *wig*? Christ, a cross-dressing mountaineer!' She leaned closer. 'Wonder what's in the parcel.'

Buchanan restrained himself from grabbing her arm. 'Please, Fizz,' he said quickly. 'Please don't touch anything else. We're going to have to report this to the police and you know they don't like outsiders mucking around with the evidence.'

That caught her attention. 'How long would it take for tomatoes to go this mouldy? Five weeks? Just about the same time as . . .'

Buchanan had no intention of going down that road. Any connection to Bessie Anderson's disappearance had to be incredibly tenuous and not worth arguing about. It was perfectly obvious that what they were looking at here was yet another mountaineering tragedy, and there was no reason to suspect foul play.

At the same time, he was conscious of a deep uneasiness. In a tiny place like Am Bealach *two* mysteries were at least one too many.

Chapter Two

Fizz felt fairly confident, as they made their way back down to the crossroads, Luath racing ahead, that things were going according to plan. She had been convinced that, once she had Buchanan here in Am Bealach, she could rely not only on his curiosity, but on the still small voice of conscience – which, in Buchanan's case, was a stentorian and unremitting roar – to prod him into action.

He wasn't so easy to bamboozle these days, so it had taken weeks of subliminal programming to imbue him with the idea of Am Bealach as an earthly paradise, and she was unashamedly self-congratulatory at her success. It was a bit unfortunate that she had lost her cool for a minute and blurted out the story of old Bessie's disappearance like that, instead of breaking it to him gently, but it looked as if she had got away with it.

As they emerged from the trees she could see the Stronach bridge below them, and she pointed it out to Buchanan.

'The police searched the woods for days when Bessie disappeared, but in the end they decided she must have toppled over the bridge there into the Stronach river and been swept out to the loch.'

Buchanan frowned down at the road and seemed to be measuring the distance from the bridge to the crossroads. It was obvious to Fizz that he had questions he wanted to ask but he evidently wasn't yet ready to admit an interest, so he just grunted and said, 'Seems a reasonable assumption.'

'Not to me, it isn't,' Fizz told him. 'And not to anybody who knew Bessie's habits. She hasn't walked as far as the bridge in years. Her cottage is on the far side of the crossroads, about maybe a quarter of a mile beyond the Clachan inn, and if she were to walk down the hill to the bridge she'd have the hill to climb on her way back. You think about things like that when you're in your eighties.'

He shrugged, looking across the loch in a bored manner, as though he were only keeping the conversation going out of politeness. 'There must be a dozen reasons for her going as far as the bridge. Maybe she felt particularly energetic that day; maybe she had some reason that seemed important to her—'

'If that's so, why hasn't her body washed ashore?'

'Snagged on a submerged log,' Buchanan suggested, in the pedantic manner that annoyed the hell out of Fizz. 'Swept all the way down the River Tay to the sea. Jammed under an overhanging bank. Lying under a pile of jetsam in some deserted cove. Take your pick.'

This was not what Fizz wanted to hear. She had listened to all these theories before and couldn't subscribe to any of them. She called Luath to heel, waited for Buchanan to close the gate across the forestry track and then led the way down the road towards the bridge.

The Stronach today was only half the river it had been five weeks ago when Bessie had disappeared. The melting snow that had swelled it into a torrent in early April was now, at the beginning of May, confined to the higher peaks, but ridges of broken branches and river wrack along the banks still showed how far the water level had dropped from its spring high. Even in May, Fizz had to admit, it was no place to take a dizzy turn.

Buchanan leaned a fist on the parapet and looked down

into the pool below. 'Deep,' he said, in an almost awed tone.

'At least fifteen feet,' Fizz admitted. 'And by the time the current has whirled you around for a few hours with a barrowload of rocks there's not much of you left to bury. A shepherd fell in there about twenty years ago, trying to save a ewe, and he came out – as Alistair, the keeper, told me – "the sizey a fitba".'

'The size of a football?' Buchanan tried translating it into standard English and evidently found it no more palatable. He stuck his hands in his pockets and turned his back on the pool, looking up the hill to the roof of the inn, which could be seen beyond the crossroads. 'That's the Clachan up there, isn't it? Lord, I could use a pint of their real ale.'

'Me too,' Fizz said, experiencing an anticipatory illusion of sharp-nutty flavour in her taste buds. 'We can phone the police from there.'

They found a dozen people in the lounge bar, where the smell of tobacco smoke, beer and pine logs was almost thick enough to be visible. Fizz could identify most of the patrons as local farmers or people from Killin but she knew none of them well enough to exchange more than a friendly nod. One or two couples had chosen to sit outside the french windows on the patio and Myra and her dad were out there collecting glasses and generally jollying things along.

Simon, Myra's husband, was behind the bar, poncing about in tartan trews like something out of *Braveheart*. His thick black hair fell over his forehead in carefully arranged disorder and the collar of his baggy shirt was unbuttoned to show an inch or two of tanned and hairless chest. All that was missing was the claymore.

It was a bit much for a man who, Fizz estimated, was probably knocking fifty, but she had seen Simon looking even more offbeat on occasion in the past. He took his position as the Clachan's front man very seriously and believed in dressing the part.

Cutting short the dramatic monologue with which he was boring a party of anglers into a state of stupefaction, he switched on a bright smile for the new arrivals and zapped up to their end of the bar.

'Fizz! Glad to see you home again.'

'How you doing, Simon?' returned Fizz and said to Buchanan, 'This is Simon Burroughs and if he doesn't know who you are, why you're here, and how long you're planning to stay, the grapevine isn't what it used to be around these parts.'

Simon flashed his capped teeth in a grin and offered a hand across the bar. 'Good to meet you, Tam.'

'Listen, Simon,' Fizz pressed on quickly, before he could take command of the conversation as he usually did, 'I have to make a phone call. We just found a tent up in the forestry plantation and I think I should report it to the police.'

Simon took a moment to assimilate this news. 'The police?' he said, glancing from Fizz to Buchanan and back again for elucidation. 'Why the big rush? If someone has lost a tent—'

'No, Simon it's not lost.' Fizz couldn't be bothered going into long-winded explanations. 'Buchanan – Tam – will explain it all to you but, in the meantime, I want to use your phone, OK? Not the public phone in the hall. We don't want everybody to know about it right away.'

Simon pushed the black curls away from his brow with the back of his hand and glanced over his shoulder at his other customers, most of whom had taken the opportunity to fade unobtrusively away. He raised the flap at the end of the counter.

'Come away through then, Fizz. You know where the phone is, but you'll have trouble reaching Gavin on a Saturday

26

afternoon. He'll be out on his boat on the loch like he always is at the weekend.'

'I'll leave a message for him.' Fizz passed through the bar and into the kitchen beyond. This was Simon's kingdom: pristine as an operating theatre and glittering with white tiles and stainless steel. The only touch of colour was the vivid blue of the electric fly catcher, which went *tsszt* once or twice as she dialled.

Gavin, who was the sole representative of the Law in the area, was, as predicted, fishing on the loch, but his wife was at home and claimed to be expecting his return at any minute. Fizz dictated detailed instructions as to where the tent could be found and left the number of the Clachan inn in case Gavin needed to speak to her in the next half-hour or so.

When she got back to Buchanan she found that Myra and her father had joined the group. Old Malcolm was looking even grimmer than usual, which meant that his bad leg was giving him gyp. Buchanan had, apparently, already passed on the basic facts of their afternoon's adventures and they were all discussing the matter with avid curiosity.

'I don't understand it,' Simon said, when Fizz had made a start on her pint. 'Tam says the tent must have been there for weeks but there have been no reports of someone missing on the hills. You'd think we'd have heard if the police were looking for a climber.'

His father-in-law nodded his big head in agreement. He had his pipe in his hands and was stuffing it with what smelled to Fizz like ripe silage.

'We're always the first to be contacted,' he said to Buchanan, 'because we see most of the climbers going by. They either leave their cars in the car park, or drop in for a pint, or stop to ask what the conditions are like on the ridge.'

'There haven't *been* all that many climbers this year,' Myra said. She got out a tea cloth and started polishing glasses as though she felt that somebody ought to be doing a little work around here. 'The conditions were very poor on the high ground right up till the beginning of last month. There's been almost no one around since the last of the cross-country skiers so we'd have noticed anyone heading for the ridge. Even if someone had gone by on foot you'd have thought one of us would have seen him, wouldn't you, Simon? I mean, you've been preparing the ground for the new lawn, out at the front there. If anyone had passed by you couldn't have failed to notice.'

Fizz suspected this was scarcely an exaggeration. Simon was the local Reuters. He had to be *au fait* with everything that was going on in the area and slipping anything past him was like trying to smuggle daybreak past a rooster.

She said, 'Well, it's just possible this guy may have approached from the other end of the loch or even come over the glen road from Lochearnhead.'

'It may not have been a climber, of course,' Buchanan admitted. 'Fizz and I jumped to that conclusion because it seemed the most obvious one but, in fact, there was nothing in the tent to confirm it. The owner could just as easily have been a first-time camper who met with bad weather, say, and got so disgusted that he never wanted to see his tent again. I've known people do funnier things.'

'Yes, so have I,' Fizz put in, remembering a Japanese guitarist she'd shared a flat with in Toronto who'd had a habit of going apeshit once a month and burning all his boyfriend's clothes. 'And this guy who was camping up there was definitely something of a four-pound note. Call me old fashioned, but I wouldn't have thought a long blonde wig was standard gear for campers.'

She caught the faint twitch of Buchanan's brows as she

spoke but it was too late to call the words back. Evidently he was trying to tell her not to complicate matters by blabbing too much at this stage, which was, of course, something she should have considered. However, it didn't make a lot of difference. Whatever one did to prevent it, news always seemed to spread around Am Bealach as though there were some sort of group consciousness in operation. One thing his reaction had revealed, however, was that Buchanan was starting to take a personal interest in the mystery.

The management team of the Clachan inn registered unanimous incredulity.

'You mean there was a long wig in the tent?' Myra passed a hand over her own frizzy ginger topknot, apparently to illustrate that it was a hairpiece that she was visualising rather than some other use of the word 'wig' that she had never encountered.

'We're not really sure, actually,' Fizz back-pedalled as best she could. 'That's what it looked like to me but, to be honest, it might have been something else. We didn't nose around too much.'

Simon, at least, found this explanation easier to accept than Fizz's previous assertion, and considered the matter dropped. 'It's not usual for climbers to cut through the woods to get to the Ardoch Ridge,' he pointed out. 'Is the tent close to the road or further in, towards the forestry track?'

'It's difficult to describe,' Buchanan said, making it clear to Fizz, who could have pinpointed its position to within ten paces, that he didn't want anyone else nosing around the area till the police got there. 'It's in a bit of a hollow surrounded by undergrowth. In fact, we'd never have found it if it hadn't been for the dog.'

Fizz let him go on chatting about how they'd been chasing Luath and other innocuous matters, gradually leading the conversation away from the contents and specific whereabouts of the tent, and in a minute she was able to pursue her own agenda by asking a question to which she already knew the answer.

'I don't suppose there's any further news about old Bessie?'

Myra shook her head. Much of the animation drained from her face, allowing her jawline and the faint bags under her eyes to sag. She wasn't in great shape for forty-five, Fizz thought, but a life spent washing sheets or pulling pints in a haze of tobacco smoke wasn't going to help anybody in a search for eternal youth.

'If there is any further news, Fizz,' she said, 'it won't be good news. Not after all this time. I think we have to face the fact that Bessie's gone for good.'

Fizz shook her head. 'I just can't believe she fell over the bridge, can you? I mean, she knew it was dangerous.'

'We all knew it was dangerous,' Myra agreed. 'All of us were warned, from the day we could toddle, to keep away from the bridge. We all knew the parapet was too low.'

'Something should have been done about it years ago,' Simon said grimly, and moved down the bar to pour more whiskies for the fishing fraternity.

Buchanan sipped his beer. 'I'm sure there's no other way Miss Anderson could have disappeared so completely, Fizz,' he said lazily, fingering the condensation on the side of his glass. 'The surrounding woods must have been well searched.'

'I can vouch for that,' Malcolm said. He used his walking stick to drag a bar stool closer and clenched his teeth hard on his pipe as he lowered himself on to it. 'We all searched for her for at least an hour before we called the police. I wasn't much help because of this damn leg of mine but we kept on till it was too dark to see where we were going.'

'Everyone in Am Bealach was here at the Clachan for lunch,

you see,' Fizz explained to Buchanan. 'Everyone except Alistair, the gamekeeper, whose mother was ill at the time. It was the Sunday that Rowena's baby was christened so they had all been to the church in Killin for the ceremony, and Lindsay had arranged a celebratory lunch here, afterwards, for all the locals.'

'Bessie didn't go to the church ceremony, I suppose you knew that, Fizz?' Myra put in.

'I don't believe I did,' Fizz lied, having heard the whole story from Auntie Duff, parts of it several times. Allowing Myra to put Buchanan in the picture was, however, less didactic than briefing him herself. She could see he was becoming interested in the mystery, but he didn't like to be pushed.

'She was supposed to be going in our car,' Myra was saying, 'but when Dad and I called in for her she said she'd decided to give the ceremony a miss. She'd been having a little trouble with her waterworks, so she said, and she didn't want to be too far from a toilet. But, as far as I could see, she was looking forward to coming to the party.'

Malcolm shook his head. 'No way she'd have missed Briony's christening party. Bessie Anderson was more a mother to Rowena than her real mother ever was. They were very close.'

'So, it must have been quite late in the afternoon when you started to worry about her,' Buchanan suggested.

'I kept waiting for her to turn up,' Malcolm said. 'She often had a nap in the middle of the day and we suspected for a while that she had simply overslept. It was about three o'clock that Simon decided to go over and see if anything was wrong and he discovered the house empty. Bessie's coat and outdoor shoes were gone and so was the trivet she used for collecting mushrooms and brambles and stuff like that.'

'She'd been talking about getting ready to plant up her hanging baskets,' Myra said. She was carefully smoothing and folding her tea cloth as though it needed all her concentration, but you could see her mind was on other things. 'I'm sure she must have gone out to pick some sphagnum moss to line them with. We found a few tufts of moss at the crossroads as though she might have dropped her trivet there, but the trivet never turned up. And nor did Bessie.'

There was a burst of somewhat forced laughter from the fishermen at the end of the counter and Simon drifted back to slip an arm around his wife's waist, grinning from jaw to hairline and glowing with the consciousness of being a born raconteur and superb host.

'I was just telling the lads about Zander and his school pullover,' he told Myra, and turned immediately to Buchanan, who was probably the only person in the area who hadn't heard the story already. 'Zander's our boy, by the way, Tam. He's ten now but, a couple of years ago Myra took him down to Killin to get him a new school pullover. There wasn't a crew-necked one in his size but he absolutely refused to have a V-neck. He wouldn't give a reason but he dug his heels in to such an extent that Myra had to bring him home without buying one. Well, that evening when she was putting him to bed she insisted he tell her what he had against V-necked pullovers and he said, real disgusted like, "Mrs McDonald," – that's his teacher – "Mrs McDonald wears a V-neck and when she bends down you can see her *lungs*!" '

As Buchanan chuckled politely, Fizz finished her pint and gestured to him to do the same. Once Simon got himself into 'mine host' mode there was no stopping him. He was able to go from one anecdote to the next without drawing breath and this was not the time to encourage him.

'We have to go,' she announced. 'Auntie Duff will have our dinner on the table by the time we get down the road. If Gavin should phone here for me, Simon, will you tell him he can reach us at the farm in about half an hour?'

Buchanan wasn't wonderfully happy about being deprived of a second pint and said so when they got outside.

'It's only twenty past five,' he complained, flashing his Rolex. 'I thought I heard your grandmother say dinner would be around seven?'

'Listen, I just saved you from death by boredom in there,' Fizz said, pausing in the car park to untie Luath from the fence she had left him tethered to. 'Simon feels it incumbent upon him to provide entertainment as well as booze and he just doesn't know when to stop. If it weren't for the fact that he's such a brilliant chef – and for the real ale he stocks – people would avoid him like the plague. He sees himself as a cross between Billy Connolly and Mrs Beaton but to everyone else he's just a plonker.'

'Hardly, Fizz. I'm sure he's really a very . . .' Buchanan halted and grabbed her arm as two boys whizzed by on mountain bikes, dangerously close. Luckily, Luath had his own agenda and was exploring round the gatepost.

'That's Zander, Simon and Myra's brat,' Fizz told him as they watched the cyclists park their machines against the wall. 'The one with the red jacket.'

Zander had grown an inch or so since the last time Fizz had seen him, several months ago, but his appearance hadn't improved much. He had never been a singularly well-favoured child and his pale, bulging eyes and wide-nostrilled nose were never going to make his fortune.

Buchanan was taking a good look at him. Probably he was struck by Zander's unusual appearance but, of course, he would never admit that. 'He doesn't take after either of his parents, does he?'

'No,' Fizz agreed. 'That's because he's adopted. Simon and Myra can't have kids of their own but they think the sun shines out of Zander's left ear. So does his grampa.'

They crossed the main road and turned down the farm track, passing between head-high hedgerows that were just coming into full leaf. Buchanan picked up a bit of dead branch and used it to swipe the heads off dandelions as they walked along.

'One thing you have to bear in mind about Am Bealach,' Fizz told him, 'is that every one of the locals is a bit nutty, one way or another.'

'Present company excepted, of course,' Buchanan remarked. 'Something in the water, is it?'

Fizz shook her head. 'It's called the Am Bealach Effect. Living in a place like this, with no stimulation to speak of, you lose about one IQ point per year. Also, if you don't have any hassle in your life you get to the state that you have a panic attack if your library book is overdue. An imagined insult – like someone forgetting to pass on a piece of interesting news – becomes a hanging offence and can result in months of ill feeling. That, basically, is why I did my bat-out-of-hell impersonation when I did.'

'So, you haven't actually lived here since you were – what? – seventeen? Eighteen?'

It always made Fizz uneasy when people started asking personal questions. She liked to keep herself to herself but, in this case, she supposed it wouldn't do any harm. Buchanan could always find out all he wanted to know about her background by asking anyone in Am Bealach – but then, maybe he wouldn't do that. It wouldn't conform with his complicated, and very personal, moral code.

Finally, she said, 'Other than school holidays, and the week I spent with Grampa when I came home last summer, it must be something like thirteen years since I've made more than an overnight stay. I was fourteen when I went away to school in

Edinburgh and, after that, I did a year at Edinburgh College of Art before I got myself booted out. I was eighteen at that point, and that's when I set off round the world with my rucksack to seek my fortune.'

Buchanan decapitated a few more dandelions and then threw his stick away into the trees, scaring the shit out of a snoozing red squirrel. 'In that case,' he continued after watching his victim's retreat with shamefaced awe, 'you don't know any of the locals really well, do you?'

'Oh, I don't think that's true,' Fizz said, and then wondered if it were. None of the neighbours seemed to her to have changed much over the years, but then, who could tell? 'I did know them well before I left. Very well. I still think of them more as family than as neighbours.'

'Excluding Lindsay and Simon. I take it they're both outsiders?'

'Lindsay is, he's from Glasgow. But Simon is from Killin. His folks owned the Glen Dochart hotel at one time. They sold it about twenty years ago so I doubt if there was much money left for Simon to inherit by the time they snuffed it. There used to be quite a few Burroughs around here, but they've all moved away now.'

Fizz had a momentary recollection of how the inn used to be before Simon took it in hand and Buchanan, seeing her smile, raised his eyebrows at her.

'The Clachan was a complete dump when Simon arrived,' she told him. 'Old Malcolm hadn't a clue how to run a hotel. He'd been a farmer all his life and when he turned the original farmhouse into an inn it just stayed much the same as it was – dingy, damp and, since his wife died, none too clean. They used to say that Malcolm kept a pig in the bath as an air freshener.'

'What made him give up farming?'

'A slight difference of opinion with one of his bulls. He

made the mistake of getting into a stall with it and the big bastard just leaned against him and squashed him into the wall. His wife started doing bed and breakfast to make some money while he was out of commission and the business just grew into a guesthouse and then into a small hotel. It was Simon who developed it. He had trained as a chef, and of course he'd grown up in the business, so really it's thanks to him that the Clachan is so well listed.'

Buchanan nodded thoughtfully and paused for a moment to enjoy the distant prospect of the farm buildings, all golden brown in the light of the setting sun, with the blue of the loch and the grey-green of the mountains beyond. Fizz had seen that view a thousand times but sometimes she needed to see it through a visitor's eyes to appreciate it as it deserved. Her own vision, she realised, was too thickly overlaid with images of the same scene on rainy winter evenings when, from the age of five, she had trudged the two miles from the end of the track, where the school bus dropped her off.

'And what about Rowena's husband?' Buchanan said, setting off again, rather faster than before, as if he could already smell his dinner. 'What does he do for a living? I imagine he's quite affluent?'

'Affluent, no. Effluent, yes,' Fizz opined, and giggled at her own wit. 'When he and Rowena got married Rowena's mother sold him what remained of the estate for a nominal sum and buggered off back to her family in Northern Ireland. Lindsay Crawford was some sort of financial adviser or chartered accountant at that point, but he has been the local MP here for years.'

'Mm-hmm. The name's familiar, now that I think about it. Why don't you like him?'

'Ask me that – if you need to – after you meet him.' Fizz smiled in anticipation. 'I'll introduce you to Lindsay and

Rowena before I go back to Edinburgh on Tuesday. That's a treat in store for you, compadre, I guarantee it.'

Buchanan accepted this assurance with his usual po-faced stoicism, but at least he hadn't issued any formal declaration of noncooperation, so Fizz could assume that he was, mentally at any rate, on the case.

Chapter Three

All day Sunday there were Land Rovers buzzing up and down the forestry tracks and uniformed policemen crashing about in the undergrowth with sticks.

Buchanan watched them through binoculars from the loch, where he and Fizz were fishing for trout, and couldn't help feeling just a trifle out of things. No one had even spoken to either him or Fizz since the brief phone call from Gavin, the evening before, when Fizz had expanded on her original message, but it was clear that the search for the missing camper was being taken seriously. There was even a possibility, Fizz had reported, with a certain noninfectious glee, that Gavin would be phoning round for volunteers to help with a foot search, should today's efforts be unsuccessful.

When the threatened phone call came through at eight thirty on Monday morning Auntie Duff took it and passed on the message to Buchanan. He had just embarked on a plate of scrambled eggs with smoked salmon and the last thing he'd have chosen to do with his day was to spend it raking through the heather for the missing camper.

Fizz had eaten two hours before, with her grandfather, and had taken off up the hill with him in the morning mists to discover how many new-born lambs had fallen victim to foxes or hoody crows during the night. Grampa – aka Archibald

Fitzpatrick or 'Auld Erchie' to the locals – was anything but geriatric. Buchanan had seen him only in brief glimpses since his arrival on Saturday, because the old man had been out on the hill with his late-lambing ewes virtually all the time.

For a man of eighty-one, Grampa was totally phenomenal: small, slightly built but possessed of the energy of a man half his age. His hearing was seriously impaired, his knees were audibly rheumaticky, and he now needed a four-wheeled motorbike to reach the highest pastures, but he still managed a flock of four or five hundred sheep with only occasional help. Although he spread the lambing out over a long period, for ease of handling, there was still, at the moment, enough work to keep Auntie Duff occupied with attending to orphaned and sickly lambs. She seemed glad of a moment's respite as she sat down across the table from Buchanan and poured herself a cup of coffee from the pot.

'Now then, Tam, are you enjoying that? Would you like another tomato with it?'

Buchanan said no, he was fine and it was delicious.

'Good, I'm glad you're enjoying it.' She smiled at him in a motherly way and motioned him to eat up. Her plump face was seamed with deep, soft wrinkles but there was still a little black among her silver hair.

'And what do you think of S. & M.?' she asked comfortably.

Buchanan stared at her, the food lying like a stone on his tongue. Placidly, she stared back.

'I'm sorry . . .?' he said, swallowing his mouthful unchewed.

'Simon and Myra. Fizz calls them S. & M. and she's got me doing it too. You met them up at the Clachan inn, she tells me.'

'Oh . . . yes. They seem very nice.'

'Simon's a clever laddie. The difference he's made to that place up the road, you wouldn't believe it. He's made his father-in-law a rich man, they say.'

Buchanan looked interested. 'Really?'

'Och yes, Malcolm told me so himself. You met Malcolm too? Poor soul. Money isn't everything, is it? He used to be a farmer, yes, and his father before him. All the low ground to the west of the glen road used to be Malcolm's, right up to the beech woods. He had a good Aberdeen Angus herd and his beasts always took the top prizes in the Killin Agricultural Show.'

Buchanan swallowed a mouthful preparatory to making some suitably impressed rejoinder but Auntie Duff shot off on another tack without waiting for, or apparently expecting, any reply.

'Fizz says she's taking you up to the big house to meet Rowena today.'

'She did say something about that . . .'

'Rowena's not good with strangers, so you're not to take it personally if she doesn't talk much.' She stretched across to refill Buchanan's cup. A conversation was clearly a rare luxury for her, no doubt because communicating with her deaf husband strained both throat and patience. 'Such a shy lassie. I remember her when she was a wee thing at the Sunday school, always in tears, always wanting home to her mummy. What she was doing getting married to Lindsay, I'll never know.'

Buchanan ate his eggs and forbore to comment.

'Flora Cameron, Rowena's mother, she was always a right bossy woman. Irish as the pigs of Docherty, Flora is, with an accent you could cut with a knife. She was for ever sending Rowena down here to play with Fizz. Hoping Fizz would bring her out of herself. But, of course, nothing could have been worse for the lassie.'

'Why's that?' Buchanan asked in spite of himself.

41

Auntie Duff's plump cheeks wobbled as she shook her head. 'Och, it just made Rowena worse, trying to make her something God never intended her to be. Trying to force her to be like Fizz. That was before I came to the farm, of course. Fizz was away at school in Edinburgh when I married her grampa.'

Buchanan saw a flash of green pass the kitchen window. 'Talk of the devil,' he said as Fizz stomped in, kicking off a pair of muddy wellington boots and throwing her green jacket over a chair.

'Morning all,' she said, and liberated her hair from under the old flat cap. 'I've got a pair of skinny wee twins out there for you, Auntie Duff. I brought their mummy with them. Grampa says to put them in the barn under a light.'

'Oh, sod it,' said Auntie Duff and bustled out muttering to herself.

Buchanan watched her go, his fork halfway to his mouth and the scrambled eggs dropping off it back on to his plate. Slowly, he dragged his eyes back to Fizz who met his look with a grin.

He said, 'I bet that expression wasn't in your grandma's vocabulary till you came into her life. Don't you think you should tell her what it means?'

'You tell her,' Fizz said, feeling the weight of the coffeepot and getting herself a mug off the Welsh dresser. Golden ringlets danced around her waif-like, pseudo-fourteen-year-old face as she sat down.

'It's not my responsibility, Fizz. What if Grampa hears her – well, maybe he's too deaf to notice, but aren't you afraid she'll come out with it in front of the neighbours?'

'So what? Everybody in the world uses colourful language nowadays. Everybody but you, Buchanan.'

'She just asked me if I liked S. & M.'

Fizz blinked at him for a moment and then she cracked up,

42

leaning over the table and laughing till tears came into her eyes. 'Oh God . . . I bet that gave you palpitations.'

Buchanan chose not to reply to that one. 'The policeman was just on the phone,' he said as she wiped her eyes. 'Auntie Duff spoke to him.'

Fizz sobered up quickly. 'Gavin? Is he organising a foot search?'

'Apparently. All interested parties to meet in the Clachan car park at ten o'clock. I suppose you're going to tell me that includes us.'

'Damn tootin', I am. I wouldn't miss it for the world. Are you having this piece of toast?'

Buchanan caught her wrist in the nick of time. 'Yes, I am, actually,' he said pleasantly. 'If you want toast you can make it yourself.'

'Bastard.' She put two slices in the toaster.

He said, 'You're obviously very happy about this foot search. Surely you're not hoping it will turn up Bessie Anderson's remains?'

'No chance. Not that far off the road. But who knows what we might find? And if we don't find any sign of the camper – well, that's *two* unexplained disappearances round about the same time, isn't it? In which case they might decide to reopen the investigation.'

One could only marvel at her persistence. 'What more could be done? There has already been a thorough search for Bessie Anderson and nobody has seen or heard anything suspicious in either her case or the camper's. I don't see the police wasting any more time on either of them, frankly.'

'Well, you can say what you like,' Fizz assured him, piling marmalade on her toast, 'but it's bloody fishy the way nobody at the inn noticed that camper going by. I'm telling you, nothing happens around here but Simon knows about it –

43

nothing! And another thing. Simon must have been in the Clachan inn that Sunday morning when the others were at the christening, because somebody had to have that lunch ready for them when they got back. Yet he didn't notice Bessie walking by towards the crossroads.'

'Which might indicate that Miss Anderson didn't pass till later in the day when they were all in the dining room at the back of the house.' Buchanan thought for a minute. 'And, if so, why didn't she go in and join in the celebrations? Had she fallen out with Lindsay or Rowena? Or was it one of the Clachan folk she was avoiding?'

Fizz shrugged. 'I can't see any of them falling out with Bessie. She was a real old sweetie.' She twisted round to look at the kitchen clock. 'Look at the time. Are you planning to change before we go?'

Buchanan grabbed a last cup of coffee. 'I've just to put my walking boots on. Won't take a minute. But maybe we should take the car as far as the Clachan. If we're expected to do a lot of climbing I might be glad of it at the end of the day. I'm still not back into fighting condition after my op.'

'You'll be fine,' Fizz stated with airy confidence, exhibiting her usual sympathetic understanding of another's weakness. 'We'll be moving very slowly.'

'I think I'll take the car all the same,' Buchanan said. 'I'm feeling a bit fragile. To tell you the truth, I didn't get much sleep last night thanks to a visiting cat.'

'A wee sleekit tortoiseshell thing? That's Selena.'

'Well, I wish you'd lock her in tonight. She kept insisting on getting under my duvet all night and every time I put her outside in the yard she got back in again. God knows how.'

'Oh, she's not our cat,' said Fizz, embarking on her second slice of toast. 'I think she started life at the big house – it was Rowena who christened her, at any rate – but she's now peripatetic. Everybody feeds her.'

Buchanan too had felt compelled to contribute a saucer of milk but had not intended his offer of hospitality to extend to a night's accommodation. Only a few months ago, he reflected as he went to get the car out, he had made a similar mistake by allowing Fizz to get a foot in the door. One never learned.

There were already quite a few people in the Clachan car park when they arrived, most of them from Killin and the surrounding farms. Three or four of them had mountain bikes and there was a small contingent on horseback which Fizz identified as coming from the local pony-trekking stables. The few holidaymakers who had come along were noticeable by their colourful attire and stood out like birds of paradise among a flock of starlings.

The proceedings were being organised by a weedy chap in a check deerstalker, assisted by a middle-aged policeman, whom Fizz identified as Gavin.

'The smaller gentleman,' she muttered, 'or, as Grampa would put it, the shilpit wee nyaff, is Lindsay Crawford. His lady wife, Rowena the Wimp, is over there at the doorway, talking to Myra.'

Buchanan zeroed in on Myra's flaming orange frizz and surveyed her companion discreetly. Rowena was wearing walking breeches and a pair of boots that looked several sizes too big for her and certainly too heavy for her matchstick legs. A bulky waxed jacket served only to accentuate her painful thinness and her pale face was half hidden by dark, wavy hair that hung down lifelessly at each side of her head like a pair of spaniel's ears. She was rocking a wheeled carrycot to and fro and regarding its occupant with a worried frown as she and Myra conversed.

'Ha! There you are, Fizz,' said a voice at Buchanan's shoulder. 'I was hoping you would turn up. Good to see you, and you too, Mr Buchanan – Tam, if I may? Lindsay Crawford. Delighted to make your acquaintance.'

The accent was an anglicised Scots that sounded, to Buchanan's ears, affected and pseudo genteel, a mish-mash of narrowed vowels and blurred consonants. The voice was consciously deepened and the man himself failed to awaken an instant rapport. He looked like a self-satisfied little prig and his toothbrush moustache and falling lock of hair gave him the look of a shorter, thinner Hitler.

Buchanan's hand was taken in a double-handed politician's grip. 'You've been in hospital, I understand, Tam? Gall bladder, did I hear? Dashed painful. And how about you, Fizz? Fit, I hope? We need someone to lead a team up to the Carlin's Loup and Gavin says you've been up there before.'

'More times than I've had hot dinners,' Fizz agreed. 'And I'm not fond of salads.'

'Good, I'll tell Gavin you'll do it then, will I?'

'What d'you think, Buchanan?' Fizz said, turning to look at him. 'We can take a Land Rover up to the end of the forestry plantation but it's a bit of a slog for the next thousand feet or so.'

Buchanan hesitated to make any promises. He wasn't too keen on pushing his luck so soon after leaving hospital but he could see that Fizz was raring to go and it was clear that her experience was important to the success of the search.

Lindsay didn't wait for his answer. 'Don't worry about Tam. There's no need for him to tire himself out. I'm sure he'd be happier tagging along with Rowena and me on the forest tracks. Wouldn't you, Tam? And we can all meet up later at the big house for a jar or two. How would that be?'

Buchanan said it would be fine with him. Although he doubted whether he could stand Lindsay for a whole afternoon.

'Excellent. That's that settled then.' Lindsay patted Fizz on the shoulder, blind to the flinty stare with which she received this sign of his approval. 'You had better report to Gavin, Fizz, and I'll get our little team together. Come and meet Rowena, Tam. She's just parking our baby with Myra for a few hours so that she can come with us.'

Fizz looked for a moment as though she were about to give Lindsay the benefit of her extremely acid tongue but she saw Buchanan's pleading face and restricted her response to an expression of distaste. 'Have fun,' she said, with profound pessimism, and strode away across the car park like a trial-size SAS man.

Rowena, at close range, was even thinner than she appeared at a distance. Her cheeks curved inwards below her cheekbones and the layer of subcutaneous fat around the lower part of her face was thin enough to show the underlying muscles and tendons like an anatomical illustration. Her dark brown eyes were quite lacking in spirit, and they rested on Buchanan only in darting glances as her husband performed the introduction.

'How do you do?' She offered a limp hand that trembled nervously in Buchanan's, and made an obvious effort to find something else to say. 'You're Fizz's boss, I hear.'

'Well, as much as anyone is Fizz's boss, yes, I suppose you could say I am. But don't quote me on that, will you?' Buchanan whispered, and won a small appreciative glimmer in reply. 'I try to run a benign dictatorship but Fizz insists on a participatory democracy, and she usually wins.' He leaned over the carrycot. 'And this is your new baby?'

'Briony, yes.' Rowena's voice gained a little strength now that the baby, and not she, was the centre of attention. She had a slight, rather attractive Belfast brogue, inherited, no doubt, from her Irish mother. 'Myra is going to look after her

47

today so that I can help with the search.'

'Rowena isn't much of a hillwalker,' remarked her husband, 'but I keep telling her that, as the wife of the local MP, she has to make an effort to be part of the community. There's no need for her to be tied to Briony twenty-four hours a day.'

'But she's a little restless today,' Rowena breathed. The whites of her eyes gleamed as she glanced sideways at the baby. 'I think she may be teething.'

'Rubbish,' Lindsay said impatiently, squashing his wife like a beetle. 'She's barely four months old, for goodness' sake! Far too young to be teething.'

Myra took firm charge of the carrycot. 'Don't worry about Briony, Rowena. She doesn't care who gives her her bottle, and Zander will happily keep her amused till she falls asleep. It will do you good to think about other things for a while.'

'Well, then.' Lindsay rubbed his hands together briskly to indicate that, in his opinion, this exchange of pleasantries had gone on long enough. 'Better get things moving.'

He set off, clearly expecting the others to fall in behind him, but Buchanan pretended to misunderstand and let him go. Rowena's eyes followed her husband uncertainly for a second and then returned to Buchanan with a faint smile. She appeared more at ease without Lindsay breathing over her shoulder so Buchanan got her talking about local places of interest and found that she wasn't as repressed as he had been led to expect.

He stayed chatting quietly with Myra and Rowena till he could see the crowd begin to coalesce around their respective nuclei of five or six experienced hillwalkers. One by one the groups left the car park and debouched into the surrounding hills.

Fizz, he noticed, had Simon in her team plus a couple of middle-aged Killin hoteliers with well-worn boots and calves like Clydesdales. Buchanan himself, together with Lindsay and Rowena, was lumped in with a group of riders from the pony-trekking stables. They set off, led by Gavin, to scour the strip of woodland that lay between the Stronach river and the glen road.

One of the riders, leading a mean-looking chestnut that stood a couple of hands taller than the other hacks, moved up to Buchanan's shoulder as they left the car park.

'You are staying with Fizz's people, I think,' she said, in a husky northern European accent. 'Simon is just now telling me.'

Buchanan registered caramel-coloured hair and a prominent bosom in a yellow sweater as she added, 'I am Gerda Modder out of the trekking centre in Killin. And you are Tam Buchanan, I think.'

Buchanan admitted this and said he was delighted to meet her, which was no less than the truth.

'Simon is telling me you were being sick in hospital so today I am taking care to you and sharing my horse with you when you are getting tired.'

Buchanan wondered if she meant one at a time or both of them at once. The horse looked big enough for either option.

He said, 'That's very thoughtful of you but I'm fairly confident I'll manage to keep up without too much difficulty. I'm told we've been given the easiest route.'

'Yes. It is going up.' Her hands illustrated rising ground. 'It is not so flat but there is a path all beside the river where the fishermen are walking so much for many years so we will not be going into the bushes.' She performed a delightful little mime of hacking through undergrowth to clarify her point.

Apart from the phenomenal bosom, she was very slim and the tight-fitting breeches she was wearing outlined legs that were long and shapely. Buchanan began to be doubly glad he had decided not to go with Fizz's party.

They turned right at the crossroads and walked up the gentle rise of the glen road into the wide U-shaped valley that separated Sgurr Bodach from the end of the Ardoch Ridge. In a little over a mile they reached the entrance to Stronach Lodge, a wide gateless drive with the gamekeeper's cottage to one side. Around the cottage, for perhaps a square acre, the grounds were laid out in a stunning garden.

Spring, Buchanan had already noticed, came late to Am Bealach. By the beginning of May the Edinburgh daffodils had already passed their best but those around the farm, some five hundred feet above sea level, were only now reaching their peak. This garden, however, was ablaze, not just with daffodils but with tulips, rhododendrons, cherry blossom, forsythia, flowering currant, and a mass of blooms that Buchanan could not identify. Each flowerbed was immaculately edged with dwarf box, and a background of variegated conifers and architectural greenery betrayed the hand of an artist.

The whole group stopped for a moment to admire the display and, as they moved on, a stocky man in a wax jacket emerged from the house and fell in beside Lindsay and Rowena.

'This is Alistair Munroe,' Gerda mentioned, pointing at his back. 'He is gamekeeper for Lindsay Crawford, you know.'

'I'd heard of him, yes, but I didn't know he was the gardener as well.'

'Oh no. This is the garden of Alistair's mother. She is making it all from the rough grass and weeds in many years. Alistair is cutting the grasses and digging for her but the mother, she is making the prettiness. In June, there are the roses. All drives by for just looking over the hedge. But now Mrs Munroe has dying – has died of a . . . a . . .' Her hands mimed furiously in the vicinity of her rampant bosom.

'Pneumonia?' Buchanan hazarded.

'No . . . in the breast . . . the heart. Heart attack it is, yes, and Alistair will only be keeping the garden nice to be remembering her.'

Buchanan looked at Alistair walking just in front of him and estimated him to be somewhere in his late thirties. He was a stunted giant of a man, not much taller than the weedy Lindsay but thickset and muscular with a square head and virtually no neck. His black eyebrows grew in an unbroken line from temple to temple half hiding brown, unsmiling eyes. Not, at first glance, an intellectual, Buchanan thought, but appearances could be deceptive.

They left the road at that point and followed Gavin into the woods where they were spaced out some six feet apart and told to get on with it. Conversation languished as they paced slowly up the hill, slashing at undergrowth with their sticks and wading through long ditches filled with dead leaves. Buchanan was responsible for one side of the fishermen's path which was covered with low scrub, and Gerda, on her horse, was on the other side, checking out the deeply undercut banks of the river.

From time to time the whole group was brought to a halt as something that might be considered significant came to light. All of these discoveries turned up within a few feet of the roadway and were pronounced by Gavin to be rubbish thrown from passing cars, but around eleven o'clock Gerda spotted what looked like a short length of fencing wire snagged on a low branch. She was unsure whether to blow her whistle or not but Buchanan, on being asked for an opinion, suspected it might be a tent peg, and if so it could be important evidence. They duly alerted Gavin who marked its position on his map and folded it carefully away in a plastic bag.

Two hours later, when they stopped for lunch, nobody had found any further traces of recent human presence and the fun, such as it was, was beginning to pall.

Gavin had chosen their stopping place carefully. A large outcrop of rock afforded adequate seating for them all and there was an excellent view of the higher ground where the other teams were searching. While the search party broke out their packed lunches, Gavin and Alistair produced binoculars and patiently scrutinised the search area.

'Can you see anything of the others?' Lindsay asked.

'Aye. Robbie and Donald McMartin are out of the forest and working their way round under Allt Benan.' Alistair raised his head, squinted up at the ridge and then peered through his binoculars again. 'And there's wee Fizz and her lot coming up the left side of the Cauldron.'

Buchanan followed his pointing finger and could just discern four specks ascending a snowfield under a curling cornice of snow. From this angle the skyline of the ridge looked like an ECG of a massive coronary. One precipitous cleft cut deep into the ridge: the Carlin's Loup, the ravine which, reputedly, a witch had once leaped across to safety, leaving an enraged populace baying impotently on the other side.

'That looks dangerous,' he heard himself saying like an old mother hen.

'Fizz knows fine what she's doing,' Alistair's perpetual scowl eased marginally as he held out the binoculars. 'Take a look for yersel', Mr Buchanan.'

'The name's Tam,' said Buchanan. 'Thanks, Alistair.'

It took a moment to refocus, and by the time he had a clear view Fizz's party had already moved to the side of the snowfield and were edging round the cornice to the firmer ground. They were moving slowly and carefully, hacking out footholds with their ice axes, and Buchanan watched, virtually without breathing, till they were above the cornice before handing back the binoculars.

Alistair looked faintly amused. 'They'll no' come to any harm, ye ken. Wee Fizz grew up in these hills. Winter and summer.'

Buchanan had never before heard anyone daring to refer to Fizz as 'wee Fizz' and could only be glad she wasn't present to hear it.

Gavin sat down beside them and stretched his legs out with a groan. 'Och, yes, Fizz is not the one to be taking any chances. Her own parents were killed in an avalanche just about this time of year, you know, so she'll be careful what she's about.'

'I didn't know that,' Buchanan said. 'I knew she was orphaned young but I didn't know how.'

'Aye. It was a tragic business and both of them so young and full of life.' Gavin ran a hand through his greying hair, smoothing it in an absent fashion over the balding bit at the back of his head. 'In Glencoe it was. They had left the two children at the farm with their grampa and gone for an afternoon's walk on Buchaille Etive Mor. Fizz was no more than a wee toddler at the time and her brother – what age would Colin be then, Alistair?'

'Just started at the school.'

'Aye. About five or six.'

'It didn't put her off hillwalking, however,' Buchanan said, unable to take his eyes off the distant specks that were already preparing to abseil down the steep ravine of the Carlin's Loup to the river of scree and tumbled rocks below.

'Not Fizz,' Gavin agreed. 'It's in the blood, like. Every time she comes home she's off up the hills half an hour after she arrives.'

Buchanan reflected that that had been the case on Saturday at least. The thought reminded him of the tent and its mysterious contents. 'I meant to ask you, Gavin. Did anyone have any ideas about why the camper might have been carry-ing a window model's hand and a woman's wig?'

Gavin chuckled and finished his mouthful of roll before he answered. 'No. It's a mystery altogether. I thought at first that the wig might also be part of a window model but my wife says it isn't. She used to work in a dress shop in Stirling before we were married and she says that wigs for window models are totally different. They're made much stiffer, so she says, and they're too small for a human head.'

'Maybe the climber was a lassie, then,' Alistair suggested.

'Aye, mebbe,' Gavin grinned. 'But, if so, she took a size ten in trainers and wore Y-fronts.'

Buchanan watched Fizz's team picking their way across the treacherous slope of scree. Fizz, in her green jacket, was out in front with the others in single file behind her, and even without the binoculars he could see dislodged rocks rolling and bouncing down the slope from her feet. He said, 'There was a brown paper parcel, wasn't there? That's not something you'd find in the average camper's pack, is it? Did you find out what it contained?'

'Aye, and that was another surprise,' Gavin nodded, wiping his mouth on the back of his hand. 'Would you believe me if I told you it was jeweller's rouge? Four ingots of jeweller's rouge! Now why on earth would a camper want to carry something like that around with him?'

That, Buchanan thought, was a tough one.

'Jeweller's rouge?' Alistair said. 'What would jewellers be needing to wear rouge for?'

'It's not make-up,' Gavin told him. 'It's some sort of cleaner for jewellery.'

'They use it for polishing silver and precious metals, I think,' Buchanan agreed. 'It's a very mild abrasive.'

Gavin and Alistair thought about that for a minute, looked

speculatively at each other and at Buchanan, and gave up.

'I never saw the like,' was Gavin's only comment before he turned away to repeat the whole conversation to Lindsay, who had overheard only the final words and wanted a recap.

Gerda, who had been talking to Lindsay and Rowena, now moved over to Buchanan's side of the rocks and sat down beside him. 'I am seeing you properly from across there and I am thinking you are maybe not Scottish at all.'

'Not Scottish?' Buchanan smiled at her, somewhat at a loss. 'Certainly I'm Scottish. What makes you think I'm not?'

'Those eyes,' she said, nodding positively but with a little giggle in her voice. 'I am thinking they are Irish eyes, no?'

'And what are Irish eyes, then?' he said, playing her game. Beyond her shoulder he could still see Fizz's party. They were now gathered together at the foot of the scree slope, apparently resting from their efforts for a while before crossing the short stretch of heather that would take them back to the end of the forestry track.

'Irish eyes.' Gerda edged closer. 'This dark blue with the long lashes so black.'

Buchanan couldn't remember seeing his eyelashes since the age of thirteen when he had clipped them off with his mother's embroidery scissors because they didn't fit the macho image he was cultivating at the time. 'And yours,' he said, giving her the slow smile that had worked for him in the past, 'must be Nordic eyes. Like the eyes of the Viking maidens who used to nip smartly up the estuaries and dash off again with poor Scottish chaps like me slung over their shoulders.'

She gurgled happily and laid a hand on his arm. 'Maybe, while you are here, Tam, I will—'

Suddenly Gavin's walkie-talkie started squawking and he stood up to answer it. Buchanan and the others watched him and tried to decipher the distorted gabbling that came through.

'You what? Where?' Gavin shouted back, a finger stuck into his free ear. 'Dead, is he? How long do you think he— What? My God! Are you sure, Fizz? Christ! Right. But one of you had better stay with him. No, you and Simon come down by the Benan burn to where Simon left his Land Rover and I'll come up to meet you.'

Buchanan caught Lindsay's eye and saw him mouth the word 'dead'. He nodded, suspecting that that was the least of it.

Gavin switched off his walkie-talkie and looked round at the attentive faces. 'Fizz and her party have found a body in a wee bittie crevice below the scree slope at the foot of the Carlin's Loup. That's all I know at the moment, but at least it lets you all off the hook for the present. You're free to go now but I'd appreciate it if you would keep off this end of the ridge for the rest of the afternoon so that the police can get on with bringing the body down. Thank you all for your co-operation.'

'So, it was a climber after all, then?' Lindsay asked. 'Lost his footing on the scree?'

Gavin shook his head slightly and moved aside as the majority of the team started to pack their gear away and set off back down the hill. 'It's a bit early to be saying for sure,' he said quietly, 'but it looks like it – just possibly – wasn't accidental.'

'Suicide?' Lindsay frowned, twitching away from Rowena, who was pressing close to him to hear better.

Gavin shook his head. 'No,' he said. 'Not suicide either, I'm afraid. Fizz says she's pretty sure we've got a murder on our hands.'

Buchanan closed his eyes. It struck him as sinister that, no matter how dire a situation might be when Fizz arrived on the scene, one could usually rely on things becoming, within days, infinitely more serious.

Chapter Four

Fizz was operating on adrenaline alone by the time she and Simon got back to his Land Rover, which he had left parked in the turning circle at the top of the forestry track. Since neither of the two Killin hoteliers had been too keen on remaining all alone with the body, they had both stayed behind, huddled in the lee of a massive monolith and ignoring, as best they could, the mashed and mutilated corpse a few feet lower down the slope.

Fizz had done no more than glance into the makeshift grave. It was quite obvious that, even if they had found him sooner, there was nothing they could have done for the chap. He was lying on his back, stark naked as far as Fizz could see, and a layer of heavy boulders had been pitched into the fissure on top of him. Animals had been at him – foxes, perhaps, or wild cats, or even raptors – dislodging the smaller stones and tearing at his flesh. Her immediate edict that nothing was to be touched was a waste of breath since none of the other three would have touched a single boulder for less than a month's wages.

She would have preferred to leave Simon behind to guard the body, rather than the two hoteliers, because he had been getting up her nose all day. He had an inflated opinion of his own mountaineering skills and questioned Fizz's leadership at every turn, till she was forced to point out, in quite bald terms, that she knew the ridge better than any of the Killin locals and particularly him. She had suffered his delusions of adequacy thus far with a patience that, she felt, deserved canonisation, but by the time they reached the Land Rover she was itching to be rid of him.

Simon made a beeline for the driver's door and produced a flask of whisky from under the seat.

'No way,' said Fizz when he offered it to her. 'I don't drink on the hills and if you're planning to drive down that track I don't think you should either.'

'The hell with that,' Simon retorted, unscrewing the cap. 'I've driven these tracks a hundred times.'

Fizz looked him in the eye. 'Not with me aboard, you haven't, Simon, and I'm not bloody well walking home. OK?'

In the few seconds Simon took to consider this Fizz could hear a grouse croaking in the heather at least a mile away. She wondered if Buchanan had already gone back to the big house with Lindsay and Rowena for the promised 'jar or two'.

Simon made a face and recapped the flask, shoving it in his pocket. 'You're probably right, Fizz. But, I don't mind telling you, I could do with something to wipe out the thought of that . . . that mess up there.'

'Me too,' Fizz admitted. 'But I can wait till I get back to civilisation.' She walked to the edge of the turning circle and found a spot where she could watch for Gavin's approach. Simon followed her, turning up the collar of his jacket against the breeze that was, now that they'd stopped walking, suddenly quite chilling.

He said, 'I suppose it has to be murder.'

'Well, it's not the way *I'd* choose to commit suicide,' Fizz said. 'I mean, crawling into a hole and pulling rocks in on top of you isn't exactly the nicest way to go.'

Simon put on a sick expression as though he felt that this

was not a suitable subject for humour. He was wearing a woolly hat that hid his hair and without its usual frame of black curls his tanned face was an unlikely orange. He said, 'I mean, it's interesting that he was at the bottom of the scree slope. As if, maybe, he'd fallen down and killed himself and someone else had buried him there.'

'Could be.' Fizz didn't want to talk about the body. The grave was no great distance away from where they stood and, although she knew she was imagining it, she could have sworn that there was a detectable smell of rotting meat on the breeze. The sight of the corpse, particularly so soon after the episode of the detached hand on Saturday, had shaken her more than she cared to admit.

'Maybe there were two of them camping in that tent.' Simon sat down on a boulder, straddled his legs and propped an elbow on each knee. 'Either that or somebody trailed that poor guy here with the intention of killing him.'

'I hope you're right, Simon,' Fizz told him frankly. 'I hope he turns out to be some crooked drug dealer on the run from the Edinburgh Mafia. Me, I just can't help wondering if old Bessie's disappearance is connected with this in some way.'

He straightened up to look at her. 'You're getting carried away, Fizz. This has a different feel to it altogether. Violent. Deliberate. Not like Bessie's disappearance. I'm sure that was an accident.'

It was easier for Simon to believe that Bessie had had an accident than for someone who had grown up with the old lady, so Fizz didn't bother to argue. But it made her sick to her stomach to think that dear old Bessie might have met a similar brutal and undignified end.

It felt like hours before they heard the police Land Rover coming up the track, although it was probably no more than twenty minutes, and by then they were both impatient to finish steering Gavin in the direction of the scene of crime and absent themselves from the vicinity.

Simon was all for dropping Fizz at the big house and heading for home but Rowena opened the door as they drew up outside and beckoned them both in.

'Myra's in here, Simon. She brought Briony round and she's waiting for you to run her home. Come in and have a drink. I'm sure you need it, and everyone is dying to hear about what you found.'

Simon slid out from behind the wheel and Fizz forced her stiff legs to follow him up the steps. A familiar pale-maned chestnut horse was tied up at the side of the house, making a vain attempt to nibble the cropped turf.

Rowena was still in her walking breeches but had changed her boots for a pair of court shoes, which looked ridiculous. She propped the tray of glasses she was carrying on one hip and held the door wider. 'Come on in. Everyone's in the drawing room, Simon,' she said, catching Fizz's eye for a second. 'Just go on in.'

Fizz took the hint, followed her through the dark, panelled hallway to the kitchen and watched her unload the glasses into the dishwasher. Loki, the ancient black poodle that ruled the household, slung his head over the rim of his basket and snarled in a half-hearted manner.

'Same to you, you little rat,' said Fizz.

'So,' Rowena asked without turning round. 'You found the climber? It must have been dreadful. Gavin said it might be murder.'

Fizz collapsed on to a chair at the table and started to unlace her boots. 'Probably. Someone tried to bury him, at any rate. I didn't examine the body too closely. Mind if we talk about it another time?'

Rowena leaned her back against the sink and looked at her. 'You don't look too good.'

'I'm fine. Just a bit out of training. Actually, you don't look so wonderful yourself.'

'Lindsay asked the search party back for drinks,' Rowena said, straightening up and pushing her hair back from her face with both hands. The action pulled the skin tight across her eyes and made her look ready to scream with tension. 'The lounge is full of people in muddy boots, half of whom I don't even know, I haven't a thing to give them to nibble except a few salted cashew nuts, I've had to use my good crystal glasses, and Briony was due to be fed half an hour ago.'

She took two tumblers out of a cupboard and half filled them with gin. 'Cheers,' she said, taking a large gulp from one before passing the other to Fizz.

'Sod the lot of them,' Fizz said, raising her glass in a toast. She waved at the chair on the other side of the table. 'Sit down, Rowena, and relax. If Lindsay can invite people round he can bloody well help to look after them.'

Rowena sank into a chair and let her shoulders droop. It occurred to Fizz that this was not her first gin of the day.

'It doesn't work like that, Fizz. When you're married to an MP you're supposed to be an accomplished hostess. You have to be able to talk to people and arrange dinner parties and always be ready for surprise guests.' She rattled her glass against her slightly protuberant incisors and siphoned up about a gill of gin. 'That's never been my scene – *you* know that – but Lindsay says he has to move in the right circles, know the right people, have house parties and dinner parties, invite these appalling supercilious people for fishing weekends—'

Sudden tears sprang to her eyes as though she'd just received an unexpected bikini wax.

61

'So, let him pay for it,' Fizz told her firmly. 'It's not as if he's short of a bob or two and the Clachan wouldn't say no to a bit of extra business. Tell him to do his own brown-nosing.'

Rowena giggled through her tears. Evidently the gin was beginning to work. 'I wish I could, Fizz. I'd love to see his face.'

'Why can't you? You don't have to be nasty about it, just tell him you've got enough to do right now with looking after Briony. And tell him you need an au pair while you're at it.'

'But I don't need an au pair,' Rowena said. 'Mrs Connor comes up from Killin Mondays, Wednesdays and Fridays.'

Fizz sighed. 'I've told you a hundred times, Rowena. When you're bargaining you start high so that you can come to a compromise and still end up with what you wanted in the first place.'

Rowena got up and went to the doorway to scan the passageway, then she reached up to the ledge above the door and brought down a packet of cigarettes. Before sitting down again she demolished the remainder of her gin and refilled her glass.

'I wish you still lived here, Fizz,' she muttered, lighting a cigarette. 'There's not a soul I can talk to any more.' Sometimes, usually when she was under strain, you could hear the lilt of her mother's Irish accent overriding her natural Perthshire burr.

'You can talk to Lindsay,' Fizz said.

'No. Not really. He's not interested in my life and – to tell you the truth, Fizz – I'm not much interested in his. I thought it would be better when Briony came along but, if anything, we're even further apart. He doesn't want to hear "baby talk" as he calls it and he only wants to play with her when she's just been fed, not when she's screaming with colic.' She dangled her head over her drink and sniffed. 'I don't know why I married him.'

That was something Fizz had wondered about too, but now was not the time to say so. She said, 'All marriages go through bad patches. Just hang on in there and things will get better. If you can just make the effort to let Lindsay know how you feel—'

Through the open doorway the sound of voices suddenly swelled as the drawing-room door opened. Hurriedly, Rowena slid her drink across to Fizz's side of the table and motioned her to take the cigarette.

'Christ!' Fizz grabbed Rowena's drink and held it under the table as Lindsay's voice, behind her, said, 'What's taking you so long, Rowena? There are people waiting for— Is that Fizz?' He came round the table to face her. 'Fizz, my dear, what are you sitting in the kitchen for, for goodness' sake? Come on through to the drawing room. Everyone's waiting to talk to you. Rowena, glasses, please, as soon as you can.'

Fizz had no intention of being interviewed by the assembled locals. Simon was good at being centre stage and there was no point in both of them having to relive their nasty experience oftener than was necessary. Besides, she couldn't move without exposing her extra glass.

'I'll be through in a minute, Lindsay,' she said. 'I'm just talking to Rowena about something at the moment.'

His moustache bristled a bit at that. 'Girls' talk, eh?' He took a bottle of Highland Park out of a cupboard and held it up to the light to check the level. 'Oh well, don't keep the hostess from her guests too long, will you?'

Fizz merely smiled, contenting herself with mouthing a few obscenities at his retreating back.

'Listen,' she said to Rowena, who was feverishly pouring detergent into the dishwasher. 'Don't bother about that, just run the glasses under the tap. The whisky will kill any germs.'

'Oh . . . yes. Right. I suppose that would be quicker.'

'That lot through there would drink Highland Park out of a bedpan so don't worry.'

They did a quick rinse-and-polish job, topped up their gins, and carried the loaded tray back through to the lounge.

It was a long, narrow room with a bay window and there were about fifteen people in walking gear standing or sitting about in groups, the largest of which surrounded Simon, who was still being debriefed by Lindsay. Buchanan was sitting on the window seat twinkling his eyes at the Hunchfront of Rotterdam, alias Gerda from the pony-trekking stables, a lady whose path had crossed Fizz's on more than one occasion.

Fizz sent them a cheery wave and went straight over to join them, ignoring both Buchanan's lack of enthusiasm at the sight of her and a bout of imperative beckoning from Lindsay.

'Hi,' she said. 'How's it going, Gerda?'

Gerda's smile stretched her lips no more than a dud face-lift. 'It is going good. Is it going good for you?'

'Fine.' Fizz turned to Buchanan. 'You OK, Kimosabe? Still firing on all cylinders?'

Buchanan drew in a long breath as though he were resigning himself to something. 'Yes, I'm fine, Fizz. Unlike your team, we had a very uneventful walk.' His eyes examined her face closely as though he were looking for signs of strain.

Fizz smiled at him brightly.

'Simon is telling how you are noticing the grave place from up high,' Gerda remarked. 'Maybe you are knowing the body, Fizz, yes? Maybe a person from Killin?'

Buchanan made a small quick movement as though to stop Fizz answering too graphically. 'Evidently identification is likely to be difficult. Isn't that so, Fizz?' He glanced aside at

Gerda in a pointed way and added obliquely, 'His killer didn't want him to be identified too quickly.'

'You bet,' Fizz assured them both. 'His face was like a pizza, what I saw of it.'

Buchanan looked at her with a sort of sad amazement as Gerda feigned imminent blackout. 'That's the impression we got from Simon,' he said, with a faint sigh, 'although, I have to say, he didn't feel the need to be quite so explicit.'

'Not only was his face puréed into baby food,' Fizz elaborated happily, anaesthetised by her two large gins, 'but, as far as I could see, he was bollock naked, so somebody had gone to a lot of trouble to make sure he was virtually unidentifiable.'

'Really?' said Buchanan a touch drily, as one who felt the subject had outlived its interest.

'Which makes me think that the killer didn't know his victim had a tent in the woods, otherwise he'd have destroyed that as well.'

Gerda was leaning forward with her mouth open, evidently experiencing some difficulty in following the conversation. Her talents, much extolled by every bachelor in Killin and by quite a few husbands as well, did not lie in the field of linguistics. Buchanan smiled at her kindly and gave her a brief résumé, then looked at Fizz.

'So . . .' he said, thoughtfully, 'if somebody went to all that trouble to prevent his being identified . . . does that mean he must be somebody we – or at least the locals – *would* have identified if they'd seen his face? Could he be a local after all? No, someone would have missed him by now, and anyway, a local wouldn't be camping.'

'That's not impossible,' Fizz remarked. 'My brother and I used to go backpacking all over these hills during the school holidays—'

'Yes, but I'm sure you didn't camp so close to the road.' Buchanan broke off with a polite smile as Lindsay appeared, towing Rowena firmly by the wrist. Rowena's face was fixed in an inane grin and she was clearly having trouble focusing her eyes. Almost everyone but Lindsay must have noticed that she was completely pissed.

'That was Gavin on the phone again, Tam, to see if you and Fizz were still here.' Lindsay treated them all to an affable nod. 'There's an Inspector Cullen from Callander CID wanting a word with you both. He'll drop by the farm first thing in the morning, if that's OK with you. I told him you'd ring him back if it wasn't suitable.'

'No problem,' said Buchanan. His face barely flickered as he took in Rowena's condition with a glance. 'I was planning to go for a pony trek tomorrow – Gerda has been selling me on the idea – but I can postpone that till later in the week.'

'You'd be well advised to have a quiet day tomorrow anyway,' Fizz said firmly and, as Buchanan stood up to give Rowena his seat, she made use of his momentary distraction to flash Gerda a quick smile and add, 'Buchanan had a bad night last night. Selena kept taking all the duvet to herself, didn't she, Buchanan? And anyway, the weather forecast is for showers coming from the west. If you wait till Saturday I'll come with you. Haven't been on a garron for years.'

'And you must make time for some fishing too, Tam,' Lindsay was rattling on. 'I'll get Alistair to ghillie for you if you like. He knows the river like the back of his hand and he'll get you a fish, all right.'

Buchanan was only half listening. He had moved round so that Lindsay had to look away from Rowena to address him and he was probably hoping that Fizz would leap into the breach in some unspecified manner to save the situation.

Gerda, ignoring the drama, smiled at someone across the

room and, without comment, stood up and drifted away to talk to him.

'That's extremely kind, Lindsay.' Buchanan's eyes darted sideways to watch Gerda go. 'I'd appreciate a cast or two on the Stronach. What flies—'

Rowena, who had sprawled on to the window seat like a length of wet spaghetti, suddenly blurted out, 'Let's *all* go f'r a pony tr – a pony trek. Used t'have a pony when I was a kid, 'member, Fizz? Heather Bell. You used t'call her Merry Hell, dinchyou? Died, y'know. Foot rot or suthing. Broke m'heart.'

Lindsay had his back to her but his head swung round so fast he almost looked over his shoulder like an owl. Incredulity fought with horror in his eyes.

'Well,' he said briskly, making a grab for her arm, 'must circulate, Rowena.'

His plan was, clearly, to circulate her straight out of the door but Rowena wasn't having any. 'You cir . . . circul-l-l-late, Lindsay,' she smiled blearily. 'They're your fren's not mine. Don' need the hassle. Nex' time y'can take 'em to th' Clach'n, OK?' Her head waggled cheekily. 'OK, chum?'

Lindsay caught her by the arms. 'Rowena, my dear, you sound a bit weary. You'd better come and lie down.'

'Nex' time y'can eat out too. No more dinnnn'r parries. Righ'?'

'Whatever you say, dear. Now come along upstairs.'

Rowena allowed herself to be led away adding, with a wink over her shoulder for Fizz, 'An' 'nother thing, chum. Need an au . . . au . . . au pair.'

Backs were studiously turned as the Crawfords paced steadily towards the door, and the background conversation continued, stilted but loud.

When they had gone Fizz said, 'Well, I suppose we ought to be going, huh?'

Buchanan said nothing, just stared at her, wearing his amazed expression again.

'Oh, gimme a break!' Fizz snapped, suddenly fed up with having him constantly judging her. 'I'm not to blame for *everything* that happens, you know! If you had your way I'd be done for breaking the Portland Vase, assassinating Kennedy and dropping the atom bomb on Nagasaki. You're always telling me a lawyer should keep an open mind – well, why not try it for once?'

'Who gave her the booze?' he said.

'She gave herself the booze and, if you're going to ask me why I didn't stop her, I didn't stop her because it's none of my business how she lives her life. She may be a wimp but that doesn't mean she's stupid. She knows, better than I do and certainly better than you do, whether she needs a drink or not, so don't bug me, OK?'

'But you primed her to stand up to Lindsay, didn't you?' Buchanan said. 'How does that fit in with your policy of nonintervention?'

'She asked for my opinion and I gave it. What she did with it was up to her. I certainly wouldn't have advised her to do it the way she did, but there you go. I wouldn't have advised her to marry the boring fart in the first place, would you?'

Buchanan looked austere, which he was good at. 'I dare say she had her reasons.'

'Sure. Maybe she fell for that bristly wee moustache of his. Maybe she likes kissing him good night and getting her teeth brushed at the same time. Or, who knows, maybe he has a todger like an aubergine.'

As she expected, he put on his maiden aunt face and did a quick recce of the nearest groups to see if anyone had overheard.

'Well,' he muttered, grinding his teeth, 'whether you had

anything to do with that little contretemps or not, Fizz, I think it would be a good idea if you weren't here when Lindsay comes back. I doubt if you'll be flavour of the month as far as he's concerned.'

'I don't know why he should be so mad at her for getting pissed,' Fizz said, unable to stop needling him now that she had started. 'I bet it's the only time he ever gets a shag.'

'I'm going now,' Buchanan said tersely, putting his half-finished glass of white wine carefully on the table beside him. 'Do you want a run home or have you still more havoc to wreak?'

She was tempted to tell him to get stuffed but wasn't quite ratty enough. 'Nothing I can't put off till another day,' she said sweetly. 'I'll take the run home.'

She saw him having a good look round, presumably for Gerda, but the Hunchfront was nowhere to be seen and her gawky chestnut was gone from the front door.

As they walked back to the Clachan to pick up the car a thought occurred to her. 'If I have to hang around tomorrow waiting for Inspector What's-his-face to drop by,' she said, 'it's going to make it awkward for me to get back to Edinburgh. It takes hours by public transport and I want to be there by tomorrow night because I've got a lecture at nine thirty on Wednesday morning.'

'Lindsay said Inspector Cullen would be calling first thing in the morning,' Buchanan pointed out. 'You could be on your way by ten o'clock.'

'Yes, but the school bus will be gone by then so I'll have to wait for the post bus at eleven. It would be so much easier if you would drive me into Stirling and I can get a train there for Edinburgh.'

He made a face but she could see he wasn't going to refuse. After a minute he said, 'Actually, I could take you to

Edinburgh. It's only a two-hour drive and I wouldn't mind dropping into the office just to keep an eye on things. Dad gets a bit excited if the work gets on top of him.'

'The office ticked over very efficiently while you were in hospital, you know,' Fizz told him.

'Yes, but I was on hand if Dad needed to discuss anything with me. He can't drop everything and run up here so easily and I told him not to phone me unless in an emergency since the only phone in the farm is in the kitchen.'

'Are you telling me he took work into the hospital for you?'

He turned his head away, pretending to be following the flight of a pair of crows. 'No, no. Just discussed a couple of things with me. He likes a second opinion sometimes.'

Fizz glared exasperation at him but he pretended not to notice. Buchanan's father had been officially retired for almost a year now. He had given up his duties as an honorary sheriff but he still managed to totter into the office three or four times a week and cream off all the best cases for himself, mostly the ones that would normally have gone to his son. Alan Stewart, the third partner, wasn't much affected since he specialised in Family Law, but Buchanan must have been aware for some time that his own career was virtually on hold.

'Big Daddy', as Fizz thought of Buchanan senior, was a darling man and she got along with him just fine, but he was spoiled rotten by his entire family and needed a short, sharp shock. He didn't realise how much his son did to make life easy for him but it was already apparent to Fizz that Buchanan's current leave of absence could, if properly managed, provide a salutary lesson.

'Buchanan,' she said carefully, 'don't you think you should just allow your father to get on with it in his own way, this time? Don't you think it might do him good to have a little stress in his life now and then? As long as you keep sheltering him from every wind that blows he's never going to retire. Why don't you let him find out how hard it is for once? In two weeks, with a little encouragement, he'll be so pissed off he'll never want to see the place again.'

Buchanan turned his head to look at her. 'When you say "a little encouragement", Fizz, I hope you don't mean a little encouragement from you.'

'Nothing he'd notice—' Fizz started to say, and then realised that he was as near angry as she'd ever seen him.

'My father will retire when he decides to do so, OK?' Buchanan said, clearly holding himself in check. 'If I wanted to elbow him out of his own practice I'd have done so before now so, please, Fizz, just mind your own business for once, would you?'

'OK, OK,' she said. 'Handle it your own way.'

'One would have thought, after all the trouble your interference caused last time, that—'

'Oh *puleeze*! Gimme a break. I'm sorry I ever thought about it, all right? You want tears? I'll cry!'

She could hear him grinding his teeth but he evidently didn't trust himself to discuss it further. At the same time, however, she received the distinct impression that, if it weren't for his tender conscience, he'd have welcomed her assistance in edging the old boy into retirement.

Well, she thought, she had planted the idea in his mind. He might not like it right now, but it would be interesting to see whether or not it took root.

71

Chapter Five

The clouds were well down over the hills when Buchanan woke the following morning, and the surface of the loch was dimpled with a fine rain. However, the break in the weather didn't bother him unduly, since it was going to be a wasted day in any case, what with hanging about waiting for the CID Inspector and then having to drive Fizz at least as far as Stirling.

He hadn't yet made up his mind about pressing on to Edinburgh and dropping in at the office, although Fizz's remarks on the subject kept floating back into his mind. It had come as something of a surprise to him to learn that even the part-time staff were aware of the problems his father was causing but it only confirmed what he had known for many months: that the practice would suffer if the old boy didn't bow out pretty soon. His memory was definitely not what it had been and it was only due to his son's constant vigilance that the loss of his legendary acuteness had not been noted by the Edinburgh legal fraternity at large.

The thought of deliberately leaving the old boy without support for two weeks made Buchanan's conscience squirm but, in fact, it could turn out to be the lesser of two evils: better by far than telling his father, to his face, that he was past it. Alan Stewart would be around to avert any major disasters

73

but he certainly wouldn't provide the backup the senior partner was used to.

It wasn't the sort of problem he felt he could contemplate before breakfast so he expelled Selena, who had stayed the night, and ran across the cobbled yard to the farmhouse kitchen.

Fizz was still at the table, Auntie Duff was stirring porridge at the Aga and Grampa was standing at the fire in damp waterproofs with a mug of tea in one hand and a bacon roll in the other.

'Just look at you, Tam,' said Auntie Duff, in exactly the tone his mother would have used. 'Could you not have taken a minute to slip on a jacket? That's how you get rheumatism, you know, sitting around in damp clothes all day.'

'It's hardly raining,' Buchanan said, noting Fizz's amusement.

'We don't want you landing up back in the hospital, do we?' Auntie Duff riposted, transferring his place setting to the side of the table closest to the Aga. 'Sit you down here and get dried out.'

She bustled out into the pantry and Fizz sent him a wicked grin. 'She'll be dandling you on her knee by the end of the fortnight, wait and see.'

'The river's up a bit,' said Grampa at the same time, having apparently not heard Fizz speaking. 'If this rain continues it might be worth trying a cast or two tomorrow. Alistair is supposed to be taking you out sometime, isn't he?'

'Yes,' Buchanan said loudly and clearly, as he had quickly learned to address the old man. 'I'm told he can practically guarantee me a salmon.'

'Aye well, if they're there Alistair will find them, no doubt about that. There's been four generations of Munroes at the Stronach estate and every one of them famous fishermen.

74

Alistair knows every stone in that river, every submerged rock that will snag your line, every wee hollow where a fish will lie.' Grampa gave a short, affirmative grunt that sounded like a bark, a habit of his which Buchanan found quite intriguing, given that he looked like a greying Scottie dog.

Fizz said, 'For God's sake don't get him started, Buchanan, or he'll talk fishing all day.'

Buchanan glanced at Grampa but the old man gave no sign of having overheard.

'Oh aye,' he was saying, 'Alistair will tell you where to cast and he'll tell you what fly to use, depending on the state of the water. The Red Munroe is a killer when the water's rising. That one's called after his father's uncle, Robbie, who was shot in the Dardanelles.'

'Bet that made his eyes water,' Fizz said with a blank face.

Buchanan pretended to be as deaf as her grampa, knowing that if she saw he was embarrassed she'd only get worse. 'Can I buy flies around here?' he shouted.

'Down in Killin, aye. But you'll get a better selection in Stirling.'

'I'll show him where the fishing tackle shop is,' Fizz said, raising her voice a couple of decibels. 'There's a train for Edinburgh every half-hour so I won't be in any hurry.'

Grampa glared at her. 'It would suit you better, my lady, if you got yourself back to Edinburgh and put in a bit of work for your exams. That's what you got the time off for and I've seen very little evidence of it over the weekend. When are you going to learn some sense?'

'Buggered if I know,' said Fizz.

'Speak up, lassie!'

'I said, I'll study tonight,' she yelled, smiling with frightening innocence.

Auntie Duff came back in with her hands full of eggs. 'I see a car coming,' she told them. 'It'll be the man from the CID.'

Grampa walked over to the window, his rheumaticky knees clicking at every step, and looked up the farm road towards the crossroads. 'Well, they'll not be wanting to talk to me,' he said, hastily finishing his roll. 'I'm away back up the hill.' He rushed out and a minute later the drone of his quad bike faded away into the distance just as the sound of the approaching motorcar became audible.

'Let the policeman in the front door, Fizz,' said Auntie Duff, getting ready to serve the porridge, 'and put him in the front room till Tam is finished his breakfast.'

'I will not,' Fizz said calmly. 'He can talk to us in the kitchen like everyone else. I'm not finished my own breakfast yet so if he wants to talk to me he can do it while I eat.'

Auntie Duff looked at Buchanan. 'I can hold your second course if you like, Tam, and you can talk to him in the front room.'

'It's all the same to me,' Buchanan said. 'If you don't mind them in here we might as well let them get on with it. It would save a bit of time and let Fizz get on her merry way back to Edinburgh.'

'Oh, that reminds me,' Auntie Duff said, as Fizz went to open the front door, 'I have some shopping I want Fizz to do for me in Stirling before she gets on the train. Could you bring it home for me in your car, I wonder?'

'No problem.'

'Just one or two things I can't get in Killin. We don't have a chemist's shop in the village, you see, and if you want anything at all out of the usual you have to depend on somebody picking it up for you. I've run out of wool for the cardigan I'm knitting—'

She broke off as Fizz came back into the room leading two men in raincoats, one of them probably in his early forties and the other some ten or fifteen years his junior.

'Detective Inspector Cullen and Detective Sergeant McLaren,' said Fizz, ushering them to seats at the table. As they shook hands she said, 'They've had their breakfasts, Auntie Duff, but they wouldn't say no to a cup of tea while Buchanan and I finish ours.'

'If we're not being a nuisance,' added Cullen politely, draping his coat over the back of his chair and sitting down. McLaren followed suit, watching the delivery of Buchanan's poached eggs and kidneys, and his eyes were those of a starving puppy.

'I hope you don't mind watching me eat,' Buchanan said, 'but we're on a tight schedule today, as I'm sure you are, and we thought that preferable to keeping you waiting.'

'Please.' Cullen waved a magnanimous hand. 'We shouldn't have to keep you long. Just one or two small points I have to clear up.'

'Of course. Only too happy.' Buchanan transferred a slice of kidney to his mouth under the close and speculative gaze of the sergeant. 'What can we tell you?'

DS McLaren took out a notebook, flipped it open and started painstakingly checking all the information that Fizz had already given to Gavin: how had they come to stumble across the tent in the undergrowth, had it appeared to them to have been ransacked, had they touched anything other than the hand and the tin of tomatoes, etc., in the midst of which Auntie Duff dumped a pot of tea on the table and went off to visit her lambs.

Fizz took it upon herself to answer most of the questions and Buchanan left her to it, giving only the occasional nod of confirmation and concentrating on his breakfast. It was amusing to see the way she handled the interrogation, offering her evidence with the wide-eyed gaze she kept for bamboozling people in authority into viewing her as sweet and innocent and none too bright. The sergeant immediately changed his tactics and the tone of his questioning became almost conversational.

'So, in fact,' Cullen put in, with an irritable glance at his disarmed junior, 'neither of you saw the interior of the tent until after your dog had disarranged it. A pity about that. It makes our work so much more difficult.'

'Not as difficult as it would have been if Luath hadn't found the tent at all, though,' Fizz said, with an enthusiasm that dazzled them while she got her dig in. 'If it hadn't been for Luath you wouldn't even know there had been a murder.'

McLaren was so anaesthetised by Fizz's girlish charm that he didn't even know he'd been needled. He gave her the sort of smile Buchanan had seen directed at her in the past, the smile that is usually reserved for a cute little four-year-old poppet, while the DI pushed back his chair and said, 'I take it you will both be around for the next day or two in case we need to ask you any more questions?'

'I'm going to Edinburgh today,' Fizz said, 'but I'll be back on Friday evening for a couple of days.'

Seeing Cullen preparing to depart, Buchanan said quickly, 'I take it you have managed to establish a firm connection between the body and the tent? Or is that still only a probability?'

'It's more than a probability,' said the Inspector. 'We found an elastic hair toggle on the corpse. It appears that, whoever he was, he wore his hair in a ponytail and, although it had come loose, the toggle was still entangled in a few strands at the back of his neck. Luckily, we found an identical toggle in the tent. However, I'm hoping our forensic department will be able to come up with some more evidence to strengthen the connection.'

McLaren slipped his notebook into his pocket and finished his tea. 'Also,' he said, looking at Buchanan, 'the tent peg you and Miss Modder turned up yesterday matches the ones used to pitch the tent in the clearing. That makes it seem likely that the camper entered the woods from the direction of the glen road. That could turn out to be a valuable piece of evidence.'

Fizz leaned an elbow on the table. 'And what about the disappearance of Bessie Anderson, five weeks ago? That must have happened round about the same time as the camper died and I'm sure you don't believe in coincidences any more than I do. Will you be reopening that inquiry?'

Cullen stood up and struggled into his waterproof coat. 'We'll certainly be bearing that incident in mind, Miss Fitzpatrick.'

'Is that all?' she said, looking as belligerent as her baby face permitted. 'What if we're dealing with a serial killer here? Do we have to wait till somebody else disappears?'

Both policemen smiled at this, Cullen with an amused twist of lip, the sergeant with a soppy look like a doting father.

'I don't think you have to lose any sleep over that possibility, miss,' McLaren told her. 'But you can be sure we'll be looking into all the circumstances surrounding the death of this young man. If there's any connection to Miss Anderson's disappearance, we'll find it.'

Buchanan said, 'You haven't identified the body yet?'

'No. It's not proving easy,' Cullen said, waiting for McLaren to stop smiling at Fizz and get his coat on.

'What do you know about him?' Fizz asked, directing her question at McLaren on the clear assumption that she'd get more out of him than from his superior.

'Not a lot,' he told her. 'He appears to be between eighteen and twenty, about five eleven, tanned, and with brown, shoulder-length hair. The food in the tent was bought in a Stirling supermarket. According to the brand labels, his underwear is British, his socks and one of his T-shirts were made in France. The sell-by date on the milk carton was the eighth of April and his paperback had been bought in London.'

Cullen coughed pointedly, bringing McLaren hurriedly to his feet, and then said, 'We mustn't take up any more of your time but I'll leave you a phone number where we can be contacted if anything else occurs to you. It's possible we may need your fingerprints just to eliminate you from our inquiries.'

Fizz saw them out and returned looking suspiciously smug. 'Things are looking up,' she announced as she resumed her seat at the table and reached for a slice of toast. 'There will be another full-scale search for Bessie Anderson any day now, mark my words.'

'You think so?' Buchanan said.

'Bound to be. She must have gone missing within days of—' A thought struck her and she jumped up to check the calendar beside the fireplace. 'Let's see. Bessie went missing the Sunday Briony was christened which must have been the . . . seventh of April. *The seventh!* What was the sell-by date on the milk carton? The eighth, wasn't it?'

'It was,' Buchanan admitted and added before she could beat him to it, 'You told me there had to be a connection, didn't you?'

'I sure did, and I told Gavin too, so I'm damn sure Cullen must have been told.' She chewed a mouthful of toast and then turned to look at Buchanan through narrowed eyes. 'He knows that Bessie Anderson and the camper died within days of each other – maybe even on the same day – but he's not admitting it to us.'

'Maybe he didn't want you to worry about it. All that talk

about a serial killer! He probably thinks you're likely to start a panic.'

'I was only trying to concentrate his mind a little,' she said, licking jam off her thumb. 'Besides, why shouldn't we be worried? The guy who killed a harmless old lady like Bessie has to be seriously unbalanced, wouldn't you say? And if he's still hanging around Am Bealach, who knows which of us will be next?'

'Serial killers don't work like that,' Buchanan said. 'They like to advertise their work. They leave the bodies where they can be found. They arrange them in a certain way or mark them so that the police know all the killings have been done by the same perpetrator. This killer is quite different. He tried to hide the camper's body, he left no "signature" at the scene of the crime and, if he killed Miss Anderson as well, he has succeeded in disposing of her remains without alerting the police to the possibility of foul play. None of which is typical behaviour for a serial killer.'

She nodded, rolling her eyes impatiently. 'OK, already. But why did he pick those two: a dottery old biddy and a nutty camper with a tent full of weird objects? There's no sense in it.'

'Let's not get fixated on the idea that the same guy killed them both,' Buchanan suggested. 'I admit that it does look like they both met their end around the same time but, as you say, who would pick those two? I think we have to remember that there is no proof either way. Maybe, if the police could find out who the camper was, they'd know why he was killed. And, when they know why he was killed, they'll be a step nearer to knowing who did it.'

Fizz made a face at him to let him know what she thought of a logical approach and said, 'And how do you propose to find out who he was?'

Buchanan set down his cup and nailed her with a look.

'Let's just get this straight, Fizz. I do not propose to find out who he was. I never at any time promised you or anybody else that I'd make this affair my business. I've no objection to discussing it with you but if the police are now looking into the matter there's not the slightest need for anyone else to get involved.'

Her expression was one of hurt disbelief. She didn't say a word, just stared at him, but he received the impression that she might start to shed tears at any minute.

'However,' he heard himself say hastily, 'one can't help being curious, so – this is not contractually binding and does not constitute an offer, OK? – so I don't mind keeping my ears open while I'm here.'

'That's your decision,' she said sadly, and let the subject drop. However, the words, *'but you'll have to live with it'* hung unspoken in the air like a banner.

Chapter Six

As soon as her Wednesday morning lecture was over Fizz made a beeline back to her flat. She rarely socialised much with her fellow students since most of them were still at the dressing crazily/drinking heavily/screwing everything stage, which she found very boring.

It was raining, so it wasn't too difficult to stay in and transcribe her lecture notes, after which she finished off an essay she had to hand in before Friday. With that off her mind she felt better about having taken the weekend off but she knew she'd have to put in some serious work between now and the end of the week if she were to get away with doing the same thing next weekend. Her first-year exams were only weeks away and she was determined to do well. She still had to earn her living, however, which meant clocking in at Buchanan and Stewart by 2 p.m.

When she got there, everyone was in a flap because Mr Buchanan senior needed the file on Hamilton Holdings, with whom he had a meeting in half an hour, and it had disappeared without trace.

His secretary, Margaret, bore down on Fizz before she had a chance to take off her jacket.

'I think it was among the papers I gave you to file last Friday,' she said, eyes flashing with malice. 'I can't imagine what you've—'

'Wrong,' Fizz interrupted sounding, to her own ears, like Big Ben striking one o'clock. 'The papers you gave me to file were all Mr Stewart's, as I'm sure you remember, so don't let's play silly buggers, OK, Margaret?'

'Well now, I'm not sure you're right about that—'

'No, but *I'm* sure. And another thing I'm sure about,' Fizz told her sweetly, 'is that I'm not carrying the can for your mistakes, or anybody else's, so don't even think about trying to pin this one on me or Mr Buchanan will be learning things about *you* that he didn't know before.'

Margaret's eyes narrowed as she brought her face down to Fizz's level. 'Like what?' she hissed, the consonants cracking like whips.

'Like who buggered up the photocopier last month, for a start.'

Margaret straightened with a jerk and turned away. 'Oh well,' she said, over her shoulder, in unconvincingly scathing tones, 'if that's your attitude!'

Fizz smiled at her retreating figure. She rather enjoyed these little spats with Margaret, who had never made any secret of the fact that she regarded Fizz as an abomination. That was OK with Fizz. One couldn't please everybody, after all, and Margaret was always going to be one of her little failures. As the senior secretary in the practice, she thought of Mr Buchanan père as her own property, and she didn't like it one bit when Big Daddy took to Fizz like she was the daughter he'd never had. She didn't like it when he allowed her to use the name 'Fizz' in the office, she hated it when she heard them chatting together, and she was beside herself when he gave Fizz as many days off as she needed to study for her exams.

Beatrice, who had been Tam's secretary since he joined the firm, had also started off as something less than a fan of Fizz's. As far as she was concerned, the unfortunate incidents that had occurred while Fizz had been Buchanan's unpaid assistant at the Legal Advice Clinic had all been Fizz's fault and deserved punishment by crucifixion. It had taken months to win her over and, in the end, it was only the suspicion that Margaret had her eye on Beatrice's job, come the day the senior partner finally retired, that made her accept Fizz as an ally. Since then, Fizz had discovered that, behind the gold-rimmed spectacles and tightly permed grey hair, there lived a free spirit who sang in a barbershop chorus and had once won a ballroom dancing competition for the cha-cha-cha.

The free spirit caught Fizz's eye as Margaret strode from the room and her lips pursed the way they did when she was trying not to smile. 'Mr Buchanan's going to have a heart attack if that file doesn't turn up before his meeting. He's been climbing the walls since before lunchtime.'

'So, you've already looked everywhere there is to look, right?' Fizz spread her hands. 'Well, who had it last?'

Beatrice waved her hands in the air. 'Nobody, apparently. Margaret says she hasn't seen it since last week and it should be in the filing cabinet.'

That, to Fizz, meant only one thing: that the old boy himself had taken it out and forgotten to put it back. She went down the corridor to his office, knocked, and went in.

'Fizz . . .' He was about to make a phone call and had a finger poised to dial but dropped the receiver back in the cradle and turned to her as though she were her last hope.

'Phoning the Samaritans?' she said.

'Fizz, you didn't file—'

'Hamilton Holdings? No. If I had, it would be in the filing cabinet, which it apparently isn't.' Fizz sat on the corner of his desk and shook her head at him. 'When did you last have it?'

He rubbed vigorously at his scalp, as though to stimulate his brain, turning his immaculate steel-grey helmet of hair into a curly mop. 'I haven't seen it since our last meeting. Wednesday of last week, at their head office. Someone must have misfiled it.'

'You couldn't have left it behind after the meeting?'

He waved that away impatiently. 'They'd have returned it to me by now.'

'And you didn't take it home to read over? You've been doing that a fair bit recently.'

His eyes widened. 'Surely not.' He stared at his briefcase for a few seconds, evidently afraid to put the premise to the test, then he grabbed it and started snatching forth handfuls of papers and throwing them on his desk. The last one out was clearly the Hamilton Holdings file: Fizz could tell that by the way he kept reading and rereading the label and the first few pages, as though he were refusing to believe his eyes.

The face he turned to her was less jubilant than it might have been. 'Dear me.'

'Quite,' said Fizz. 'Will you tell them or will I?'

He sat down again behind the desk and started shuffling the papers about. 'You can tell them, Fizz. I want to give these a quick going-over before the meeting.'

Fizz didn't move. 'You sure?' she said.

After a minute he lifted his head and met her eyes. He was so like Buchanan it was uncanny. He had Buchanan's black-lashed eyes and Buchanan's stubborn chin. And, ultimately, he had Buchanan's tender conscience.

'I suppose I owe them an apology,' he said, watching her face carefully in the clear hope that she would say, no, no, not at all, which she didn't. 'I'll tell them myself then.'

They went to the door together and as he held it for her to pass through before him he said, 'And how's Tam doing? Is he settling in at Am Bealach?'

Fizz took her time about answering. 'He's very tired, I think,' she said, as though giving the matter some thought. 'He seems to me to be very much in need of this holiday and I just hope nothing happens to make him decide to come back to work before he has the chance to recover fully. I'm sure it was stress and worry that caused the trouble with his gall bladder in the first place but a couple of weeks in Am Bealach should do him a lot of good.'

Buchanan père looked profoundly depressed. 'A couple of weeks, you say? I hope you're right, Fizz.'

'Oh, I'm sure I am,' she said airily. 'All he needs is to be able to relax completely and forget about the office. You must know yourself what a lot of stress you people in the legal profession are subject to and stress can cause so many illnesses, especially as you get older: heart trouble, cancer, depression, strokes . . . all sorts of life-threatening conditions. It could be a blessing in disguise that this minor problem hit Tam before he fell victim to something serious. At least it's a warning that he's been working too hard.'

The senior partner was silent as they walked up the corridor. 'Well, keep an eye on him, Fizz, and . . . and tell him we're managing just fine without him.'

'I'll do that.'

She made an excuse and nipped into the photocopying room so that she didn't have to be around while he confessed to the others. It might be necessary to make him face up to his shortcomings but that didn't mean she enjoyed it.

It was raining in Am Bealach and had been for almost twenty-four hours. Buchanan had tried a few casts in the morning, just upstream from the Stronach Bridge, but Alistair, who stopped to chat for a moment in passing, assured him that the fish wouldn't be biting and he was right. In fact, even if he had hooked a salmon, Buchanan wasn't at all sure that he could have landed it successfully, given the weight of his line and the strength of the current. The river had risen at least three feet overnight and the pools were dark brown with a creamy foam on top like a glass of Guinness. From being a placid, sparkling mirror, the Stronach was now a raging torrent, and it looked perfectly feasible for someone falling in, especially an old lady like Bessie Anderson, to be swept down to the loch in a matter of minutes.

Buchanan was still half inclined to believe that Miss Anderson's death had been accidental. Admittedly, if she had taken a header off the bridge, one might have expected her body to have washed ashore somewhere by this time, but there was very little habitation around the seventeen-mile length of the loch and a body could easily lie unnoticed in some wooded cove for months before someone stumbled across it.

He thought about taking a walk round the shoreline after lunch but, in the end, the rain was so heavy that he scrapped the idea and drove round to Killin instead. There wasn't much to the village other than the Visitor Centre and the famous Falls of Dochart but he wandered about the gift shops for a while and bought a few postcards.

He was studying a poster for a forthcoming ceilidh when he heard the sound of hooves behind him and turned to see Gerda tying her pony to the railings by the post office.

'Gerda!'

She looked surprised, but not overly pleased to see him. 'Tam. How are you?' she said politely.

Buchanan was somewhat taken aback by this lack of enthusiasm since she had been all over him like a wet suit when last encountered.

'I'm fine,' he said, 'except for finding time a little heavy on my hands. I'd planned to try a pony trek today but the weather put me off. What's the weather forecast for tomorrow, have you heard?'

'Good, I think,' she said, lifting her eyebrows and letting her lids droop over her eyes like pale pink shells. 'Marianne takes a nice trek tomorrow morning. She is going up the back side of Ben Lawers. You will like this very much.'

'What about you?' Buchanan asked, rolling with the punch. 'Aren't you taking a trek tomorrow?'

'Yes, but by the lochside only. You will like better the Ben Lawers.'

Her face was expressionless and her eyes had a blank look that shut him out. Evidently he had done something to annoy her, but what?

'I thought we had an arrangement,' he said. 'You promised to show me Finlarig Castle and the stone circle and the burial place of Fingal. Is that now dropped from the agenda?'

She lifted her chin, reminding him for a moment of Fizz in a bad temper. 'You are bringing Selena with you?'

'Selena?' Buchanan couldn't begin to imagine what he could have said to give her that impression and had absolutely no recollection of ever mentioning the cat to her in the first place. Her English was not wonderful but he had thought her able, at least, to follow his meaning if he spoke clearly. 'No. Why on earth should I bring Selena? I doubt if she'd enjoy that sort of thing. Besides, Alistair was telling me this morning that she's moved in with him now.'

Gerda's eyes opened. 'She sleeps with Alistair and you don't mind?'

'Glad to get rid of her,' Buchanan admitted. 'I haven't had a decent night's sleep since she latched on to me. She's a cute little thing but she smells a bit.'

Gerda seemed to take an unnecessarily long time to digest this, as if the cat's welfare were somehow important to her.

Finally, her eyes focused on the letter in her hand. 'I am putting this to the post,' she muttered and disappeared into the post office.

While he waited for her to emerge it occurred to Buchanan that it was no wonder she had gone off him. If she had been under the impression that he wanted to take a stray cat on a pony trek she must have thought him seriously unbalanced. Clearly, one would have to take more care in future not to be misunderstood.

When she came out of the post office Gerda looked a little less frigid.

'Are you in a hurry?' Buchanan asked as she untied the pony. 'Maybe we could have a coffee or something.'

She pouted her lips a little. 'I do not like to be tying Brandy for very many minutes. Boys throw stones to him and he is panic.' She glanced at Buchanan sideways and added, 'But if you do not mind to walk in the rain I will show you to the castle. Is not far.'

'Sure,' Buchanan said. 'I'd like that very much.' That was something of an exaggeration, since he'd already had about enough rain for one day, but it was clearly the best he could hope for at short notice.

Fortunately, the route wasn't across country but down a leafy lane which had once, Gerda informed him, been a railway track. 'This is a long time ago, of course. There are no trains for maybe twenty years.'

'How long have you been living in Killin?' Buchanan asked.

'I come here three years now but for summertime only.' She was tall for a woman and her long legs kept pace with his stride as she marched along, Brandy's head bobbing at her shoulder. 'I am in Killin at Easter and go home to Maastricht at the back of September.'

'Why Killin?' he wondered. 'What brought you to this neck of the woods?'

'First I am on holiday and go on pony trek with Norrie Telfer, who is owner of the stables. He does not like to do trekking so he gives me room and food and I come every summer.'

'Funny people around here,' Buchanan said, grinning at the typical Highland insanity of the situation. 'Why start a trekking stable if you don't like to do trekking?'

Gerda turned her head to smile at him but the hood of her anorak remained facing forward so he could see only half her face. 'Norrie is not starting the stable, he is buying it cheap from Lara, the last owner, who sells in a hurry.' Her one visible eye took on a mischievous tilt. 'Lara and Simon are having a big romance.'

'Simon from the Clachan inn? Simon Burroughs?' Buchanan bent his head to look at her. 'He's having an affair?'

'No, no. This is a long time ago,' Gerda frowned, as though it were his fault that he'd picked it up wrongly. 'Lara is gone from Killin many years now and Simon is perfect husband again. No more romances.'

She pulled her horse's head away from a patch of buttercups and walked on. Buchanan followed. He wondered if the affair were common knowledge in the locality or if Gerda only knew of it because of her association with the stables.

'Did Myra know about this at the time?' he asked.

Gerda rolled her eyes. 'Myra is finding out OK. Oh, sure. She is coming to the stables with chef's knife and suggesting to cut Lara's liver. That is when Lara sells to Norrie and goes away for ever.'

'Really.' Buchanan compared this view of Simon's wife with the impression he had already formed of a somewhat unexceptional middle-aged woman and found it not altogether surprising. Myra was pleasant enough on the outside but one got the impression she would be an implacable enemy.

'Simon was young in that time,' Gerda said airily, peeping at him round her hood. 'In Killin is not much excitement, you know. Fishing, yes; tennis and bowling; music sometimes in the pub. Not so much good fun is boring for young people so romances happen. A little danger, a little making heart beat, you know? Romancing is good for people, you think, Tam?'

'Not for married people,' Buchanan said. He had seen enough of the divorce cases, that were properly Alan Stewart's domain, to know the misery a little extramarital adventure could cause.

'No, but for not married people? For people like you and me?' She slowed her pace and her voice sank to a husky murmur. 'I think you are liking a little danger too, no? It is in those so blue eyes, I think. Yes, and the sexy smile. This is true, Tam, yes?'

Christ! Buchanan thought, wondering exactly what she was working up to. 'That's what you think, is it?' he said enigmatically.

She tucked her free hand through his arm and smiled up at him with alarming confidence, as though she were certain of his compliance. 'I think you are old-fashioned type as well, maybe. You like ladies to be shy and men to make running. Yes, I think you are too proud, Tam. But sometimes you must put your proud in your pocket and just enjoy.'

They were surrounded by mud and dripping greenery but Buchanan could see, through the trees, the outline of the ruined Finlarig Castle. Was she proposing some sort of alfresco frolic on the battlements? And if she did, what then?

He could imagine what Fizz would say if she found out he had been 'romancing' with one of her friends, but that was nothing to what he'd have to suffer if she heard he'd had the chance and chickened out.

The sound of many voices suddenly reached them from the direction of the castle, like the gabble of distant geese. Buchanan was ashamed to discover that his first reaction was one of undiluted relief.

Chapter Seven

Buchanan was playing golf when Fizz phoned home on Friday afternoon. She had hoped that he might have offered to meet her off the train at Stirling but instead she had to take a bus to Callander, change to the school bus as far as Killin and hitch the last two miles with some holiday-makers who had a caravan at Kenmore.

She was a patient traveller, having served her time at the trade over a period of years, but it didn't amuse her to arrive home and find Buchanan stretched out on a sun lounger on the lawn with a John Grisham novel and a can of McEwan's Export.

He slipped his sunglasses down the bridge of his nose and looked at her over the top. 'Hi. You made it, then?'

'No thanks to you, compadre. I thought you were playing golf?'

'I was. I've only been back here about half an hour.'

She flopped down on to the grass and loosened the laces on her Docs. The first half-hour of being home was always the best. The silence was the first thing that hit you, then the cool, cool purity of the air, like a good Sauternes.

'So, how're things in Edinburgh?' Buchanan wanted to know.

'Fine,' she lied, affecting the pleasantly surprised tone of one who had expected to find the situation anything but. 'They all send their good wishes.'

'No major problems, then?'

'Nope. Everything seems to be progressing very efficiently and there's nothing too stressful on the calendar so you can relax and enjoy your holiday.' She closed her eyes against the sun and then opened one again to squint at him. '*Are* you?'

'Am I what?'

'Are you enjoying your holiday?'

'Sure,' he said, in a perfunctory sort of way, and then appeared to think about it. 'I think I am, actually. That's a very nice eighteen-hole golf course in Killin – I played two rounds today – and your grampa let me take his boat out on the loch yesterday to fish for trout.'

'Get anything?'

'A couple. Auntie Duff did them in oatmeal for my breakfast.'

'God! Your belly will be dragging on the ground by the time you get back to Edinburgh. Have you been for your pony trek yet?'

'No.'

He pushed up his dark glasses and turned his face to the sun. If Fizz had been a suspicious sort of person she might have thought he looked a little shifty, but if he said he hadn't been for a pony trek, he hadn't. 'So, how else have you been passing the time?'

'Fishing the river. Reading. Had a walk round Killin and saw the castle. Alistair says he'll give me a call when there's a run of salmon going up the Stronach. Oh, and we're invited to a barbecue at the big house tonight. Seven thirty for eight. Casual.'

'Oh great! You know what that means, don't you?' said Fizz in disgust. 'Lindsay boring on about politics and Rowena in the throes of a nervous breakdown. She's terrified of you, you know.'

He folded his arms behind his head and clenched his teeth over a yawn. 'I don't think so. We had a long chat on Sunday, while we were waiting for the search parties to get themselves organised, and I thought we got on together rather well.'

'With Rowena? You're joking?' Fizz could not begin to imagine Rowena tête-à-tête with Buchanan or, indeed, with anyone else whom she had known for so short a time. 'Did she speak at all?'

'Some.' He lolled his head sideways on the lounger to look at her. 'I get the impression that Lindsay is something less than the wind beneath her wings. He doesn't have a lot of patience with her.'

Fizz made a disgusted grimace. She could get seriously rattled by Rowena at the drop of a hat but she hated anyone else to do so. Particularly Lindsay.

'That fart-faced little piss artist is turning her into an alcoholic,' she said bitterly. 'She's always been shy but she's now getting to the stage where she needs three gins to get enough courage to take a Valium. Lindsay's in London half the time, when he's here he never talks to her, and since Bessie Anderson died she doesn't have another woman in the neighbourhood who she can confide in.'

Buchanan reached for his beer can and shook it to see if there was any left. 'There's Myra, surely?'

'Myra is really very self-centred, you know. She's so involved with her family and her business that she has no interest in Rowena's problems. Alistair's mother was nothing but an old grouch, and Auntie Duff – well, she's very sympathetic, of course, but to be truthful . . .'

It was difficult to put into words without sounding bitchy, but she had a mental picture of Auntie Duff at the battle of

Hastings, patting King Harold on the back and saying, 'Try blowing your nose, dear.'

Buchanan yawned again and said sleepily, 'I get the picture that Bessie Anderson was an easy person to confide in. Maybe she knew more than was good for her.'

Fizz felt a little cold breeze caress the back of her neck. 'You think Rowena killed her to keep her from talking?'

Buchanan rarely laughed and, when he did, it was usually at something nobody else would see the humour in.

Finally, Fizz had to interrupt his hilarity to say, 'I take it, my dear Watson, that Rowena isn't your prime suspect at the moment?'

'Not at the moment, no,' he said, still grinning. 'In fact, since I saw the Stronach after a day of solid rain, I'm even less inclined to discount the police theory. Five weeks ago, with the snow still melting from the high ground, it must have been a deathtrap. I don't say I necessarily agree with the theory that old Miss Anderson fell into the river, but it's too soon to abandon it.'

Fizz had abandoned it weeks ago but there was no point in going over all that again. For the present it was enough that he was considering other possibilities. 'You haven't found out anything further, then?'

'Nothing concrete, just gossip.'

'About who?'

'About Simon, for a start. Did you know that he had a torrid affair with a girl from Killin?'

Fizz's mind leaped on this previously unconsidered fact with alacrity but she was unable to get any mileage out of it. 'I knew about it, sure. Everybody between here and Lochearn-head knew about it but it was way back before I left school and it's water under the bridge now.'

'But Myra knew about it at the time. So there must have

been a lot of ill feeling – on her part and Malcolm's too, I imagine.'

Fizz thought back. It had all come out the spring before she went to art school and she'd been working furiously on her portfolio at the time, but there wasn't anyone within twenty miles who was not thoroughly conversant with the details.

'There was certainly a huge dust-up about it,' she said. 'I mean, we're talking mega here, right? Apparently it had been going on for the best part of a year and Myra was the last to know. When she did find out it was like *Götterdämmerung*. I believe Myra brandished a knife at Lara and told her to be on the next stagecoach out of town and, according to local legend, she had Simon's balls bronzed and still wears them round her neck on a chain.'

She had a flashback of sitting in Rowena's bedroom: the two of them eating peanuts and discussing the drama with a delicious sense of superiority. The evocation was so strong that for a couple of seconds she was seventeen again, tasting the peanuts, smelling the potpourri on the dressing table, re-experiencing all the background emotions of excitement and uneasiness attendant upon becoming a student. Then the bubble popped and she couldn't recapture it.

She said, 'There was a lot of real bitterness in Am Bealach. Everybody had an opinion. Myra's dad was threatening to make balloon animals out of Simon's intestines, but nothing much came of it as far as I ever heard. I think Malcolm made Myra a partner in the business, maybe to give her a little more security, but that was after she and Simon had sorted things out between them.'

'So it all blew over,' Buchanan murmured, adjusting the cushion behind his head.

'Eventually,' Fizz agreed. 'But it took time. S. & M. actually went to a marriage guidance councillor, then a while later they adopted Zander, and after a few months everything appeared to settle down.'

'H'm. Well, as you say, it was all a long time ago.' Buchanan's voice had slipped down several notches in pitch and the effort of making conversation was clearly becoming onerous. 'If there was any lingering animosity in the family it has surely dissipated by now.'

'I think it was becoming a father that made a difference to Simon's attitude,' Fizz said. 'Both he and Myra are absolutely besotted with Zander. So's Malcolm.'

Zander would not have appeared, to Fizz, to be the sort of kid to engender that sort of adoration, even as the only child of ageing parents, but then, she was the first to admit that, even on a good day, she could take kids or leave them. Particularly kids with bulging eyes and a nose that reminded one of looking down the barrels of a shotgun.

She would have shared these sentiments with Buchanan had she felt like provoking him (which was always a temptation) but when she turned to look at him he was sound asleep in an attitude of deepest unconcern, with his sunglasses sliding down his nose and his empty beer can drooping from his inert grasp.

After studying him for a few minutes she got up and went into the farmhouse to see what she could find to wear for dinner at the big house.

They decided against taking the car because it was a glorious, still, pink and gold evening and because Buchanan refused to drink and drive. This was OK by Fizz, who had been sitting all afternoon on public transport, but it meant she had to carry a warm jacket in case it was chilly walking home in the dark. The rest of her evening outfit consisted of her trusty jeans and a multicoloured shirt, which her brother had left behind at the farm on a previous visit. It was probably not up to Lindsay's expectations but she had at least blow-dried her hair which, she felt, was making enough of an effort for anybody.

The Clachan looked quiet as they passed by. There were only three cars in the car park and no one at all at the tables in the garden. In fact, in the three-quarters of an hour it took them to reach the Stronach gatehouse they passed neither pedestrian nor driver. Alistair Munroe, however, was dead-heading the rhododendrons beside his front path. Behind him, the garden glowed like some exotic piece of multigemmed jewellery. The low evening sunlight filtered through the petals of the border plants, lighting them like lamps, and a dark red Japanese maple seemed hung with rubies. The lawns were carpets of emerald velvet, not flat but gently undulating, cropped and edged with a fanatic's precision. As they approached, Alistair looked up and nodded to them with his usual brooding glower.

'Don't take it personally,' Fizz muttered to Buchanan while they were still out of earshot. 'Last time I saw his teeth he was choking on a peanut. Hello, Alistair, how's life treating you?'

'No' bad.'

'Your garden's looking magnificent,' Buchanan said, breathing in the scent of purple lilac like a Bisto kid. 'You must spend a lot of time on it.'

'Just keepin' it tidy now. I'm too busy to do it the way Mum did.' He swung a hairy arm to indicate a hole in the lawn behind him. 'She wanted a pool and a bog garden here. Once that's finished I'll have enough to do just keepin' the weeds down.'

'Why bother about the pool now, Alistair?' Fizz said. 'You'd be quicker just filling it in again.'

Alistair swung his head heavily from side to side. 'Och no.

She wanted a pool and she'll get a pool. It's to be the way she wanted it.'

Buchanan nodded as though he endorsed this sentiment, though Fizz could hardly believe he did. 'The garden is a fitting memorial to your mother, Alistair.'

Alistair's expression softened slightly. 'Come away in and take a wee look round if you like.'

'Another time, perhaps,' Fizz put in quickly, just in case Buchanan accepted the offer. 'We're expected up at the big house.'

'Oh aye,' Alistair nodded, scratching at a cleg bite on his wrist with the point of his secateurs. 'I saw the Land Rover from the Clachan going up the drive a wee while ago so I wondered if there was something on. A barbecue, is it? I was thinking I could smell cooking.'

'We should go,' said Fizz, realising that if Alistair could smell cooking they were late. 'We'll drop in another time, Alistair. I want Buchanan to see your garden while the spring colour is at its best.'

What she really wanted was for Buchanan to have a long talk with Alistair and see if his opinion of the gamekeeper tallied with her own. She had never had much to do with Alistair. He had left the primary school in the village before she was old enough to attend but she had always felt that he had more going for him than he was generally given credit for.

Admittedly, he was a bit lacking in the social skills department but then he'd had an ailing mother to take care of much of his adult life so he hadn't had the opportunity to do much socialising. Get him on to the subject of wildlife, however, and you'd learn a thing or two. He knew every wild orchid and every badger sett on the Stronach estate, he could show you the ptarmigan chicks on the bare summit of Sgurr Bodach and the mud chute among the alders where the otters slid into the loch. Of all the Am Bealach residents, Alistair was the only one Fizz could have wished to know better.

They smelled the barbecue before the house came into view and as they turned the last bend in the drive they came upon a scene that reminded Fizz of one of those fifties movies that depicted the ideal American family. Lindsay, in a butcher's apron but, thankfully, no chef's hat, was supervising the charring of various bits of dead animal; Myra and Simon were rocking gently in a garden swing and sipping something long and cool from frosted glasses; Rowena, looking distinctly Pre-Raphaelite in yards of white cheesecloth, was zapping around with plates of nibbly bits. If it had been Doris Day tripping across the grass to greet them instead of Rowena's Rastafarian poodle, the illusion would have been complete.

It was immediately obvious that Rowena had gone totally over the score as usual. One had only to look at the bowls of salads, relishes, home-baked rolls, and exotic desserts to know that she had been in a frenzy for days. No doubt the thought of cooking for an expert like Simon had spurred her on like a cattle prod.

'Rowena,' Buchanan said to her as they milled about helping themselves, 'what a magnificent spread. Is this all your own work?'

'Yes,' Rowena breathed, dealing teaspoons into saucers like Diamond Lil. 'I just hope it tastes all right.'

'Reminds me of the story about the legionnaires who ran out of food in the Sahara.' Simon, already laughing at the punchline, held up a hand in a traffic policeman's gesture to halt all conversation. 'The captain says to them, "Well, *mes braves*, I have some good news and some bad news. Which do you want first?" "The good news," say his men. "OK. We have nothing to eat but camel dung!" "Bloody hell," say the men.

103

"Tell us the good news, for God's sake!" And the captain says, "We've got *plenty*!" '

Everyone pretended to laugh except Rowena, who was clearly trying to work out if there was an insult in there somewhere and, if so, was it deliberate.

'The inn looked quiet as we passed,' Fizz remarked, this being the first remark that came to mind before Simon could get his stand-up comedian act together. 'Not many cars in the car park.'

Myra nodded, not looking as if it bothered her much. 'We've got eight residents tonight but we made them eat at six o'clock so that we could have an evening off. In another couple of weeks we'll be properly into the season and won't be able to raise our heads till October.'

Buchanan de-charred his steak with a brain surgeon's dexterity and amputated a sliver of pink flesh. 'Do you stay open all year?'

'Yes, more or less,' Myra said. 'We closed for three weeks in February, and Simon and I went off to Bermuda on our own, but for the rest of the winter there's usually just enough passing trade to make it worthwhile heating the public rooms.'

'You're lucky to have your father to look after Zander for you,' Rowena said softly, then, finding eyes upon her, she hummed the opening bars of 'Stardust' to herself and passed round the rolls.

Myra smiled. 'Yes. It was nice to be on our own for a while. Besides, Dad was never one for holidays and Zander was promised a weekend at EuroDisney to make up for being left behind. Simon's taking him next weekend, for a birthday treat. Actually, his birthday's not till Tuesday but one day off school is as much as he should miss right now.'

'That kid,' Lindsay said to Buchanan, in a half-kidding, wholly earnest tone, 'is spoiled rotten! Wants a pony – gets a pony! Wants a mountain bike – gets a mountain bike! Wants to see some pop group playing in Edinburgh – he's on his way!'

Simon and Myra smiled soppily at each other, pretending to be embarrassed.

'He's our only chick,' Simon said, 'and I can't see why he shouldn't have the odd treat if we can afford to give it to him. I really don't think it does him any harm.'

He had got himself tarted up for the evening in high-waisted trousers and a tartan bow-tie-and-braces set. Where he bought such outfits was a mystery to Fizz.

'He's not at all spoiled,' Rowena said, patently trying to make up for her husband's crass humour. 'Zander's a darling boy, and he's so sweet and patient with Briony. I don't know how I'd have managed without him to look after her for me the day she was christened. I didn't have to worry about her all afternoon.'

Lindsay moved around, topping up glasses. 'That's true. He was great with Briony. Kept her amused all the way back in the car and throughout lunch, didn't he, Myra?'

'Yes, he's fascinated by her,' Myra laughed.

Fizz found this exchange deeply interesting. 'Didn't you take your own car to the christening ceremony?' she asked Myra while the main current of the conversation flowed on around them.

'Oh, you know what it's like at those things, Fizz. A lot of our friends from Killin had come to the service and we wanted to talk, but Dad had to rush back to help Simon prepare lunch, so Lindsay gave Zander and me a lift.' Myra leaned across Lindsay to include Rowena in the Zanderfest. 'He simply couldn't take his eyes off the baby, could he, Rowena?'

'Hope he doesn't want a little sister for himself next!' Lindsay said, with his usual total lack of sensitivity.

He must have been aware, as Fizz was, that Myra and

Simon had tried to start a family for years without success and were unlikely to conceive in their late forties or, for that matter, to be able to adopt a second child at that stage in their lives. Zander might be no rosebud, but he was, as Simon said, their only chick, and likely to remain so.

S. & M. allowed Lindsay's elephantine wit to pass unanswered and concentrated on their steaks with a frigid politeness that was obvious to everyone but Lindsay. Rowena overreacted by giving a violent jolt as though she'd been goosed by a ghostly hand, jumping up, and passing round the first platters that came to hand.

'The lilac's late this year,' she stuttered, in a sort of half-cocked desperation, and for a moment it looked like no one could think of a response other than a bald agreement.

Then Buchanan said easily, 'I noticed on the way here that Alistair's lilac is in full bloom, but then it's a good deal more sheltered down there than your garden is.'

'Mrs Munroe's garden is always way ahead of everyone else's, isn't it, darling?' Myra turned to Simon for confirmation, noticed his bow tie was crooked, and straightened it. 'The trees shelter it from the wind and the high walls make it a real suntrap.'

Fizz wondered if she were the only one to recognise the faint note of disparagement in Myra's voice, as though the trees in question had just sprung up there by chance instead of being planted as a windbreak by Alistair's mother. Myra had not always seen eye to eye with Mrs Munroe, who had been, like many perfectionists, a somewhat spiky character. She had also been an outspoken atheist, which to someone as religious as Myra was probably quite offensive.

'What amazes me about that garden,' Buchanan said, 'is that it was made by a woman who was so incapacitated by heart trouble. Auntie Duff was telling me yesterday that Mrs

Munroe could barely walk as far as the gate for months before she died.'

'It's silly.' Myra gave her head a quick shake. 'We all subscribe to the idea that it was Mrs Munroe's garden when, in fact, it was Alistair who did all the work. Every spare minute he had was spent laying paths, building rockeries, cutting hedges, mowing lawns, barrowing soil from one bed to another—'

'Oh, come on, Myra,' Fizz had to say, in the interests of fair play. 'You know it was Mrs Munroe who deserves the credit. She chose the plants and said where they were to go and how they were to be treated. And I used to see her, right up to last year, sitting for hours in her greenhouse, pricking out the seedlings for her borders and her hanging baskets. Alistair was just the labourer.'

'He was happy to do it,' Rowena stated unexpectedly, giving the words an uncharacteristically bitter edge as though she were getting at somebody. Fizz looked at her in surprise and saw the bitterness reflected in her face. 'Alistair would have done anything for his mother and he knew that her garden meant more to her than anything else.'

'It certainly meant more to her than any of her fellow creatures,' Myra insisted, 'and I'm including Alistair in that remark. She kept him tied to her apron strings all her life, never let him have any outside interests other than his job. The man has never had a life of his own and now that his mother's gone it's too late. He hasn't a clue how to start meeting people and making a new life for himself.'

Simon nodded in agreement. 'This obsession he has about making the garden some sort of permanent memorial to his mother – it's not healthy. He should be thinking about getting out more, maybe getting himself a new job some place busier and finding himself a wife instead of dwelling on the past.'

'His mother has only been dead for a month, Simon,' Fizz said. 'Give him time. He'll get around to reorganising his life in a few months – but I don't see that moving away from all his friends and the home he was born in is necessarily the way to do it.'

Lindsay put a firm end to that topic of conversation by topping up everyone's glass: nonalcoholic punch for Myra, who was driving, and wine for the others. That done, he led the talk firmly on to the current political scene and the evening went rapidly downhill.

It was pleasant enough, for a while, to close one's ears to Lindsay's ranting and simply enjoy the slow progression of the sunset from ruby red to a pale, luminous turquoise. But by the time Venus appeared, low down on the western horizon, Fizz had had enough. For Rowena's sake, she toughed it out till eleven thirty, and then manoeuvred S. & M. into making the first move, thereby ensuring a lift home for Buchanan and herself.

As an evening out it ranked somewhere between carpet bowls and home movies but it had definitely had its moments, some of which she was looking forward to discussing with her learned friend.

Chapter Eight

Buchanan's biological clock was gradually becoming adjusted to Am Bealach time. For the first three or four days of his holiday he had felt it necessary to fill every minute of the day with some activity and had retained more than a sneaking suspicion that he wouldn't last out the week, never mind a fortnight. Now there were fairly long periods when he found himself happily doing nothing at all, not even thinking, and the sensation was not unpleasant.

The morning after the barbecue, he was sitting on the low windowsill of his cottage, with Selena purring on his shoulder and the early morning sun on his face, when Grampa tooled into the yard on his quad bike, trailed by two black and white collies. Luath and his mother, Bess, burst out of the barn doorway and ran to join the pack, greeting everyone with enthusiasm.

'How're you this mornin', Tam? No' a bad day again.' Grampa leaped off the bike like a youth and waded through the sea of dogs, both rheumaticky knees clicking audibly. 'I had a look at the river as I came by. It's a bit brown still, after the rain. Give it a day or two and it'll be in better condition. Have you had your breakfast yet?'

'No. I was just beginning to think about it.' Buchanan detached Selena, claw by claw, from his sweater and stood up.

'Come away in, then,' Grampa barked. 'I'm ready for a cup of tea myself.'

They found Fizz washing dishes at the sink while Auntie Duff bottle-fed the baby lamb that had spent the last two nights in a box by the Aga.

'About time, you lazy sod,' said Fizz, unheard by Grampa and unremarked by Auntie Duff. 'I was planning to take you up the ridge today but if you don't get a move on it won't be worthwhile starting.'

Her hair, which had looked so smooth and elegant last night, had now returned to its usual riot of curls, and a fresh batch of freckles had blossomed across her cheekbones. Buchanan was forcibly reminded of those Cabbage Patch dolls that used to be so popular.

'Ardoch Ridge?' he asked uneasily. The line of summits beyond the big house had a curiously menacing aspect, seen from below, and he had no particular desire to know the Carlin's Loup any more intimately than he already did.

'No. We'll keep that till you're feeling better,' said Fizz, and smiled at his obvious relief. 'The Tarmachan Ridge, on the other side of the loch, is the better walk anyway. We can take a picnic lunch with us and do it slowly. You'll love it.'

'There's a wee bit of that flan we had for lunch yesterday still in the fridge,' Auntie Duff told her. 'And you can take some of the liver pâté for sandwiches. Maybe your Grampa will have a can of beer somewhere for Tam to drink.'

'No beer thanks, Auntie Duff,' Fizz said bossily. 'Not on the ridge. We'll pick up some Coke on our way through Killin.' She made way for her grandmother to wash her hands at the sink and came over to sit at the table across from Buchanan.

'Could you take a few kidneys with your bacon and eggs, Tam?' Auntie Duff wondered. 'There's no sausages because Fizz didn't get them out of the freezer in time to let them defrost.'

'I was too busy feeding the hens,' Fizz claimed indignantly and so loudly that her Grampa heard her.

'Did you give them the layers' pellets, lass?'

'I did but the sparrows were all over the place like a plague of locusts before I had the troughs filled.' She dropped her voice and added for Buchanan's benefit, 'Hate these bloody sparrows. There's thousands of them and they gorge themselves till they can't even fly and then lie around on the grass all morning, belching and farting. Greedy little bastards.'

'And the geese as well?' Grampa said at the same time, unaware that Fizz was speaking.

'Yes. And brought the eggs in,' Fizz yelled.

Grampa clicked over to the table with a pot of tea and motioned Buchanan to help himself.

'What about those knees? Helluva racket, isn't it?' Fizz remarked as soon as he'd turned his back. 'And, if you think that's bad, you should hear him in the wintertime. He sounds like the rhythm section of a samba band.'

Buchanan winced. 'Please, Fizz, don't do this to me,' he muttered, glaring at her while keeping a wary eye on Grampa's back. 'It would be extremely embarrassing if you were over-heard.'

'No chance,' Fizz grinned. 'Grampa hasn't overheard any-thing for years and Auntie Duff, as you may have noticed, can only think about one thing at a time. While she's making your breakfast she's deaf to everything else.'

'All the same—' Buchanan broke off as Auntie Duff leaned over the table to deposit his porridge plate and jug of cream but it was clear from her expression that she hadn't been following the conversation.

'Oh my, that looks good,' Buchanan told her, covering his embarrassment with garrulity. 'Fizz says you'll be making me fat.'

'Fat!' Auntie Duff tut-tutted at Fizz. 'Look at the boy, there's not a pick on him!'

Fizz raised an eyebrow. 'Not right now, there isn't,' she said, eyeing him judiciously. 'I've seen more meat on a butcher's apron. But he won't stay that way on the diet you're feeding him. He'll have a belly on him like a poisoned pup.'

Auntie Duff closed her eyes at this profanity and withdrew from the arena to poke tenderly at the kidneys.

'So, what did you think of that conversation last night?' Fizz asked, propping her chin on her fist.

'About the need for a complete reorganisation of the land laws?' Buchanan said, knowing that wasn't what she meant.

'Land laws?' Grampa had returned to the table to top up his teacup and, bending over close to Buchanan, had caught the words. 'Was Lindsay giving you his election speech?'

'Yes,' Buchanan yelled, grinning. 'For the best part of two hours.'

'Aye, I thought he would be at his electioneering again. The man's an idiot. He hasn't a sensible thought in his head and doesn't give a damn about anyone else as long as he's all right. I'm telling you, he's not the man I'd want to be representing me in Westminster, or any place else.' He gulped down his tea and carried the cup to the sink. 'I'm just sorry for that wee lassie he married.'

'You wouldn't think he was Rowena's type. One wonders why she married him,' Buchanan shouted.

Grampa turned his head and looked at Fizz. 'That's who you should be asking about Rowena,' he growled. 'The poor lassie never did a thing in her life unless she thought *she* would approve.'

It occurred to Buchanan that he had never heard Grampa address Fizz by her nickname or, indeed, by any other name. In fact, now that he thought about it, he had never heard

Grampa address her at all except when it was necessary, and then only on impersonal matters. There was a coolness between them that was being hidden before an outsider but it was clearly more than a passing tiff.

Fizz stared calmly out of the window till Grampa had left the room and then looked at Buchanan with a rather pinched smile. 'You'll have gathered that I am responsible for every mistake Rowena has made since she left her cradle. What Rowena does with her life is my fault, not hers, and will continue to be my fault to the end of her days.'

'Why does your grampa blame you for Rowena's marrying Lindsay?'

She shrugged one shoulder. 'It's a long story. I certainly never advised her to do it. I wasn't even around when she did it but I was perceived to be the evil influence behind her decision.'

She wafted the subject away with a gesture, leaving Buchanan no choice but to list the matter among the other areas of Fizz's past that he had hopes of clarifying one of these days. He'd anticipated learning more about Fizz's background during this holiday, he remembered, but it was more likely, on present showing, that he would end up with more questions than answers.

'Anyway, what I wanted to know,' Fizz continued, 'was if you heard anything of significance in the conversation last night.'

'Significant in what way?' Buchanan asked. 'In connection with Bessie Anderson or the camper, I presume?'

'Uh-huh. Did you?'

Buchanan finished his porridge. 'I did notice that *you* saw something significant in the fact that Myra and Zander travelled home from the christening with the big house contingent.'

'Damn right.' Fizz nodded vigorously. 'But only because it showed that old Malcolm was first back at Am Bealach.'

'And that interests you, does it?'

Fizz put on her God-give-me-patience look. 'Bessie Anderson was alive and well when Malcolm and Myra called in for her on their way to church, right? Therefore she met her end between then and about three in the afternoon, when Simon found her gone.'

Buchanan smiled agreement. 'While the others were at the church, I suspect.'

'What makes you think that?'

'The sphagnum moss that was found at the crossroads. Nobody but Bessie would have been collecting sphagnum moss that day, so if Bessie went that far she must have walked past the inn, and if the party had been in progress at the time I'd have thought she would have dropped in. She had been invited, after all, and if she felt well enough to go out to pick spaghnum moss she must have been well enough to go to the party. I think she'd want to go to the celebration, wouldn't she? She and Rowena were reputedly close and all the neighbours were there.'

'Yes. I'm sure she'd have come to the party if she'd been alive,' Fizz agreed. 'So, if we *do* have to include some of the locals in our list of suspects – and let's face it, who else do we have? – we can at least narrow it down to those who were back in Am Bealach before the start of the buffet lunch. Between noon and four p.m. all of the guests were together in the Clachan, so the chief suspects have to be Simon, who was there all morning cooking the lunch, and Malcolm, who arrived back before the others.'

This line of thought had been running through Buchanan's head for days, but he didn't find it so cut-and-dried as Fizz did. He accepted his second course from Auntie Duff and spread butter on a slice of toast before he answered.

'Two points. First, there's Alistair. He was invited to the festivities, remember, but couldn't go because his mother was so ill. Therefore, he was around all day – presumably at his mother's bedside but, who knows? Secondly, any one of them could have slipped away before or during the early stages of the buffet lunch while the rest were milling around and before Bessie Anderson left home. How long would it take to reach Miss Anderson's house? Three minutes? Less?'

Fizz screwed up her face. 'You'd have to be pretty desperate to risk nipping out during the party to commit a murder. What if your absence were noticed?'

'I'm sure any of them could have come up with a believable excuse. The Clachan lot were probably coming and going all the time with food and drink, Lindsay and Rowena had the baby to keep an eye on, etcetera, etcetera.'

Buchanan ate for a few minutes in silence, wishing Fizz would go away and give him peace to enjoy his breakfast. When she showed no sign of doing so he remarked, 'I'll tell you what did intrigue me, though.'

'What?'

'The way Rowena spoke up for Alistair when Myra was belittling him. It's not like her to stick her neck out like that, is it?'

Fizz looked at him with saucer eyes. The tip of her tongue appeared and absently moistened her top lip. 'Well, flip me gently,' she said. 'You don't think there's something going on between those two?'

'No,' Buchanan sighed, wondering if he'd ever cure her of leaping to conclusions. 'Not in the way you mean but, all the same, she was very niggled when Myra was claiming he was henpecked.'

Fizz gave that some thought for a minute or two. 'It's

certainly the first time I've seen Rowena speak her mind in company, but that's Rowena, you know. She's always been unpredictable.'

She fell into a deep reverie, allowing Buchanan to give his kidneys and bacon the attention they deserved. He waited, wondering if she might comment on how Rowena had been influenced to marry Lindsay, but she merely buttered herself a slice of toast and maintained her eternal mystery.

Fizz was not best pleased to see, when they stopped to buy Coke on their way through Killin, that there were two tourist buses at the Falls of Dochart. That meant that traffic was almost at a standstill because the bridge was jammed with tourists taking pictures of the river and the background of snow-streaked peaks. Buchanan suggested stopping to watch the three locals who were fishing for salmon below the bridge but Fizz nipped that idea in the bud because she had seen it a hundred times, and because she wanted to pick up some soft drinks and press on.

She was sitting in the car waiting for Buchanan to come out of the Co-op when she saw McLaren, the young detective sergeant, strolling by on the other side of the road. In a second she was out of her seat and cutting diagonally across the road in front of him so that she could appear not to have seen him.

'Hello there,' he said as she reached the far pavement. 'It's Miss Fitzpatrick, isn't it?'

Fizz forged a blank look and then smiled warmly. 'Hello. Nice to see you again, Sergeant McLaren.'

He was better-looking than she remembered, quite dishy, actually, with russet hair and beautiful teeth, and furthermore, he looked frightfully happy to have run into her.

'You're home for the weekend, are you?' he asked.

'Uh-huh. Just till Tuesday. I'm supposed to be studying for

my end-of-term exams but it's not easy in weather like this. How's the case going? Have you made any progress since I last saw you?'

'Not a lot. We're still trying to establish the identity of the camper and not meeting with a great deal of success.'

Behind him, Buchanan emerged from the grocery store, looked in the car and then scanned the street. As he spotted her, Fizz edged round so that she could wave him away without McLaren noticing. There was no point in trying to get information out of the sergeant in front of a lawyer.

Buchanan watched for a moment, his hands on his hips, and then indicated that he was going back to the bridge to watch the fishermen. That suited Fizz just fine.

She continued to pretend an interest in McLaren's account of door-to-door enquiries in Killin and then said, 'There's something I had in my mind to tell you about the case, but I can't remember what it is. It'll probably come back to me when you've gone.'

He tipped his head at the café a few paces away. 'Why don't we go in for a coffee? By the time we've finished you may have remembered what it was.'

'Why not?' said Fizz, and was just in time to see Buchanan's frown as he finished locking the car and started back towards the bridge.

'I mustn't be long,' she said to McLaren as they found themselves a table. 'I'm meeting Buchanan. We're doing the ridge this morning.'

He held her chair for her in a manner to which she was quite unaccustomed. 'You must know these hills well, I suppose, having grown up here.'

'I spent the first fourteen years of my life on them. My daddy used to carry me on his back when I was a baby.' Fizz could see the oak-clad slopes of Stronaclachan rising sheer beyond the window, bursting with spring green, and dotted with ewes and lambs. She said, 'That's why I hate this business so much. OK, people die on the hills all the time, but they die everywhere all the time. The thought of murder happening up there where it's so distant from that sort of thing . . . it's a kind of desecration.'

The waitress arrived and McLaren ordered coffee and shortbread. 'It will all be cleared up soon and then you can start to forget it,' he said, with a spurious confidence.

'Really? But you said you hadn't made a lot of progress.'

'Ah, well . . .' He looked at his plate for inspiration. 'We're amassing a fair amount of information. Once we've managed to collate it I think you'll find it won't be long till we make an arrest.'

'What sort of information?' Fizz asked, acting all wide-eyed and fascinated.

'Oh . . .' He waved his hands vaguely, and gave her the sort of doting smile that made her want to puke. 'Just reports of the camper being seen in one or two places between here and Stirling. That sort of thing. We're now fairly sure he was in Stirling two days before his arrival here and that he stopped in Callander to buy provisions the day before. We're still not sure whether he hitched a lift to Killin from Callander or whether he walked over the pass from Lochearnhead, but the pattern of the sightings leads us to believe he was a backpacker, rather than a climber.'

Fizz nodded. McLaren was good at giving the impression of being very forthcoming but, in fact, he had told her nothing she hadn't known, or could have deduced, a week ago.

She said, 'What about the hand and the blonde wig? And the jeweller's rouge?'

'No.' He leaned back from the table to allow the waitress to put their coffee and shortbread in front of them. 'Still no explanation of why he was carrying those. We checked the jewellers' suppliers in Glasgow and Edinburgh but he didn't buy them there.'

'I'm sure there must be aspects of the case that a local would understand better than an outsider,' Fizz said, nibbling a piece of shortbread. 'People living in these remote places have their own way of doing things.'

He smiled in a fatherly sort of way. 'I don't think there's anything that you'd be able to help us with,' he said, wasting another smile on her. The smile deepened. 'Not unless you know anything about local drug pushers.'

Fizz sat up and batted her eyelashes. 'Drug pushers? Not here, surely?'

She knew damn well there were drug pushers in the area and had been for many years. Although she had never used drugs herself, considering them to be nothing more than a crutch for inadequate losers, she knew plenty of locals who did hash and one or two who she suspected of using coke.

McLaren folded his arms on the table and leaned closer, dropping his voice a little to say, 'The camper was carrying a small quantity of cannabis resin and a single Ecstasy tablet. We found them in the tent.'

'Really.' Fizz opened her eyes at him as though she thought he was terribly clever to have discovered that. 'But couldn't he have bought both drugs in Stirling or . . . or wherever he was before that?'

'The cannabis, yes. But not the Ecstasy tablet. That was from the local supplier.'

'How can you tell?'

'Easy,' he said, looking a little smug. 'Ecstasy isn't a pre-scription drug. The tablets don't have the initials of the drug company on them but each manufacturer has his own logo, embossed on every tablet: a dove, a dollar sign, a lightning bolt – whatever. The few tablets we've found around these parts recently have all come from a manufacturer using a logo in the shape of a lotus blossom, the same logo as we found on the tablet in the tent.'

'Gosh.' Fizz was well aware what Ecstasy tablets looked like. She didn't know the local pusher but she was damn sure she could find somebody who did. 'I thought Ecstasy tablets were only used by people at raves,' she said in an awed voice. 'Does that mean the camper was heading for some big city?'

'Could be,' McLaren admitted. 'But Am Bealach was definitely on his route. He had either been there or was heading in that direction.'

Fizz's spirits sank horribly at this news. It had to imply a positive connection between the camper and an Am Bealach resident, a connection that none of the locals had admitted.

'A woman in Lochearnhead came forward to say she remembered a backpacker asking directions to Am Bealach around that weekend,' McLaren was saying. 'And her description – although it was a bit vague – seems to tally with what we already know. Of course, the lad may have been heading for some place *beyond* Am Bealach, but it would appear a strange route to take to Killin or any of the other villages on the loch.'

Outside the window, the main street was deserted. The tour buses had departed and the village had reverted to its normal mid-morning torpor but now it seemed that there was a tension about the silence that sang in the air like a plucked string. For the first time since Mrs Anderson's disappearance, Fizz had a profound sense of foreboding.

She had never really believed that one of the locals was embroiled in this affair. Not really. Her inclusion of the entire community in her list of suspects had been, she now realised, purely for purposes of elimination. Or to impress herself, and

Buchanan, with her businesslike and unbiased approach. But why would anyone choose to visit a dot on the map like Am Bealach unless he knew someone there?

'Surely,' she said, in a last-ditch defence, 'if the camper was heading for Am Bealach he wouldn't have made camp only two or three miles from the crossroads, would he? He'd have kept going till he got there.'

'Possibly. Inspector Cullen has three theories.' He held up three fingers and smiled in a faintly derisory manner as though he and Inspector Cullen were not necessarily of the same mind. 'Number one is that the camper had walked through the pass from Lochearnhead and was too tired to continue. Number two is that, not having a map, he wasn't aware that he was so near his destination. Number three is that he wanted to visit someone in Am Bealach under cover of darkness.'

Fizz looked at him carefully. 'But you don't necessarily agree with any of those theories.'

His eyebrows shot up as though he felt he had been caught out, then he smiled again, flashing his white teeth. 'I think they're excellent theories as far as they go,' he said, 'but the first two are no more than guesses. We don't know that he had no map: it may have been destroyed by his murderer along with his clothes. And if he had a map he would certainly not have camped so near the crossroads. No, I think it much more likely that he wanted to meet someone without attracting too much attention to himself.'

Fizz found herself much inclined to agree with this reading of the matter. She gulped the last of her coffee. 'Must dash. Buchanan will be spitting tacks.'

He jumped up as she pushed back from the table and dashed round to hold her chair. 'If you're likely to be in Killin over the weekend,' he said, 'why not give me a ring and we could have a bite to eat together?'

'Sounds nice,' she said. 'Maybe I'll do that.'

But if she did, she knew it would be for the information she could get out of him, not for his boyish good looks.

Chapter Nine

Buchanan had seen a salmon landed only once, on the River Tweed when he was a boy of about fourteen, but the excitement of watching the battle of wills between man and fish had stayed with him for seventeen years. He wasn't just doing Fizz a favour, therefore, when he left her in peace to quiz McLaren, and the time he spent waiting for her at the Dochart bridge passed remarkably quickly. None of the fishermen had any luck while he was there but it was interesting to see how they fished an awkward lie and it whetted his appetite for his day on the Stronach with Alistair.

It did occur to him to wonder, and at some length, if Fizz's only purpose with McLaren was to pick his brains. The policeman was a good-looking chap, much about Fizz's age, and the flirtatious way she had been smiling at him might not have been entirely counterfeit.

So what? he asked himself. What's it to you? And, since there was no answer to that, he put it firmly out of his mind and watched the fishermen.

Fizz arrived back before he got bored. She looked a little subdued and even apologised for keeping him waiting, which was quite unlike her, but she didn't offer to tell him what had been discussed until he asked her about it.

'I tried to find out if they'd discovered anything new about the camper,' she said then, 'but McLaren's as tight as a duck's arse. He wasn't giving much away.'

Buchanan watched her face as she climbed into the car and was fairly sure she'd learned something that had upset her. Maybe something that implicated one of her neighbours. Something, at any rate, that dulled her usual sparkle and made her eyes focus on something only she could see. He let her dwell on her thoughts till they parked beside a narrow river at the end of the ridge and then stopped her as she reached into the back seat for her boots.

'You might as well tell me, Fizz. McLaren said something that took the wind out of your sails, didn't he?'

She glared at him for a moment and then gave a short laugh. 'I wish to God I'd never got involved in this mess,' she said bitterly. 'If I hadn't taken you up the Stronach woods last week and stumbled into that tent . . . if I'd just let things lie . . . what difference would it have made? None, probably.'

Buchanan waited, knowing she'd get around to it in due course.

'Just wait and see, Buchanan. It'll be my fault if somebody in Am Bealach turns out to have murdered that camper. Everyone will be saying, "It's all thanks to Fizz, of course. Never spent five minutes in Am Bealach without causing trouble. If it hadn't been for her it would all have blown over and nobody any the wiser." '

It was totally unlike Fizz to give a hoot in hell about anyone else's opinion. Indeed, Buchanan was quite sure, at times, that her chief motivating force was the desire to offend as many people as possible. The only person he could visualise blaming Fizz was her grampa, so he had to assume that it was his reaction she was worried about. This was something of a revelation, since she had never given any sign of being upset by the old man's grouchiness.

Fizz was glaring at him again, demanding some response, so he said, 'McLaren has grounds to suspect somebody in Am Bealach, does he?'

'He's damn sure the camper was headed in that direction anyway, because the lad asked somebody in Lochearnhead how to get there. Why would anyone want to go to a dot on the map like Am Bealach unless he knew someone there? And if he did – who was it? Probably someone I grew up with!'

Buchanan regarded her patiently. 'Is that all McLaren has to go on? Hardly conclusive proof that the camper was known to one of the residents, is it?'

'It's not proof,' she said, with a trace of sadness. 'I don't think even McLaren is taking it that seriously – not yet. But it makes sense. There's absolutely no reason for anyone to ask directions to Am Bealach unless they have business there.'

'It's a crossroads,' Buchanan suggested, with an optimism he knew was unconvincing, 'and there are farms and small villages all along the loch shore, aren't there? There's no reason he shouldn't have been visiting one of those.'

'I hope you're right.' Fizz forced a tight smile and reached again for her boots. 'Let's walk.'

She set a gruelling pace for the first ten minutes and then remembered that Buchanan was supposed to be convalescing and slowed to a steady slog. She had her own route up on to the ridge, rejecting the worn track in the heather that everyone else followed, and circling round the first low hill instead of going over the top. This was marginally less tiring but landed them in the middle of a peat bog which she claimed had not been there the last time she had passed by.

They stopped for lunch beside a small lochan, just below the high point of the ridge, where the view stretched from Ben Nevis to the high plateau of the Cairngorms. Neither of them spoke much as they ate. Fizz was clearly dwelling on her discussion with McLaren, and Buchanan's thoughts kept turning to Fizz's relationship with her grandfather.

She only had two relatives in the world: her grampa and her brother Colin, who was a wildlife photographer based in South Africa. She rarely referred to Colin, so Buchanan couldn't judge how close they were, but it was obvious that Grampa was important to her. Thinking about things she'd said in the past, it now seemed likely that it was, at least in part, the old man's advanced years and the knowledge that she wouldn't have him around much longer that had made her cut short her travels and return to Scotland.

She had always appeared to Buchanan to be such a strong character: self-sufficient, invulnerable, expecting little from other people and not, therefore, likely to be disappointed. One couldn't help but admire her for it, but it seemed doubly sad that the one person she cared about should give her the cold shoulder.

They finished eating and packed away the remains of their lunch in their knapsacks but Fizz was in no hurry to move on. She stretched out on the heather with her hands behind her head and stared up into the blue.

'Something else McLaren told me,' she said suddenly, as though her worries had put it out of her mind and she'd only just remembered. 'They found some hash in the tent and also an Ecstasy tablet that they can trace to a local supplier. It's the same kind as others they've seen around here but they don't know who's pushing them.'

'Interesting,' said Buchanan. 'And you're worried in case it's someone in Am Bealach?'

She turned her head to grin at him, squinting her eyes against the sun. 'Not unduly worried, no. I don't think even Simon – who would be in the best position for that sort of activity – could get away with it for long without one of the neighbours sussing it. They all have their binoculars, you know, even Auntie Duff, and they can tell you things about yourself you didn't even know.'

Buchanan wasn't quite so convinced about the lack of privacy in the community but there was no point in making her more depressed than she already was. The possibility of the crimes being drug related had not previously occurred to him and now merited some thought, but Fizz carried on talking.

'I don't know who the pusher is in these parts nowadays, but I know a few junkies I could ask.'

'I don't think it's just a matter of asking, Fizz. Junkies are not noted for being particularly public-spirited people, as far as I'm aware. How are you going to get one of them to betray his supplier?'

Fizz blinked her eyes innocently in the way Buchanan had come to dread. 'Maybe I'll think of something,' she said.

It was well after four by the time they got back to Killin. Buchanan wasn't too tired, which pleased him because it showed he hadn't become as unfit as he had feared since his operation, but he was parched with thirst. Fizz also claimed to be in need of liquid refreshment so they stopped at a small snack bar at the edge of the village.

The door was propped open with a grey concrete garden gnome and a plastic carpet runner protected the dingy Axminster from the doorway to the small counter at the back of the room. There were no other customers at the moment but the close-packed tables and chairs indicated that, at other times, business was brisk.

Fizz chose a table in the bay window, tipped her chair back against the wall and closed her eyes. As Buchanan started to ask her what she wanted to drink she raised one hand to silence him and he registered, for the first time, that there were voices coming from the curtained doorway behind the counter. Not only voices but giggles and little explosive laughs.

'Honestly, Fizz—' Buchanan started to say but her eyes flew open and she raised an admonitory finger to her lips just as a phrase, louder than the rest, drifted through the curtains.

'. . . really mustn't! What if someone came in?'

'Lock the door,' said an indistinct male rumble.

Buchanan was mortified at being forced to eavesdrop on this conversation and indicated to Fizz, in dumb show, that if she insisted on listening she was on her own. Unfortunately, as he pushed his chair back it banged into the table behind it, making the crockery rattle, and the conversation beyond the curtain came to an abrupt end.

'Pest!' said Fizz angrily, but she had called him worse on several occasions so he bore her ire with fortitude.

He was reseating himself at the table when the waitress emerged, which was fortunate since it must have looked, to her, as though they had just arrived. She was a woman in her late forties, not bad-looking but with a leathery, smoker's face and high colour. She was slim, but her bottom had sagged too far for the tight black trousers she was wearing, and her posture was so bad that, from the side she looked like the hands of a clock showing ten past six.

Without wasting any words, she took their order for two Cokes, brought it to them, and charged them on the spot before retreating to the back premises and, presumably, her boyfriend.

Fizz smiled a smile of deep contentment. 'This guy,' she said quietly, 'the guy who owns this place, right? He's a user. Thirty years ago, according to local gossip, he used to be one of the flower people, out of his skull most of the time on hash or acid or whatever he could lay his hands on. Nowadays it's coke, from what I hear, although I dare say he wouldn't turn down anything that could give him a hit.'

'I do hope you're not intending to ask him about his supplier?' Buchanan queried, getting ready to beat a hasty retreat. 'If so, you won't be wanting me around.'

'No, stay,' Fizz said firmly. 'I may need you. Besides, I want another drink first, don't you?'

Buchanan did want another drink. He went over and tapped on the counter, trying not to decipher the murmurings that were still going on in the room beyond, and ordered the same again.

When the waitress delivered their order Fizz gave her a wistful smile and said, 'I wonder if it would be possible to have a few words with Mr McConnachie?'

This constituted a major problem for the waitress, being an eventuality for which her training had not prepared her and one for which she had no ready response. After considering the request for some time she decided to take the matter to a higher tribunal. 'I'll just see,' she said, and retreated beyond the curtain.

Buchanan was struggling with a feeling of impending doom. 'I don't know why you need me here,' he whispered urgently. 'You wanted rid of me when you were quizzing McLaren so why—'

The curtain swung aside to reveal a grey-haired ogre of a man in a kilt; at least six foot three, twenty stone, and four point seven on the Richter scale. As he strode towards them the crockery on the counter chattered like teeth.

'Something I can do for you?' he asked Buchanan, and his bass voice flowed from word to word with scarcely a ripple like a deep river.

Buchanan, momentarily at a loss for words, indicated Fizz

with his eyes and she said, 'Sit down, Duncan. I want to talk to you for a minute.'

He hooked back a chair with a leg that would have fed a family of four for a fortnight and sat, watching her curiously. 'You're from Am Bealach, aren't you? One of the Fitzpatricks.'

'Fizz Fitzpatrick. And this is Tam Buchanan. We're looking into the disappearance of Bessie Anderson. You'll have heard of that business?'

'Oh, I've heard about it. Sure, it was in the *Killin News*.' He leaned back in his chair, his pouched eyes frowning at them both beneath curly eyebrows. 'But I never knew the woman and I know nothing about what goes on in Am Bealach.'

'No, of course not.' Fizz smiled enchantingly, her blue eyes glowing with amiability and benevolence. 'The thing is, it's all tied up with that camper whose body was found last week and I've just heard that some hash and an Ecstasy tablet were found in his tent. The Eccie was a lotus – supplied locally.'

Duncan McConnachie's face gave no sign that he had heard her speak. He just kept looking at her, expressionlessly, waiting to hear what would come next. Buchanan found this monolithic stillness wholly unnerving since his previous experience of Fizz had led him to believe that, although it was *she* who annoyed people, it was likely to be *he* who got punched in the face.

Beside McConnachie's massive bulk, Fizz looked like a kitten smiling up at a Rottweiler. Sun-bleached tendrils of hair framed a face that made Shirley Temple look depraved and her denim-blue eyes rested on Duncan with absolute faith and affection.

'Now, nobody knows anything about that camper,' she was saying. 'We don't know his name, we don't know where he came from or where he was going, we don't know what business he had in this neck of the woods. But the guy who sold him the Eccie could maybe tell us something. If we could just locate him.'

Buchanan tried to distance himself from this charade by staring out the window. There was no way this guy was going to cut off his own supply by dropping his pusher in the shit and it was just a bit embarrassing to watch Fizz making a fool of herself.

Duncan's slow voice said, with subdued amusement, 'And?'

Fizz raised her eyebrows. 'And I want you to tell me who he is.'

'Me?' He tried to keep his face straight with only partial success. 'How would I come by that information?'

Fizz's smile became even more cherubic. 'Let's not play silly buggers, Duncan. We're talking about the same guy you get your stuff from. I doubt very much if there's enough business for two pushers around here, don't you? I'm not going to spill the beans to the police, I just want a word with the guy, that's all.'

Duncan's meaty face split in a huge grin. 'You think I'm a junkie? Good God, who put that idea in your head? I haven't touched anything stronger than coffee since 1972. You've picked the wrong guy, kid.'

'I don't think so,' Fizz twinkled, totally unfazed.

'Listen. If I knew who this pusher was I'd be happy to tell you.' Duncan put on a sincere face but his eyes still held traces of amusement. 'But, believe me, it's been years . . . many years since I indulged and there isn't even anyone in the village I know for sure is using the stuff these days. Maybe you could try asking Con Douglas up at the golf course road.'

Fizz didn't know when to give up. 'I'm asking *you*, Duncan,' she insisted patiently, still smiling. 'It's better than being interviewed by the police, isn't it?'

'And why would the police want to be interviewing the likes of me? Eh?'

'As a user you must know the name of the pusher.'

Duncan threw a pained glance at Buchanan as though to say, what's *with* this idiot?, and returned his attention to Fizz. 'I keep telling you, I'm not a user.'

'Save your halitosis, Duncan. I know you are. I know it for a fact.'

Duncan leaned across the table so suddenly that Buchanan's muscles tensed. 'So, prove it.'

Fizz turned her head lazily and looked out the window. Following her eyes, Buchanan could see the local bus drawing to a stop across the road and a bunch of young teenagers surging out of it. Behind them came a plump woman of about forty carrying bags of shopping.

'There's your wife, Duncan,' Fizz commented brightly. 'She's looking well.'

'Right, then.' Duncan pushed back his chair. 'Better get on with the work.'

'I wonder,' Fizz said, halting him with a look. 'I wonder what she would think if she knew how you were amusing yourself with the hired help while her back was turned.'

Duncan's knee jerked as though someone had tested his reflexes. His face flooded with a wash of unhealthy colour that seemed to inflate his massive jowls and make the veins swell on his pudgy nose.

'I didn't hear you say that.' Duncan's lips didn't so much enunciate the words as pass them like kidney stones.

Fizz tut-tutted her disapproval of this reaction. 'I think you *should* hear me, Duncan, and hear me good. I want the name of your pusher before I leave this table. I won't have to tell him who gave it to me and I won't have to put him out of business. As far as I'm concerned you and other pathetic dopeheads like you can continue to go to hell your own way. All I'm interested in is finding out about that camper.'

There was a long, but not peaceful silence. Buchanan wanted to ask Fizz not to make Duncan any angrier but he could see that even the sight of her was doing irreparable damage to the guy's cardiovascular system.

Mrs McConnachie came in from the street, kicking the gnome aside and letting the door swing to behind her. She looked curiously at her husband who stood up and took her carrier bags from her.

'Been busy?' she asked and walked ahead of him through the curtained doorway. Duncan followed, glancing once over his shoulder at Fizz with an expression that indicated he'd be back.

Buchanan, not for the first time, felt himself totally defeated by Fizz's cavalier attitude. She had no discernible sense of self-preservation and didn't hesitate for a minute to involve any innocent bystander in her highly questionable schemes.

'You appreciate, no doubt, that he was within an inch of slapping you around the ear?' he said angrily. 'Which would have meant that I'd have had to punch him and would probably have ended up in traction. Please, will you stop getting me into situations like this? I like my teeth where they are.'

'Oh, pooh!' she said with a giggle. 'He's all blubber. You could have taken him in the first round.'

Buchanan was as moved by her flattery as he was by her more frequent insults. 'Just cool it, OK? Don't provoke him any further.'

'I won't have to.' She pushed the feathery golden ringlets back from her brow and slid up her sunglasses to hold them in place. 'I've got his balls in the mangle and he knows it.'

There was a movement behind the curtain and Duncan's

bulk filled the doorway. His colour had returned to normal but the expression on his face gave Buchanan severe stomach cramps. He walked slowly across the room towards them, his thumbs hooked into the chain of his sporran.

'Right,' he said to Fizz, in a voice like distant thunder. 'Don Taylor. His mother owns the store at the foot of Glen Earn. And if the police get their noses in there I'll find you, right? That's a promise. Now get the fuck out of here.'

'A pleasure to do business with you, Duncan.' Fizz drained her Coke and stood up. 'Give my regards to your wife, won't you?'

Buchanan got behind her and hustled her towards the door before she went too far, but they were blocked on the threshold by the arrival of new customers, giving her time to say clearly,

'And, by the way, your Coke's flat.'

'*Will* you shut up?' Buchanan snarled, propelling her firmly outside.

She was on a complete high. She was always pretty, in a ridiculous baby-doll sort of way, but right now she would have glowed in the dark. Her eyes were huge and sparkling with exhilaration and her lips curled happily upwards like the petals on a rose. If Buchanan hadn't wanted to choke the life out of her he would have been quite enchanted.

'That was a disgraceful exhibition,' he told her straight, the minute they got back to the car. 'There was absolutely no need to be so offensive.'

'But I like being offensive,' she sniggered. 'The man's a complete tosser.'

'I'm not stupid, Fizz,' Buchanan said, letting in the clutch and roaring out of the car park at a speed that pressed her back in her seat. 'I know damn well that it wasn't just Duncan you were needling. You were getting at me at the same time.

You just love to see me squirm, don't you? It amuses you to embarrass me by saying things your Grampa can't hear, and it amuses you to set me up in a potentially violent situation like you just did.'

'Bollocks,' she said, hanging on to her smirk.

Buchanan ignored the interruption. 'I've had it up to here. That's positively the last time I let you involve me in your machinations. From now on you're on your own. And furthermore, I don't like the way you're doing this. The information you just got from Duncan must be given directly to the police – certainly not followed up by you. You're getting yourself into a scene that could turn out to be very dodgy.'

She looked blankly out through the windscreen, some of her sparkle noticeably dimmed. 'I can't tell the police,' she said flatly. 'You heard Duncan. I don't want him turning up on my doorstep with a meat cleaver some dark night.'

'You don't have to follow up the lead. Just forget about the pusher and concentrate on other lines of enquiry.'

'We don't *have* any other lines of enquiry. This pusher could maybe tell us if the camper was heading for Am Bealach or just passing through, en route to someplace else. He might know where the guy came from or why he was in the area.' She turned and looked at him, challenging him to deny it. 'This is the best – the *only* break we've had all week. You can't really expect me to walk away from it.'

Buchanan's spirits sank like a concrete lifebelt. If Fizz insisted on going down that road there was no way she would be deterred. The minute he turned his back on her she'd be in there faster than the eye could follow, which meant that sooner or later he'd end up tagging along with her.

A brilliant way to convalesce.

It was beginning to appear as if staying in Edinburgh might have been a great deal healthier in the long run.

Chapter Ten

From the minute they left Duncan McConnachie's café Fizz was jumping out of her skin to come to grips with his pusher.

She was not acquainted with either Don Taylor or his mother but she had passed their small store once or twice since her return to Scotland. It was situated at the foot of the glen road, which formed the curve of a capital D that looped through Am Bealach and Killin before joining up again with the straight route to the north and west.

Off the main tourist route like that, maybe half a mile from Lochearnhead where the glen road joined the A82, there could never have been enough business to make it a viable concern. Not legitimate business. On the other hand, it was perfectly situated for the kind of clientele Don Taylor wanted to attract.

Fizz would have gone straight there from Duncan's café but for the realisation that, not only would the store be closed for the weekend before they could get there, but that Buchanan would refuse to take her. He needed a period of quiet reflection, some good food and company, and a lavish helping of ego massage before he would be human again.

So on Sunday, she took him to the Killin gun club open day where he only narrowly avoided making a complete arse of himself on the flighting pigeon but hit seven out of ten at the bolting rabbit, which was not bad for a beginner.

Malcolm was there with Zander and Simon and, later on, Rowena and Lindsay turned up with Briony in her carrycot. Only Alistair, among all the younger Am Bealach residents, failed to show, and that intrigued Fizz.

'What's with Alistair?' she asked Rowena while they were sitting on the grass watching Simon and Buchanan banging away at the springing teal. 'It's not often he's been known to miss a shoot. Particularly an open day. He's still a member of the club, isn't he?'

'Yes, I think he comes along to the club shoots most times.' Rowena looked down the grassy slope to where Lindsay was queuing at the refreshment caravan. She might have been hiding her expression, but it was hard to be sure.

'So why isn't he here today?' Fizz persisted.

'I don't know.' But Rowena, like Buchanan, had been brought up to believe that the sky would fall on your head if you told a lie, so she added, 'That is, it might be because he's avoiding Lindsay. The two of them aren't the best of friends at the moment.'

'Well now, that does surprise me,' Fizz said, reflecting that the only surprising thing about it was that Alistair hadn't slit his boss's gizzard years ago. 'What did they fall out about?'

Rowena made a vague gesture. 'I don't know. Lindsay refuses to discuss it because I criticised him for being auto-cratic with Alistair. It was really inexcusable of Lindsay – after all, Alistair is the fourth generation of Munroes to be game-keeper at Stronach estate and I'm sure his children will carry on the tradition. I don't think Lindsay really understands how Alistair feels about . . .'

'Coffee or tea, you two?' Lindsay called from the caravan. 'There aren't any scones left, just chocolate biscuits.'

'Two coffees, two biscuits,' Fizz shouted, making a uni-lateral decision to save Rowena from any stressful cost/benefit analysis, and returned to her cross-examination. 'Was that why you were being so defensive of Alistair on Friday? You were getting your little dig in at Lindsay, weren't you?'

Rowena looked uncomfortable. 'I know I ought to support Lindsay in these things but I just felt – I just feel that Lindsay can be too high-handed sometimes. After all, the lodge cottage is as much Alistair's home as Stronach House is Lindsay's – more so, since he was born there. It's not right for Lindsay to treat him as some kind of serf.' She saw Zander coming towards them, pushing Briony in her carrycot, and added softly, 'Don't say anything to Lindsay.'

Fizz felt she was unlikely to say anything to anybody about the sort of petty tiff that was all too common in Am Bealach, where people fell out and in again with each other all the time. She had satisfied herself that there was no Lady Chatterley situation in progress and that was all that interested her. She would have been quite staggered if the reverse had proved to be the case since, not only did Alistair have very little going for him in the Casanova department, but Rowena would have needed major surgery to uncross her legs.

However, stranger things had been known to happen between repressed males and losers like Rowena, and it wouldn't have been the first time Rowena had cast herself out of the frying pan into the fire.

Lindsay arrived back with refreshments for everyone – Lord Bountiful dispensing alms to the poor, Fizz thought ungratefully – and whistled – in the rest of the Am Bealach contingent to partake.

'You're out of practice, Fizz,' Malcolm said, propping himself on his shooting stick beside her. 'I was watching you at the high pheasant and thinking it's as well your grampa isn't here today or he'd be seeing all his teaching going down the drain.'

'Don't remind me,' Fizz said with a touch of grimness. 'I'm not likely to forget his teaching methods.'

Malcolm gave a short laugh. 'Aye, and nor should you, Fizz, for you're a good example of what he does well.' He winked at Buchanan and used the stem of his pipe to indicate Fizz. 'I mind he had Fizz and Colin throwing stones at tin cans for years before he would let them near a gun, but by the time they were old enough for air guns they both had a good eye in their heads.'

Fizz answered with a grunt. She had no very happy memories of her education at Grampa's hands. His methods might have been effective but he just didn't know when to stop.

'Well, it doesn't take long to lose the knack of it,' she said. 'I haven't even looked at a gun for years.' That was a lie, she realised almost as the words left her lips. She had looked at a gun very closely, only last year, and from a very alarming angle, but there were now quite long periods when she could push that memory to the back of her mind.

'You're still using your grampa's old side-by-sider, I see,' Simon noticed. 'Why don't you have a go with this Perazzi of mine? It's very light for an over-and-under.'

'I can fire it,' Zander claimed, French-kissing his ice cream. 'Grandad is teaching me. I'm to get a shotgun of my own when I'm twelve. A four-ten.'

Fizz hefted the ancient side-by-sider with which she had first learned to shoot. 'Oh, I think I'll stick to old faithful here. It's been in the family for generations. Grampa's father sold it to him on his deathbed.'

'That Perazzi is too long in the barrel for Zander, of course,' Lindsay pointed out. 'But, if you're thinking of getting him a four-ten in a couple of years, Simon, I think you're making a mistake. He'd be better to start with an air rifle, the way I started as a lad. A nice little .177 or even a .22. He'd have a lot of fun with either of those.'

'But it's a shotgun I want,' Zander complained, glancing at his father for reassurance. 'I can handle a shotgun already. I can handle the Perazzi, can't I, Dad?'

Simon gave him a big grin and a light punch on the shoulder. 'You keep on improving the way you're doing, sport, and you'll be shooting against the gamekeepers by the time you're twelve.'

'Och aye, two years is a long time,' Malcolm rumbled. 'You've a lot to learn before you're twelve.'

'There's plenty of fun to be had with an air rifle, though,' Lindsay insisted, hanging on like a bulldog. 'When I was not much older than you, Zander, I had a .177 and I remember one November morning . . .'

Fizz abandoned Buchanan and the others to Lindsay's reminiscences and turned her attention to Rowena who was now administering orange juice to her offspring. It was funny to look at Briony and see Rowena's big brown eyes and wavy hair in such a miniaturised form while, at the same time, realising that if you stuck a toothbrush moustache beneath that button nose you'd see another Lindsay staring back at you.

'Funny how like you both she is.' Fizz stroked Briony's rounded cheek with a forefinger, surprised by its swan's-down softness. 'Why did you wait so long to start a family? You must be married – what, seven years?'

Rowena threw a wary glance at her husband but found him in full flow and unlikely to overhear. 'Lindsay thought it would be better to wait. At first it was just for a year or two, till we got settled. Then it was for another couple of years, till he became more established in the party, only that took longer than he'd estimated. Then, once he'd been re-elected a couple of times, he decided that his image would be enhanced if he were perceived to be a family man, so . . .'

'So you were permitted to conceive,' Fizz supplied, deleting expletives. 'I get the picture. And are there to be any more little vote-catchers in the future?'

'Hopefully. Another one, at least.'

Rowena's Mona Lisa smile would have fooled most people. She could appear as pliable as knicker elastic but she didn't stretch for ever without snapping. And, judging on past performance, who knew which way she would jump?

If he had been going out of his way to irritate her, Buchanan could not have succeeded any better than he did the next morning. Fizz was frantic to meet and interview the alleged drug pusher but Buchanan was in laid-back mode and wouldn't be rushed.

She was standing at the kitchen window waiting for him to come for his breakfast when she saw him away along the loch shore, wandering along the beach with Selena pouncing jauntily in front of him. He was evidently on his way back from an early walk but he was in no hurry, strolling along with his hands in his pockets and his eyes on the ground.

Typical, Fizz thought. You could see he was totally oblivious to the magic of the morning, the flawless blue of the sky and the perfect reflections of the mountains on the still surface of the loch. Even Selena's playful attacks on his shoelaces didn't appear to be intruding on his thoughts.

No doubt he had walked as far as the end of Grampa's land, where the Stronach met the loch. There was no bridge there and nothing to see except the family burial plot, so it was the obvious place to turn back.

In the hope of speeding up the day's proceedings, she walked down to the end of the garden to meet him and she was only a few yards away when he looked up and noticed her. He looked so solemn that she abandoned all thought of berating him for his tardiness. If he was bored sick, as well he might be for all his polite denials, he might too easily pack up and escape back to Edinburgh, which would be disastrous at this stage in their investigation. She needed him today, not just for transport but as a witness.

This being the situation, she greeted him with a smile. 'I see your little tortoiseshell friend is visiting again. You two are becoming an item.'

He smiled back, which made a change. 'Actually, she's beginning to grow on me. If she could just do something about her BO I could get quite fond of her.'

Fizz would normally have made some remark about old maids and cats gravitating to each other, but instead she hurried him into the kitchen, without seeming to do so, and saw to it that he was fed and watered with the utmost dispatch.

'You'll have to change out of those trousers,' she told him as he ate. 'And that sports shirt is no good either. I want us to look like a couple of backpackers. If we waltz in there looking like a posse of plain-clothes policemen we'll get zilch.'

'What are backpackers wearing these days?'

'Something like this.' She had borrowed a tartan shirt from Grampa's après-lambing wardrobe and teamed it with her sawn-off denim jeans.

'Uh-huh.' Buchanan nodded, raising one eyebrow in that sardonic way he had. 'I dare say I could cut the legs off my Rohan slacks but finding a tartan shirt could pose a bit of a problem.'

'Wear your shorts, then. And surely you possess a T-shirt?'

He said he'd think of something but she wasn't at all surprised to see him appear, shortly, as spruce as a Christmas tree in tailored shorts and a pristine white T-shirt, white sports socks and Reeboks.

'Boots,' said Fizz, pointing at his feet.

'Boots and thick socks in the car,' he said. 'I'll change when we get there – or rather, before we get there, since I imagine you don't plan for us to be rolling up in a Saab?'

They left the car half a mile from the shop, in a forestry track where it was hidden by sitka spruce, donned their boots and rucksacks, and walked down the hill to the end of the glen. Loch Earn was out of sight around the curve of the hills but the loch, below them, was bluer than the sky and dotted with water skiers. The only visible building was the grey stone cottage with the ugly cement shop extension grafted on the front. There were metal advertising signs for Walls ice cream and Coca-Cola outside and an unpainted wooden bench flanked the open doorway. Among other notices on the glass door was a poster asking for information about the missing camper.

Fizz slowed her step as they approached. 'Tell you what: you sit outside on the bench and keep your ears open and I'll suss out the situation and get a couple of Cokes.'

'You don't think it might be better if I were to do the questioning this time? I'm not totally inexperienced at this sort of thing, you know.'

'Buchanan,' Fizz said kindly, 'in that outfit you wouldn't fool Stevie Wonder.' Actually, in his hiking boots and thick socks he didn't look quite so much like a tailor's dummy and his tan, after a few days of lying in the sun, gave him an authentic weather-beaten appearance, but you couldn't hide the immaculate haircut and the close shave.

Buchanan lowered his pack to the bench as though it weighed a ton and wiggled his shoulders like a man who'd been yomping for hours. 'OK. Just make sure you speak clearly enough for me to follow the conversation. I want to know if you're about to be taught a salutary lesson.'

'To hear is to obey, O Star of the Universe.'

The woman behind the counter was peeling herself a choc ice when Fizz went in. She was somewhere in her late fifties and looked every day of it, although she had made a brave attempt to improve on nature with pancake make-up and eyeliner, which had evidently been applied in a poor light. Her hair was drawn tightly back from her face and there was what looked like a dead mole pinned to it at the back of her neck. The gold chains around her neck were probably fake, as were her stud earrings, but they could have fooled most people.

'Hi,' Fizz said, helping herself to a couple of cans of Coke and putting the money on the counter. 'Is Don about?'

The woman's expression, which had been less than heart-warming from the word go, stiffened suddenly into that of a prison officer with piles.

'No, Don is not about,' she said crisply, and with a very obvious hope that the conversation would end right there.

Fizz mimed mild exasperation. 'That's too bad. I really wanted to catch him. I don't suppose you know when he'll be back?'

'He won't be back. Donald doesn't live here any more.' There was a faint quaver in her voice that told Fizz the parting had been recent and none too amicable.

'I see.' Fizz grappled with bitter disappointment. She had to be back in Edinburgh by tomorrow night so this could be her last chance of locating Don. She said, 'So where's he living now?'

'Listen, dear . . .' Don's mother looked at the ice cream in her hand, dropped it into a waste bin and folded her arms. Her colour had risen slightly and sweat glistened along her hairline and under her baggy eyes as though she were in the throes of a hot flush. 'I don't know where he's living and I don't want to know. I've had enough of his lying and cheating and his taking off to God knows where for days at a time and his "friends" turning up at my door at all times of the day and night . . .' She caught herself just as she was starting to lose the place and took a firm grip of the edge of the counter. 'So you can tell that to any of your friends who are looking for him. I don't want any of your sort hanging around here any more. Understand?'

Fizz wondered how long she had been aware of her son's nefarious activities. Probably for quite a while, if the trinkets around her neck were, in fact, real gold. They were just the sort of sweetener Don might give her to shut her up, but the discovery of the body of one of their customers must have had quite laxative effects on them both. One could imagine Mrs Taylor going totally bananas when she read the police description of the corpse in the local paper. There were so few backpackers around in March she could scarcely have failed to remember one so distinctive.

Fizz took a slow drink of her Coke and then said, 'I'm not actually one of Don's friends. In fact, I've never met him, but a guy I met in the Killin Youth Hostel last night asked me to give him a message if I passed this way. I can't remember the guy's name but you'll probably know him: a tall, tanned dude with brown hair tied in a bunch at the back. About twenty. A backpacker. He got some stuff from Don about a month ago.'

Mrs Taylor went very still. 'Last night?' she said slowly. After a couple of seconds her grip on the counter tightened. 'You saw him last night, did you say? A backpacker? Long dark hair?'

'Uh-huh. I think he said he met you.'

'Jeans and a green sweatshirt?' Mrs Taylor persisted faintly, clearly unable to believe that the rotting corpse that had haunted her dreams for the past week was still alive and well and living in Killin Youth Hostel. 'With a navy and green rucksack?'

'That's him.' Fizz awarded her a sunny smile. She hadn't a clue what the guy had been wearing but it was obvious they were both talking about the same backpacker. Watching Mrs Taylor's face was like watching the sun come up on a June morning. Her relief was so palpable that one couldn't help feeling happy for her.

Fizz waited till Mrs Taylor's grip on the counter began to relax and then hit her with: 'He bought some hash and some Eccies from Don and he wanted me to tell him—'

'I don't want to know about that.' Mrs Taylor sprang away from the counter, her eyes rolling to the doorway where the shadow of Buchanan's long legs could be seen beyond the threshold. Dropping her voice to a hiss, she said, 'What Don gets up to is no business of mine and if he's been selling . . . whatever it was you mentioned . . . it's him you want to talk to about it, not me.'

'Actually, it's not the drugs I want to talk about,' Fizz confided, making Mrs Taylor's face spasm momentarily with angst. 'It's the backpacker. I'm trying to establish his identity.'

Mrs Taylor regarded her blankly. Her mascara had dribbled black smudges on her cheekbones making her look like a baseball player on a sunny day. It took her a few seconds to formulate: 'His identity? I thought . . .'

'That I met him in Killin Youth Hostel?' Fizz helped her along. 'Nope, 'fraid not. That was just one of my little whoppers, Mrs Taylor. The poor dude ended up under a pile of boulders with his face like a pound of mince. And nobody knows who he was, where he came from or what the hell he was doing there except your son. And you.'

It looked to Fizz, for a second, as though Don's mother had

received one shock to the system too many. Her eyes rolled back in her head, then she leaned on the counter and seemed to be scanning its surface for a blunt instrument.

Finally, she fixed Fizz with a malevolent eye and hissed, 'This is entrapment!'

'You're damn right it's entrapment,' Fizz returned brightly. 'But, as I'm not a policewoman, there's not a thing you can do about it. Just be bloody grateful I got to you before the CID did because they'd have your pig's fart of a son meeting some new boyfriends in Barlinnie Prison before he could cough. You catch my drift?'

'Who are you?' Mrs Taylor's eyes rolled to the doorway. 'And who's your friend?'

'I'm the person who's asking the questions, and you are the person who's answering them, Mrs Taylor. Just bear that in mind and maybe you'll manage to keep your son out of jail. And don't give me any shit, OK? Otherwise you'll be talking to Inspector Cullen within the hour.'

Incredulity fought with alarm under the pancake make-up as Mrs Taylor nodded. 'But . . . but I don't know anything. Neither does Donald. The backpacker . . . we'd never seen him before. We never asked his name.'

'You're sure? Not even his first name?'

'Absolutely. He just said that someone in Stirling had told him that Don could "fix him up". I don't know who that was but it must have been someone Don trusted otherwise . . .'

'And you don't know where Don is now?' Fizz interrupted, cursing her luck.

Mrs Taylor's voice shook as she said, 'No. I haven't heard a word since I threw him out last week.' She produced a tissue from under the counter and blew her nose. 'I just couldn't take any more. He promised me time after time that he'd stop dealing. He kept saying he'd given up but his customers kept calling round so I knew it was lies. Then this lad that Don had supplied was found up the glen, and every knock at the door had us jumping out of our skins in case it was the police on the doorstep.'

Fizz found it hard to be sympathetic. 'OK,' she said, 'you don't know the backpacker's name. What else can you tell me about him? What did he look like? Did he say where he'd come from, other than Stirling? Did he mention speaking to anyone? Did he say where he was headed?'

'No, he didn't talk much and I hardly looked at him. He just had a Coke and asked the way to Am Bealach and then left.'

Fizz's spirits dropped into her boots. 'He asked the way to Am Bealach?'

Mrs Taylor nodded. She didn't look any too happy about answering questions but was evidently pinning her hopes on Fizz's promise of confidentiality. 'He had a map, but it didn't quite cover Am Bealach.'

'Did you get the impression that Am Bealach was his objective?' Fizz steeled herself to ask. 'Or was he just passing through en route to somewhere else?'

'I don't know. He didn't say. But the name "Am Bealach" was written in the margin of his map. In green ink.'

Great, Fizz thought bitterly. The sole piece of interesting information the interview had managed to elicit, and it had to be the news she most fervently didn't want to hear. The camper was on his way to rendezvous with one of the Am Bealach residents.

'There weren't any other place names in the margin?' she asked without much hope.

Mrs Taylor started to say, 'No' and then paused for a second. 'Not place names, no, but there was a circle drawn on the map in the same green ink. On the west coast, just north of Oban. And there was an address written on the sea beside it.

Well, it would be Loch Linnhe, at that bit, not the sea.'

'Did you read the address?' Fizz breathed.

'No. I wasn't interested. I only noticed it in passing, because we used to live near there, but I remember that the circle was between Benderloch and Connel.'

Fizz knew the area reasonably well, and if her memory served her correctly, it was very thinly populated. In fact, if there was a village between Benderloch and Connel it must be a very small one. Maybe she had uncovered a further avenue of enquiry after all. She drained her Coke and chipped the can into the waste bucket.

'Right, Mrs Taylor. With any luck you won't be seeing me again, but if Don contacts you, you can give him a message from me. Just tell him to get a new hobby, 'cos if I hear he's still doing business at the old stand I'll drop him in the shit. OK?' She gave Mrs Taylor her sweetest smile and rubbed a little salt in the wound by adding, 'And listen – thanks for your help.'

Outside, Buchanan was leaning against the wall beside the doorway with an expression on his face that Fizz had seen him wear more than once.

'What's wrong with you now?' she said shortly. She felt that, not only had she handled the interview rather well, but that her politeness could be held up as a model to little girls for generations to come.

'This gets to be more of a paper chase at every turn,' he said glumly. 'I don't suppose for a minute it's to be "Home, James, and don't spare the horses"?'

'No chance,' Fizz assured him. 'It's only a two-hour drive to Benderloch. Nice part of the country. You'll love it.'

Buchanan hoisted his pack. 'I had a feeling you'd say that.'

Chapter Eleven

After consulting his road atlas, Buchanan took the main road north from Lochearnhead which was quicker than looping back to it via Am Bealach and Killin.

He could feel Fizz throwing him curious glances every few seconds as though she were puzzled by his willingness to taxi her around Scotland at the drop of a hat. He was fairly puzzled himself, truth to tell, but he suspected his motives had their roots in the discovery he had made during his early morning walk.

He had awakened at six fifteen to find that Selena had made herself a comfortable nest in the downie, within the angle of his knees, preventing him from straightening his legs and driving him, eventually to the edge of the bed. She had arrived sometime in the middle of the night, damp with dew, and went on to stake her claim to the lion's share of the bed. Nothing short of direct violence would dislodge her.

Around about 7 a.m. Buchanan abandoned the unequal struggle and got up and, because it was such a superb morning, he decided to take a stroll along the lochside before breakfast.

He left Selena unconscious on the bed but had barely quitted the farmyard before he discovered that she was accompanying him. She appeared suddenly on the deer track a few yards ahead, leading the way, as though the outing had been her idea, not his. He had still not discovered her means of entrance to and egress from his cottage but he was close to concluding that she could pick locks.

He couldn't quite put his finger on it but there was something about her – something more than the fact that she was hard to get rid of – that reminded him of Fizz.

The water of the loch was still as glass, except for patches where it was dappled with the rings of feeding trout, and the range of peaks beyond Killin was reflected as perfectly as in a mirror. Last night, in the long twilight, the hills had been tawny beige with cornflower-blue shadows, but now they were lime green and grey, splotched with dark brown where the heather grew.

He was within sight of the dry-stone wall that marked the boundary of Grampa's farm when he spotted what he thought was a ruined cottage surrounded by trees. It was only when he left the loch shore to investigate it that he discovered it to be a private graveyard. There was a wrought-iron gate set into the high wall surrounding it, and inside were some twenty or thirty gravestones in various stages of decrepitude. Selena, without waiting for Buchanan to open the gate, oozed through the interstices of the wrought iron and disappeared into the long grass.

Buchanan followed.

Almost all of the inscriptions were sacred to the memory of a Fitzpatrick and those that weren't were marking the last resting places of married females of that clan. A tall column of grey slate listed the four members of the family killed in the First World War and the two who were lost in the Second.

One grave stood out from the others. It occupied a plot a few paces from the gateway, partly shaded by the branches of a wild cherry tree, and here the turf had been cleared from a long rectangle in front of the headstone. A ground-cover plant with variegated leaves and tiny pink flowers grew thickly there and the green shoots of some sort of bulb were just beginning to poke through. Around the edge, the leaves and headless stalks of daffodils still formed a border and a narrow stone edging gave some protection against encroaching weeds.

Knowing already whose grave this must be, Buchanan leaned forward to read the inscription.

In loving memory of Gregor McLellan Fitzpatrick, born 1938 and his wife Rhona Mhairi Fitzpatrick, born 1941. Departed this world 11 January 1974. *GUS AM BRUS AN LATH.*

There was no time to explore the other graves properly but the place was worth earmarking for another visit. It would be interesting to know which of the living Fitzpatricks was tending Gregor and Rhona's grave. It wasn't easy to picture Grampa giving much time to it at this season of the year and Auntie Duff would have found it hard going to walk that far along the pebbly shore. That left Fizz, and if she had done the work she must have started it after her return to Scotland last year.

This was a side of Fizz she had kept well hidden from Buchanan. She had never shown any sign of affection for anyone, living or dead: on the contrary she exhibited a deep-seated horror of emotional ties of any description. Fizz was one, and all alone, and ever more shall be so. Or was she?

As he followed Selena back to the farmhouse Buchanan couldn't help imagining Fizz as a toddler, growing up here in the care of a loveless old man, never knowing a daddy's hug or the healing kiss of a fond mother. There was no escaping the comparison with his own childhood, wrapped in the cotton wool of affluence and parental affection.

He had wondered what made Fizz the way she was, and now he was beginning to find out.

As they passed the end of the road that approached Killin from the north it occurred to Fizz that they ought to let Auntie Duff know that they might not be home in time for dinner. Accordingly, Buchanan pulled into the nearest garage and waited while she made the call. Within seconds of her departure, a Land Rover pulled into the parking space beside him and Gerda got out. She saw him right away and smiled, but not with any particular degree of warmth.

He felt immediately guilty for not phoning her, if only to arrange a pony trek. He hadn't seen anything of her since her come-on last week, when that fortuitous group of American sightseers had arrived on the scene just in time to save his virtue or her feelings.

He had an in-built horror of rapacious females. A gentle, take-it-or-leave-it intimation of willingness was one thing, but an approach bordering on attempted rape was another. Subconsciously he was convinced that some degree of affection between sexual partners was what distinguished Homo sapiens from a lower order of primates, but Gerda had nipped affection, very effectively, in the bud.

Good manners, however, dictated that he get out of the car and act glad to see her. 'Gerda. How're you doing?'

'I am doing extremely well, thank you, Tam. Are you doing good? How is your bladder?'

'My gall bladder is just fine. I'm feeling much better now. Fit enough for that pony trek you promised me. Do you have a trek going out tomorrow afternoon?'

'We have treks going all afternoons,' she said, defrosting slightly round the edges. 'If there are persons wishing to go we make a trek at two thirty. But for you, Tam, we go any time. On Saturday we take a new first-time trek. A special, all-day trek by the drove road to Crianlarich. I think many people will like to go.'

'Great,' Buchanan said. 'The new trek sounds very interesting but, unfortunately I won't be able to make it because I'll be driving back to Edinburgh in the afternoon. But, I'll probably see you tomorrow if the weather's reasonable.'

He made a mental note to drive past the stables before he booked in, to ascertain that there were other riders waiting to go. A one-to-one personal interface situation with Gerda, particularly off in the woods somewhere, could get very complicated.

'You are being much in the sun, I see,' she said, ogling his bare legs in a roguish manner, 'and being nice and brown. Also I am burning a small part yesterday.'

She hauled the wide neckline of her blouse aside to expose one pinkly tinted shoulder striped with a white strap-mark, plus quite a lot else besides.

Fizz chose that precise minute to reappear.

'You ought to be careful,' Buchanan told Gerda, a little too loudly. 'You don't want to end up with a melanoma.'

Fizz gave no sign of having noticed anything untoward. 'Hi there, Gerda,' she said chummily. 'What's happening in Killin these days?'

Gerda adjusted her clothing and smiled a smile that didn't reach her eyes. 'In Killin nothing is happening much.'

'Roger in the garage told me he saw an osprey fishing near Fiddler's Bay this morning.' Fizz turned to Buchanan. 'What time did you and Selena go for your walk on the shore this morning?'

'About seven thirty, I think. It could have been earlier when we started out, but I didn't see anything the size of an osprey.'

155

'Selena?' Gerda said with sudden interest. 'She is not sleeping with Alistair any more?'

Buchanan tried not to meet Fizz's eye, knowing that she would find Gerda's not quite perfect English hilarious. He could have predicted that she would reply for him, as she did.

'No, she's sleeping with Buchanan again. They are becoming inseparable, those two. I suspect he's planning on taking her back to Edinburgh with him.'

Actually, the idea had already begun to take firm root in Buchanan's mind. If he could find an effective feline deodorant he might seriously consider it. She was a cute little thing with a character all her own and he'd miss her when he left.

'Must dash,' Fizz was saying. 'We have some business to get on with this afternoon.'

'I am also dashing,' said Gerda, tossing her head in a manner that looked strangely petulant. 'Goodbye.'

She turned on her heel and walked into the garage without another glance at Buchanan.

Her abruptness struck him as exceedingly odd, but then so did a lot of things about her. Much of it was undoubtedly due to her foreign ways but, even taking that into consideration, she did seem to be a very strange girl. Her fixation about cats, for instance. And her propensity for taking her clothes off in public places.

Fizz had a one-word verdict.

'Slag,' she said, as she got into the car, but Buchanan pretended not to hear.

Plochaig, as their destination proved to be called, was just as isolated a hamlet as Am Bealach and, although there were a few more houses, they were closer together, in a single line along the loch shore. They drove straight through and back again in about a minute and a half.

'OK,' Buchanan said when he had parked in a lay-by, 'there

doesn't appear to be anything out of the usual here, does there? Nothing that looks like a natural destination for a backpacker. So, door-to-door enquiries would appear to be the only option. There are eight houses. That's four each.'

'*Mais oui, mon capitaine!*' Fizz readjusted the elastic band that was keeping her hair under some sort of control. 'Let's get this show on the road!'

Seconds later she was deep in conversation with a middle-aged housewife on the doorstep of the first house in the row. Buchanan took his time in following suit. The heady aroma of peat, seaweed, bog myrtle and wood smoke that was so characteristic of the west coast was so strong that he would have known where he was if he had been parachuted there in darkness from the other side of the world. The only sound was the lapping of waves on the shore and the hum of Fizz's voice a hundred yards away.

The first house he tried was empty. So was the second. At the third, a shout summoned him to the back garden where he found an elderly chap in black trousers and waistcoat and a collarless shirt baiting a fishing line with lugworms. He looked pleased to see a visitor and insisted on shaking hands, a courtesy which Buchanan would willingly have dispensed with since it resulted in the transfer of a good deal of blood, seaweed and segments of lugworm.

Having seated his guest, with great urbanity, on his own stool, the fisherman perched himself on a low wall and crossed his legs, exposing cream wool long johns tucked into his socks.

Buchanan stated his business as briefly as he could, pretending to blow his nose at the same time so that he could clean his hand on his hankie.

'It's not often we see a backpacker around here,' his host informed him apologetically, as though he wished he could be less negative. His diction was soft and sibilant with liquid vowels, and he showed his Gaelic roots by pronouncing all his ds as ts. 'In fact, I ton't know when I last saw a petestrian on this stretch of roat, with or without a pack on his back. They go whizzing straight through in their motorcars and the only ones that stop are the ott one or two who have B & B with Mrs Carson.'

'It occurred to me,' Buchanan suggested, 'that perhaps one of the locals could have met this backpacker somewhere – perhaps when they were on holiday – and invited him to visit if he were passing through Plochaig.'

'When you live in a place like Plochaig, son, you ton't feel the need of holidays. That sort of thing is for young people and folk who live in the city.'

'And there are no young people at all in the village?'

'Not a one. Not permanently, no. I've seen the McLeans' grantchildren here now and again, from Inverness, and Mrs Sweeney's son stays with her, on and off, but he's in his forties. The young folk have to go where the jobs are. There's nothing here for them. Not any more.'

That was clearly as much information as this call was going to yield, but Buchanan found himself pinned down by politeness while his host expounded on the depopulation of the Highlands, the fishing industry, the scourge of low-flying jets, and the decline of manners in modern society.

When he finally escaped he saw Fizz leaning against the car with her arms folded, gazing out across the loch. She turned to watch his approach and held up one hand with fingers spread.

'Five,' she said. 'I've done five houses while you did three – and two of yours were empty, don't think I didn't notice. I just hope you learned something of interest.'

'I did. A little lugworm goes a long way,' he said, and walked down to the water's edge to scrub his hands, and his hankie, with sand and sea water. As he turned to walk back up the beach he noticed the outline of another house, high up among the trees, on the other side of the road. It was hidden from the road below by the slope of the hill but from the beach he could discern a faint outline against the sky.

'So, you didn't achieve a major breakthrough either?' he asked Fizz.

'Nope. Backpackers are an endangered species around here and the only "young" person in the area at present is Mrs Sweeney's son who is forty-one and home from London for the summer. He and his mother have both gone off to Oban today because Mrs Sweeney has a dental appointment and Ian went along for the ride. The other empty house belongs to Mr Armstrong who is out in his boat, which he does a lot since his wife died, the year before last, of a stroke.'

Fizz, as usual, had managed to elicit more information than he had, Buchanan had to admit, but none of it was particularly valuable.

'There's another house up there among the trees,' he said. 'Do you want to suss it out or do you want me to do it?'

Fizz about-turned and squinted up the hill. 'I like it,' she said. 'Yes. I like the look of this one. Nice and private. You could get up to all sorts of devilry in there and nobody any the wiser.'

'Devilry is not necessarily what we're looking for,' Buchanan reminded her.

'No, but if we find it, it wouldn't surprise me. Besides, that place has an aura about it. It smells of money. Let's both go.'

Buchanan wondered at himself giving Fizz her head like this. Either he was still feeling sorry for her lost childhood, or the Am Bealach Effect had made considerable inroads into his brain cells, or he was beginning to respect her instinctive aptitude for investigative work. It would never have occurred to him to barge in on perfect strangers and start questioning them without any authorisation whatsoever, but here he was, tailing this crazy woman up a private driveway to do just that.

A screen of conifers hid the house till they were at close range, when it was revealed to be a row of converted farm steadings. Painted Germoline pink with black paintwork and embellished with wrought iron, it stopped Buchanan in his tracks. Fizz homed in on it like a pointer dog.

The door was opened by a six-foot blonde wearing tight white hipsters and a blue satin shirt open almost to the waist. Under the make-up, she could have been any age between twenty and thirty and her loosely curling golden hair hung in careful disarray almost to her shoulder blades. The expression on her spoiled and pretty face was not welcoming.

'Yes?'

Buchanan waited for Fizz to answer and only realised that she wasn't going to when he felt a sharp dig in his spine.

'I do apologise for intruding on you like this,' he said, hurriedly filling the hiatus. 'We are making enquiries about a . . . a missing person . . . and we wondered if you could help us.'

Her cool demeanour shattered. 'A missing person? But that's *priceless*! Ghislain!' she shouted over her shoulder. 'Sweetie! These people are looking for a *missing person*! *Do* come in, won't you? Ghislain will be *thrilled* to talk to you – he's out on the terrace. We're having some champers, would you like some?'

'I'd be delighted,' Fizz responded with speed.

'It's only *pretend* champers, actually—'

'OK, I'll pretend to be delighted.' Fizz twitched an eyebrow at Buchanan as she followed the blonde through a panelled hallway, across an oak-beamed, chintzy and french-windowed lounge on to a sheltered terrace.

Ghislain was lying on a sun lounger with a bottle of

champagne in an ice bucket on the ground beside him and the *Financial Times* over his face. A large orange-clad gut and a pair of fishbelly-white legs in Bermuda shorts was all that could be seen of him.

'Ghislain!' cried the blonde shrilly, snatching the newspaper away. 'Do wake up, sweetie. We have guests. Guess what, these lovely people are here to talk to us about a missing person! Isn't it utterly *hilarious*! Ivana will *die* when I tell her!'

Buchanan watched with horror and embarrassment as Ghislain straightened his toupee and floundered to his feet like a loosely packed sack of blancmange. He was at least fifty, with a plum-red face and fat-lipped mouth. Around his neck, in the shadow of a roll of fat, he wore a gold chain with the word 'Booboo' hanging from it. His eyes were screwed up against the painful and sudden assault of the sunlight but he managed a huge grin and shook hands all round.

'Frightfully nice to see you both! Delighted you could drop in!'

'Ghislain,' said the blonde in gravelly tones. 'Do listen. These people are here to ask us about some missing person or other.'

'Buchanan. Tam Buchanan. I'm a solicitor and this is my assistant, Miss Fitzpatrick.' Buchanan took the bamboo chair the blonde was waving him into while Ghislain held another for Fizz. 'I hope you don't mind this informal visit but we were just passing through . . .'

'Glasses, sweetie,' said the blonde settling herself on a canopied swing and sweeping her heavy curtain of hair off her face with both hands. 'We're all going to have some champers while we talk. And bring the strawberries that are in the fridge.' She turned to Buchanan. 'I'm Saskia, by the way. I'm very much in the soft drink brigade, actually. Alcohol is simply *oozing* with calories, you know. Once a month I have a Dutch

Mouden, which is *so* naughty – full of liqueurs and cream and chocolate. It's the most outrageous thing in the world but one must be naughty some times. Actually,' she giggled, 'I've been naughty since the day I was born, but Ghislain likes me to look nice. He's like: who needs cream anyway? So I stick to tonic water most of the time but I'm going to be grown up and have one *teeny* glass of champers today because you're our first guests at The Steading. Imagine! This place is just *so* back-of-beyond—'

'How long have you been here?' Fizz wedged in as Saskia drew a quick breath.

'Two years, but not all the time, naturally. Ghislain has his business in London and I am forever dashing off on modelling assignments.' One ruby-tipped hand swept the fall of blonde hair from the right of her head to let it tumble to the left. 'We have our place in Wimbledon, of course, but I'm a country girl at heart and I said to Ghislain, I said, Look, sweetie, I have to be somewhere peaceful to let the creative side of my character grow and develop. I have to *breathe*, do you know what I mean?'

Ghislain arrived back with a tray of glasses and straw-berries, plus some frosted bottles of tonic water which Buchanan opted for since he was driving. Saskia went on talking in an unbroken stream of inanities while Ghislain opened a fresh bottle of 'champers'. By 'pretend' champagne Saskia clearly meant anything nonvintage since the labels on both the new and the half-empty bottle were nothing to be ashamed of.

'This place has been a godsend to my writing, hasn't it, sweetie? I simply could *not* have found the time to create anything if we'd been in London all week. Even when we're here it's bad enough: I have to go shopping in Glasgow tomorrow, then we have a dinner with some people from LA at

Gleneagles on Wednesday, then I'm flying to Dublin for a TV ad.'

'What do you write?' Buchanan asked. He had a feeling that she had left a pause so that somebody could ask that question.

'I write about people.' Saskia's voice dropped to a deeply serious level. 'Society. The inside story behind all the glamour and luxury.'

'Ever sold anything?' Fizz asked.

Saskia popped a strawberry in her mouth and chewed busily while Ghislain galloped to the rescue. 'We have friends in TV who are very interested in Saskia's work. There's a three-part drama under discussion at the moment and possibly a fly-on-the-wall documentary series some time next year. They're desperate for something fresh, something different, by someone who knows what it's really like up there.'

'We've had meetings,' Saskia stated, as though this proved her standing in the artistic community.

'Really?' Buchanan cast around desperately for some way of stopping her. 'Anyway . . .'

'If it weren't for my mother taking Miles, my darling baby, off my hands, I'd simply *buckle*, wouldn't I, sweetie? Of course, I absolutely *worship* him, we both do, well obviously, but, three-year-olds are utterly exhausting and one has one's own life to lead, hasn't one?'

'Actually,' Fizz said, overlapping Saskia's last words just a fraction. 'We have to be moseying along shortly and we do have a couple of questions to ask you, if you wouldn't mind.'

'But of course.' Saskia's large and lustrous eyes grew even bigger. 'I am *dying* to be questioned! This is *positively* the most exciting thing that's happened to us in months.' She gave an anticipatory giggle and sat up straight like a schoolgirl. 'Please do go ahead.'

Buchanan could see that Fizz was wishing she'd brought a

rubber truncheon and a bright spotlight, so he cleared his throat to let her know that he was doing the questioning for the moment.

'We're looking for information about a young man who has disappeared while he was backpacking around Scotland. We know he was intending to visit Plochaig at some point in his itinerary but we are not sure whether he had actually reached here or not. Hopefully someone either saw him when he was here or is still expecting him to arrive.'

Saskia and Ghislain took several seconds to respond to that. They both seemed to be expecting him to go on talking and had not quite caught up with the storyline before an answer was required of them.

'A backpacker,' Fizz prompted, reducing the crux of the matter to two words.

'A backpacker?' Ghislain was now in full command of the situation. 'You mean one of those chappies with tin mugs and rolls of mattress dangling from their haversacks? My dear people, I don't think I've ever had contact with one of those in my life. We don't move in those circles, if you follow me.'

'You might have noticed him passing on the road,' Fizz insisted.

'Poppet, we can't even see the road from here, and I can tell you, we don't do a lot of socialising down by the lochside.' Ghislain topped up the champagne glasses and opened another bottle of tonic water for Buchanan. 'Very strange people down there.'

'Strange?' said Fizz quickly. 'In what way?'

'Absolutely no social skills whatsoever,' Saskia sniffed. 'Typical working class. None of them has two pennies to rub together but they don't want to earn some honest cash by doing a few hours' housework a week or digging our garden once in a while. I've never met such *scandalously* unsociable people in my *entire life*!'

'I offered to buy a scrap of land from one of them,' Ghislain complained, 'so that we could build a jetty for our power boat instead of having to drive all the way to Connel every time we wanted to take it out. Offered him a decent price too, but the silly old codger wouldn't sell.'

'They've stolen every shrub we've planted – or cut it off at ground level,' Saskia took over. 'They ignore us when we wave at them from the car.'

'They roar up and down on their motorbikes at crack of dawn.'

'They watch us through their telescope,' Saskia said, but Ghislain felt that was going too far.

'Well, no, bunny, that's an astronomical telescope, but they do stare up the drive every time they walk past and they're never looking our way when we drive by.'

'People are funny,' Buchanan smiled, his sympathies entirely with the locals. Saskia's difficulties in getting plants to grow were almost certainly caused by hungry deer, and it would take a deeply insensitive man to disturb the peace of the lochside with a power boat. 'Do you happen to know any of the neighbours who might have been away from home recently? Perhaps abroad. Anywhere that they might have run into this young chap and invited him to look them up if he were in this vicinity?'

Saskia's laugh was like breaking glass. 'I doubt if any of them have been further than Benderloch since the day they were born, have they, sweetie? They certainly don't holiday abroad, I can promise you that.'

Ghislain nodded in confirmation. 'There's not one of them under fifty and even if they did meet a backpacker somewhere, I don't see any of them offering him the time of day, never mind hospitality.'

'Mr and Mrs McLean go to Inverness sometimes to see

their grandchildren,' Saskia remembered suddenly, but not even Fizz found that particularly galvanising.

'Well, there are still a couple of people we haven't talked to yet. Maybe we'll come back another day.' Buchanan stood up. 'We've taken up enough of your time and you've been most hospitable. Now we really must be on our way.'

'Sorry we couldn't be more of a help to you, old chap,' Ghislain said, lurching somewhat unsteadily to his feet and, quite unnecessarily, assisting Fizz to hers. 'If you pay Plochaig another visit you must drop in and see us.'

'Yes, do,' Saskia insisted. 'We'll keep our ears open for anything that might help. Not that we hear much local gossip – not that there ever *is* any – but anyway . . .'

She kept calling after them till they were halfway down the drive, wishing them luck with their investigations and urging them to let them know how things were progressing.

Fizz said nothing at all. She appeared to be in some sort of psychogenic fugue and Buchanan was content to leave her so till they were in a situation where she would be constrained to mind her language.

By unspoken but mutual agreement they headed back to the car.

'Well,' said Fizz, 'on a success rating of one to ten I reckon this afternoon scored about nought point five. And I'm awarding that for the view.'

'I think that's a bit parsimonious,' Buchanan said judiciously. 'After all, you've met two of the beautiful people and some – according to Saskia – *scandalously* unsociable, working-class people. You can't call that a wasted day.'

Fizz blew him a raspberry. 'Listen,' she said tersely, 'if you're planning on sending me in to talk to those two weirdos again just tell me now, right? It'll take me a day or two to have a cyanide pill implanted in my tooth.'

Chapter Twelve

It was raining by the time they got back to Am Bealach, in fact it looked to Fizz as if it had been raining for hours. That end of the loch had a weather system all its own, independent from, and frequently bearing no relation to, conditions on the other side of the surrounding mountains.

She wasn't particularly bothered by the rain, except for a nagging worry that it might incline Buchanan to pack up and return to Edinburgh, leaving the current mysteries unsolved. That would be a real bummer because the near certainty of an Am Bealach resident being involved in the deaths was weighing heavily on her mind and she wanted the matter settled, one way or the other.

Fortunately, they ran into Alistair in the evening, as they walked up to the Clachan for a pint, and he had just been assessing the condition of the river.

'I'll no' be surprised if we get a few fish coming upriver in the next few days,' he told Buchanan.

'Fish', to Alistair, were salmon. Fizz had once heard him inform a tourist who had claimed to see a fish under the Stronach bridge, 'Och, it wouldn't be a fish you were seeing, lassie, it would be a broon trootie.'

'Well, I'll be ready to go any time you say the word, Alistair,' Buchanan told him. 'Just give me a bell and I'll be on your doorstep in a quarter of an hour.'

'Maybe no' the morrow. The river's still rising so if it keeps raining overnight it should be just nice by Wednesday or Thursday. I'll keep an eye on it.'

'Either day's fine by me. Just let me know,' said Buchanan and, as they were at the Clachan by that time, he added, 'Come in and have a pint.'

Alistair hesitated, glancing up the glen road towards his cottage. 'A half-pint maybe. I have a hind hanging there in the cold room that should be getting butchered and into the freezer by tonight, but, och, it'll wait a wee while.'

'You're not still culling hinds, at this time of year, are you?' Fizz said, as they went into the bar.

'No. This was a young one I found at the deer fence when I was up there taking a look at the grouse. It had a broken foreleg so I had to put it out of its misery.' He held open the door for the others to pass into the lounge. 'You can tell Auntie Duff I'll be handing in a bit haunch to her some time through the week.'

'She'll appreciate that,' Fizz said. 'Thanks, Alistair.'

'Just don't mention it to his nibs,' Alistair muttered, with a malevolent glance towards the fireplace where Lindsay was making political capital with a couple of his constituents.

Myra was behind the bar, and while Buchanan chatted to her and ordered the drinks it occurred to Fizz to try to find out what had caused the rift between Alistair and Lindsay. The chance of turning up anything of interest was slight but one could never tell.

'You haven't forgiven Lindsay yet, have you?' she said quietly, trying to look as though she was already *au fait* with all the details.

Alistair's black eyebrows lifted as he turned to look at her. 'How'd you know about that?'

'Oh, come on, Alistair,' Fizz flannelled. 'You know you can't keep a secret in Am Bealach. Isn't it about time you let bygones be bygones?'

She was quite prepared for Alistair to show surprise that anyone should be interested in a small difference of opinion between him and his employer. The impression she had received from Rowena had given her no reason to suppose that the row had been a serious one. Admittedly, now that she thought about it, Rowena had claimed to know none of the details, but her references to Lindsay being autocratic and treating Alistair like a serf had implied that it was just a clash of personalities.

But there was something in Alistair's face right now that made her wonder if it had been rather more than that. The look he threw at Lindsay's back would have burned a hole in his cashmere sweater.

'Let bygones be bygones!' he muttered under his breath. 'The way he treated me won't ever be bygone, as far as I'm concerned. If I wasn't stuck here working for the wee shite till the day I die, I'd have told him what to do with his job.'

The trouble with pretending you already knew the facts of the matter under discussion, Fizz reflected, was that, thereafter, you couldn't ask any direct questions about it without proving yourself a liar. She now had to attempt a circuitous approach by saying,

'You don't *have* to work for him, do you, Alistair? I mean, just because you're the fourth generation of Munroes to look after Stronach Estate it doesn't follow that you have to put up with a balloon like Lindsay all your working life. You're a free man now and there's a whole lot of world out there. You shouldn't even be contemplating staying in Am Bealach.'

Alistair answered with a noncommittal grunt but Fizz could see no sign that her advice had penetrated his gloom.

'Who was it that told you about it? Was it him?' Without turning round, he tipped his head at Lindsay. 'Is he blabbing it around?'

'No, no. He's not blabbing it around,' Fizz said hurriedly, perceiving that Alistair was taking the matter much more seriously than she had expected. It had clearly been a big mistake to claim she knew what their quarrel had been about and there was going to be further trouble if she didn't back down fast. 'I just noticed a coolness between you two and put two and two together,' she said lightly. 'I suppose he was acting monarch of the glen again, was he?'

Alistair's gaze narrowed and, after a minute his expression changed for the worse. 'You always were a nosy wee besom, Fizz,' he said nastily. 'You don't know a damn thing about it, do you? Well, just don't try any more of your joukery-pokery with me, d'you hear, or you'll be sorry. My business is my own.'

Fizz assumed her best expression of deeply outraged innocence but she was saved, by the arrival of the drinks, from having to waste her breath on a denial. It was irritating to be caught out but she was comforted by the thought that one couldn't win them all. She had at least elicited the fact that Alistair was no more willing to discuss the recent breakdown of diplomatic relations than was Lindsay.

In such matters of general interest, everyone in Am Bealach would normally be able to quote both viewpoints word for word, complete with historical footnotes and in-depth analysis. So, if both the protagonists were managing to keep everyone in the dark about the matter, as it would appear they were, it stood to reason that the facts must be worth knowing.

'Simon having an evening off, is he?' she asked Myra, when Alistair had stopped talking about fishing and taken himself off home to butcher his hind.

'No, he should be back any time now. He went to Glasgow this afternoon to pick up the tickets for the EuroDisney trip.' She took a large sip of something the same colour as her frizzy hair. 'They could have reached us by post in plenty of time but, no, he had to go and get them. Wouldn't take the chance that they might be lost in the post.'

'Well, better safe than sorry,' Buchanan said, predictably approving behaviour as pedantic as his own. 'I'd imagine it would be a painful blow to Zander if the trip had to be cancelled at the last minute.'

'Oh God! We'd never hear the end of it! He's been going on about it for weeks and, to be honest, so has Simon.' Myra widened her big eyes in pseudo-amusement. 'Me, I'd rather spend a weekend in a leper colony than put a foot in the place but Simon is absolutely raring to go. Some men never grow up, do they?'

'Is this Zander's first time abroad?' Fizz asked.

'No, we've taken the car over to France a few times on the ferry, but this is his first time on a plane.' She rolled her eyes to indicate that this was another big deal and sent a with-you-in-a-minute wave to a waiting customer. 'Tell you the truth, I'll be glad to see the back of both of them by the time Saturday comes!'

Her warm laughter as she moved down the bar gave the lie to this statement. Whatever ups and downs her marriage had suffered in the past, it certainly appeared to Fizz that she had put them all firmly behind her and settled down to being a loving and contented wife and mother.

'What d'you think?' Fizz asked Buchanan, shielding her lips from Myra with the rim of her glass. 'Does she really trust Simon virtually on his own in Gay Paree or does she simply not give a shit what he gets up to?'

'Fizz! I do wish—'

'Because, frankly, I wouldn't trust that liver fluke as far as the front door. I'll lay you ten to one that the minute he's off that plane—'

'I'm going over to have a word with Rowena and Lindsay,' Buchanan interrupted, getting all shifty as usual, although Myra was chatting busily with her other customer and couldn't have heard a word. 'Are you coming?'

'Wouldn't miss it for the world.'

Lindsay's audience had dwindled rapidly to an itinerant farm labourer and the Killin half-wit so he wasn't too distraught about being interrupted.

'Tam! Good to see you. Come and sit here, Fizz, where you and Rowena can get on with your girls' talk. How's the holiday going, Tam?'

Fizz's hackles rose at being thus confined to purdah, but seeing that Buchanan was holding his breath, she decided to disappoint him and sat herself down where she was told to like a good little girl. She wanted a quiet word with Rowena, in any case, before she went back to Edinburgh tomorrow, but that could wait till Lindsay was out of earshot.

'I can't believe I've been here only ten days,' Buchanan was saying. 'Another four days and I'll be headed back to the smoke.'

'You don't have to go back on Saturday,' Fizz said. 'The cottage is vacant for another week.'

'Unfortunately, I have to earn my living, Fizz, otherwise, I admit it, I'd be sorely tempted. I could get used to this place.'

'For short periods,' Rowena whispered, keeping her chin well down and smiling at him from under her brows.

'Yes, I suppose you're right there, Rowena. It's one thing being on holiday here and quite another to live here all the time.' Buchanan smiled at her with that special rapport that seemed to have developed between them. Fizz had never before seen Rowena so relaxed with a man, particularly one so . . . well . . . personable. In a boring sort of way.

'You should see it in the winter—' Rowena started to say but Lindsay had been out of the conversation long enough.

'So, we've a chance of a run of salmon this week, I hear,' he put in, leaning back in the couch and stretching an arm out behind Rowena's shoulders. 'Alistair says it looks promising if the rain keeps up.'

'So he was just telling me,' Buchanan nodded. 'I'm really looking forward to it.'

'I thought I might join you,' said Lindsay, snuffing the light in Buchanan's eye like a candle. 'I don't get the chance much these days but I'll be here for a few days to attend to some constituency business, so I might as well take the chance while there's a bit of company.'

'Great,' said Buchanan, and if you hadn't known him you'd never have guessed he'd just had his ice lolly swiped. 'What about you, Rowena? Don't you fancy joining us? Or don't you fish?'

'Rowena doesn't—' Lindsay started to say, but a miracle happened.

Rowena laid a light, restraining hand on his arm and leaned forward, looking into Buchanan's eyes. 'I do fish sometimes, Tam, but I'm a fine-weather fisherman. I don't enjoy standing all day in the rain getting soaked.'

Buchanan replied in his calm, unemotional way, but Fizz was too stunned to register what he said. It was several seconds before she even noticed that Lindsay was in a similar condition, sitting there with his lips apart and blinking at his beer as though he was unable to focus his eyes.

It was a one-off, however. As soon as Lindsay re-entered the conversation Rowena became monosyllabic again and sat staring dreamily at Briony, who was asleep in her carrycot beside her. Maybe, Fizz thought, it was the effect of having a baby that had brought about that momentary sign of change in a condition that had been chronic since childhood. Maybe Rowena felt she had to be strong to protect Briony from her father's unhealthy influence. The lioness-in-defence-of-her-cubs syndrome. Stranger things had happened.

When Lindsay announced that it was time to head for home Rowena said she had to powder her nose first and Fizz saw her opportunity for a private chat.

The loo was about the size of a phone box and not wonderfully congenial so she waited till they were emerging into the lobby before she said, 'Hang on a sec, I want to ask you something.'

Rowena showed the whites of her eyes. 'About what?'

'About Lindsay and Alistair.'

Rowena glanced at the toilet door as though she suddenly had the urge to go back in. 'What about them?'

'This fight they had. It was pretty serious, wasn't it? But neither of them has spoken about it since. They are even pretending to be on reasonable terms with each other. What's going on?'

'Nothing's going on.' Rowena fidgeted from one foot to the other, trying to edge past Fizz and make good her escape. 'Don't make mountains out of molehills, Fizz. They had a little disagreement, that's all, and now it's over.'

'But it's not over,' Fizz insisted. 'Not for Alistair anyway. Far from it. What was it all about?'

'Nothing! I . . . I don't know what it was about. Lindsay wouldn't tell me and Alistair clearly didn't want me to ask.'

'How did you know about the row, then?'

'I heard . . . Alistair called round one evening and I heard them arguing – on and on – in the library and then Alistair went storming out and slammed the front door. I asked

Lindsay what had happened but he just cut me off. Said *he* was running Stronach estate now and he would make the decisions.' She sniffled a bit and glowered in the direction of the lounge as though she could see Lindsay through the wall. 'He doesn't understand how things are here in Am Bealach. I tried to explain that we all grew up together and he can't come swanning in at this stage in the game, throwing his weight around as if he were God.'

'Did you really?' Fizz said, wondering if Rowena's confidence had started to bud earlier than she had realised. But Rowena looked embarrassed.

'Well, not in those very words, maybe,' she mumbled unwillingly, 'but you know what Lindsay's like. I doubt if he even heard me.'

Fizz prayed for patience. 'Lindsay is a problem that's going to have to be solved one of these days, Rowena, you realise that, don't you? Either you dig your heels in and demand a change in the way he treats you or you walk out the door. He wouldn't like you to dump him – not good for his image – so you have him over a barrel. Just tell him to shape up or ship out.'

'I don't think I could do that, Fizz . . .'

'Sure you could. You gave him a real jolt this evening when you stopped him from answering for you. I was proud of you, kid, and if you can do it once you can keep on doing it. It's just a matter of trying a bit harder. Nothing succeeds like trying.'

'Well . . . we'll see.' Rowena started back towards the lounge but Fizz held her by the back of her cardigan.

'I want you to find out what Alistair and Lindsay were rowing about,' she said. 'I'm sure it's something significant.'

Rowena stopped and turned. 'What d'you mean, "significant"? Signifying what?'

'How do *I* know, dammit?' Fizz snapped. 'Christ! You're getting as bad as Buchanan, always wanting everything typed out in triplicate and filed under F for facts. I just feel there's something fishy about it and I want to know what's going on between them, OK? So, see what you can squeeze out of Lindsay.'

Rowena gave an acquiescent sigh but Fizz held out little hope of getting anything out of her. She was obviously ashamed of Lindsay's part in the altercation and, besides, she had always been one for letting sleeping dogs lie and keeping the shit well away from the fan. Probably the best hope of getting the lowdown on the quarrel was to persuade Buchanan to see what he could find out during his day's fishing with the combatants.

She broached the subject as they marched back down the farm road in the rain and, for once, Buchanan seemed moderately interested.

'You don't have any inkling yourself of what they might have been fighting about?' he asked.

'Well, there are lots of possibilities,' Fizz said, 'but Rowena, I gather, heard enough to give her the impression that it had something to do with the running of the estate. I'm sure it would incense Alistair if that jumped-up, city-bred little Hitler started telling him how to run a grouse moor or interfering with his deer management. But, if that were the problem, Alistair would have taken it to arbitration in the Clachan bar and everybody would know about it, which they evidently don't.'

Buchanan digested this slowly, wiping raindrops off his nose with the back of his hand. A few paces ahead of them a barn owl dropped off a low bough and sailed away into the beech woods, motionlessly and without a sound, as though it were blown on the wind.

Buchanan stood staring after it but Fizz's mind was fixed on the matter in hand. 'Why should they both keep it a secret? That's the question,' she said. 'And there was something else Alistair said that made me wonder a bit.'

'Yes? And what was that?' said Buchanan, giving up hope of a second sighting of the owl and walking on.

'He said he'd be working for Lindsay till the day he died. Weird, huh? It was as if Lindsay had something on him . . . some sort of hold over him. I told him he should be thinking of getting out and seeing a bit of the world but you could tell he didn't take it on board.'

'Is it really strange?' Buchanan watched his feet splashing through the puddles and appeared to be debating this question inwardly. 'After all, his father and his grandfather both lived and worked all their lives on the estate. Did Alistair plan to leave here when his mother no longer needed him?'

'No, I don't suppose he did,' Fizz admitted. 'He may want to leave now, of course, if he's had all he can stand of Lindsay, but surely, if there's so much friction between them, Lindsay wouldn't insist on his staying. You'd think he'd be glad to get shot of him.'

'H'm. It's a very interesting situation,' Buchanan admitted. 'How was Alistair reacting to it? Was he frustrated? Violent?'

'Not really. He was a little bitter about it and, right now, Lindsay is not necessarily the person he'd save first in a fire, but he's not about to put out a contract on him, if that's what you're thinking. As far as being stuck on Stronach estate goes, I'd say he was more resigned than anything else. In fact the suspicion that Lindsay might be blabbing about the row seemed to annoy him more than anything else.'

They walked on for a while, wrapped in their own thoughts, the only sound the hiss of the rain on the leaves and the occasional rustle of wild things in the hedgerows.

Then Buchanan said, 'Do we assume that it was the altercation Rowena overheard that started the unpleasantness, or was that just an incident in an ongoing feud? When did that altercation take place? Do we know how long this coolness between them has been going on?'

'Not long,' Fizz said, applying her exam technique of answering the easiest question first. 'It can't have been going on for a long time or other people would have noticed.'

Suddenly the impossibility of untangling the recent mysteries weighed on her like a lead poncho. How was one supposed to tell which facts were important and which weren't? It wasn't at all easy to envisage a connection between the Alistair/Lindsay fracas and either Bessie's disappearance or the murder of the camper. The spat was more likely to be totally unconnected to either mystery, but Fizz was unwilling to dismiss it from her mental list of possible leads.

'What do you think, Buchanan? Is the fight significant?'

It was too dark to see his face but she could tell by the sound of his voice that he had turned his head towards her and that he was smiling. 'That depends on when it happened.'

'Like . . . if it happened around the time . . .'

'Like . . . the time everything else happened?' he finished for her. 'Maybe. Who knows?'

Fizz had a feeling *he* knew, but that didn't necessarily mean he was going to tell her.

Chapter Thirteen

Fizz took so long to get ready to leave for Edinburgh the next day that Buchanan could have choked her. He ended up sitting in the car with the engine running, threatening to leave on the dot of twelve whether she were with him or not.

She knew perfectly well that he had a pony trek planned for two thirty but she insisted on washing her hair and ironing her jeans and picking some parsley and chives to take with her. Then she found she had mislaid some lecture notes she needed for the next day and turned the whole house upside down before she found them in her shoulder bag.

Had they been held up by a tourist bus or a tractor on the long, winding road through Glenogle or along the shore of Loch Lubnaig, it could have cost them an extra half-hour on the journey. That would have meant little to Fizz, who could get a train every thirty minutes to Edinburgh, but would have demolished Buchanan's plans for the afternoon.

Missing the pony trek was no big deal. Apart from the chance it would give him to see otherwise inaccessible areas of the surrounding wilderness, he would just as soon not have bothered. But it did irritate him that, having promised that he would do it, Fizz's go-slow was in danger of making him seem a liar.

He felt bad enough about rejecting Gerda's advances

without appearing to be the type who would string her along with promises he had no intention of keeping, and it was quite possible he wouldn't have another free afternoon between now and his departure on Saturday, since he would be fishing either tomorrow or Thursday.

Fortunately, he made it to Stirling and back without any serious hold-ups and was back in Killin by two fifteen, in time for a swift recce of the stable yard to make sure he would have plenty of company on his trek.

The riding centre was located in a square of old, but beautifully renovated farm buildings on the edge of the village. It was a beautiful spot, overlooking the loch, and the cluster of houses that comprised Am Bealach was visible on the far shore, looking like a scatter of nuts on a green tablecloth. Behind them the jagged peaks of the ridge were hidden by rolling grey clouds but the rain had stopped and flitting beams of sunlight were illuminating small areas with a *son et lumière* effect.

The break in the weather had tempted a half-dozen or so holidaymakers to turn out for the afternoon trek. They ranged in age from ten or so to the mid-fifties, and were in the process of being allocated suitable mounts by Gerda, a teenaged girl, and a weather-beaten guy with a beard who, Buchanan surmised, must be the owner, Norrie Telfer.

Gerda looked around at the sound of the car engine and sent Buchanan a perky wave as he got out of the car. She was looking extremely fetching in cream riding breeches and a blue polo-necked sweater that fitted her like clingfilm. Her hair swished and sparkled as she bent to shorten the stirrups on a fat Shetland pony and her even teeth looked uncannily white against her tan. But while Buchanan could appreciate all that in a detached manner, he remained perversely unattracted.

He rather wished he knew the reason for this and was

horribly suspicious that he was getting old. In another six months he would be thirty-one: not exactly geriatric, but perhaps past his prime. He had to admit that there had been a time when he would not have kicked Gerda out of bed, rapacious or not, and the sad fact was that he had been living like a monk for nine months and one could take choosiness too far.

Ever since Janine had ended their long partnership – over nothing more than her insane misconception of the role Fizz played in his life – he had doubted his ability to handle relationships. He might be heartily glad, at this stage in the game, that Janine had run mad before he had made a fool of himself by marrying her, but the appalling acrimony of their parting had made him wary.

Gerda put an end to these depressing ruminations by waving him over and introducing him to her boss.

'Here is Tam, I am telling you of, who recovers from his . . .' Her hand mimed a disembowelling. 'Who is getting weller in Am Bealach.'

'Norrie Telfer. Nice to meet you, Tam.' Buchanan's hand was gripped in a fist with skin that felt like the bark of a Scots pine. 'I hope you're making a speedy recovery?'

He had a haughty, almost Arabic face, with a hooked nose and dark, hooded eyes, but when he smiled his eyes tilted up at the corners and he looked shifty. 'You're long in the leg,' he said, with the air of a Savile Row tailor. 'I think it had better be Rossack for you. Have you ridden before?'

'Occasionally. Long time ago.'

'Fine. Rossack needs a firm hand but he won't give you any trouble.'

Rossack appeared, from sea level, to be no more than about fifteen hands but once you were up there the stable yard seemed a hell of a long way away. The other riders all looked supremely confident, however, and ambled about the place in a relaxed manner that Buchanan found almost reassuring. The presence of the ten-year-olds also seemed to indicate that anything other than a sedate pace was not on the schedule, which suited him fine.

Gerda donned a helmet and sprang aboard her usual mean-faced chestnut. 'OK,' she announced, sidling up beside Buchanan. 'We go now.'

The rest of the troop fell in behind them and they meandered out of the yard and took a rough track leading uphill into a spruce forest. Rossack, in spite of a bit of head tossing and mane shaking, seemed to manage quite well on his own without any outside interference, so Buchanan let him get on with it.

'I am taking a nice trek for you today, Tam,' Gerda assured him. 'We come out from the trees soon and see some good sights to the loch. Then we go up and up, maybe to the Stone Age axe factory. You are hearing about the Stone Age axes?'

'No. Have some been found around here?'

'Many.' She pointed up to where, but for the trees, they would have been able to see the end of the Tarmachan Ridge. 'The peoples who are living on the islands in the loch, hundreds of years then, they are taking the cows to the high pastures in summers and having no things to do, so they snick, snick, snick.' Her hands made chipping movements, as though she were whittling an invisible stick. 'They are making stone axes and all the time breaking some, so now there are piles of broken pieces.'

She rattled off this presentation with uncharacteristic fluency, probably having memorised it word for word, and then lapsed into her familiar pidgin English.

'Selena is not liking to come pony trekking with you today?'

Buchanan looked at her to see if she was smiling and found

her eyes fixed on him with keen interest. It occurred to him that she might be slightly mad.

'What *is* this fascination you have with Selena?' he said, hauling Rossack away from a patch of vegetation he was determined to investigate. 'Every time I see you you ask me about her.'

She shrugged and looked away and rode on for a second or two without answering. Then she said, 'First I am thinking it is Fizz with you, then I am thinking it is Selena, then you are telling me Selena is sleeping with Alistair, then she comes back with you again. You say she comes with you to Edinburgh but I am never seeing her beside you.'

Buchanan tried to translate this into something resembling sense. He could see she had a problem but exactly what it was escaped him totally. He had a suspicion she was accusing him of being cruel to animals.

'She has her own life,' he tried to reassure her. 'She goes off in the morning and I don't see her again all day. She doesn't miss my company, if that's what's worrying you.'

Gerda made a faint explosive noise with her lips. 'So you are only taking her to bed, yes? You are not loving her at all? So why do you bring her to Edinburgh again?'

'You think she wouldn't like to lose her freedom?' Buchanan hazarded wildly.

'I think,' Gerda said forcefully and then ran out of vocabulary. She waved her hands. 'I think Selena is a . . . she is a . . .'

Buchanan tried to read her mind. 'A nuisance?'

'No . . . she's a . . . it's a long word . . .'

'A tortoiseshell?'

'I don't know tortshell. I think . . . yes! She is a Protestant!'

Before Buchanan could attach any meaning to this remark Gerda suddenly announced,

'*Prostitude*!' She jabbed a finger out in front of her as

though pointing out the word in the air beyond her horse's nose. 'I am thinking she is a prostitute!'

For about three seconds Buchanan was inclined to agree with her, thinking that her intention had been to use the word as a simile for Selena's wandering ways, then the mists cleared and the absurdity of the situation became clear. He threw back his head and howled with laughter.

Gerda didn't think it was funny. 'This is the wrong word, yes? You are bad for laughing.'

'I'm not laughing at you, Gerda.' He tried to sober down but couldn't stop chuckling. 'It's the right word OK – at least, it's the word you intended, I suppose. It's just that you've got the wrong end of the stick.'

'The stick? I do not have a stick.'

'Selena isn't a prostitute,' he said, and then, out of the blue, it came to him that if Gerda thought Selena was a woman it would be folly to enlighten her. Once she discovered that it was a cat they'd been discussing he'd never get her off his back. He thought for a minute and then said carefully, 'When I said she was sleeping with Alistair I meant only that she was staying overnight at his place. They are old friends and she often stays there. She has a lot of friends in Am Bealach and she likes to stay with all of them.'

Gerda's delicate brows twisted as she digested this. She took a look back at the other riders strung out behind them and motioned the teenage girl, who was bringing up the rear, to round them up a bit.

'So,' she said, after a minute or two. 'But, at Edinburgh she will be only with you, yes?'

'Yes,' said Buchanan, omitting to add a codicil to the effect that he hadn't decided whether to take her or not. He wanted no lingering doubts as to his availability to remain in Gerda's mind.

'And you will be only with Selena?'

Buchanan nodded. 'We will be living together, yes. Just the two of us.'

Gerda frowned and her hand seemed to be grasping for words that were just out of reach. Clearly, Buchanan's interpretation of her question was not quite what she had intended to convey.

'Norrie Telfer seems a nice chap,' he blurted out, snatching at the first topic that would serve to divert her. 'What's he like to work for?'

Gerda took a moment to come to grips with this sudden change of topic. She seemed reluctant to part with the old one but wasn't adept enough to manage the conversation to her satisfaction.

'Norrie . . . he is OK. He is being with his cows and sheep most days so there is no trouble. But I am not liking his wife one bit.' She made a bored face. 'She is not liking me also.'

Buchanan found that not altogether surprising. 'How long have they been in business?' he said, to keep the conversation going in a manageable direction.

'Twelve years. Maybe less.' She thought about it. 'Eleven years, nearly. But Norrie is only getting married last year. Maybe I go some place else next summer.'

They broke clear of the forest at this point and the view of the mountains was so spectacular that the trek came to a halt. Gerda gave the riders a minute or two to take photographs and then chivvied them along the track to point out some ruined shielings. Buchanan took this opportunity to latch on to a middle-aged couple and managed successfully to keep them between him and Gerda for the rest of the trek.

Norrie was working around the yard, hefting feed bags, when they got back. He walked over and held Rossack's head as Buchanan dismounted.

'Enjoy that?'

'It was superb,' Buchanan said. He could see Gerda watching him as she led the horses away. She looked as though she half expected him to waylay her so he gave her a grin and an obscure hand signal and tried to look as though he couldn't get away. To keep Norrie standing there he went on, 'I only wish I could manage to do it again before I go home but I'm afraid I won't have time now.'

'When do you go home?'

'Saturday, unfortunately. I'd have liked to stay longer, but we can't all be like you.' Buchanan waved a hand at the view. 'You've got it made here: beautiful house, terrific situation, nice little business . . .'

Norrie smiled, looking suddenly like a confidence trickster. 'Not much of a business, really, except for the summer months. We're fairly busy in July and August but there's not much doing for the rest of the summer and by the time you pay staff and feed the ponies all winter it's not the Rockefeller Foundation, I can tell you.'

'Still, I imagine you'd get a good price for it if you chose to sell up,' Buchanan suggested.

'More than I paid for it, you mean?' Norris grinned wolfishly. 'Gerda was telling you I got it at a bargain price, no doubt? Oh, I don't mind. It's common knowledge in the village, like everything else.'

'Lara was lucky that she found somebody with the cash to buy the business. Even at a bargain price,' said Buchanan, trying out Fizz's trick of implying one knew more than one did.

'You knew Lara?' Norris looked surprised.

'Not really,' said Buchanan, as though he were only slightly acquainted with her. 'But I knew she was in a hurry to sell.'

'Damn shame,' Norrie nodded. 'I never felt the same about

Simon Burroughs after the way he treated her. Oh, I know his
wife found out and created stink, but you don't drop a girl in a
state like that and never give her another thought, do you? A
nice lassie like Lara.'

Buchanan said, 'Did you ever hear what happened to her?'

'Never heard another word from her after she left. She never
wrote to any of her friends here or came back to see us.'
Norrie thoughtfully stroked Rossack's nose. 'Damn shame.'

Buchanan went on thinking about Lara as he drove home.
The deeper he probed into the cupboards of the Am Bealach
residents the more skeletons emerged.

Fizz found the office in a satisfactory state of chaos when
she arrived at work on Wednesday afternoon. There had
been several harrowing incidents since her last visit and the
atmosphere was not one of enthusiastic achievement.
Buchanan's secretary was already talking about looking for
another job.

'Listen, Beatrice,' Fizz told her, 'when Buchanan gets back
to work next week you'll find everything will return to normal
in no time. In fact you may find it will be better than normal.'

Beatrice regarded her over the top of her gold-rimmed
glasses. 'You know something I don't know?'

'Nope. I just have a feeling the old boy will have had about
enough by that time. I wouldn't be surprised if he decides to
call it a day at last.'

Beatrice leaned back in her chair and doubled the front of
her cardigan across her chest, folding her arms across it as
though she felt a sudden chill. 'I've thought that once or twice
myself, this past week, listening to the way he goes on when
he's in one of his moods.'

'You sound as if you're not wild about the idea of losing
him.'

'Not wild about it?' Beatrice gave a humourless hoot. 'It can't happen soon enough. The only thing that bothers me is: which of us gets the boot? Margaret or me?'

'Why should either of you get the boot? Margaret will just transfer her secretarial expertise from Buchanan senior to the new partner they'll be taking on.'

Beatrice looked over her shoulder as though she suspected that Margaret were hovering in the doorway. 'She'd never put up with that, Fizz, you know that yourself. It would be demotion.'

'Well, I wouldn't worry about it if I were you. Buchanan junior thinks the wind and tides obey your bidding. There's no way he'd swop you for Margaret.'

'I hope you're right.'

'I know I am.' Fizz made a mental note to weight the scales a little next time she was speaking to Buchanan. Meanwhile, she still had work to do on his father.

Buchanan senior looked at least five years older than he usually did. In actual fact, he was very fit for his years and still an attractive man but right now his eyes were distinctly baggy and there was a faint air of uncertainty about him that smote Fizz's conscience somewhat.

'Fizz,' he said, looking surprised to see her. 'Heavens, is it that time of the week already? Where does the time go? Sit down and tell me how things are in Am Bealach. Is Tam still improving? He phoned home twice through the week but I was out both times and I know he doesn't like to inconvenience your grandparents by having me phone him.'

'He's a lot better,' Fizz told him. 'He's eating extremely well and I think he is a lot more relaxed. He's been doing a bit of clay pigeon shooting with the local landowner and the two of them are planning to get a couple of salmon tomorrow. He seems to be really enjoying himself; golfing, reading, seeing a bit of the countryside.'

'That's good to hear,' said the senior partner almost tremulously. He riffled the edges of the papers on his desk. 'And, is he still planning to come back to work next week?'

'He hasn't said what his plans are,' Fizz answered, implying there was a distinct possibility that he might take another week. She saw her boss shiver as though he had been holed below the waterline. 'So what's been going on here this week?'

'Everything,' he muttered darkly. 'I've never known us to have so much on our hands. And now – just this morning – I hear that Victor Jardine has been arrested again, this time on a conspiracy charge. So that will mean I'll be up to my ears for God knows how long.'

'Victor Jardine?' Even Fizz remembered the famous court case of two years ago when Jardine had been cleared of embezzling nearly two million pounds. 'I didn't know he was one of our clients.'

'Buchanan and Stewart have been looking after his affairs since the fifties. The stories I could tell you about *him*.'

Fizz looked at him with wide eyes. 'I bet you could tell some wonderful stories about lots of people; all the famous trials you've been involved in. Haven't you ever considered writing your memoirs? They would make fascinating reading.'

A hint of a smile touched the corners of his mouth. 'There have certainly been some interesting cases over the years: the Calderwood poisoning... the Morningside murders... Emmanuel Libby – he was before your time but, my word, what a character! And Jeremy Neal, remember him? The chap who took an axe to his wife's lover, with two policemen watching him, and walked free? Now there's a story and a half!'

'There must be hundreds,' said Fizz, becoming genuinely enthused. 'You really must get it all down on paper while it's still fresh in your mind. Imagine, the inside story on the Calderwood sisters! The publishers would be cutting each others' throats for it.'

Buchanan senior withdrew his unfocused gaze from a vase of carnations and looked at the pile of work on his desk. 'One of those days, maybe. If I ever get around to retiring.'

'That's life, isn't it? There's always something getting in the way of our doing what we want to do.' Fizz stood up. 'For instance, the pile of filing that's waiting for me out there. I'd better get on with it.'

But as she closed the door she glanced back at him and he was staring at the carnations again.

Chapter Fourteen

Alistair phoned the farm on Wednesday to tell Buchanan that the river was still too high. There had been torrential rain through the night and the resulting flood had brought down too much mud with it to make fly-fishing anything but a waste of time. But by tomorrow, if the rain held off, the Stronach would be in perfect condition. Buchanan contained his impatience and treated himself, instead, to two rounds of golf at Taymouth Castle.

By Thursday the dry weather had returned, with a light cloud cover and a fresh breeze.

'Just what you want,' Grampa said at breakfast time. 'When it's too clear and the surface of the water is too calm the salmon can see you. You need a wee wind to give you a few ripples and not too bright sun. A day like today is just perfect.'

'Put on your green waterproof jacket,' Auntie Duff advised from the Aga where she was stirring porridge. 'Alistair always wears his old green jacket when he goes fishing.'

'What's that you're saying?' said Grampa.

'I'm telling him to wear his green jacket.'

'What?'

'I was just telling Tam that he should—'

'*What?*'

'Sod it,' said Auntie Duff, and shouted, 'If you would take

yourself into Stirling and get a hearing aid we wouldn't all
have to go around shouting our heads off all the time.'

'If you take yourself into Stirling and get a new set of
dentures,' Grampa returned, bridling, 'maybe I'd be able to
make out what you say!'

Auntie Duff had no intention of taking this lying down. 'It's
not my teeth, it's your ears—' she was starting to yell when she
was interrupted by the ringing of the telephone. 'That'll be
Alistair for you, Tam,' she said, instantly forgetting her indignation. 'Just get it yourself, will you, dear? If I take my eye off
this it'll burn.'

It was indeed Alistair, confirming that all systems were go
for the day's fishing.

'The boss says he'll meet you here at the lodge at ten
o'clock, if that suits you,' he said. 'Don't worry about bringing
sandwiches because Rowena is going to bring a picnic and
meet us at the Minister's pool round about lunchtime.'

'Sounds great,' Buchanan said. 'Anything else I have to
bring?'

'Och no, don't you be bothering about tackle or anything
like that. I'll have all the gear in the Land Rover. See you at
ten.'

Buchanan returned to his orange juice and reported these
arrangements to his hosts. Grampa was not overly impressed.

'In the old days,' he asserted vigorously, 'when Alistair's
father and grandfather were keepers on the estate, there used
to be fishing parties of fifteen rods or more, and a salmon for
each of them at the end of the day. The staff from the big
house would be down at the river at lunchtime with the big
picnic baskets full of hot game pies and fine wines and all your
orders.'

'All the maids in their black dresses and white starched
pinnys,' Auntie Duff elaborated. She put Buchanan's porridge

and cream in front of him and stood with her arms folded on top of her generous bosom while she enjoyed the memory. 'And the young ladies of the party walked down to join them – the older ones were driven down in the shooting brakes. Oh yes, they knew how to do things in those days. Mrs Munroe would be up to high doh getting her menfolk all spick-and-span – the first Mrs Munroe, that was, not Alistair's mother.'

Buchanan looked up. 'His father was married twice?'

'Both of them were – his mother and his father. Isn't that right?' She turned to Grampa and raised her voice. 'Alistair's parents – it was a second marriage for both of them, wasn't it?'

'Both of them were widowed, that's right,' said Grampa with a short bark of confirmation. 'Alice Munroe must have been near forty when she came to the Stronach estate. A damn sour besom she was too, from the day she arrived.'

Seeing the conversation about to die, Buchanan said, 'So she wasn't popular with the other women?'

'Och, they got along fine right up to a few months back,' Grampa said, eating his porridge in the traditional way: dipping each spoonful into a separate bowl of cream. 'Alice Munroe was always short-fused and the last few weeks of her life she had no time for any of us. Just wanted to be left alone to get ready to meet her maker.'

'She even turned her back on me,' Auntie Duff said over her shoulder as she returned to the cooker. 'I walked that road two or three times a week to make sure she was being looked after properly – not that Alistair didn't do his best but he had his work to do and his mother wouldn't have the district nurse in the house. But, at the end, she turned her face to the wall and wouldn't have anything to do with any of her friends.'

'How long had she been without her second husband?' Buchanan asked.

Auntie Duff referred the question to Grampa who had to

work it out by association with sundry other events of local importance. Finally it emerged that Alistair's father had died the same year that Malcolm was crushed by his bull, which was fourteen years ago.

That, by Buchanan's calculations, was also the year Fizz left home but nobody appeared to think that was worth a place in the annals of the family. There had been a lot of change in Am Bealach around that time. He thought about that for a while and came to the conclusion it didn't mean a damn thing.

He walked up to the Stronach gatehouse and got there well before ten but Alistair was already sitting on a bench in the garden waiting for him, a book of fishing flies open on his knee.

'Just working out what lures we'll be needing,' he said as Buchanan sat down beside him. 'I wouldn't be surprised if we saw a blink of sun later, so if we do, we'll need to change our tactics.'

'Grampa thinks there's a good chance of getting a fish today,' Buchanan said. 'Is he right?'

'Oh aye,' said Alistair with calm assurance. 'I saw five going up this morning in as many minutes so if we don't get one the day, we never will.'

Buchanan crossed his ankles and leaned his head back against the house wall behind him. The scent of grass clippings and damp earth was reminiscent of Scout camps and school rugby matches. In front of him a small lawn sloped gently down to a bed of early-flowering shrubs surrounded by miniature box hedging. On each side and spilling on to the lawn itself was a profusion of border perennials and variegated ground-cover plants with bulbs poking through. Most of them were not yet in bloom but already there were splashes of vivid colour everywhere and in another month or so it would be a scene straight out of *Homes and Gardens*.

'It's a superb view of the garden from here,' Buchanan commented. 'You get a much better idea of the layout than you do from the gate.'

Alistair jerked a thumb over his shoulder at the window behind him. 'This was my mother's room. Her last few weeks, she spent most of her day sitting at the window or, on warm days, she'd have a wee while out here on the bench, so it was this stretch that she kept improving.'

'She never stopped changing her garden around?'

One side of Alistair's mouth curved upwards in a wry smile. 'She used to say that a garden's never finished. Things get overgrown and take up too much room, or they get leggy and straggly, or the frost gets them – there's always something. We used to have a rockery down there where I'm digging the pond but it got completely overgrown and the soil was exhausted.'

'So, that was your mother's last project, was it? To scrap the rockery and replace it with a pool?'

'That's what she wanted,' Alistair nodded. He looked down the gentle slope to the hole under the lilac tree and smiled with gentle satisfaction as though he saw his work complete. 'Couple of weeks before she died she told me what to do and I started ripping out the rockery the same day. She didn't live to see it finished but she knew it would be there all the same. That's what mattered.'

'I'm sure she died happy,' Buchanan murmured. 'And she left something behind her that will give others great pleasure for years to come.'

'That she did,' Alistair agreed. 'As long as it's looked after.' He paused and cocked his head as the sound of a Land Rover engine made itself heard from the direction of the driveway to the big house. 'Here's his nibs.'

Lindsay was full of enthusiasm for their day on the river

and if his manner towards Alistair was a trifle offhand, it was not curt enough to spoil the ambience of the occasion. They piled into the Land Rover and drove up the glen road for about a mile. At that point the river was so close to the road that they could hear it through the trees, and a couple of minutes' walk brought them to a magnificent dark brown pool beneath a high ridge of waterworn rock. At one end was a cascade of white water spilling down over the ridge, and at the other an open, gravel-bottomed run with a few loose boulders close to the banks.

'You take the pool, Tam,' Lindsay directed, without reference to Alistair, 'and I'll take the tail run. Then we can swop over later for a while.'

He stomped away downstream with his waders flapping and was soon lashing the water to a foam with more energy than skill. Alistair made no comment, other than a deeply drawn sigh, and set about advising Tam where to cast his fly.

'See where the water swirls round at the far side there? That's because there's a big flat rock just under the surface, and that's where you'll find a fish resting for a wee while before trying to get up the falls. Just you put your fly in upstream a bittie – about a yard above that birch tree on the far bank – and you'll see it drift down past that stone as easy as you like. Take your time now.'

It took Buchanan a few casts to catch the current Alistair had his eye on, then he settled down to a steady cast and drift, cast and drift, expecting, every single time, to feel the sudden tug that would mean he had a fish on. After an unsuccessful quarter of an hour, Alistair picked out another likely spot and the drill started again.

The movement of the water was hypnotic and it wasn't easy to remain alert but Alistair, from his seat on a dry rock, kept putting in suggestions and making comments, which helped

Buchanan to keep his mind on the job.

Lindsay gave it another half an hour and then marched back up the bank and announced it was time for a changeover. 'Bugger all happening down there so far,' he commented. 'Haven't had a nibble.'

'Well, I suppose they're coming up river all the time,' Buchanan said hopefully.

'Och, yes. We'll give it a bit try anyway,' Alistair agreed and off they went.

'See these boulders in there near the bank?' Alistair said as they approached. 'Well, I put them there myself to make a groyne – a nice wee place for a fish to rest, just out of the current, but the sort of place where worms and flies might get swirled in. I'll want you to set your fly down where it will drift in there and tap a nice cock fish on the nose.'

Tam did his best to follow these instructions, but without any marked degree of confidence, so he was taken utterly by surprise when, on his fourth cast he felt an authoritative *tug-tug-tug*.

'It's a bite!' he yelled, and struck instinctively, to tighten the line and draw the hook into the fish's jaw.

Alistair was at his elbow, speaking low and calm. 'It's mebbe a wee snag, Tam. There could be submerged branches in there, come down with the flood, but just wait still a minute and see if it tugs again.'

Buchanan waited, his heart racing, his finger feeling the line for vibrations, then, with a sudden splash, a black back broke the surface and a broad tail flicked a spray of diamond droplets into the air.

'*Kee-rist!*'

'It's headed upstream, Tam. Keep your point up and give it a bit line.'

For the next ten minutes Buchanan fought it up and down

197

the run, sometimes running down the bank, sometimes in water up to his thighs with the strength of the current threatening to push him under. Alistair kept up a steady flow of advice and Lindsay came hurrying up with the tailer and landing net.

Gradually the fish's frenetic struggle weakened and a gleam of mother-of-pearl underbelly showed as it broke surface. Feeling no less exhausted, Buchanan drew it gently in towards a sandy bay where Alistair was ready to snare it by the tail and tap it neatly on the pow.

'Fourteen pounds if it's an ounce,' he claimed, holding it up by the gills and examining its skin. 'Straight out the North Sea within the last couple of days. A fine fish.'

Buchanan's knees were shaking with excitement. He felt compelled, while Alistair took the salmon back to the Land Rover, to give Lindsay a blow by blow account of the contest, just in case he had missed any of it, and felt he could go on talking about it for the rest of the day. However, Lindsay was now fired with the hope of getting a fish for himself so they all had a quick nip out of his silver-topped flask and set off downstream to the next pool.

Alistair strode on ahead and Buchanan was hard on his heels, still light-headed but raring to come to grips with another fourteen pounder. Just downstream of the gravel run they came to another pool, deeper and wider than the first: the Minister's pool, named after some forgotten cleric who had found his heaven here. Ten feet above the pool the river had carved a smooth notch in the bedrock, forging a spout that channelled the whole width of the torrent into a powerful jet, no more than six feet wide, that sprang clear of the rock before dropping into the pool below.

There were stepping stones a few paces upstream but these were now some three inches underwater and Buchanan's jaw was set as he followed Alistair across.

'Just mind the third last one. It's a wee bit unsteady and the moss is slippy.' As Buchanan teetered ashore, Alistair leaned out from the bank and proffered a steadying hand. He looked up the river for sight of Lindsay who had stopped to answer a call of nature. 'You go on down, Tam, and pick your stance and I'll wait for his nibs.'

Buchanan had a good look at the pool on his way down the bank but decided, in view of his previous success, to try the tail run. He was negotiating the trailing branches of an alder when he heard a cry from beyond the waterfall, and although it was almost drowned out by the noise of the river he knew instinctively that it was a cry of terror.

He threw down his rod and whipped round to run back up the bank but, in the instant he turned, he saw something big rolling in the cataract and knew that he was too late, bar a miracle, to do anything. None the less, he waded in as far as the middle of the tail run where the rocks gave some kind of protection against the thrust of the water and from where he could scan the roiling surface of the pool.

And there, a second later, something rose, spinning, to the surface.

Looking up, he saw Alistair, above the fall, staring down at the slowly revolving body as though he were frozen into immobility. It was all wrong. Alistair should have known what to do. Alistair was the countryman. Alistair knew the river like nobody else did.

Buchanan put his hands to his mouth and bellowed above the roar of the water.

'*Alistair!*'

He didn't know what he expected Alistair to do – it was just a plea for instructions or a cry for help – but it served to wake Alistair from his trance. He looked round at Buchanan and shouted something unintelligible, then, moving with lightning speed, he raised the spare rod he was carrying, whipped it in the air above his head to let out a long stretch of line, and cast the fly at Lindsay's body.

The hook lodged first time in his jacket and Alistair let out more line and came scrambling and sliding down the bank to the beach. The line went taut as he gradually increased the tension and the rod bent till it was virtually right angled. At first there was no change in the position of the body but slowly it yielded to the pull and moved towards the edge of the vortex. But, at that second, the rod snapped and the loose end, with a whirr of line, was catapulted into midstream like an arrow.

Buchanan, who had been holding his breath, howled with anguish. He staggered forward as though he thought he could do something useful but stopped as he realised his helplessness. Alistair was shouting something and waving an arm, and, when he looked back at the pool he saw that the traction had been enough to tug Lindsay out of the vortex and into another current which was now carrying him downstream.

Buchanan had no time to choose his route back towards the bank he had just left. He launched himself forward, waders slipping on the slimy rocks, and got one desperate handful of Lindsay's jacket as he shot past. Water burned into his lungs as he went under, then he was up again with both hands twisted into Lindsay's clothing and the current sweeping them both downstream at a menacing rate.

Buchanan kicked for the bank but one leg was trapped beneath Lindsay's body as though wrapped in waterweed. Taking in water like the *Titanic*, he grabbed Lindsay by the collar and used one arm to propel them both out of the main current. It felt as though he were swimming through treacle and there were points where drowning seemed to be an imminent possibility, but when he managed to look round, he appeared to have made a little progress.

Just don't let there be another cataract right now, he prayed silently, with visions of a sudden drop through twenty feet of foam and a plunge into one of Mother Nature's food processors. The phrase, *'the sizey a fitba'* sang in his mind like a mantra.

Then the force of the current slackened abruptly and he was able to reach out his free arm and grab hold of a half-submerged spike of root that appeared an inch from his left eye. He could hear Alistair shouting now and, in a few seconds, he saw him come scrambling through the trees and leaping into the water beside them.

'Jesus, look at you!' he exclaimed. 'You're trussed up like a pair of chickens with nylon gut!'

It was the gut that had slackened their speed, looping on to the tree roots as they hurtled past. It was also the gut that had cut deep into Buchanan's leg and nearly drowned him and Lindsay both. Alistair slashed them free with a few swipes of his knife and then grabbed Lindsay under the arms and heaved him bodily up on to the bank, leaving Buchanan to make his own way to safety.

By the time Buchanan crawled ashore Alistair had turned Lindsay on his face and was hefting him up by the middle to force the water out of him.

'Is he still alive?' Buchanan choked out.

Alistair didn't pause to answer. He flipped Lindsay over on to his back and started blowing into his mouth and working his arms, but by the look of his face Buchanan doubted if he had much hope of a happy outcome.

Lindsay's face didn't inspire confidence either. It was waxy white and there was blood welling out of a deep gash above his ear. If he wasn't dead, Buchanan thought, he was damn near it. He started to say, 'I'll take over when you get tired, Alistair—' but Lindsay suddenly moaned and a gush of foul-smelling water and vomit belched from between his lips.

Alistair sat back on his heels, panting, as he watched Lindsay's chest begin to rise and fall of its own volition. 'He's no' looking good,' he said. 'Concussion, like as not. We'll need to keep him warm while I go back for the Land Rover.'

Standing up, he whipped off his wet jacket and threw it to the ground. Beneath it he was wearing a body warmer, a sweater and a flannel shirt, all of which he removed. 'You'll need to try and get these on him as fast as you can.' He resumed his jacket, shuddering as it hit his bare skin. 'Keep his head turned to the side in case he's sick again and see if you can get something between him and the ground. I'll be back in five minutes.'

Buchanan was, himself, as close to hypothermia as he'd ever been in his life. His fingers were all toes as he tried to undress Lindsay and get him into the dry clothing. Lindsay was no help at all and his flaccid limbs, skinny as they were, seemed to weigh a ton and bend in all the wrong places.

Buchanan could find nothing to put between him and the ground except wet clothing, but remembered Auntie Duff giving him a plastic bin liner in which to bring home his catch so he was able to make a fairly damp-proof course. After that there didn't seem much he could do but chafe Lindsay's hands and feet and swear silently at Alistair for taking so long.

After a couple of minutes, Lindsay's eyes half opened and he threw up again, missing Buchanan's knees by millimetres.

'Gordon Bennett,' he said, which struck Buchanan as showing extraordinary restraint under the circumstances. He looked forward momentarily to quoting the remark to Fizz as an example of how a gentleman dealt with a near-death experience.

'You're OK, Lindsay,' he said, and dragged him a couple of feet away from the pool of vomit. 'We got you out.'

Lindsay's eyes opened properly and he lifted a hand to wipe a regurgitated piece of waterweed off his moustache. 'Out of what?'

'The river. You fell in.'

Lindsay absorbed this in silence and closed his eyes again while Buchanan resumed work on his extremities. In the ensuing silence the sound of an approaching vehicle became audible over the thunder of the falls.

'That's Alistair back,' Buchanan said, thankfully. 'We'll soon have you into a warm bed.'

But it wasn't Alistair who appeared through the screen of trees that hid the road, it was Rowena, carrying a basket on one arm and Briony on the other.

Buchanan leaped to his feet and strode across the turf to intercept her before she saw Lindsay and panicked. 'Rowena – Lindsay's had a bit of a fall. Nothing to worry about, but he's a bit groggy.'

Rowena's smile fell from her lips. Without a word she thrust Briony into Buchanan's arms and ran down the bank to drop to her knees beside Lindsay. Her voice drifted back, carried by the breeze, and although the words were not intelligible, the distress and alarm came over loud and clear.

Buchanan was somewhat surprised at this show of affection, the existence of which was something he had never suspected, but he left her to it. He was feeling the need of some tender loving care himself, and now that the crisis was over he was also aware of a deeply disturbing uneasiness.

There were forces at work here in Am Bealach that he felt unable to understand and it began to look as if Fizz ought to be informed of the latest developments before things went any further.

'What d'you think, Briony? he asked the miniature Rowena in his arms. 'Is it time to hit the panic button?'

Briony stared at him with an expression of horror and alarm, went bright red and started to scream blue murder.

Chapter Fifteen

Fizz had been studying at her kitchen table since six in the morning without a break when, at twenty to three in the afternoon, her doorbell rang. She debated with herself whether to answer it or not, since it was unlikely to be anyone she wanted to see, just at that point in time, but when it rang again with trenchant insistence her curiosity was aroused.

On the doorstep she found Mrs Auld, who lived across the landing. She was wearing her husband's slippers and possibly the last crossover apron in regular use in the western hemisphere.

'Phone call for you, luvvie.'

Fizz's stomach gave a sudden lurch. Grampa and Auntie Duff were the only people who knew Mrs Auld's number and she was sure they wouldn't use it unless there was an emergency.

Mrs Auld led the way across the landing to her open door, her casual footwear slapping the concrete like flippers.

'It's a Mr Buchanan. Just wants a few words, if it's not too inconvenient. You don't come across manners like that very often these days, *I* can tell you. Did you hear those lager louts going by last night? And where were the police? Plenty of them lounging about in the daytime whenever you're looking for a place to park, but never a one to be seen when we're getting eighteen verses of "The Ball of Kirriemuir" at three in the morning. Here you are, luvvie.'

'Buchanan?'

'Hi. I hope it's OK to use this number. Auntie Duff said you wouldn't object—'

'Never mind all that,' Fizz cut in impatiently. 'What's up?'

Buchanan hesitated briefly. 'There have been one or two developments that I think you ought to know about. Basically—'

'What do you mean "developments"?'

'If you'd just listen, Fizz—'

'OK, OK. Shoot.'

'I'm beginning to worry about Alistair Munroe—'

'Christ! Alistair!' A stony silence answered her. After a second or two, she said, 'Sorry. What's worrying you about Alistair?'

'Just answer me one question: did Mrs Munroe ever say anything to anyone about wanting to be buried in her garden?'

Fizz stared at the receiver. 'No – not that I ever heard. What makes you ask that, of all things?'

'I just got to thinking . . . I found the Fitzpatrick family graveyard when I was walking along the shore the other day and I thought . . . I thought it must be comforting for Grampa, for instance, to know that he'll lie there, on his own ground, when he passes on. Which led to Alistair's mother, and what she would have wanted.'

'Right.' Fizz nodded to herself. 'Well, I know she never liked Killin churchyard. Every time we were all at a local funeral she used to say it gave her the creeps, but Alistair's folks didn't have a family plot; they were always cremated. Still, now that you bring it up, sure, if it had occurred to her she might have wanted to be in her own garden.' The wheels of her mind were spinning but she wasn't getting any traction, and Buchanan was being annoyingly obtuse. She said, 'But she wasn't buried in the garden, she was cremated. Auntie Duff could have told you that.'

Buchanan said nothing, but said it to such effect that it was as if he had shouted it.

'You surely don't suspect that Alistair . . . that he faked the cremation because she . . .? You're mad, Buchanan! Why should he do that when there's no law against burying her in the garden?' Fizz stared out the window at the distant hills of Fife but it was Am Bealach she was seeing: the rolling lawns of Alistair's garden and the hole he had dug for his mother's memorial pool. She shook her head as adamantly as if Buchanan could see her. 'It's quite common around there to have family plots on your own land. Heck, people do it all over the place nowadays, even in housing estates. They're even selling biodegradable coffins for do-it-yourself burials.'

She heard Buchanan draw a slow breath, then he said, 'The thing is, it's not the Munroes' land, is it? Alistair would have needed Lindsay's permission to inter his mother in the grounds of a tied cottage.'

'Uh-huh. I suppose he would, but Lindsay wouldn't be too keen on that, I bet,' Fizz said, and then realised that, of course, Lindsay, the obnoxious little reptile, would have refused. Probably *had* refused.

The truth seemed to be opening out in front of her eyes like the pages of a book. All those references to the cottage being as much the Munroe family home as Stronach Lodge was Lindsay's, Rowena's impotent anger at Lindsay's insensitivity, they all tied in. It was obvious, no matter what Rowena said, that she at least suspected what the row had been about.

'You could be right about Lindsay refusing permission for the interment,' Fizz admitted, 'but there's no reason to suspect

207

that Alistair went ahead and did it anyway. I think that's pushing it a bit.'

'Why, then, is he talking about being stuck on the Stronach estate for life?' Buchanan asked. 'Doesn't it look as if he might be afraid that a new tenant of the gamekeeper's cottage might dig up his mother's coffin?'

It did, Fizz had to admit, appear hellish likely. She began to wish she had not shared that particular piece of information with Buchanan.

'And there's something else that made me jumpy,' he was saying. 'We went fishing this morning; Alistair, Lindsay and myself. The river was in spate, and when Lindsay was crossing over, just above the Minister's pool, he fell over the falls and cracked his head – and not necessarily in that order, if you follow me. He was alone with Alistair at the time.'

Fizz was speechless with shock. Burying one's mother on someone else's property might be said to show a certain lack of moral principles, but precipitating that someone into the Minister's pool was edging towards the unacceptable. Even if the precipatee was Lindsay.

'Is he dead?' she got out, surprising a swift glance out of Mrs Auld who was getting on with her ironing and trying to pretend she wasn't listening.

'No, but it's a miracle he survived. Alistair and I managed, between us, to fish him out, but he was in a bad way. He has concussion and needed three stitches in his head.'

'So, tell me the bad news: has he said what happened to make him fall in?'

'He says he can't remember.'

'Oh, great,' said Fizz, tempering her response to avoid bruising Mrs Auld's sensibilities. 'And what's Alistair saying about it?'

'Not a lot. You know Alistair. Naturally, I haven't said

anything to him regarding my suspicions – they really are very flimsy, after all – but in view of Lindsay's accident, I'm nervous about doing nothing.'

Fizz took a short break to think about that. As far as she personally was concerned, if Alistair had managed to bury his mother in the garden without anyone else knowing about it, jolly good luck to him. It didn't do anyone any harm and nothing would be achieved by doing a Burke and Hare on Mrs Munroe's remains at this stage in the game.

However, that didn't mean that Buchanan would keep his mouth shut about it. He did not take the view that the law was for the blind obedience of fools and the guidance of right-minded men. To Buchanan, the law was the law and not to be questioned and, as a lawyer himself, which he never forgot for a second, he would almost certainly insist that Alistair should be dropped instantly in the shit. Furthermore, there was the little matter of Lindsay's accident. If that had been engineered by Alistair the police would have to be told.

The trouble with telling the police was that, if Alistair were *not* guilty of murder, or attempted murder, the truth about his mother's burial would still come out and she would be disinterred. Which would be a damn shame. Clearly, a delicate touch was needed before things got out of hand.

'Tell you what,' Fizz said finally. 'I can jump on a train and be in Stirling in about an hour. Can you pick me up at the station?'

She expected him to give her an argument about it but, to her surprise, he succumbed without a struggle and said he'd be there by four. This easy victory made her more worried than anything else, since it seemed to suggest that Buchanan wanted her there, and if that were so, it must mean that he didn't want to take the responsibility of uncovering something that would upset the whole Am Bealach apple cart.

'Something wrong at home, luvvie?' asked Mrs Auld as Fizz rang off. She was trying to look as though she were only asking out of politeness but there was an avid gleam in her eye.

'One of my friends has had a nasty accident,' Fizz told her and set a firm course for the door, talking in an unbroken stream that prevented Mrs Auld from getting a word in. 'I'm going to have to dash up there right away, I think there's a train at half-past and Buchanan is meeting me at Stirling, thanks for taking that call for me, Mrs Auld, see you when I get back, by-ee.'

It took her ten minutes to throw some underwear and textbooks into a bag and another five to sprint down North Gray's Close to Waverley Station, but for the next hour she had nothing to do but watch the passing scenery and worry. The more she thought about it, the more convinced she became that Buchanan's suspicions were spot-on, at least as far as the burial was concerned.

It was less easy to accept that Alistair might have tried to top Lindsay. It didn't seem like the Alistair she had grown up with. But now Lindsay was probably the only person who knew that both mother and son had been set on burying her in the garden. Alistair certainly wouldn't have blabbed it around, not if he had made up his mind to go ahead with the unlicensed interment, so if any questions were asked at a later date, Lindsay would be the only one to point the finger.

Was that why he'd had to have an 'accident'? Was his mother's resting place so important to Alistair that he'd go to that extent to avoid discovery? No, absolutely not! It was quite inconceivable that Alistair could think like that. He might go a little over the score out of love for his mother but not that far.

When her train arrived at Stirling Fizz found Buchanan waiting on the platform. He was looking even grimmer than

usual, which was saying something, and seemed to limp a little
as he stepped forward to take her bags.

'So,' she said kindly, 'how are you enjoying your rest and
recuperation?'

He almost smiled. 'It's been . . . interesting. I particularly
enjoyed the underwater cruising and the shock therapy. Very
character-building. I could have done without the two stitches in
my leg, but I had a nice chat with the doctor, who turned out to
be a particularly decent sort of chap, so one mustn't grumble.'

'Shit, you get all the fun. How come nothing happens when
I'm around?'

'Guess I'm just lucky.' He threw her bags in the back of the
car and held the passenger door for her. 'Before we head for
home there's something I want to look at.'

'What's that?'

'A jeweller's shop. I noticed it on the way here, while I was
stopped at a traffic light. There was a sign in the window that
said they did specialist repairs and made up pieces to individual
designs, etcetera. I just wondered if they sold jeweller's rouge.'

'You're not still bashing your brains about that, are you?'
Fizz said. She had ceased to hold out any hope of learning
anything from the bizarre objects the camper had carried with
him, and was less than optimistic about making a breakthrough now.

'I'm just curious,' Buchanan said. 'The guy had to have
bought the stuff locally, wouldn't you think? If you were
buying it for somebody else, say, you'd pick it up at the last
possible place, you wouldn't buy it before you set out and
carry it further than you needed to.'

'Well, no, an experienced backpacker wouldn't carry a milli-
gram more than absolutely necessary. Heck, I've known guys
who halved the handle of their toothbrush and trimmed the
margins off their paperbacks – yes, and used the pages they'd

read as toilet paper so's they didn't have to carry that as well. But he wouldn't have left buying the stuff till the last minute either. Not unless somebody told him to pick it up here.'

'Well, we're virtually passing the door of the goldsmith's anyway, and if they don't stock jeweller's rouge they may know somebody locally who does. It won't take a minute to pop in.'

There was a parking spot right at the door of the shop, which seemed to Fizz an omen of sorts, so she changed her mind about letting Buchanan go it alone and accompanied him into a gloomy interior, illuminated only by the lights from glass showcases.

A surprised-looking youth of about seventeen emerged from the back shop. Fizz's first impression was that maybe they didn't get many customers at this late hour of the day, but she soon discovered that his surprised expression was due to his arched eyebrows rather than to astonishment.

'Can I help you?'

'I hope so,' Buchanan said. 'Do you sell jeweller's rouge?'

The youth's eyebrows became even more arched. 'Jeweller's rouge? No, I'm afraid not. You'd have to go to a supplier for that. We only stock it for our own use. You could try Cochrane's in Glasgow.'

'I suppose it's not something you're asked for very often?' said Buchanan.

The youth smiled, squeezing shut his eyes and exposing an engaging gap between his front teeth. 'Nobody's ever asked for it before. Not since I've been here.'

That seemed to be that as far as Fizz was concerned, but as she moved to the door she heard Buchanan say, 'Has jeweller's rouge any other uses that you know of apart from polishing precious metals?'

'Not really. We just use it to buff up gold, mostly. It's just a polishing agent. Or lenses – I think they use it to put a smooth finish on spectacle lenses and lenses for telescopes. That's all I've ever heard of it being used for. Sorry.'

'Not at all,' Buchanan said, with more sincerity than the answer seemed to warrant. 'That's very useful information. Thanks very much.'

Outside in the car he was all smiles. 'You didn't find that interesting?' he asked.

Fizz frowned at him. 'Riveting,' she said, totally unable to see anything of interest in a word the lad had said. 'OK then. Tell me what I missed – but just remember, Buchanan, nobody likes a smartass, OK?'

'Lenses for telescopes,' he said, with what Fizz would have termed a smirk. 'Where did you last hear mention of a telescope?'

Fizz had no memory of anyone mentioning a telescope in her company at any time in the last fortnight. 'You sure I was present at the time?'

Buchanan nodded. 'You bet. Maybe you had severed the connection between your ears and your brain at that point but you were definitely present in body.'

'OK. Remind me.'

'The fragrant Saskia. I told you our trip to Plochaig deserved a better score than nought point five, didn't I? Don't you remember Saskia saying something about the neighbours spying on them through telescopes, and Ghislain telling her it was an astronomical telescope?'

That did sound familiar to Fizz but she had barely registered it at the time. She considered this new piece of information as Buchanan pulled away from the kerb and edged out into the stream of rush-hour traffic. 'I suppose it's a bit of a long shot,' she decided, 'but the fact that there's a connection to Plochaig . . .'

'Exactly. And I rather suspect we'll discover that the guy with the telescope is Mrs Sweeney's son. I think we have to talk to him, don't you?'

'Oh, sure. As long as we don't have to get involved with Saskia again. I dare say the Sweeneys are on the phone—'

'No,' said Buchanan decisively. 'I don't want to speak to this guy on the phone. I want to see his face, his body language, his lifestyle. Also, I don't want to warn him that we're coming in case he disappears before we get there. No, we'll take a run over tomorrow morning, first thing.'

'*Jawohl, mein Führer.*'

Fizz wasn't sure whether to be pleased with this new development or not. Establishing the identity of the anonymous camper was, she felt, not too likely to solve the mystery of his death but, on the other hand, concentrating on that aspect of the mystery might serve to keep Buchanan off Alistair's back till she had a chance to investigate him herself. If it turned out that the illicit interment of Mrs Munroe formed the extent of Alistair's misdemeanours there was always a chance that, between them, he and Fizz could find a way to hustle it past Buchanan. It was a very small crime, after all and must have been a big help to Alistair in coming to terms with his bereavement. It had also, no doubt, been a comfort to Mrs Munroe to know that she would be contributing to the fertility of her own memorial.

It was probably too much to hope that Buchanan had not already asked himself the question: if Mrs Munroe was now in the garden, what – or *who* – had been cremated in her place? However, he was pussyfooting around that particular topic, doubtless because he hoped Fizz would face up to it before he had to twist her arm.

Buchanan spoke suddenly, out of a long silence. 'I phoned the office this afternoon – before I intruded on your neighbour

– just in case you were putting in some overtime.'

'Oh yes?' Fizz said warily. 'Who did you speak to?'

'Beatrice, initially. She tells me my father has been running around in ever decreasing circles for the last two weeks and could implode at any second.'

'Really?' murmured Fizz. 'He hides it well.'

'Not from Beatrice, and not from Alan, who I also spoke to. I suspect you're the only one who hasn't noticed that he has been having a pretty rough time.'

'Well, I'm only there for a couple of hours, Wednesday and Friday, and I don't see a lot of him.'

'That's not the impression he gives.'

'You spoke to him too, then?'

'I did.'

He left it at that while he negotiated a flock of sheep that filled the roadway, flowing round both sides of the car like a foaming river.

Finally, Fizz was forced to ask, 'And did your dad admit that things were getting on top of him?'

'No. In fact, he did his best to hide it from me. He was very anxious that I make sure I'm back to full health before I return to work.'

'Really?' That was a bit of a facer, really, because Fizz had hoped to have the old boy ready to leap out of the window by this time.

'Really. He gave me a long lecture about stress: how it can build up over the years, the illnesses it can trigger, etcetera, etcetera. Life, I understand, is not a rehearsal. I should learn to take more care of myself before it's too late.'

'Cor,' said Fizz. 'Was he implying, do you think, that it was too late for *him*?'

'Apparently not.' From the side it appeared to Fizz that he was trying not to smile, but she wouldn't have sworn to it.

'When I had convinced him that I had fully recovered my customary rude health he admitted that, of late, he had begun to think that it was time for him to turn his hand to other things – primarily, his memoirs. Evidently, his experiences of the past fifty years in Scottish Law are unique, and not to be allowed to slip into obscurity, so he has to get them down on paper before it's too late.'

'Well, that's true, you know,' Fizz said carefully, still not sure if she was suspected of interfering. 'He has been involved in some of the most interesting cases of his generation and he has known all the famous characters in Scottish Law – barristers, judges, forensic experts as well as villains. He could write a bestseller.'

'I don't know that he's worried about making a lot of money but he was certainly all fired up about it this afternoon.'

The muscles at the side of his mouth tightened a little. One could call it a smile, Fizz judged, if one were in a generous mood.

'Well,' she ventured, 'I just hope he doesn't change his mind.'

'Quite.'

Typical of Buchanan to say nothing that could be quoted but, all the same, to give the impression that he knew the score. Well, that was enough for Fizz. If he was aware that it was she who had brought about this change in his father's plans, he also realised that he owed her a favour. So, maybe there was a hope of making him keep his mouth shut about Alistair as well.

Chapter Sixteen

Grampa had been out on the hill since mid-morning and had returned only minutes before Fizz and Buchanan drove into the yard. He knew, therefore, only the briefest outline of what had occurred at the Minister's pool and he was, to Buchanan's embarrassment, infuriated to find that Fizz had used the accident as an excuse to take more time off her studies.

'It'll be a different story when you have your exam paper in front of you, let me tell you! You'll wish then that you had got your head down and done some work this past fortnight instead of lounging around here as though you had all the time in the world. They don't hand out law degrees like lollipops, you know.'

'I've studied for six hours today, Grampa,' Fizz said, happily warming her bottom at the Aga.

Grampa either didn't hear this or chose to ignore it. 'Is it some kind of genius you think you are, that can pick up a degree in your spare time? It was the same thing at art school – wasting your time with student politics and parties every night till they threw you out. You never learn, do you?'

Fizz amazed Buchanan by remaining blank-faced and unriled. It occurred to him that the dull red flush creeping across her grampa's brow might be warning her not to goad him any further.

Feeling uncomfortably *de trop* he edged towards the door and escaped to his own cottage but as he crossed the yard he could hear Grampa yelling, 'And what about your job? Who's going to employ someone who takes days off every time something interesting happens elsewhere? You'll never amount to anything, lassie! Hitchhiking around the world like a vagrant is all you'll ever be any good for . . .'

Buchanan closed his ears and fled.

Selena had spotted him, from wherever she had been hiding, and came racing across the cobbles to rub against his legs as he unlocked the door. Buchanan picked her up and stroked her but even her ecstatic purring failed to dispel the cloud of guilt that had settled around him.

It was his fault that Fizz was here, even if neither Fizz nor Grampa would have accepted that view of the matter. OK, he hadn't asked her to come but he had hoped she would, and he had been mightily relieved when he heard her say she was coming. He had wanted her here to share the responsibility – and the decisions – when the truth came out, as appeared imminent.

Alistair might well be totally innocent of all their suspicions, but Lindsay's fall that afternoon had made Buchanan jumpy and he wouldn't feel easy in his mind till he knew what was going on. He was well aware that Fizz would be furious if he did anything that resulted in Mrs Munroe being unnecessarily disinterred, but some sort of action would have to be taken if the illicit burial was only the tip of a very nasty iceberg.

Having convinced himself that he'd had no option but to alert Fizz to the developing situation, he propped his sore leg on a footstool and, with Selena spread-eagled across his chest, slept soundly till dinnertime.

Fizz was her usual chirpy self during the meal, and

Buchanan could see no sign that she was at all affected by her grampa's tongue-lashing. However, she took herself off to her room to study before the others had finished their coffee and, as Auntie Duff thereafter rushed off to the Women's Guild in Myra's car, Buchanan and Grampa were left alone at the table.

Grampa took a sip of his coffee and looked into the cup. 'Ach well, since it's just the two of us, Tam, I think we'll have a little something in this, just to give it a bit flavour.'

He clicked across to the Welsh dresser and came back with a bottle of Grouse. 'Now then,' he said, topping up Tam's cup to the brim, 'that'll take the sting out of your stitches. *Slàinte mhath!*'

'*Slàinte mhath!*' The hot liquor burned a trail down to Buchanan's stomach, making him realise that he had needed a stimulant all afternoon to dull the memory of the struggle in the river. 'Well, if it doesn't cure my wounds it certainly takes my mind off them.'

Grampa set the bottle on the table. 'A fine carry-on that was to happen when you're still convalescing from your operation. I don't know yet how you managed to beat that current below the Minister's pool. In a spate like we saw today I'd have said you didn't have a chance.'

'I was downstream from the worst of it,' Buchanan said. 'Almost at the bend, where it's wider and shallower, and I had a good footing on gravel.'

Grampa's eyes were bright blue in the shadow of his bushy brows. 'So, you were quite a distance away when it happened?'

'I'd gone ahead to take a look at the tail run and Alistair had waited for Lindsay, to give him a hand across the stepping stones above the pool.'

'I know the place fine. I never liked that crossing.' His eyes bored into Buchanan's as though they could read his thoughts and it looked, for a moment, as though he might have suspicions of his own. 'How did Lindsay come to lose his footing with Alistair there to help him?'

Buchanan took a minute to choose his words and made a unilateral decision to take Grampa into his confidence. Somebody was going to have to speak to Alistair: someone he trusted. Not Fizz: too dangerous. Not himself: too official. Therefore, Grampa would have to do it.

He said, 'One of the stepping stones was very unsteady. If Lindsay lost his balance there, it's possible that Alistair didn't feel like risking his life to save him. You know they've been at loggerheads recently?'

'At loggerheads?' Grampa's eyes narrowed. 'What about?'

'I don't know,' Buchanan said. 'Nobody knows for sure except the two of them. They're keeping it very quiet.'

Grampa's gaze wandered thoughtfully around the table top and then homed in like an Exocet on Buchanan's face. 'But, you have your suspicions, I'm thinking?'

Buchanan, for an instant, felt it was Fizz he was facing. He couldn't think of anyone else who possessed that uncanny facility for reading him like a book. He wished he had another whisky.

'I took a walk down the lochside one morning and came across your family graveyard,' he said carefully. 'It made me wonder if Mrs Munroe would have wanted to be buried in her own garden.'

Grampa's sudden stillness was a sign that he had heard enough. Buchanan watched the play of expression across his face and knew the moment when the pieces finally clicked into place.

'Lindsay wouldn't have that,' he said, after a long period of clearly painful consideration. 'But if you're thinking Alistair is trying to kill out of revenge for being refused permission, then you're wrong, Tam. I don't believe Alistair would do a terrible thing like that – not unless his mother's death has tipped his reason.'

'Lindsay's fall could have been completely accidental,' Buchanan assured him. 'I was telling the truth when I said I didn't see what happened. But there is a strong possibility that Alistair went ahead with the burial without permission, which would give him a stronger motive for silencing Lindsay.'

He gave the old man a minute or two to digest that news and then added, 'It's none of my business where Mrs Munroe is buried, of course. As far as anyone else is concerned, I don't know a thing about that.'

Grampa leaned across to grip Buchanan's arm for a second, nodded grimly, and went for the bottle of Grouse and two glasses. 'Aye. I thought there was something going on, the way you and Fizz were asking questions, but I never suspected this.'

'But, it's all speculation,' Buchanan stressed, wishing he could conduct this conversation at a more discreet pitch. There might be no one around to overhear it but it made him feel uncomfortable none the less. 'We might be barking up the wrong tree entirely, but if Lindsay *is* in any danger, we can't afford to do nothing.'

'You're right, Tam. There have been too many terrible things happening in Am Bealach this while back. How do we know they're not all connected? I still don't think Alistair could have lost his reason to that extent but the police will have to be told.'

Buchanan nodded, accepting a measure of whisky that gladdened his heart. 'It may come to that but it would be a pity – if Alistair had nothing to do with the other offences – if we caused his mother to be exhumed.'

'Aye. God knows, Mrs Munroe deserved to be buried where she was happiest. That garden gave us all so much pleasure, over the years, the least we can do is turn a blind eye if we possibly can.' Grampa rubbed a hand over his jaw with a sound like someone wire-brushing a chain-link fence. 'But we don't have any choice, Tam. If someone else is murdered while we shillyshally it'll be too late to be sorry.'

'We'll have to talk to Alistair – or somebody else will,' Buchanan said. 'We'll have to find out the extent of his involvement before we land him in any trouble. I'd do it myself, but he wouldn't trust me to keep my mouth shut about his mother, if what we suspect about her burial turns out to be true, and furthermore, the less I admit to knowing about the business the better.'

Grampa seemed to subject the likely candidates to review and came to the same conclusion as Buchanan. 'I'll talk to him myself. I'll catch him tomorrow afternoon, when he's back from the hill.'

Buchanan leaned back in his chair and stretched out his legs. His stitches were still smarting but the whisky was starting to glow like a campfire in his belly, warming the cold, empty space that had been yawning under his ribs since his brush with death.

He said, 'I think we could afford to leave it till Saturday, since Lindsay is going to be bedridden for a few days. I'd like to be around, in the background, while you quiz Alistair but tomorrow Fizz and I are going back to Plochaig to talk to someone there who has a telescope. We discovered today that jeweller's rouge is used in the polishing of lenses.'

Grampa drained his glass and gave Buchanan a glowering look. 'You've been interesting yourself in that matter too, have you?'

Buchanan sensed a certain dryness in his tone as though he thought the mysteries were a purely Am Bealach concern. He said, 'Fizz asked me to see what I could find out—'

'That lassie!' Grampa exclaimed, with an expression of annoyance. 'She's into everything like a ferret, that one! Can't keep her nose out of anything. And the trouble she causes!'

'I do believe that she was genuinely worried about Miss Anderson's disappearance and also its effect on you,' Buchanan couldn't resist saying. 'She thought you would be happier if you knew what happened to Bessie Anderson.'

That stopped Grampa in his tracks. He said nothing for a while but sat fingering his empty glass and looking at nothing, then he pushed back his chair.

'What's your malt, Tam?'

Buchanan looked at him in surprise. 'Glenmorangie.'

'Aye, well, you could do worse. Come away through.'

Buchanan followed him across the lobby and into the lounge, a shadowy room with a piano in one corner and a grandfather clock in another, where a fire was smouldering in the brass canopied grate. Grampa kicked the logs into life and threw on another pine knot.

'Sit yourself down, Tam,' he said, throwing open a cupboard to display a staggering collection of bottles. 'Malt whisky is a wee hobby of mine. Not that I treat myself very often, but when I do, I like to have one that suits my mood. Now then, Glenmorangie... I know I have one somewhere... Aye, here we are.'

He chose a Talisker for himself and settled into the armchair across the hearth from Buchanan. 'So, what else have you been finding out about Bessie Anderson's disappearance?'

'Not a lot,' Buchanan admitted. 'She appears to have been held in respect and affection by everyone in Am Bealach and hadn't had much contact with the rest of the world for years. It's difficult to see anyone having a motive to kill her.'

Grampa held his glass to the fire and looked through it at the flames. 'You're maybe wondering, like I am, if it was her body that was cremated instead of Mrs Munroe's. Och, it's a wicked thing to be thinking of Alistair, but somebody was in that coffin they burned, for it was sealed by the undertaker.'

'It crossed my mind, yes, but I don't quite see how Alistair could have achieved that.' Buchanan extended his legs and gingerly crossed his ankles to avoid pressure on his stitches. 'I'll be interested to hear what he has to say when you question him about it.'

There was a long silence while Grampa considered that. Buchanan sipped his Glenmorangie and watched the flames and smelled the scent of burning pine sap and listened to the hissing of the logs.

'There's a lot of questions I'll want answered before we go to the police,' Grampa muttered.

Buchanan nodded. 'Exactly my own thoughts. I suspect, in fact, that Fizz was afraid we might turn up something that required a certain amount of discretion. That's why she wanted me here.'

Grampa made an irritable movement with his free hand. 'What was she needing to get involved for in the first place? What goes on in Am Bealach is none of her business any more. She goes wandering off to the ends of the earth for years on end and, the next thing we know, she's back here trying to run the place. I don't know who she gets it from – certainly not her father, I can tell you that – but she has this notion that nothing is ever done right unless she does it herself.'

Grampa tossed off the rest of his whisky. There was clearly more in the mouthful than he had calculated and it took him a moment to get his breath. 'It would suit her better if she got her life in order instead of worrying about what doesn't concern her,' he growled. 'Twenty-seven years old and she's never had a proper job – not for a day longer than it took her to earn enough money to buy a ticket to some place else. And don't be thinking it's the way she was brought up, because it wasn't. I took good care, with both her and Colin, to give them the best start in life I could afford.'

'It can't have been easy,' Buchanan murmured, picturing a man approaching sixty, with no wife or close relations, saddled with two young children.

'No. It was not easy, but I did my best.' He looked at Buchanan's glass. 'Drink up your malt, Tam. I want to introduce you to one you may not have tried. It's a wee bit sweeter than Glenmorangie and maybe a touch heavier, but it's worth the tasting. Lochnagar. Matured in sherry casks and I think you'll detect the extra bit peat they use in the malting of the barley.'

His wrinkled hands moved slowly as he poured, like a priest performing an ancient and arcane ritual. Buchanan sipped, rolled the liquid round his tongue, and was enchanted. Grampa continued to talk about the whisky and the differences between it and Glenmorangie but Buchanan wanted to hear more about his early days as a surrogate parent.

'You have a reputation in Am Bealach for being a first-rate teacher,' he said, when he got the chance. 'Malcolm was talking about your methods the other day.'

'Och,' Grampa glowered, brushing away the compliment with an impatient gesture. 'I didn't know a damn thing about bringing up children when I was landed with those two. Not wee ones, no. My wife took to do with that when Fizz's father was a laddie, so I had it all to learn.'

He hitched himself round in his chair and nodded towards the glass-fronted bookcase behind him, and Buchanan, following his lead, picked out volumes by Montessori, Carl Doman, Rudolph Steiner and other authors that rang a bell as respected educationalists.

'I'm not saying I didn't enjoy it, mind,' Grampa admitted. 'But it was a responsibility I hadn't looked for at that stage in my life. And it was a worry too, knowing that I had to have them standing on their own two feet before I kicked the bucket.'

Buchanan had to smile. 'You succeeded there with Fizz anyway,' he said. 'She's the most confident, self-sufficient person I think I've ever met.'

Grampa looked into the fire. In the silence, the resonant tick of the grandfather clock in the corner sounded like a kettle drum. 'There was no use getting them too tied to an old man who could go at any time. They had to go away to school and learn to rely on themselves.' He drank some of his whisky, closing his eyes to savour the taste. Then he smiled. 'Colin, now. He turned out a credit to me. Stuck in at school and at university, got himself a good degree and a good job, never gave me a moment's worry in his life.'

Buchanan was beginning to feel the effect of the spirits. The only lighting in the room was from a standard lamp and, in the resultant gloom, it was becoming increasingly difficult to focus on Grampa's head. He was also feeling increasingly saddened by Grampa's attitude to his granddaughter. He said, 'You didn't do too badly with Fizz either.'

'Fizz?' Grampa barked, beetling his brows again. 'She never made a damn bit of use of anything I ever gave her – piano lessons, private schooling, art school – money down the drain! I wanted her to have a career so that she would be independent financially, but no, she wasn't interested in that. She should have a husband and children of her own by this time, but there's no sign of that either.'

Buchanan chose one of Grampa's two heads and squinted at it. 'She's determined to get her law degree. Actually, she puts in a lot of work—'

'Pshaw! She'll never stick to it, mark my words. I give her another term at the most.' He stood up and went to the cupboard for another bottle. 'Highland Park. This one's from Orkney. They still have their own maltings and their own peat cuttings beside the distillery for drying the barley, and you can smell the heather through the peat. Tell me what you think of it.'

Buchanan, having throughout this lecture tried to refuse the glass, found himself unable to resist. But this was definitely the last. Definitely.

'I know it's not for me to say,' he heard himself utter, before he took time to consider what he was about. As he caught himself, Grampa waved a magnanimous hand for him to continue and he thought, what the hell?

'It's none of my business, right? But it seems to me that . . .' The words he meant to use floated out of his mind, leaving it totally void, and then came back to him like an echo. 'She's OK, you know. Fizz. You wanted her to be independent: well, she is. She can look after herself better in this world than anybody else I know and she doesn't let just anybody close enough to hurt her. She knows exactly what she wants from life and she knows how to get it. The only trouble is: she doesn't want what you want for her.'

'She wants to waste her life floating around the world till she's too old to do anything else,' Grampa grumbled into his glass. 'What's she going to fall back on when she's too old to do that sort of thing? Eh? She's not going to be twenty-seven and pretty all her days.'

Buchanan, having promised himself he wouldn't, took another mouthful of Highland Park. That was the crucial mouthful. That was the one that kicked down the gates of reason and let in the forces of folly.

He sat forward in his chair in the hope of improving his

focus. 'You made her what she is,' he said thickly. 'You taught her to live her own life . . . make her own choices . . . y'taught her not to be swayed by other people's opinions. Now you want to dictate to her and you don't like it when she goes her own way.'

Grampa shook his head. He seemed to Buchanan to go on shaking it a trifle longer than was strictly necessary. 'I only want her to be happy.'

'But, she *is* happy,' Buchanan grinned, this enigma striking him as frightfully amusing. 'She does exactly what she wants to do at any given time and she wants for nothing. Thing is . . . thing is . . . ha-ha-ha . . . she's perfectly adapted to her environment.'

The sound of his own laughter shocked him into momentary sobriety but, as Grampa had nothing to say in reply, he rambled on, graciously sharing his sudden clarity of vision.

'See . . . it's a different world out there today. Even if she'd got her art degree, chances are she'd be unemployed anyway. And marriage? What kind of man could Fizz promise to love, honour and obey? Do people still do that, anyway?'

Grampa began nodding with exaggerated sagacity, his head wobbling about like one of those fake dogs you see on the rear windowsills of passing cars. Buchanan, by this time, saw nothing strange in this.

'Things change, Tam, and you don't always notice them changing here in Am Bealach. Maybe Fizz knows better than I do how to live out there.' He performed a strangely balletic gesture towards the window. 'But it's hard to stand back and let her make her own mistakes.'

'They may not turn out to be mistakes,' Buchanan said, but he had a little difficulty with the tip of his tongue and had to repeat the words for Grampa's benefit. His throat was becoming irritated with speaking so loudly and he had a great longing to lay his head on the back of his chair and have a short snooze.

'That's true,' Grampa said, blinking owlishly at the far wall as though deeply moved by the revelation. 'That's very true, you know. It's the absolute truth. My God, Tam, that's the truest thing I ever heard in my life . . . What was it again?'

Buchanan couldn't remember. He heard himself saying, 'People can't all be th' same. Easy f'r you'n me t' say . . . shouldn't do this 'r that . . . we've got . . . we've got backup . . . we've . . .' The thought escaped him and he fell abruptly silent.

Grampa was slumped in his armchair opposite with his chin on his chest and his arms dangling to the floor. His eyes appeared to be closed.

Buchanan smiled gently to himself, kicked off his shoes and gave himself up to euphoria. He had never before heard a clock with such a rich, dark brown, satisfying tick, or known a room so imbued with calm and comfort. His armchair cradled him like a mother's arms and the warmth of the fire on the soles of his feet was utterly delicious. As his eyelids started to droop he felt himself drift blissfully into nirvana.

'Tell you what,' Grampa said, lurching to his feet with startling alacrity. 'There's a bottle of ten-year-old Macallan in that very cupboard. I was keeping it for a spesh . . . special occasion, but och . . .'

He produced a golden bottle that sparkled like a lit fuse in the firelight. The red warning label on its side proclaimed, 'THIS WHISKY IS 100% PROOF', but the words wobbled before Buchanan's eyes and had no meaning.

Chapter Seventeen

Around about the time Buchanan was starting on the Highland Park Fizz was in the kitchen, phoning Rowena.

'What's the latest bulletin on Lindsay?' she was saying.

Rowena's voice was so weak and shaky you'd have thought it was she who'd cracked her skull. 'He's sleeping quite peacefully, the nurse says.'

'The nurse? What nurse?'

'Oh . . . Lindsay refused to go to hospital so Dr Downie sent a nurse to sit with him tonight, just in case there are any complications. He gave me some tablets so that I could get a night's sleep.'

Fizz made a rude noise. 'Tablets! What do you need tablets for, Rowena, for God's sake? There's bugger all wrong with you, and if you're going to need tablets every time Lindsay or Briony get a tap on the head you're going to be brain dead by the time you're forty! Throw them away.'

She heard Rowena sigh.

'Maybe I won't need them.'

'You won't,' Fizz felt confident in assuring her. By the time Rowena hit her pillow tonight she'd be ready to sleep like a log. But, first things first.

'Listen,' she said, 'what I wanted to ask you . . . did you ever hear Alistair say he would like to bury his mother in their garden?'

231

Silence.

'Did you, Rowena?'

More silence, then Rowena coughed delicately and said, with perhaps just a little too much emphasis, 'No, I never did. He never said anything like that to me, Fizz.'

'But that's what Alistair and Lindsay quarrelled about, right?'

'I don't know what they quarrelled about.'

'Just stop acting the cretin, OK, Rowena? You can put two and two together as well as I can, and I can tell you're not surprised at the suggestion, so you must have thought about it.'

Silence. Then, 'Mrs Munroe did say to me once, a couple of years ago, that she'd love to be buried in the garden and I said I thought it was a good idea. But that's the last I heard of it. OK, I admit it did cross my mind that Lindsay and Alistair could have fallen out over that, but I really don't know.'

'All right,' Fizz said, satisfied that Rowena knew the score. 'But there are two questions we do have to ask, and those are: (a) did Alistair bury his mother in the garden without Lindsay's permission: And (b) is he now so scared that Lindsay might suspect him that he's willing to shove him in the Stronach to shut him up?'

Rowena sounded for a moment like she was gargling with sawdust. 'What are you thinking of, Fizz? Alistair wouldn't dream of hurting Lindsay! He helped Tam to save him, for goodness' sake!'

'I hope you're right, Rowena,' Fizz told her. 'But are you willing to take the risk? If Alistair has flipped his lid Lindsay could be in danger. And what about Bessie and the camper? Doesn't it make you scared?' She paused as a loud burst of laughter echoed down the passageway behind her, and then she went on, 'We can't let things continue like this, can we? We either tell the police or we find out whether our suspicions are correct. Maybe Mrs Munroe isn't in the garden after all.'

'But, how can we find out? Alistair would deny it.'

'We dig, of course.'

'Dig?' Rowena squeaked. Fizz could picture her reeling backwards. 'You and *I*? The whole *garden*?'

'Not the whole garden, you plonker. I've got a pretty good idea where she is, if she hasn't gone up in smoke like we're supposed to think. It won't take us long. The rain's stopped.'

'*Tonight*? Are you asking me to dig up Alistair's garden *tonight*?' Her voice kept getting higher and higher and her diction faster and faster till it sounded as though she'd been sniffing helium. 'You're mad, Fizz!'

'It has to be tonight,' Fizz told her calmly. 'Buchanan's wondering about Alistair as well and you know what he's like. Official channels. He'd drop Alistair in the shit whether he were sure Mrs Munroe was in the garden or not. If we want to prevent her being disinterred we have to find out for ourselves.'

'But . . . but Alistair will see us . . . or hear us digging.'

'No he won't. The place where I think he buried her is well away from the house and we'll wait till it's good and dark. About one o'clock.'

Rowena made choking noises followed by several false starts before she stuttered, 'You must see that's quite impossible, Fizz. I don't know what you're thinking of to suggest it! I mean . . . I mean . . . to propose that I leave my baby and my sick husband and start digging up someone's garden in the middle of the night . . .!'

'You mean, you have a better idea? Or maybe you're in favour of letting Alistair stew in his own juice?'

'No, not that. Of course not but . . . I can't, Fizz. I just can't do it.'

'Why not? Lindsay has a nurse to look after him. Tell her

you're going to take your sleeping pills and ask her to keep an eye on Briony. Easiest thing in the world. It won't take more than a couple of hours.'

Rowena said nothing, but Fizz could hear her breathing fast and shallow. In the silence the sound of a car engine swelled and died as headlights panned across the window. 'That's Myra bringing Auntie Duff back from the Women's Guild,' she told Rowena. 'I'll have to go. See you at Alistair's gate at one o'clock.'

She rang off quickly, before Rowena could put forward any more arguments, and was making herself a cup of cocoa when Auntie Duff and Myra came in. 'Hi, you two. Had a nice evening?' she said.

Auntie Duff kicked off her shoes and sat down, wriggling her chubby toes. 'Very nice. Quite a few there tonight.'

'Elspeth McBain showed us the slides of her holiday in the Holy Land and then we had a selection of music-hall songs from the ladies of the committee.' Myra draped her jacket over a chair and put the kettle on with the air of one taking part in a long-established ritual. 'The minister's wife won the competition for the best jar of home-made chutney.'

'Sounds like an absolute rave. Sorry I missed it,' said Fizz.

Buchanan's voice, loud but indistinct, echoed across the passageway from the lounge. 'I said . . . no, listen . . . listen . . . whassit matter in the end, right? Whassit goin' t'matter in a hundred years?'

He was answered by a burst of hysterical laughter from Grampa which ended in a noisy fit of coughing.

Auntie Duff's face froze. 'Who's that in there with your grampa? He's not going through his malts with Tam, is he? The last time he did that – when Colin was here the Hogmanay before last – he was ill for a week! You'd better go and put an end to it.'

'Who, me? No way!' It suited Fizz's arrangements just fine
to have Buchanan and Grampa conveniently stoned and, quite
apart from that consideration, it was nice to see Grampa
having a bit of fun. The times she'd heard him laugh so
heartily could be counted on the fingers of a three-toed sloth
and still leave it able to order two beers.

'Well, *I'm* certainly not going in there,' Auntie Duff said
hotly.

'Why should you?' Myra said, spooning tea into the teapot.
'It's not as if he makes a habit of it, and I'm sure Tam won't
take more than is good for him. He's a very moderate drinker
but I dare say he might feel the need of a medicinal dram or
two after his nasty experience today. Goodness knows, he
earned it.'

'Indeed he did.' Auntie Duff beamed as though it was she
herself who had been complimented. 'We're all very proud of
him, aren't we, Fizz? He was lucky to – there's a nice date and
walnut loaf in that tin, dear – he was lucky to get off with
nothing but a cut leg.'

Myra glanced over her shoulder at Fizz and turned back to
the teapot before she said, 'I've never known you to bring a
boyfriend home before, Fizz. Are we to assume there's something special about Tam?'

Fizz narrowly avoided choking on her cocoa. 'He's my boss,
Myra. That's all. Just my boss.'

'Oh . . . sorry! Did I put my foot in it? I just thought—'
Myra fluttered her hand apologetically, but the gesture looked
a little exaggerated. 'You seem to have such a nice relationship
I naturally—'

'Well, you were quite wrong. We exist in a state of armed
truce, most of the time, so don't start saving up for a set of
Tupperware.'

It was a fortunate turn of phrase since it reminded Auntie

Duff that someone was coming from Stirling to give a Tupperware demonstration in a few weeks' time and the conversation took a more comfortable turn.

Fizz escaped as soon as she could and headed for her room, pausing momentarily at the lounge door to listen to Grampa confiding soulfully that he'd always wanted to be a doctor.

In her bedroom she tried to bone up on the law of delict for a while but gave up when she'd read the same page three times without absorbing anything. It was by then after midnight so she tidied away her notebooks and looked out an old pair of navy trousers and her hiking boots. With the hood of her dark green jacket pulled over her hair she felt fairly well camouflaged as she stepped out into the pitch-blackness of the yard.

It was still dry, but the sky was completely overcast and a cold wind was whipping in across the loch, bringing a scent of snow from the high tops. She had to feel her way around the corner of the steadings to the barn where she had, earlier, placed a piece of polythene and a couple of spades where she knew she could put her hand on them without switching on her torch. Luath and Bess came rushing at her from their beds in the straw, barking like werewolves, but they shut up as soon as they smelled her hands and skulked back into the shadows. She thought it unlikely that anyone would bother investigating the cause of the disturbance – certainly not Grampa who, judging by the silence in the lounge as she had passed, was probably dead to the world.

The farm road posed no difficulty to Fizz, even with neither moon nor stars to guide her step. She had walked its length a thousand times in darkness and knew every bend and pothole like the lines on her grampa's face. She didn't have to use her torch till she was well past the crossroads because the outside light in the Clachan car park was still on and gave enough illumination to guide her to within a five-minute walk of

Alistair's cottage. As she approached, she was afraid of falling into the ditch so she slowed to a careful pace and used the torch in short bursts to check her heading.

Rowena was late. Fizz had been lurking in the bushes opposite Alistair's gate for about ten minutes when she heard soft footfalls on the roadway and saw a patch of deeper shadow move against the outline of the lilac tree.

'Psst!' she said, and the shadow gave a galvanised leap.

'Where are you?'

'Over here in the bushes.'

Rowena stumbled across the verge, put one foot in the ditch, and fell against Fizz, pushing her into a bramble bush.

'Listen,' she said, when Fizz had finished swearing, 'this is madness, Fizz. Please tell me you're not going through with it. What if we're found out? We're bound to leave traces and—'

'Be quiet,' Fizz told her sternly. 'I'm not totally simple, you know. Nobody is going to find out.'

'How can we dig up a garden without leaving a mess?' Rowena demanded, pushing her face close to Fizz's in an effort to see her better. 'It's impossible!'

'You don't think he buried her in a flowerbed, do you? Don't be such a plook, Rowena – she's under that pile of earth that he dug out for the pool or I'm Bugs Bunny.'

'*No*! I don't believe it!' hissed Rowena, hyperventilating against Fizz's cheek. 'Are you sure? He told me he was going to plant heathers on it!'

'That proves it. Anyone else would have used it as topsoil elsewhere in the garden. If he's leaving it where it is, it must be because his mother is underneath. Come on, let's take a look.'

'I really don't want to do this,' Rowena pleaded, hanging on to Fizz's jacket, her faint Irish accent stronger now she was upset. 'Apart from anything else, I don't think it's right to disturb a . . . a corpse.'

'We're not going to disturb her,' said Fizz. 'We're just going to establish whether there's a coffin in there. If there isn't, we'll put the soil back and come away, and nobody will be any the wiser. There's absolutely no danger.'

The possibility that they might find not just one corpse but two had not escaped Fizz but she felt it wiser to airbrush over these minor details for the time being in case Rowena took off up the glen road like a startled mustang.

They let themselves into the garden by the double gates that opened on the driveway at the side. The estate Land Rover was parked just inside and a *leylandii* hedge hid them from anyone with superhuman night vision who might have been watching from the cottage. Using the torch as little as possible, they scuttled, staggered and slid down the slope of the lawn till the smell of wet loam told them they had reached the empty pool.

Alistair had already lined the cavity with thick black polythene and appeared, also, to be making a start on planting the heather hillock. There were twenty or thirty heather plants in pots standing beside a white sack of ericaceous compost and a few small conifers had already been planted but, luckily, not at a point where they might get in the way of an exploratory excavation of the type Fizz visualised. She handed Rowena a spade and unfolded the piece of polythene she'd brought with her, spreading it out on the grass at the foot of the mound.

'Right. I think you should dig straight in at this angle and put the soil here on the polythene sheet. If you hit anything solid let me know. I'll do the same here, in the middle.'

It wasn't as easy as Fizz had expected it to be. Instead of the pile of loosely packed earth that it should have formed, the soil had been trampled firm and was now set like cement. Every time the spade hit a stone it transmitted a shock wave right up her arms into her skull, making her teeth rattle and doing terrible things to her *joie de vivre*. Rowena, who was taking the job somewhat more slowly, suffered less from this problem and appeared, now that she had resigned herself to being involved, to be applying herself quite resolutely to the task.

'She's not in this mound,' she panted while they were having one of several rest periods. 'I'm certain we're wasting our time with this.'

'Well, I hope you're right,' Fizz said, wiping away a trickle of sweat that was dripping off the end of her nose. 'I'd be delighted to know that we were wrong about Alistair.'

'I've been thinking about it and I'm certain that Alistair dug out the pond weeks before his mother died. Way back in the springtime. Before Bessie went missing. You'd think, if he meant to bury his mother here, he'd have waited till she died before excavating the pond.'

'Yes, but it might have been Mrs Munroe's wish to have a pond here, as Alistair claims,' Fizz suggested. 'Or . . . even if they'd picked out this spot as her burial place she might have wanted to see it started before she slipped away. It would be easy enough for Alistair to dig a hole in the newly dug earth and put his mother's real coffin in it in the dead of night.'

'I suppose so,' said Rowena, and they set to again, piling up their diggings on the square of polythene. It was hot work and Fizz, who had long ago discarded her jacket, was glad when the wind picked up. However, a little later she discovered that the breeze was not only cooling her but breaking up the cloud cover. Large patches of starry sky were appearing along the western horizon and it looked like it was only a matter of time before the moon came out.

'Rowena,' Fizz said, between spadefuls, 'I think we'd better get a move on, if we can. The moon's going to appear any minute now, and I know it's unlikely Alistair will be awake, but if he were, it's just possible he could spot us from the house.'

'Maybe we should stop now,' was Rowena's solution to the problem. 'I'm on my last legs and there's no sign of anything here where I'm digging.'

'We'll give it a couple of minutes more,' Fizz decided, 'then we'll call it a day, OK?'

Rowena slammed her spade into the earth in a tiny display of bad temper. 'What difference – *aaaaarrgh*!'

'*What*? What is it?'

'I hit something . . .'

Fizz pushed her out of the way and switched on the flashlight for a swift appraisal. A couple of scrapes with her spade disclosed a smooth surface that looked like wood.

'Shit!'

For a few seconds the only sound she could hear was the rustle of the leaves and Rowena panting in her ear.

'It's *her*, isn't it?' she asked Fizz eventually. 'It's her coffin.'

'I bloody hope it's hers,' Fizz told her, and tapped the wood to make sure she wasn't looking at a piece of old timber. It sounded hollow.

Rowena straightened. 'OK. What are we waiting for, Fizz? For heaven's sake, let's put the earth back and get out of here.'

There didn't seem much else to do, other than open the coffin, which even Fizz didn't much fancy.

They started throwing earth back into the holes they'd made, trampling it firm and trying, in so far as speed permitted, to keep the mess to a minimum.

The moon came out when they were only half finished but they ignored it and kept shovelling. They were stamping down the last few spadefuls when the garden gate clicked open behind them.

Fizz whirled round and gaped to see Alistair starting to

walk up the path towards the house. He was half turned away from them but his route would take him, within a few paces, barely ten feet from the hillock and he couldn't fail to see them. As she cast around frantically for cover, Fizz was just in time to see Rowena springing up the sloping lawn like a gazelle and darting behind the hedge. There was no time to weigh possibilities: she grabbed at the spades and polythene and followed suit.

She caught up with her abettor at the double gates, only because Rowena was struggling ineptly to unfasten the catch. Fizz did it for her and they sprinted up the drive towards Stronach Lodge and safety.

Fizz would have been quite happy to pause halfway to listen for sounds of pursuit but Rowena was going for gold and couldn't be halted. They were both completely winded by the time they staggered into the kitchen and rushed for the gin bottle.

Rowena was spitting tacks.

'Damn you, Fizz! You said there was absolutely no danger!' She sounded so Irish that Fizz half expected her to say "begorra". 'I could *kill* you! You've been doing this to me all my life! I wish I had a pound for every time you've got me into serious trouble! No danger, you said! We might have been in danger of our *lives* out there! You should have *realised* that Alistair might be out at night – it's his *job* to look out for poachers, dammit! I will never *ever* let you talk me into one of your insane schemes again, so don't dare try it!'

Fizz blinked her eyes at her innocently. 'Do I detect the subtle undertones of angst in your voice? Dear me! And I thought *I* was the injured party, having been left standing there like a dork with two spades and a polythene sheet in my hands, and egg all over my face. Where was my doughty companion then, might I ask? Hightailing it like all-get-out, that's where, with a hey nonny nonny and to hell with *you*, Guinevere, *I'm* over the drawbridge! Well, thanks a bunch!'

Rowena splashed gin into two tumblers and glugged half of hers before she answered.

'It was you who taught me to look after numero uno, Fizz. Anyway, there wasn't a thing I could have done to save the situation so don't start acting the martyr.'

Fizz had a strange feeling reminiscent of having dialled the wrong phone number and started a conversation with the wrong person. This was not the Rowena she had known for twenty-seven years. It wasn't even the Rowena she had come home to last summer. This was a new, improved-recipe Rowena, who had suddenly begun to learn the lessons her best friend had been trying to teach her since childhood. Is this what motherhood does to people, she wondered, and raised her gin in a silent toast.

'I'll tell you something, mavourneen,' she said, carrying her glass to the fridge and topping it up with Briony's orange juice. 'You do a hell of a lot of bleating before the event, but when the chips are down, you don't mess around.'

Rowena took that without noticeable gratification. 'If you've got to do a thing,' she shrugged, 'you might as well do it and get it over with. Tell you what though,' she added with a snigger, 'I couldn't help but see the tabloid headlines: "MP's Wife in Body Snatch Scandal". That would have given Lindsay's career hopes a real boost, wouldn't it?'

Fizz found this absolutely hilarious and for some minutes they were both rendered helpless by a fit of galloping giggles in which, no doubt, the release of tension played a predominant part.

'Well, at least Alistair doesn't appear to have seen us,' Fizz commented when they had got their breath back. 'He'd have come after us if he had, and I'm pretty sure he didn't do that. However, I don't see our cover-up job fooling him for long. If he goes out on the hill early tomorrow I think it would be a good idea for you to nip in and smooth out the earth a bit.'

White appeared all round Rowena's pupils. 'I wouldn't go back there if you put a gun to my head! I told you, Fizz, I'm finished with this business.'

'Not by a long chalk, you're not,' Fizz told her kindly. 'What if Alistair really is a killer? If he sees that grave mound all untidy he's going to know that somebody is on to him and who knows what he'll do? Maybe kill somebody else. Can you be sure you didn't leave anything behind that could point to you?'

Rowena's glass rattled against her teeth. 'Stop it, Fizz. You're just trying to frighten me.'

'OK. Forget it. But if he turns up here with a shotgun—'

'All right! I'll do it! Just stop going on about it, will you? But that's the last thing I'll ever do for you, Fizz. I mean that.'

'Well, actually, there is one tiny little favour I have to ask—'

'No. Absolutely not. I don't even want to hear about it.' Rowena got up, walked to the door and listened, then came back to her seat.

'It's not for me, it's for Alistair,' Fizz murmured.

Rowena regarded her suspiciously out of the corners of her eyes. 'You're sure about that?'

Fizz was about to say, Would I lie? and then decided to rephrase it. 'Of course, I'm sure. If we want to be certain that all he's done is bury his mother in the garden we're going to have to confront him—'

'No no no no no no no no no,' said Rowena like a machine gun. 'I'm not confronting anybody. No. Finish. Don't even think about it.'

Fizz looked at the ceiling. 'I'll do the confronting, Rowena, OK? All I want from you is backup.'

'No no no no . . .' etc.

'Listen, all you have to do is stand outside on the road while I talk to him. If the worst comes to the worst and he *is* a killer, he won't be able to do me any harm if he knows you're a witness. You could take your car if you like. All I need is for you to be there. If Alistair can clear himself to my satisfaction there may still be a chance that his mother can stay where she is.'

Rowena poured more gin into her tumbler. 'Why me? Couldn't Tam back you up?'

Fizz rolled her eyes. 'You are being facetious, I assume. Buchanan the Magnificent, friend of all, would have a fit of the vapours if he ever caught a whiff of what we've been up to. And who else would you want me to inform about what we found tonight? Simon or Myra? Old Malcolm? How do you think Lindsay would feel about them knowing the whole story? No, I think not, Rowena. I'm afraid you draw the short straw.'

'OK. But I want your promise that you'll never ask another favour of me as long as you live. Not this kind of favour.'

'Sure.'

'And not tomorrow. I just couldn't face it tomorrow.'

'No, tomorrow's out for me too. Buchanan and I are going to Plochaig and I don't know when we'll get back. We'll have to try to corner Alistair on Saturday morning. That's his day off – isn't it? – so he'll probably be about the garden. You'd better make sure you've tidied up the mound before then.'

Rowena nodded unhappily. She got up and peered out into the darkness before drawing the curtains carefully across the window. Then she locked the door and slid the bolt across.

'You could sleep here tonight, if you want to,' she said, with a lightness that sounded a little forced. 'It would save you walking home in the dark.'

It would also, Fizz thought, save walking past Alistair's cottage and wondering if he was waiting there for her with a gralloching knife or a knotted scarf.

'OK, Rowena,' she said. 'If it'll make you feel any safer.'

Chapter Eighteen

Conversation at breakfast time was, to put it mildly, sluggish. Grampa made no reference to the night before, other than to pour Buchanan an aperitif of Barr's Irn-Bru, the traditional Scottish cure for a hangover. Auntie Duff was patently in the huff with her husband and even Fizz appeared subdued, yawning and dreaming over her porridge as though she hadn't slept well.

Buchanan himself was suffering less physical punishment for his evening of indiscretion than he felt he deserved. There was a headache hovering in the wings when he awoke but it never quite got its act together and, although his stomach quivered at first sight of his porridge, he felt better once it was down.

Mentally, however, he was extremely tender. He winced every time he was scalded by the recollection of yet another of his inane utterances, and could only hope that Grampa had not been paying close attention. There had been times in the past when he'd had a skinful but, apart from the occasion of his brother's stag night, when he had won a packet of Day-Glo condoms in a karaoke contest, he had never been quite so blootered.

The only plus was that Fizz had retired early to her room and knew nothing about the business. He felt fragile enough this morning without having to face her *Schadenfreude*, and the possibility of her being in possession of material that she could use to blackmail him would have caused him acute uneasiness.

He felt safe enough to admit to her that he felt the need of some fresh air before they set off for Plochaig. This was perfectly true, but he also wanted to be sure that no lingering traces of alcoholic poisoning remained to put him above the driving limit.

'OK, Kimosabe,' Fizz said amicably. 'I wouldn't mind a walk.'

'Up to the crossroads and back? Is that enough for you?' Buchanan suggested.

'Um . . . no,' she said quickly, as though she had taken a sudden dislike to that locale. 'Let's go along the loch shore. It's more sheltered.'

There wasn't much wind, as far as Buchanan could tell, but one route was as pleasant as another so they headed for the beach and turned in the opposite direction to that which Buchanan had covered before. Luath and Selena had both joined the party before they had gone a hundred yards.

'I suppose,' Buchanan said, as the thought occurred to him, 'that we should phone and find out how Lindsay is this morning.'

'He's fine,' Fizz said, and was immediately overcome with a fit of coughing. When she recovered she added, 'I phoned before breakfast and Rowena said he'd had a good night and there didn't seem to be any complications.'

'Well, thank God for that anyway,' Buchanan said.

'You mean, thank God it's not another murder?'

Buchanan supposed that was what he did mean. It reminded him of something else he wanted to ask Fizz. 'Did you know that Alistair's parents had both been married twice?'

'Had they?' She squeezed her hands into the pockets of her jeans and frowned at the path ahead. 'Yes, his father had, I'm pretty sure, but that was well before my time. I've heard Grampa speak of his first wife. She had a lovely singing voice, I believe, and always sang at the ceilidhs. Alistair's mother? No, I didn't know it was a second marriage for her as well. Who told you that?'

'Grampa and Auntie Duff. I remembered just last night that one of them said she was nearly forty when she came here, so she must have been no chicken when she had Alistair. Do you know what age she was when she did?'

Fizz was hopping from boulder to boulder across a stream and didn't answer till she'd reached the other side. 'Haven't the remotest clue. Of course, I've been away for years and, as far as I was concerned, she was an old lady all my life. She was like Bessie Anderson: we always meant to have them carbon dated but they wouldn't stand still.'

'Did they look alike?' Buchanan carried Selena across while Luath splashed through the shallows with great enjoyment.

Fizz stopped and looked back at him with speculation. 'No, not at all. Bessie was wee and plump with thick, silvery hair: Mrs Munroe was skinny, an inch or two taller, and had black brows like Alistair's.'

'But they were around the same age, no?'

'They looked it, yes.' She watched Selena tidily burying a small deposit in the sand and then said, 'I suppose, if Alistair is – what? Thirty-eight? – and his mother was forty-ish when she married his dad, she could easily have been knocking eighty, so you're probably right, there can't have been much between them.'

'Mm-hmm. That's interesting. I had imagined Alistair's mother to be no more than twenty-odd years his senior. Maybe late fifties, early sixties.'

It was obvious to Buchanan that she could follow his line of thinking but she didn't make any comment. Anything to do with Alistair's culpability was apparently a no-go area and she wasn't going to say anything that might help to incriminate him. However, he knew she wouldn't lie about facts that could be corroborated by other people.

'Were you at Mrs Munroe's funeral?' he asked.

'Uh-huh. It was lashing with rain but at least it was in the crematorium, not in the churchyard and there was a nosh-up at the Clachan afterwards.'

'Did anyone view the corpse? Was there a sort of "lying in state" sort of thing? Or a wake?'

Fizz made a noise that sounded like 'Ptchaw!' and added, 'We don't do any of that macabre nonsense around here. Just a quick service, sling them in the ground, or in the incinerator according to personal preference, and straight back home for a ham sandwich and a sweet sherry. No messing about. When I pop my clogs they'll probably just chuck me on the compost heap.'

Buchanan had a momentary vision of the little walled graveyard at the far end of the beach and felt a pang to think that there would be a stone for Fizz one day.

They reached a point where they could go no further without getting their feet wet, turned without a word and started to retrace their steps. Fizz launched into an enthusiastic dissertation about the edible mushrooms to be found in the beech woods, intending, no doubt, to guide the conversation on to more neutral topics, but when she wound down, Buchanan started to edge back on to his previous tack.

'You came home for Mrs Munroe's funeral but not for Briony's christening,' he remarked. 'Weren't you invited?'

Fizz wrinkled her nose and grinned guiltily. 'Officially, I had flu,' she said, 'but actually, I just couldn't face it. You know what these things are like. Well, you probably don't – not like they are in a small community – but I can tell you, they are mind-blowingly boring. But, I did send a pressie.'

Buchanan threw a stick for Luath who studiously looked the other way. 'Was Mrs Munroe invited?'

He heard Fizz sigh with resignation. 'If she was, it was only out of courtesy. So was Alistair, naturally, but neither of them came. Mrs Munroe was too ill and Alistair had to look after her. But Alistair did leave her for an hour or so, later in the afternoon, when Lindsay called him out to help look for Mrs Anderson. That, of course, was an emergency and he knows the immediate area better than anybody.'

'And it was about a fortnight later that his mother died?'

'About that, yes.' She stopped to check that Luath was following them and then looked Buchanan in the eye. 'So, you see, it doesn't tie in.'

'What doesn't tie in?'

'What you're thinking.'

'And what am I thinking?'

She drew her brows together. 'That Alistair killed Bessie Anderson and substituted her body for his mother's.'

'Well, if that's what I'm thinking, you're right, it doesn't tie in.'

'OK, smartass,' she snapped, with a glare that would have been lethal at close quarters. 'If *that's* not what you're thinking, what is?'

'I really don't know, Fizz. I'm just trying to get it straight in my head. Did Alistair really bury his mother in the garden? Did he kidnap Miss Anderson and keep her prisoner till his mother died before bumping her off? Did he kill the camper too? Or does Alistair have nothing to do with any of it?'

'Don't ask me,' Fizz said lightly, abandoning her irritation. 'I hate multiple choice questions. I vote we talk about something else till we see what we turn up at Plochaig.'

Buchanan was quite happy to go along with this suggestion since Fizz was clearly determined not to share any of her personal insights with him at this stage and he had gone about as far as he could go on his own. He had hoped to have made more progress before the end of his holiday but, unless they turned up something surprising at Plochaig, or Grampa's talk with Alistair bore fruit, he would be going home tomorrow with his tail between his legs.

It was late in the morning when they finally set off for Plochaig, which meant that they had to stop for lunch at Taynuilt. Buchanan ate sparingly, in deference to his beleaguered digestive processes, but Fizz worked her way assiduously through three courses, which meant that it was twenty past two when they finally drew up at the home of Mrs Sweeney and her son.

The doorbell awakened no response from within the house but a moment or two later, just as Fizz was starting to peep through the letterbox, they heard footsteps approaching at the side of the building.

Buchanan walked to the corner to meet them and found a fine-featured woman of about sixty-five wearing a baseball cap and a pair of painters' white overalls.

'Hello,' she said, in a surprised tone.

'Hello,' said Buchanan, and introduced himself and Fizz. 'Sorry to intrude, but we were hoping to have a word with your son. It's possible we may have a mutual acquaintance.'

'Really? Well, that's very nice.' Her deeply pitched, Gaelic intonation reminded Buchanan inexplicably of the peaty taste of Highland Park. She redirected her smile to include Fizz. 'Ian's working in the back yard. Why don't you come round?'

They followed her back down a side path that was overgrown with moss and weeds and found themselves in a cross between a farmyard and a refuse tip. There were animals everywhere, dogs, cats, goats, three lambs and a variety of fowls. They were climbing over, perching on, crawling under and swinging from a collection of metal rubbish that seemed to include everything from a vintage Ford to an old iron bedstead. The smell was something else.

'Ian,' said his mother, 'you have visitors, dear.'

A pair of legs slid out from below the Ford, followed by an oily T-shirt and a tanned face. Ian was very thin, with floppy, jaw-length, blond hair parted in the middle.

'Hi,' he said uncertainly, as his mother disappeared into a dilapidated shed. 'Do I know you?' His mouth was extraordinarily wide and smiley, but in speaking he appeared to make use only of the middle third, leaving the corners to carry on smiling.

Fizz shook her curls. 'No, but we're rather hoping you might know someone we're looking for.'

His smile widened till it was pointing at his ears. 'I hardly know anybody in Scotland now. I've lived mostly in London for over twenty years and I've been working in France since last September. I only got back last month.'

'That's OK,' said Fizz, fending off a border collie who found her perfume irresistible. 'Maybe you met him in France.'

'Oh, right. What's his name?'

'Ah . . . well, actually, that's one of the things we were hoping *you* could tell *us*,' Fizz said, twinkling at him on full beam. 'All we know is that he was carrying jeweller's rouge and we think it might have been for somebody in Plochaig.'

'Oh, Travis? Sure.'

Fizz started to say something – probably more explanation – but stopped and gawped at him as though she were afraid to believe her ears. Buchanan realised that he was doing the same. For three or four seconds the world stopped revolving, the dogs stopped sniffing, the hens stopped squawking, and the smell ceased to assault the nostrils.

Then Buchanan started to speak, cleared his throat and said, 'Travis? You knew him?'

'Sure. He's coming to visit me here any day now.'

'Well, actually . . .' Fizz started to say, but Buchanan poked her in the back and substituted, 'Is there somewhere we can sit down and have a talk?'

Ian looked quickly from one of them to the other and used one forefinger to flick his hair back from his brow. His smile faded. 'Come on into the house.'

They went through a stone-floored laundry, dotted with feeding bowls, and crossed a passageway to a rather attractive sitting room with a low ceiling and small windows. Buchanan used the hiatus to introduce himself and Fizz.

'Look . . . I hardly knew this guy,' Ian said, getting immediately agitated by the revelation that the law was involved. He twitched a hand towards the chairs grouped about the fire. 'If he was caught carrying drugs—'

'No, no. There's no question of his being guilty of any law infringement,' Buchanan said.

Ian continued to look uneasy. 'What's up, then?' he asked.

'Well, for a start,' Buchanan said, beating Fizz to it by a short head, 'I have to tell you that your friend . . . Travis . . . died last month.'

Ian looked sombre but not unduly upset by this news. 'What did he die of?' he asked.

'I'm afraid he appears to have been murdered.'

Fizz leaped in at this point to elaborate. 'He'd been camping quite close to Loch Tay, but his body was found up in the hills a couple of weeks ago. The police say there must have been foul play. There was a package of jeweller's rouge in his tent and Plochaig was circled on his map so we thought . . .'

Ian clasped his hands between his knees and regarded them glumly. 'I wondered why it was taking him so long to show up. He phoned at least six weeks ago, saying he was on his way north and I asked him to pick up some jeweller's rouge so that I could finish the new mirror I'm grinding for my telescope. I kept waiting for him to show up but . . . this is a bit of a shock.'

Buchanan gave him a moment to think about it, then said, 'The unfortunate thing about it is that because there was very little left behind in the tent he'd been using, it's been impossible to establish his identity. That's where you can help us.'

'Sure. Anything I can do,' Ian nodded, and then thought about it and added, 'Except . . . I don't know that I actually knew him that well. I don't think I even knew his second name.'

Fizz started to say, 'Shhhiii—' but caught Buchanan's eye and stopped herself.

Buchanan chewed the side of his lip. 'Maybe it will come to you,' he said, accepting the bludgeoning of fate with saintly stoicism. 'Why don't you just tell us where you met him and anything else you may remember about him? It's surprising how small a detail can sometimes help to put us on the right trail.'

'Sure.' Ian thought for a minute and said slowly, 'He was backpacking around France, working his way up towards the Channel. I ran across him in February, in a bar in Provence. He was trying to ask the barman if he knew of a campsite nearby, and the barman hadn't a clue what he was going on about, so I offered to translate. We had a couple of beers together and, in the end, I said he could set up his tent in my garden for the night.'

He stopped and looked at his hands again, picking at the

dirt under his nails as though it had suddenly become important to be tidy. Then he said, diffidently, 'I don't know if I ought to be saying this, but he was one of those guys you can't get rid of. At the start, all he needed was a camping site. Then I found myself offering him a bath. Then the one night had become a week and he was tapping me for a loaf of bread or a bottle of milk or a can of beer every damn day. You know the scene. Finally, I had to tell him the party was over but, by then, he knew I was going home in a couple of weeks and he knew my mother's address, here in Plochaig. Actually, I was pretty sicked off when he phoned to say he was coming to visit, but he said he'd probably only come for a couple of days as he'd be staying with someone else. He didn't say who, but I think it was in some place with a Gaelic name.'

'Did he tell you anything about his background?' Fizz prompted, disappointment still showing in her face.

Ian did his best to cheer her up. 'His mother had just died and left him a little money so he was bumming around as long as it lasted, I gathered. His father was dead – he'd been a shopkeeper of some sort.' He stopped and furrowed his brows. 'To tell you the truth, we didn't talk much after the first evening. I got to avoiding him if I could.'

'Was he headed anywhere in particular?' said Buchanan.

'London, initially.' Ian's puckish smile returned, showing his relief at being able to supply definite information. 'That's where he was going when he left France. He didn't expect to get to Scotland till a couple of weeks after that. Then he intended to look up somebody in that place I mentioned. I forget—'

'Am Bealach?' Fizz asked, before Buchanan could prevent her from putting words into a witness's mouth. 'Is that where his friend was?'

'That's right – Amb . . . Amb Yallick . . . what you said. I think he planned to stay there for a long time – till the autumn at least, he said – but I suspected he wasn't sure of his welcome and that was why he was contacting me again. In case he needed a fail-safe, you know?'

Buchanan looked at Fizz. She was staring fixedly at the floor as though she were trying to decide which of the Am Bealach inmates she could connect to this wandering boy.

'Can't you think of anything else he told you?' she roused herself to say, which wasted a further ten minutes while Ian dredged up a wealth of useless details mainly concerning Travis's opinions of French plumbing, the *gendarmerie*, and the propensity of French dogs to bite first and ask questions later.

'What did he look like?' Fizz demanded.

'Jeez . . . it was weeks ago.' Ian pursed his lips. 'Big guy. Heavy for his age. He had darkish brown hair that he wore in a pigtail, or sometimes just in a bunch at the back. A bit of an ape.'

'Not good-looking, you mean?'

'Definitely not. And scary when he got riled.'

Fizz leaned back in her chair, her posture signifying to Buchanan that she had asked all the questions she could think to ask at the moment. He too felt that he had scraped the bottom of the barrel but he made no move to wind up the conversation because he could see that Ian was still thinking about Travis and there was always the hope that he could still come up with something.

He didn't, but Fizz did.

'Did you ever see Travis with a fake hand and a woman's blonde wig, Ian?'

'Uh-huh,' said Ian calmly, as though he were waiting for the second part of the question.

'You *did*?' exclaimed both Fizz and Buchanan in perfect unison.

'Sure.'

'What did he carry stuff like that around with him for?' Fizz asked, and waited, open-mouthed, for his answer.

'It was his burglar-proofing,' Ian said. 'Every time he went off for the day and left his tent behind he used to fake up a body in his sleeping bag. Just stuffed it full of clothes and put the wig and hand in position. I don't mind telling you, the first time I looked in, it gave me a helluva fright.'

Fizz pointed her chin at the ceiling and laughed till she was red in the face and Buchanan had to join in, leaving Ian smiling companionably but somewhat in the dark.

'We've been puzzling over that for weeks,' Fizz explained, when she got her wind back. 'It was Buchanan and I who found the tent, you see, but my idiot dog got in first and dragged out the sleeping bag, so we didn't see the setup as Travis left it.'

Ian's smile widened. 'Well, I'm glad I managed to solve part of the mystery at least.'

'It's been most helpful to talk to you,' Buchanan said and stood up, making all the usual polite noises as he led the way to the door. There was no sign of Ian's unconventional mother as they wended their way through the menagerie but the blue-white light of an oxyacetylene welding tool was glinting beyond the windows of the wooden hut.

'Mum does metal sculpture,' Ian said, as though it were a matter of little interest. 'You have to have a hobby here or go mad.'

'Metal sculpture and astronomy,' Fizz said, making conversation as he walked them to the gate. 'Interesting hobbies. You must get a good view of the western sky from here. No streetlights to bother you.'

'It's pretty good, yes. I'm actually an industrial photographer, and when I was in France—'

He broke off and halted for a moment as though a thought had struck him. 'You know, I do believe I took a snap of Travis – maybe two with my small camera. If so, the film is still in there. I haven't used it since I got home.' He looked at Buchanan and Fizz, nodded, and started back to the house. 'Won't be a minute.'

'We should have thought to ask him about photos,' Buchanan said, irritated with himself.

'Oh pooh! The silly fart should have thought to tell us before now. He knew we were interested in what Travis looked like.'

Ian came trotting down the path with a roll of film in the usual black tube. 'You can keep it,' he said, handing it to Buchanan. 'There's nothing of interest on it or I'd have developed it long ago. In fact, I've only taken a couple of shots and I think they must both have Travis in them. I hope they're of some use to you.'

'I'm sure they will be,' Buchanan said, overstating the case a tad in the interests of politeness. 'You must let me pay you for the film.'

There was a short argument which ended in Ian trousering a fiver.

'You realise we're going to have to take this evidence to the police?' Buchanan said. 'I'm afraid they're probably going to be dropping in on you this weekend sometime.'

Ian didn't seem to be at all perturbed by this information but Fizz was blazing with suppressed indignation and could scarcely wait till they were back in the car before exploding.

'Take it to the police?' she raged 'You're not going to give this to those CID tossers before we've even had a look at it, are you? All this work – all this honest-to-God sleuthing we've put in to get this bloody snapshot – and you're going to drop it in their laps just like that? Buchanan, if you do this to me, I'll never forgive you, you swine, I swear—'

'Listen,' said Buchanan.

'What?'

'Do you know what the penalty is for withholding evidence? Do you really want to have that on your record when you sit your final exams?'

That shut her up for a second; but only for a second.

'Nobody knows we've got it. We don't even know whether there's a decent shot of Travis on the film. Surely there's a case for making sure of that before we waste police time?'

Buchanan wiggled the gear stick in neutral while he fought with his conscience. He was just as curious as Fizz was to see what Travis looked like and besides, there was really every chance that they could talk their way out of it. It did, however, smack of a certain moral turpitude which he found distasteful.

'We can find one of those fast-print services,' Fizz insisted. 'What possible difference could a few hours make? Don't be such an old fuddy-duddy, Buchanan. Live dangerously for once!'

'On your head be it,' Buchanan sighed, and let in the clutch.

The thought that really niggled him was that he was getting to be more like Fizz every day.

Chapter Nineteen

Fizz was rabid to see the photographs developed as soon as possible. There was a twenty-four hour service in Killin which would return them by noon the next day but there was no way they could make it back to Killin by 4 p.m., which was as late as they could leave it to hand in the film.

In the end, they stopped at Crianlarich, about twelve miles from home, and dropped if off there. This meant that Buchanan would have to drive back to get the prints in the morning, but that was better than waiting till Monday.

Buchanan showed no interest in walking up to the Clachan after dinner, probably because he still had enough alcohol in his system to last him a fortnight. He flopped out in front of the TV with Auntie Duff, seemingly unaffected by the constant, 'What did she say there? Turn it up a bit,' from Grampa and Auntie Duff's irritating practice of commenting on everybody's clothes, complaining at length about any bad language and spotting John Gielgud in every crowd scene.

Feeling she wasn't missing anything, Fizz put in four hours' study in her room and fell asleep planning what she'd say to Alistair in the morning.

Since Buchanan left early to do a bit of last-minute shopping before picking up the film, she was able, on the pretext of enquiring after Lindsay, to get a lift with him as far as the big house. He wanted to come in with her but was dissuaded without too much difficulty, it being unlikely that he'd see Lindsay anyway.

Rowena opened the door looking so pale she was almost translucent. She was still in her dressing gown and Briony was asleep in her arms.

'Hi. How's Lindsay?' Fizz asked, getting that out of the way first, because she had told Buchanan that's what she was there for and she had a preference for telling the truth when it wasn't too much of an inconvenience.

'He's much better but the doctor wants him to stay in bed for another day. What are you doing here? I thought we were to meet at Alistair's cottage?'

Fizz followed her into the kitchen and sat down at the table. 'Buchanan gave me a lift. We located a couple of photographs of the dead camper yesterday at Plochaig and we left them in Crianlarich to be developed. He's gone to get them.'

'Photographs? Of the camper? Where did you—'

'It's a long story, Rowena. I'll tell you all about it later. For God's sake go and get dressed, I don't want Buchanan back here and looking for me before we've seen Alistair.'

'You're sure you still think it's a good idea—'

'It's the *only* idea, Rowena. Can you think of any other way of handling this thing without going to the police and having them digging up Mrs Anderson? 'Cos I can't.'

'But, if he turns nasty—'

'He's not going to turn nasty with you standing outside with Lindsay's mobile phone in your hand and two nines already dialled, now is he? Alistair may – just possibly – have gone over the score a bit, but he's not a madman. Now go and get ready.'

'I'm scared—'

'JUST DO IT, ROWENA!'

Rowena gave a small bleat and fled from the room, cradling Briony's head to her shoulder. Fizz could hear her bare feet pattering away across the parquet flooring of the hallway. In about five minutes she came back wearing something brown and droopy and carrying her car keys.

'I think I'd feel safer in the car,' she said. 'That's OK, isn't it?'

'Of course. As long as you park it where Alistair can see you from the window.'

'What if he has a gun?'

Fizz closed her eyes. 'He has a gun, Rowena, you know that. He probably has several. But, believe me, he won't use them. If it worries you, you can park at the front wall where you'll be almost completely screened. You'll be perfectly safe, I promise you.'

'Don't *promise* me, Fizz, OK? Just don't promise me anything. Every time you promise me something, everything starts going wrong.' She scrambled into Lindsay's Mercedes and barely allowed Fizz time to get in before speeding down the drive with an alarming graunching of gears. 'Just don't take all day, that's all. I'm supposed to be going to Killin for nappies so if I'm not back in an hour . . . And if you ever tell Lindsay – if you ever tell *anybody* I had a hand in this . . . this is the last time, I'm telling you, Fizz, don't ever do this again—'

There was no shutting her up. By the time they stopped outside the cottage it sounded like she was on fast forward and you could hardly make out the words. It was a relief to get out and slam the door on her.

Alistair was sitting on his bench beside the front door. Fizz's heart started bungee jumping as he spotted her and stood up, but he didn't come to meet her, he just stood there soberly watching her come up the path towards him. She attempted a smile but it wasn't much of a success.

'Morning, Alistair,' she said a bit throatily, and saw instantly, by his expression, that he knew what she was there for.

'Hello, Fizz.'

'You know what I'm here for?'

His eyes left her for a moment to glance at Rowena in the car, and then he looked back at her and sighed.

'Aye. So it was you?'

'It was us,' Fizz admitted, indicating her partner in crime with a tilt of her head. 'You noticed, then?'

'I'm no' daft, Fizz. No, nor blind either. Why's Rowena not coming up?'

'Oh, you know Rowena,' Fizz said vaguely. She sat down and, after a minute, he sat beside her and rested his head wearily against the wall behind him.

'What are you going to do?' he said.

His attitude encouraged Fizz to hope that things were going to go as smoothly as she had promised herself. Her heart gradually stopped fibrillating and she was able to say gently, 'For the moment, Alistair, all I'm going to do is to ask you to tell me the truth. After that we can work out what's best to be done.'

Alistair lifted his head to read her face and then looked back at the car. 'How many folk know about it?'

'As far as I know, just Rowena and I, and we'd both like to have your mother remain where she is.'

Alistair said nothing. He looked neither grateful nor relieved.

Finally, Fizz said, 'I wish you'd tell me how you managed it, Alistair.'

He seemed to come back unwillingly from some deep meditation and didn't answer straight away. 'It just happened.' He sat up and leaned forward to rest his elbows on his knees.

which indicated to Fizz that he wasn't planning on turning violent, at least, not for the moment.

'I didn't plan anything. All Mum wanted in the world was to know that her last resting place would be here.' He spread his hands as though to indicate that, as far as he was concerned, that was the end of the story, and then added in a firmer tone, 'She deserved that much, dammit! She'd lived with the fear of death hanging over her for years and the only comfort I could give her was to promise her she'd lie in her own beautiful place.'

'And then that wee bastard up at the lodge refused his permission?'

Alistair smiled on one side of his mouth. 'Aye. His nibs refused permission – but I never told Mum that. It didn't make any difference. We just went ahead and chose her resting place and I started to make her coffin. I never saw Mum so content as she was those last few weeks.'

Fizz looked at him in amazement. 'She didn't know that you were going to fake her cremation?'

'No.' Alistair's brow wrinkled as he lifted his eyes to the distant hills. 'She never knew that. But I knew it, and it worried me for weeks. It would have to be a cremation, you see, like the rest of our family, or everyone would have thought it damn funny. And they all knew how much Mum hated Killin kirkyard so everyone in Killin would have been shocked if I had pretended to lay her to rest there. It would have looked so heartless that even Lindsay would have been suspicious – and that was the last thing I wanted.'

'What's so difficult about faking a cremation?' Fizz wondered. 'You did it in the end, didn't you?'

'It's a matter of weighting the coffin,' Alistair said. 'You can't cremate rocks, Fizz. No, nor sand, either. And ten stone of wood make a suspicious amount of ash.' Alistair's hands were kneading each other constantly, his thumbs rubbing at his nails and smoothing the skin over his knuckles. 'I'd made up my mind that the best substitute would be to use a young hind. It would have been chancy because, if the incineration wasn't complete, there could be bits left whole and it wouldn't take a forensic scientist to tell the difference between deer bones and human.'

'And I suppose you can't fake any sort of funeral without calling in an undertaker, right?' Fizz remarked, as the thought occurred to her.

Alistair pressed his lips together and nodded. 'That's why it seemed like a gift from God when I found Bessie Anderson's body lying in the middle of the crossroads.'

'Jesus Christ, Alistair!' said Fizz, more in sorrow than in surprise.

Alistair lurched to his feet and started walking up and down, his big brown hands performing weird jerky gestures in front of him. 'There wasn't a mark on her. I think she'd had a heart attack and just dropped dead on the spot. There wasn't any time to think about it – someone could have left the christening party to look for her at any minute – so I put her in the Land Rover and brought her back here and put her in the cold room where we hang the game.'

'Oh my God!' Agitation brought Fizz, too, to her feet and she stood there with her head swinging from side to side as though she were at Wimbledon, watching Alistair pacing up and down in front of her. 'You mean, your mother was already dead and buried when—'

'No! Mum was still alive, but she was so far through that I couldn't see how she could last the week.'

'But the funeral ... the funeral they thought was your mother's ...' Fizz's head felt as though it were full of tapioca. 'It didn't take place till a fortnight after Bessie disappeared,

266

right? Are you telling me you kept Bessie in the cold room for a fortnight?'

'I did!' Alistair growled, and Fizz was shocked to see his eyes redden with sudden emotion. 'I didn't like doing it to old Bessie any more than you would have but . . . but she was *dead*, dammit! She didn't know what was happening. I thought it would be for a couple of days at the most but Mum held on and held on till I thought I'd have to put Bessie in the freezer. Thank God, it didn't come to that.'

Fizz, personally, would have thought that two weeks, even in a cold room, would have left perceptible signs on a corpse but Alistair would know about that better than most. He must comprehend, none better, the efficacy of his own cold room and he would have known precisely how long he dared to wait.

'When Mum died,' he said, sounding profoundly weary, 'I had the undertaker put the lid on the coffin right away, as soon as he had laid her out, and I told him I wanted her left here, in the house, till the cortège left for the crematorium.'

'Uh-huh,' Fizz nodded, visualising the scene with no difficulty at all. 'And then you unscrewed the lid, swapped the bodies, and laid your mother to rest in her home-made coffin under the hillock of newly dug soil. No problem.'

Alistair stopped his pacing, stuck his hands in his pockets, and leaned a shoulder against the trunk of a rowan tree that grew a pace or two away. Looking beyond him, Fizz could see Rowena's face pressed whitely against the side window of the car, so she gave her a cheery wave to reassure her that everything was going smoothly.

'Is that all then, Alistair?' she said.

'What?'

'Is that all you have to tell me?'

He lifted a shoulder. 'What else do you want to know?'

Fizz wet her lips. 'What about the camper?'

267

He swung round on her with a suddenness that made her jump. 'What camper? The chap that—' His finger, pointing up at the Ardoch Ridge completed the sentence. 'What's he got to do with it?'

He seemed more concerned than guilty, to Fizz's mind, and she was quick to say, 'Nothing, I suppose, if you say so, Alistair. I just thought . . . well, he must have died round about the same weekend as Bessie Anderson did. I thought at first that there must be a connection, but if Bessie died of a heart attack, well, I've probably been way off the track all along.'

Alistair didn't look at all happy at the thought of this possibility – which appeared to be striking him for the first time. 'Who told you it was the same weekend?' he asked gruffly.

'The CID chap, Cullen, I think. Didn't you know?'

'No. I never connected that business to Bessie Anderson till you mentioned it.'

Fizz looked at him with interest. 'But now that you think about it . . .?' He didn't answer, so she added, 'Are you sure it was a heart attack?'

'I'm not a doctor!' he snapped angrily, and Fizz saw at once that he was now seriously uneasy. 'All I know is that Bessie had knocked her head a wee bit when she fell, but there was just a scrape, nothing—'

He broke off at the sound of a car engine and a moment later the Clachan Land Rover trundled down the glen road and drew to a halt beside Rowena. Fizz could hear Simon's merry hail and watched as Rowena rolled down the window to talk to him.

'I'd better go, Alistair,' she said quickly. 'We don't want anybody asking what I'm sitting here chatting to you about, do we?'

'You mean . . . you're not going to take this any further?' Alistair's face was as wooden as always but his voice shook a fraction on the last word.

'No way,' she said firmly. 'And neither is Rowena. Um . . . but, there is just one thing I'm curious about. Your esteemed boss. Just between ourselves, Alistair, was Lindsay's fall a hundred per cent accidental?'

Alistair hesitated. 'I'll be honest with you, Fizz. Yes, it was accidental, but I knew the stepping stones were a bit shoogly. I should have told him.' He rubbed a hand hard across his face and drew a deep breath. 'There was a split second when I think I could have caught him and I didn't. I don't think I meant to let him go to his death . . . I don't know. But it makes me sick to think about it.'

'Forget it,' Fizz advised him. 'Self-flagellation went out with codpieces.' She headed down the path and called back, as much for Simon's benefit as anything, 'See you at the Clachan tonight?'

Alistair smiled and waved and she was pretty sure that it must have looked to Simon as though she'd just been chatting to Alistair in the passing.

The Land Rover was starting to pull away as she reached the car but Simon braked and rolled down the side window. 'Back home again, Fizz? This is getting to be a habit. You'll be joining the WRI next!'

'If I do,' Fizz told him earnestly, 'you have my permission to shoot me in the head.' She noticed Zander sitting in the back seat wearing a Walkman, and gave him a wave. 'Where are you two rushing off to?'

'Just stopping in Killin for petrol and then we wave goodbye to sunny Perthshire and head for EuroDisney. What's the time?' He took a look at his watch and revved reflexively. 'Twenty-five to twelve. Better not hang around.'

269

'Bye, then. Bye, Zander. Have a super time. Send us a postcard.'

Rowena, still in the car, sat through this exchange with palpable impatience. 'What happened?' she demanded as Fizz took the seat beside her.

Fizz said, 'Well, for a start, I'm as sure as I can be that Alistair isn't guilty of anything more serious than burying his mother in the garden.'

'You're sure? Oh, thank heaven for that, anyway! Oh, that's wonderful! Wonderful!' She started giggling and sniffling and putting her hands to her cheeks and generally going to pieces.

'Listen,' Fizz said in quelling tones, 'you might as well run me home while I tell you the rest. I want to be there when Buchanan arrives back.'

Rowena let in the clutch obediently, still beaming with relief. 'You have plenty of time,' she said sunnily. 'Simon told me Tam won't be able to pick up his photographs till twelve noon.'

Fizz fixed her with a hard look. 'He what?'

'The twenty-four-hour development service,' Rowena said patiently, as though speaking to Briony. 'Simon has used it before. You can't get the prints back before twelve noon, so Tam won't be—'

'You didn't – please tell me you didn't tell Simon about the photographs of the camper, Rowena?'

Rowena was negotiating the crossroads at that point and, although there was no traffic in sight in any direction, it seemed to be taking all her attention.

'Rowena?' Fizz said. 'You sodding did, didn't you?'

'It's no big deal, Fizz. He wasn't at all interested in the photographs. I wouldn't have mentioned it but he said he felt he should go down to the farm to say goodbye to Tam before he went back to Edinburgh and I had to tell him Tam wasn't there.'

'Did you mention the camper?'

'Why not? The camper has nothing to do with Alistair, surely?' Rowena's nervous giggle was an admission of guilt. 'Heavens, what does it matter anyway? Simon won't tell anybody. He won't see anybody to tell – his plane leaves at three o'clock.'

Fizz was gripped by a sudden nameless fear. The speed at which Simon had pulled away from Rowena's car was now not just strange, but seriously disquieting. She glanced down the loch in the direction of Killin – and Crianlarich – and suddenly screamed, 'STOP!'

Shocked into instant compliance, Rowena stood on the brakes and skidded into the verge. Fizz fell out and leaped the ditch to stand on the dry-stone dyke beyond. In the distance, maybe three miles away, a stretch of the Killin road emerged from the trees and ran close to the loch shore and, on that stretch, she could see the unmistakable white Land Rover that belonged to the Clachan inn. It was clear, even at this distance, that its speed was little short of suicidal.

Rowena was just getting out of the car when Fizz took a flying leap back to road. 'Get back in the car!' she yelled furiously. 'And get down to the farm. I need a telephone.'

Rowena took off in a shower of gravel and a screeching of tyres. 'What-what-what . . .?'

'I don't know what's happening,' Fizz panted, trying to think. 'I just don't like the way Simon's speeding down that road. He didn't go back to the inn for his cases, and his flight's not for nearly three hours, so what's his rush?'

'Oh God . . . oh no . . .' Rowena screwed up her face as though she were in pain. Her colour had now faded from pale ivory to a poisonous eau-de-nil. As she slowed the car to a standstill in the farmyard she fell back in her seat as though she were about to pass out.

'Turn the car,' Fizz snapped at her. 'I'll be back in a minute.'

She sprinted into the kitchen and clawed the telephone directory off its shelf, leafing through it feverishly to find the number of the gift shop in Crianlarich, where they had left the film to be developed.

'I thought we'd have a nice bit of roast venison for lunch, dear, seeing it's Tam's last meal with us,' said Auntie Duff, peeling potatoes at the sink. 'And, we mustn't let him go away without his salmon. It's in the big freezer in the pantry.'

Fizz tuned her out as she found the number and dialled it with shaking fingers. It seemed to take hours to explain what she wanted and make sure it was understood. As she rang off, she heard Auntie Duff rambling on about getting a barbecue for the next time Tam came for a visit.

'Listen, Auntie Duff,' she said, grabbing her by the shoulders and turning her round so that she could see her face. 'Listen. You know Tam's gone to Crianlarich?'

'Yes, dear. He going to—'

'Well, I've asked the assistant to get him to phone you right away and, when he does, I want you to give him a message, OK?'

'You'd better write it down, dear, or I'll forget it. You know what I'm like.'

'No time for that.' Buchanan, Fizz reckoned, should be phoning within the next ten minutes or so, unless Simon had got to him first. Even Auntie Duff could remember a few words that long. 'All I want you to say is: "Look out for Simon." You'll remember that, won't you?'

'Look out for Simon.' Auntie Duff blinked her pale eye uncertainly. 'Yes, but what does it mean?'

'He'll know what it means. I'm going to meet him now – Rowena's driving me.'

Auntie Duff stuck her hands on her hips and called afte

her as she hurtled back out to the yard. 'Well, your lunch will be on the table at one sharp so if you're late you'll get it cold.'

Rowena had turned the car and was standing leaning against the side door taking deep breaths.

'OK, kid,' Fizz told her. 'Let's see how you can drive.'

Chapter Twenty

Buchanan was not ill pleased with his shopping trip. He had found small gifts for his family, a bottle of Isle of Jura for Grampa and a rather fetching silk scarf for Auntie Duff. He had also spotted a half-sized fishing rod which he couldn't resist buying for Zander, seeing as his birthday was on Tuesday. That made it necessary to find something for Briony too, which was less easy. In the end he settled for a multicoloured glass mobile which he found in the last shop in the village, about half a mile from the gift shop where he had parked his car.

It was starting to rain quite heavily as he began the walk back but he had gone no more than a few paces before the Clachan Land Rover pulled up beside him and Simon leaned an elbow out of the window.

'Hi there, Tam. D'you enjoy walking in the rain or do you want a lift?'

Buchanan stepped over to the kerb. 'I'm parked along at the gift shop. If you're passing it, yes, thanks, Simon, it would save me getting wet.'

'No problem. Hop in.'

As he walked round to the passenger door, Buchanan saw Zander in the back seat and wondered if he should give him his present now or gift-wrap it and leave it at the hotel for him to open on Tuesday.

Simon more or less decided the matter by saying, as he pulled away, 'We're on our way to Paris for Zander's birthday treat. Just picking up some travel sickness pills before we head for the airport.'

'What time's your flight?' Buchanan asked, looking in his wallet for the receipt docket he'd need to produce when he picked up his prints.

'Three.'

Buchanan asked Zander if he was looking forward to the trip, which was an inane question, but Zander replied to it politely in the affirmative, and continued to make conversation for the remainder of the drive by listing all the rides he planned to go on when he got there.

'Picking up some snaps of your holiday?' Simon asked, as he backed into a parking slot. He neatly removed the docket from Buchanan's fingers, together with the fiver he was holding with it, and passed it over his shoulder to Zander.

'Nip in and get Mr Buchanan's snaps, there's a good lad. I want to have a wee chat in private.'

Buchanan looked at him in surprise. 'What's up, Simon?'

Simon waited till Zander was out of earshot and then turned sideways in the driving seat, laying an arm across the steering wheel.

'I'm a bit worried about something, Tam, and I've got a feeling you're the man to talk to.'

'Anything I can do to help,' Buchanan said. 'What is it that's concerning you?'

Simon smoothed his fingers across the shiny surface of the steering wheel, studying them thoughtfully. 'There's something going on in Am Bealach . . . something I don't like.'

'Uh-huh?' Buchanan sat up. 'Like what?'

'I'm not sure, to be perfectly honest, but I think Alistair is involved. He's been acting very strangely for the past few

276

weeks. Out at all hours, digging in his garden at two in the morning.'

'Well, I suppose his job would entail his being out at night from time to time, wouldn't it?' Buchanan asked, experiencing mild disappointment.

'Yes, but there are other things. He gets visitors late at night. A man and a woman. People I've never seen around here before.' He frowned at his restless fingers again and gave an embarrassed twitch of the shoulders. 'I'm not usually so nosy about what my neighbours are up to but I don't sleep well and I can see Alistair's cottage through the trees from my bedroom window.'

'Even in the darkness?' Buchanan doubted that somewhat.

Simon smiled without humour. 'OK, I admit it: I saw the lights of the car and had to take a walk up the glen road to satisfy my curiosity. I wouldn't have bothered but . . . with Bessie Anderson's disappearance and the murder up in the woods . . . I suppose I felt I ought to find out what Alistair was up to.'

'And did you?' Buchanan asked, saddened by this further confirmation of Alistair's involvement.

Simon chewed his upper lip and nodded. 'I followed him last night and he went all the way to—' He stopped talking as Zander emerged from the shop with a photographic envelope in one hand and an ice lolly in the other. 'Look, Tam, I don't want to talk about this in front of Zander but there's something I want to show you before I leave for Paris.'

'What is it?'

Zander's hand was already on the door handle, but Simon said quickly, 'I'd rather not say – I don't want to influence your opinion before you've seen it for yourself. It's just up the road here. Won't take minutes.'

Zander started to say something about a telephone message

for Mr Buchanan, but as he slammed the door shut, the Land Rover leaped forward, throwing Buchanan back in his seat and making the boy cry out as he fell on to his knees in the back.

'Take it easy, for God's sake!' Buchanan gasped.

Simon careened out of the car park, spun right and covered two hundred yards of main road in about three seconds before swinging off on to a wide, curving forestry road.

'I haven't much time if I'm to be in Edinburgh by three,' Simon said, his foot flat to the floor, and his arms wrestling with the wheel of the bucking Land Rover as though he were on the trail of a stampeding rhinoceros.

Both Buchanan and Zander were hanging on with both hands, the former swearing under his breath and the latter emitting a loud and frightened wail. Only at that point did Buchanan realise that Simon had not run mad, but was probably kidnapping him and must, therefore, be under the impression that he, Buchanan, was about to finger him for involvement in one or both of the Am Bealach deaths.

Buchanan's hand went instinctively to the door handle, but at the same time his eyes registered the sheer drop of maybe fifteen feet, inches from the edge of the track. Even if Simon slowed down for an instant, it would be a brave man who would leap out into space.

'Simon . . . you're going to get us all killed,' he said, reaching backwards to support Zander. 'What's the point of getting away if you've killed your boy? You'll never forgive yourself.'

Simon eased up on the speed marginally, but not enough to make a bid for freedom a viable option. Buchanan looked at the hills ahead. The track seemed to swing back round in the direction of Killin. He could see Ben Lawers and the Tarmachan ridge in the far distance.

'What do you have in mind for me, Simon?' he yelled, above the roaring of the engine and the squalling of Zander in his ear.

'Nothing lethal,' Simon grated, glaring with concentration at the hideously crumbling track ahead. 'I just want you out of the way for a few hours while Zander and I disappear. Sorry, Tam, but we're too close to freedom now to let you get in the way.'

Buchanan could hardly hear him over the noise, so there was no point in trying to question him. It was obvious that all that twaddle about Alistair's nocturnal guests had been merely a stratagem to hold Buchanan in the Land Rover till Zander got the photographs. Did it, therefore, follow that Simon somehow knew the photographs might hold a clue to his involvement? A clue he couldn't risk leaving behind?

Fighting the seismic lurching of the vehicle, he dragged himself round to see what Zander had done with the envelope and saw it skating about on the floor at the boy's feet. Simon made no move to prevent Buchanan reaching for it but it took several seconds and a disproportionate amount of effort for him to trap it and haul himself back into a stable position.

He fell back into his seat and pulled out the two prints. They were good, as one would have expected of a professional photographer. One showed two young people sitting on a low wall: a girl of about twenty, grinning toothily at the camera, and a young man, in profile, speaking into her ear. In the second shot, the young man was on his own, squatting outside a green tent, and this time he was staring straight into the lens.

He was not Hollywood material, was Buchanan's first thought, then he looked again and the resemblance hit him like a punch in the throat. Those bulging, pale green eyes and the unfortunate, wide nostrilled nose, had a double in Am Bealach.

And if he turned his head he would see that double, slobbering and wailing, in the back seat.

Fizz could see, in the moment they screeched into the car park of the gift shop, that Buchanan's Saab was still parked there but, when she had satisfied herself that Buchanan himself was neither inside the gift shop nor in its immediate vicinity, she began to lose her cool. A young boy, she had elicited, had picked up the photographs about half an hour ago, but Buchanan had not been with him.

There were only six shops in Crianlarich so, within ten minutes, they knew that Buchanan was in none of them and had not been seen by any of the shopkeepers for more than half an hour.

Fizz was appalled to discover that her knees were shaking. 'That's it,' she told Rowena, when they had eliminated the café and the hotel bar. 'Buchanan wouldn't just walk away and leave his car there in the car park. Simon's got to him.'

'Where—'

'Shite! How do I know where, Rowena?' Fizz felt she had enough to suffer without Rowena's stupidity. They had been stuck behind a tractor for a five-mile stretch of winding lochside road where overtaking was out of the question and she was now ready to bite through the jugular of anyone who got in her way. 'All I can swear to is that Simon's Land Rover didn't pass us on the road – which is damn funny.' She leaned over to look at the clock on Rowena's side of the dashboard. 'It's half-past twelve, dammit, and if Simon was heading for Edinburgh Airport – as he should be, by this time – we'd have passed him on our way here. So where the hell *is* the bastard, and what has he done with Buchanan?'

'If I were Simon,' Rowena said, positively, 'I'd be worried that someone from Am Bealach – like you and me, for instance – might come looking for Tam, and I wouldn't want to run into them on the road. The only way Simon could reach Edinburgh without passing the Killin turn-off would be to go via Loch Lomond.'

Fizz thought about that. 'Y'know, kid, that's the most sensible thing you've said today.' She snatched the road map out of the side door pocket and, with the help of a good deal of vile language, found the right page. From Crianlarich, the two routes formed a triangle. You could either go directly southeast via Stirling, passing the Killin turn-off en route, or you could head south to Loch Lomond and then turn east to Edinburgh.

She said, 'The Loch Lomond route is a bit longer but he could still make it that way in time for his flight. There's no other explanation. The question is: can we catch up with him?'

'We have the Merc, he has a Land Rover,' Rowena pointed out.

'OK, we'll go for it,' Fizz decided. There were no firm indications on which to base a logical decision but this was clearly a case for doing *something*, even if it was *anything*. Fizz, right at this moment, didn't give a monkey's chunky about nailing Simon but she needed to know what had happened to Buchanan. He was either already dead, held as a hostage, or tied to a railway line somewhere, so sitting around worrying about it was not an option.

'Shouldn't we phone the police?' Rowena said.

Fizz knew damn well they should, but she was raring to go, the adrenaline sparking and fizzing through her veins like the effect of three tequila slammers on an empty stomach, and her brain screamed at the thought of wasting a few precious seconds.

'Shite!' she howled, and sprinted across the car park to the phone box.

The police presence in Crianlarich was no more substantial than that in Killin and she knew as she dialled that any attempt to contact him on a Saturday would only end in a one-sided conversation with an answerphone.

Simon brought the Land Rover to an abrupt halt at the end of the track and told Buchanan to get out. But, as Buchanan laid a hand on the door catch, he added, 'And move slowly, Tam, OK? We don't want any accidents.' With a smooth movement, he gripped his fancy shotgun, which had been jammed down between his seat and the door, and laid it across his knees, the business end inches from Buchanan's groin. 'Let's keep it friendly, all right? Just walk round to my side.'

He slid out of the driver's door as Buchanan crossed in front of the vehicle and stopped, in response to a curt gesture, a couple of paces away from him.

'Just stay there, Zander,' Simon said over his shoulder to the snotty-nosed face in the shadows. 'Don't get out. I'll be right back.' He smiled. 'This way, Tam.'

Buchanan preceded him along a sheep track that wound round the base of a hillock so that, in a couple of minutes, they had lost sight of the Land Rover. They were now on a level pathway that was recognisably another disused railway line similar to the one in Killin. Buchanan could feel the presence of the shotgun at his back, even though it wasn't, in fact, touching him, and the thought of Simon's finger on the trigger was severely stressing his sweat glands.

There was no possibility of doing anything heroic, like smashing an elbow in Simon's face and taking the gun off him. Simon wasn't daft enough to come that close and there was no cover at hand that Buchanan might have attempted to put between him and his assailant. All he could do, at least for the moment, was try to undermine Simon's concentration by making him talk.

'So, the camper was some relation of Zander's, was he, Simon?'

Behind him, Simon made a noise that might have been a chuckle. 'Curiosity killed the cat, Tam. You should have learned that by now.'

'Is there any reason why you shouldn't tell me?'

Simon hesitated a moment. 'I'm not worried about you knowing the truth, Tam, since it's all going to come out now, thanks to you and Fizz. It makes no difference anyway. Zander and I will be stepping into our new life in a few hours and there's no way anyone's going to trace us. I've only had a few weeks to set things up but I reckon they're just about foolproof.'

Buchanan would have liked to believe Simon's earlier assurance that he had nothing lethal in mind for his prisoner, but it wasn't proving easy. His eyes were combing the landscape for anything he could use to his advantage, a rock he could snatch up and hurl at Simon, a fast-flowing river he could dive into, a passer-by he could yell to for help. There was nothing.

He said, 'If Myra knows nothing about this it's going to hit her hard when she finds out. Don't you think it would be easier on her if she heard the truth from me, rather than from the police?'

'I never meant to hurt Myra. She need never have known anything if it hadn't been for . . .'

'If it hadn't been for Travis?' Buchanan prompted.

'Ah.' Simon's voice sounded impressed. 'You know his name? I didn't realise you were quite so adept at this game, Tam. You'll be flattered to know, you're quite a bit ahead of the police.'

Buchanan heard the steps behind him slow a little and he

shortened his stride to match them. 'I know his name; I know he must be closely related to Zander, but I don't know why you killed him. I suppose he was trying to claim Zander back from you?'

'Travis,' Simon said heavily, 'was my nephew: my brother's son.'

That threw Buchanan completely. Travis looked nothing like Simon except, perhaps, in build, whereas he was the double of Zander, who was no blood relation.

'My brother, so Travis informed me, has been dead for thirteen years,' Simon was saying, 'and his wife died this January. I hadn't seen any of my family since I was in my twenties and I wasn't even aware they knew I lived in Am Bealach now. Then, out of the blue, that Sunday morning when the rest of Am Bealach was at Briony's christening, Travis appeared on my doorstep.'

There was a long pause while Buchanan wrestled with the paradox, his mental faculties seriously impaired by the presence of the shotgun barrel ogling his kidneys. Then he heard Simon clear his throat and go on.

'The shock nearly bloody killed me, Tam, I swear to God. It was like looking at Zander. The resemblance was uncanny, and I knew right away that, if Myra saw him, my cushy life here would be over. I'd be out on the street without a penny.'

'If Travis was a blood-relation of yours, so was Zander. You adopted a relation, but Myra didn't know?' The surprise stopped Buchanan in mid-stride. He stared blankly at the path ahead as the jigsaw fitted together. Zander was ten next week. Around about ten or eleven years ago Simon had been in the throes of a passionate affair with Lara. For a second it took his breath away.

He turned in amazement and looked at Simon. 'He's your son. Yours and Lara's.'

Simon's eyes were red and haunted with some unidentifiable emotion.

'I loved Lara,' he said simply, lifting the shotgun to level it at Buchanan's chest. 'She died having our baby and her parents were awarded custody. There was no one else with a legal claim to Zander but they were in their late fifties, Lara's folks, and they knew it was a bad scene. I'm damn sure the last thing they wanted was to be landed with a screaming infant at their stage in life.'

'So you persuaded them to let you adopt the child?'

Simon shook his head and motioned Buchanan, with the gun, to go on walking. 'There was no chance of a legal adoption and, in any case, I doubt if I could have swung it to be allowed to have Zander. We'd tried to adopt before but I was over forty at the time and we didn't stand a chance. No, it was never official. Lara's folks and I came to an arrangement that seemed to them the best for Zander and gave me the son who was part of the woman I loved.'

'And what about Myra and Malcolm? What version of the story did you give them?'

'The truth – as far as it went. I told them that I knew of an elderly couple whose daughter had died and left them with a baby they didn't want. Myra was so desperate for a child that she'd have bought one in Thailand if she'd known how to go about it. We'd been going through a rough patch and she hoped a baby would solve all our problems.' Simon's voice shook, with laughter or emotion, Buchanan couldn't tell which. 'And it did. I made an effort, for Zander's sake, and after a while Myra started to trust me again. We've had ten good years.'

'But Travis's arrival put all that in danger,' Buchanan reasoned as Simon fell silent again. 'Malcolm and Myra were co-owners of the inn and you would have had neither your son nor a means of subsistence if they threw you out. But, why kill him, Simon? Couldn't you simply have given him a bung and sent him on his way?'

Simon gave a harsh laugh. 'You don't know this guy we're talking about! He was a bloodsucker. A leech. He knew right away that I was panicked at the sight of him. He didn't know why, but he knew there was money in it. I gave him fifty quid and told him we were too busy in the inn to give him houseroom but he simply pocketed it and said he'd be back when it was gone. He knew he'd struck a gold mine.'

Simon's voice faded and for a while Buchanan could hear nothing except the gravel crunching underfoot and the sound of his own heart thudding in his ears.

Then there was a long intake of breath and Simon said, with a sort of helplessness, 'I hit him. I just picked up the brass bell from the reception desk and let him have it with all my strength. He went down like a felled ox.'

'Was he dead?' Buchanan asked, but Simon ignored him.

'I didn't want to kill him. I don't know what else I could have done. All I could think of was that Myra and her dad would be back from the christening in an hour and I couldn't have Travis hanging around for them to see. Even if he had left right then I could never have predicted when he'd turn up again. It was the only way I could think of to get rid of him for good.'

Buchanan heard the footsteps falter behind him. He stopped and turned. Simon was only a pace away but he had the shotgun in both hands and looked as if he meant business.

'How did you get the body up to the scree slope?' Buchanan said.

Simon motioned him, angrily, to walk on, which he did, but kept twisting to look back as much as he could, still hoping for a chance to jump him.

'I put him in the back of the Land Rover and drove up the forestry track as far as I could go, then I toted him across country, till my strength gave out, stripped him and hid him where he was found. Later, I burned everything he had on him – but I didn't know he'd camped in the woods the night before. The way he'd been speaking, I thought he'd come from Stirling that morning.'

Buchanan hadn't realised that Simon was quite such a fit hillwalker but remembered that he had been in Fizz's team for the assault on the Carlin's Loup. That must have been quite an experience for Simon: trying to avoid finding the body he himself had hidden. 'You did all that in an hour?'

Simon looked haggard. 'Just over. I was only minutes ahead of the christening party by the time I got back down to the crossroads, covered with blood and stamping the accelerator into the floorboards. It's always deserted there on a Sunday – *always*! And with all the locals in Killin at the christening—' His voice wavered and died. They had gone about ten paces before he went on, 'God knows what the silly old fool was doing, standing there in the shadows with her basket of moss. I didn't see her till it was way too late.'

Buchanan was too stunned to speak. He kept walking on, like a zombie, subconsciously aware that Fizz would be upset by this news.

'I didn't stop. To tell you the truth, Tam, I was going at such a lick that I was past before I even registered her properly, but I saw her in the driving mirror as I pulled in to the Clachan car park so I stopped and ran back. She was stone dead.'

A small wooden structure appeared on the side of a slight incline ahead of them. It looked like an animal shelter of some sort, or perhaps a shooting butt. Simon, if he noticed it, made no comment but went on with his story.

'I could have sworn I didn't hit her, Tam. Maybe she tried

to jump out of my way and fell, or maybe the shock killed her, I don't know. Hell, maybe I did just brush her in passing.'

'At least it was quick,' Buchanan said, already planning how to break the news to Fizz. Which was silly, he realised, because it was just as likely that someone else would be breaking the news to her about *him*, regardless of Simon's promises to the contrary.

'I had to leave her there,' Simon said, almost aggressively, as though he were replying to an unspoken criticism. 'If I had done anything else I'd have had to explain what I was doing at the crossroads when I was supposed to be rushed off my feet preparing the lunch. Someone else had to find her.'

Buchanan, in spite of everything, was tempted to smile at the thought of Simon's consternation when the body turned out to have disappeared. 'Do you know what happened to her body?' he asked.

'I worked it out eventually,' Simon said, 'as you did too, didn't you, Tam?'

Buchanan stopped and turned. 'Maybe.'

'But you're saying nowt to nobody, huh?' A slow smile curved Simon's mouth. 'You're OK, Tam. I'm glad I don't have to bump you off. Just get in there and we'll leave it at that.'

Buchanan looked over his shoulder at the hut. It was barely four feet by four and had scarcely enough headroom for Danny De Vito. At this distance he could see it wasn't an animal pen but probably had once held tools for men working on the now defunct railway line.

'Let me get this straight, Simon,' he said, in a tone of mild enquiry. 'You're planning to fly off into the bright blue yonder leaving me in that hellhole there? And how long for?'

'It's the best I can think of, Tam, and it's only for a matter of hours, I swear it. I'll phone Fizz from Orly airport as soon as I arrive there.'

These assurances fell on deaf ears. Buchanan thought it unlikely that Simon would feel safe to phone anyone anywhere till he was safely at his final destination – which was unlikely to be Paris. However, it was patently obvious, by the way Simon was holding the gun, that he would use it if he had to, so Buchanan had no option but to squelch into his prison and hope it wasn't as secure as it looked.

He heard the door thud as Simon wedged something heavy against it and felt the reverberations as he appeared to jump up and down on the wedge to make it secure. It was pitch-dark inside so he could see nothing, but he heard his captor's voice through the door.

'Goodbye, Tam. Wish me luck.'

Buchanan made no reply at all. Under the circumstances, he felt that was the nicest thing he could say.

Chapter Twenty-One

Somewhere between Crianlarich and the head of Loch Lomond, Fizz and Rowena underwent an inexplicable personality swop.

Rowena adopted an air of calm determination and settled down to driving as she had never driven – or, probably, thought to drive – in her life, while Fizz went slowly to pieces.

She started off as, perhaps, two-thirds angry, and one-third scared: angry at Simon for having the audacity to interfere with Tam Buchanan in any way, scared in case Buchanan was not merely in a hostage situation, as she was forcing herself to hope, but already dead. But as they careered south to Ardlui on a wet and twisty road, her optimism deserted her and she found herself wringing her hands and ranting like Rowena on a bad day.

There were stretches of the road from where they could see the way ahead for several miles but never once were they rewarded by the sight of the white Land Rover. Fizz was distraught at the thought of Simon's half-hour-plus head start but Rowena stuck doggedly to the theory that it would do Simon no good to drive dangerously since his flight didn't leave till three and he could make the airport comfortably by then. Furthermore, his Land Rover was an old, long wheelbased model and didn't have the turn of speed that she could achieve in the Mercedes.

This was true as far as Ardlui, where they joined one of the busiest tourist routes in the Highlands. The traffic from there onwards beggared even Fizz's invective and the only comfort was that Simon, up ahead somewhere, was probably making no better progress. The scenery wasn't quite at its best in the pouring rain but the mountains and the islands in the loch were still spectacular enough to make tourists want to take their time on the twenty-mile stretch.

Rowena kept one thumb on the horn and charged past everything that would allow it. Those who didn't get over were subjected to continual harassment till, sooner or later, Rowena managed to squeeze past – usually on a corner or a blind summit – and not always without leaving her mark on her adversary's vehicle.

During one brief, unavoidable snarl-up she indicated the road atlas which Fizz had thrown on to the back seat. 'I'm not sure of the route at the end of the loch. Take a look at the map and tell me which road we take from Balloch.'

It took ages to find the right page and, with the car swaying from one side of the road to the other Fizz could hardly focus on the tiny print.

'Christ! It's like electrical wiring,' she howled, pointing furiously at the tangle of green and red lines that scribbled their way from Balloch to Edinburgh. 'We're never going to make it in time!'

'Don't panic,' Rowena said, placidly overtaking two tour buses, a caravan, and a McEwan's ale lorry while bringing the opposite lane to a hooting, gesticulating standstill. 'Look for the quickest way to Falkirk, it's a straight road to Edinburgh from there.'

Fizz held the map closer to her eyes, absently returning a passing V-sign with her free hand. 'Turn left on to the A811 at

Balloch and, about eight miles further on, you have to turn right on the A809 then left at Carbeth. It'll probably be signposted to Strathblane.'

The road from that point onwards was marked in yellow, which was less than reassuring but she had to assume that Rowena, being a driver and familiar with the territory, must know better than someone who hadn't seen this part of Scotland for seven or more years. It was a new experience, putting her trust in Rowena, but she had very little option. There was no other way they could catch up with Simon, and there was no opportunity of trying to get help from the local police, since there were no sizeable centres of population at any point along the loch shore.

Speeding through Balloch, Rowena spotted a telephone box. 'What d'you think? Should we have another go at phoning the police?'

'No, no, keep going!' Fizz yelled as Rowena momentarily took her foot off the accelerator. Stopping for anything that was not a certain and immediate move towards extricating Buchanan from trouble was simply unthinkable. 'The police here won't know what we're talking about and it'll take half an hour to explain it and, even then, they won't move their arses. What time is it now?'

'Ten past two.'

'Will we make it?' Fizz asked, hating the tone of helpless anxiety she heard in her own voice.

'It'll be tight, but we've still got a chance. Whether the police will listen to us at the airport is another thing entirely.'

'I don't give a hoot in hell whether they listen to us or not,' Fizz said savagely. 'I'll claw that two-faced murdering bastard off the plane with my own hands!'

Ten minutes later they discovered that they were hopelessly lost.

★ ★ ★

As Buchanan listened to the fading sound of Simon running back along the track, his first thought was not that his present surroundings might prove to be his sepulchre, but that Fizz might be in danger.

The matter of the phone message that Zander had mentioned had been shoved well into the background by subsequent events but now that the Spectre of Death was taking a short breather it loomed suddenly back into importance.

Only Fizz would have tried to contact him at the gift shop like that and, if she had deemed it necessary to go to so much trouble, it was unlikely that all she wanted was for Buchanan to pick up a packet of aspirins. The only logical conclusion was that she had found out something during the course of the morning and had been trying to warn him that Simon was on his track. If that were the case – and Buchanan could think of no other explanation – Simon would know, as soon as he got the gist of the message from Zander, that Fizz was a threat to his future plans.

He couldn't see his watch in the darkness so it was impossible to estimate whether Simon still had enough time in hand to hunt Fizz down at the farm but, if she had induced someone to give her a lift to Crianlarich – and, being Fizz, she *would* have – her path would be crossing Simon's as soon as he got back to the main road.

The door was at least two inches thick with butt hinges that would have resisted an hour's work with a jemmy, so a minute or two of trying to kick it open was enough to teach Buchanan the advisability of taking time to think before going off half-cocked and doing himself a severe injury.

He forced himself to pause and make a quick examination of the inside of his prison. It was made entirely of railway sleepers securely bolted together, and an exploratory kicking of various possible weak spots had no effect whatsoever.

It wasn't, as he had at first imagined, totally dark inside. There were several small chinks, where wall met ceiling, which let in enough light, once one's eyes had become accustomed to the gloom, to see that the place was totally empty. There were no implements he could use to prise the sleepers apart; no heavy stones with which he might even hammer out an SOS. Even the floor was constructed from railway sleepers, so there was little point in trying to tunnel his way out with his bare hands. It was thick with mud and dead leaves, but by feeling amongst the litter he found a piece of fencing wire about four feet long, jammed down between the sleepers.

It was difficult to imagine getting much mileage out of a piece of wire, but that appeared to be the extent of his options. While he tried to think of a better plan, he started to use it to widen a small hole at the edge of the door where the wood had begun to soften.

It took about ten minutes of scraping to get a field of vision that allowed him to see how Simon had achieved such a rigid wedging of the door. It looked – it *was* – depressingly effective, but in fact it was only a length of rusty rail that had survived from the days when this was a working branch line, and it had been wedged firmly between the door, just alongside his spy hole, and a nearby outcrop of rock. It must have been cut to fit the distance so someone – surely not Simon? – was using this hut.

Buchanan crouched painfully on his heels. His shoulders and thighs were screaming from the continued bending and squatting, and blood from his cut leg was now soaking into his trousers, but the mental torture was infinitely worse.

He was trapped here in the back of beyond while Fizz was about to walk into extreme danger, and the best he could hope for was that whoever had been using this hut might chance to pass by.

★ ★ ★

'I told you to turn left eight miles out of Balloch,' Fizz snapped, glaring at the map. 'We must have passed the junction ages ago. We must be bloody near Buchlyvie by now.'

'Well, it's your fault for keeping me talking! You're supposed to be the navigator. You should have been watching for the crossroads instead of waving your arms about and ranting on like a fishwife!'

Fizz couldn't believe this was Rowena talking to her. 'It's all right for you,' she returned hotly. 'You've at least got something to do while I'm just sitting here with my bum biting the buttons off the seat and going quietly mad! Anyway, no matter who's to blame, we're going to have to turn back.'

'I think we should stop and ask someone if we're on the right road. We could be wandering about all afternoon.'

'Rowena, take a look about you – there isn't a living soul in sight! You'd think Scotland was playing England at Murrayfield!'

'Well, we should stop and phone the police,' Rowena said, doing a screeching U-turn and hurtling back the way they had come. 'We have to try that, Fizz, it's our last chance of stopping Simon. We haven't got a cat's chance in hell of making it to the airport now.'

'They won't listen to us,' Fizz said, taking a handful of hair at each side of her head and yanking it painfully as a sort of counterirritant.

'Well, it's all we can do now, Fizz. There's a phone box back here, I saw it as we passed.'

'Look,' Fizz said suddenly, 'that signpost says Balfron. I'm sure that's on our route.'

'It's too late now,' Rowena said wearily. 'We've lost nearly half an hour wandering around country roads. Here's the phone box. You're better at that than I am.' She pulled in to the side of the road and looked at Fizz, waiting for her to get out.

Fizz felt a strange calm descend on her as though, now that there was no rush, she was able to think clearly again.

'No, Rowena. The police aren't going to leap into action and arrest a peaceful citizen on the say-so of a screaming woman. Even Cullen and McLaren – if they get the message I left for them – are unlikely to declare a red alert. It's not as if we're being physically attacked or anything and we haven't time for the red tape. We have to do this another way.'

Rowena narrowed her eyes. 'Yes?'

'Yes. And you have to do it, Rowena. Thank God I've got you with me. Just a short phone call ought to be sufficient.'

The idea of trying to get the fencing wire looped around the length of rail started off purely as an exercise in occupational therapy. Buchanan had not one iota of hope that he could succeed, given that the hole he was working through was only a centimetre wide and barely an inch long. However, ten minutes into the proceedings he decided that it might be worth spending time on widening the aperture and, that done, he reckoned the odds against succeeding had improved to something like a thousand to one.

It was a process of trial and error, of minute modification, and of patient repetition. At times he was mesmerised by the same rhythm as the cast-and-drift of salmon fishing, at other – more frequent – times he was swamped by a frenzy of impatience and frustration. His mind, as he worked, was tirelessly exploring other possibilities of escape but it was difficult to be optimistic.

The chances of anyone passing by this spot were probably virtually nil. Simon must have been pretty certain of that, although the fact that he had chosen the hut without much forward planning could indicate that it might be less perfect than he could have wished. However, the old railway track showed no trace of frequent use so if he were ever to escape from here, Buchanan concluded, it was up to him.

It had to be more than an hour before he got the end of his now shortened and curved length of wire around the rail.

Buchanan was simultaneously jubilant and terrified that it would slip loose again. The free end of the wire had curved away from the door but he was able to use the spare length that he had broken off to hook it closer and, after a long and bloody struggle he finally had both ends in through the hole and bent sideways to prevent them slipping back out.

Scrabbling in the mud at his feet he found a short length of branch which he twisted into the ends of the wire to give him a better grip. By now his hands were sticky with blood, so he wiped them dry on his trousers, braced a knee against the door, and yanked with all his strength.

It was a miracle. Not only did the rail fall, but it landed sufficiently sideways to let the door open about nine inches, which was just enough to allow Buchanan to squeeze himself through.

He stood for a moment, groaning and trying to straighten up, then he started running back along the railway line in the direction Simon and he had come. His watch said two twenty, so, even if he were too late to save Fizz, there was still time to have Simon stopped at the airport.

It seemed at first as if every part of his body were on fire with pain: his hands, his cut leg, his neck and shoulders, his surgery wound. But by the time he got into his second wind he had forgotten all that and felt that he could keep going as long as it took.

As he circled the low hillock where the railway line joined up with the track he thought he heard the sound of someone laughing in the distance and, to his utter amazement, his first view of the track showed a line of pony trekkers ambling along it, led by a familiar figure in a yellow sweater and cream breeches.

He tried to shout but managed only a husky growl, so he staggered to a halt and whistled as loudly as he could. When one or two of the riders looked round he waved furiously and croaked, 'Help!' a few times. At last the trek ground to a ragged halt and a handful of riders detached themselves and trotted across the heather, led by Gerda, looking more beautiful and radiant and desirable than Buchanan had ever seen her.

'Tam! How are you coming to here?' She swung a long leg forwards, over her horse's head, and slid down its shoulder to the ground, leaving Brandy to get tucked into the fresh grass of the verge. 'What is this happening? Who is doing this to you? How are you starting to be bleeding on your hands?'

Buchanan didn't have either the breath or the patience to answer questions. The utter impossibility of explaining things to Gerda, or to the ring of shocked faces that surrounded him, reduced him to an arrogant brevity that, hopefully, brooked no argument.

'Simon shut me in a hut back there,' he snapped. 'It was Simon who murdered the camper and now he's getting away. I'm sorry, Gerda, but I'm going to have to take your horse. He's faster than the garrons.'

'No!' cried Gerda, shocked indignation flashing from her eyes as Buchanan tweaked the reins from her grasp. 'Is not possible, Tam. Brandy is Norrie's horse. I am needing him to be leading trek. Stop, Tam! Norrie will be sacking me if I do not bring Brandy home!'

'Norrie will understand,' Buchanan said. He had to hold her off as he got into the saddle but a couple of sharp kicks in the butt woke Brandy to the realisation that lunch was over and his surprised leap broke Gerda's hold on the bridle. As they galloped away, Buchanan could hear her shrieking.

'*Schotse perverse idioot! Ik hoop dat je van mÿn paard valt en je nek breekt!*'

Unfamiliar with the language though he was, Buchanan could translate these remarks loosely to infer that their relationship was at an end.

It took Brandy twenty-three painful and alarming minutes to reach the end of the forestry road and for many of these he was only marginally in control of the situation. It was anything but a comfortable ride as the track was covered with loose stones and potholes and Brandy was none too surefooted. There were times when Buchanan was within inches of going off on his own, which would have been nasty, if not fatal, but he was, astonishingly, still in the saddle as they exploded on to the main road and ploughed into a small crowd of people who scattered in every direction.

Brandy staggered to a trembling halt and Buchanan fell off into the arms of a muscular chap wearing a Day-Glo waistcoat and a motorcycle helmet. He looked to Buchanan like a traffic cop and, indeed, as he began to register the situation he realised that the place appeared to be choked with uniforms.

'Cullen,' Buchanan gasped out hoarsely. 'Detective Inspector Cullen. Can you contact him? I need to talk with him . . . urgently.'

The eyes below the helmet clicked open. 'You're not Mr Buchanan, are you?'

Buchanan admitted this to be the truth and found himself ushered through the crowd like a VIP. There appeared to be some sort of Search and Rescue Services open day in progress.

'What's going on?' he asked the policeman.

'We're just setting up a search for you, sir. There was a

phone message to the effect that you were in danger of your life.'

He tipped his head towards the field on the far side of the road and Buchanan saw a helicopter with its blades slowly rotating. Close to it, talking to what looked like the pilot, were Cullen and his sidekick, McLaren. They both turned and stared at Buchanan as he and the cop approached.

'Ah . . . good to see you looking so well, Mr Buchanan,' said Cullen with an unpleasant smile. 'I had a feeling that Miss Fitzpatrick might be exaggerating slightly when she claimed you were being murdered. Apparently I was right.'

'Where is she?' Buchanan croaked, scanning the gallery of faces in the hope of spotting her bright hair.

'According to the rather garbled message she left on the police answerphone, she and Mrs Crawford are driving to Edinburgh via the Loch Lomond route in the hope of intercepting Simon Burroughs, against whom she has lodged some very serious accusations. What she plans to do with Mr Burroughs, if and when she catches him, she did not think fit to inform us. Nor did she mention her reason for taking the tourist route.'

In spite of Cullen's pedantic and long-winded style of conveying information, which was painfully frustrating to someone in Buchanan's state of mind, the information itself was, on inspection, quite heartening. There was no reason that Buchanan could think of why Simon should risk missing his plane by denying himself the direct route through Stirling, and he could only conclude that Fizz had guessed wrong there.

'She knew that Simon had followed me to Crianlarich so, when she couldn't find us there, she must have wondered why she hadn't passed him on the road on his way to Edinburgh,' he told the DI, and gestured urgently towards the hills. 'But she must have been in Crianlarich while Simon and I were scorching up that track back there. He had me trapped in a tool store on the old railway line. You know he's catching a flight from Edinburgh airport at three o'clock?' He looked at his watch and swore as he realised it was two minutes past the hour.

'We are aware of that, yes, Mr Buchanan. Thanks to Ms Fitzpatrick's information, much of which we were in a position to substantiate, we will be looking to interview Mr Burroughs as a matter of extreme urgency. If our colleagues at Edinburgh airport have missed him you can be quite sure that he will be detained for questioning at Orly when he disembarks.'

Cullen's tone was not at all what Buchanan might have wished but the adrenaline rush that had been driving him for the past three hours was now draining away and he couldn't be bothered getting miffed. All he wanted now was to be sure that Fizz was, indeed, safe: the rest of the drama had ceased to interest him.

He found the photographs of Travis in his jacket pocket and handed them over. 'I think there's enough evidence to arrest Burroughs, not just question him,' he said. 'This is the dead camper, Simon's nephew, Travis. The reason he looks like Simon's adopted son is that Zander is Simon's son by his one-time girlfriend, Lara.'

McLaren glared from the photographs to Buchanan's face. 'Where did you get these? No – I'll hear all that later. I suppose you have some proof of these relationships?'

Buchanan nodded and the DI went back to studying the photographs.

Sergeant McLaren had been listening to a message on his radio and relayed it to the pilot before turning to his superior. 'Burroughs is on the flight list, sir. And it appears that the flight has not left yet. If you want to question him yourself,

Campbell here says he can taxi us down to Edinburgh airport in the chopper.'

There was a short discussion on which Buchanan wasn't able to eavesdrop but, when he saw Cullen and the pilot turn towards the helicopter he grabbed the DI's arm.

'I want to go too,' he said urgently. 'Somebody's going to have to take care of Zander and, besides, I want to know if Miss Fitzpatrick is there – or . . . or what's happened to her.'

'I'm afraid—' Cullen began with a pitying expression.

'Come on, Cullen. You owe me this! You wouldn't be making an arrest today if it weren't for Fizz and me.'

Cullen looked from Buchanan to the pilot who shrugged willingly. 'Oh . . . come on then. I'll need some more information from you anyway.'

It was Buchanan's first flight in a chopper and he didn't particularly enjoy it. He found a dressing for his leg in the first-aid box and bound up the cut, after which he spent the rest of the trip worrying about Fizz and answering Cullen's questions.

They landed close to the terminal building and were shown into the offices of the airport police where there was still an air of commotion surrounding the personnel as though they had only just brought in their prisoner and were still under some sort of tension. Buchanan was ignored as Cullen was brought up to date with the current state of affairs but the pilot beckoned him into a side room where there were some easy chairs and the means of rustling up a hot drink.

Rowena was standing at a telephone hood, with the receiver in her fist and a resolute expression on her face. Fizz was stretched out in an armchair with her Docs on a coffee table, leafing through a *National Geographic* magazine.

'Buchanan!' She bounced to her feet with an expression of such relief that, for a split second, Buchanan thought she might be going to cast herself into his arms, as she had done once before on a similar occasion. It was almost a disappointment when she didn't.

Rowena turned and waved at him, with the phone to her ear, but went on speaking into the mouthpiece.

'Well, too bloody bad, Lindsay,' she was saying, 'but Alistair deserves better than that and so did his mother. And I don't know what happened to Bessie's ashes but you'll have to arrange some sort of memorial stone. Why? Because it was your fault . . .'

At the words, a strong sense of unreality assailed Buchanan and he sat down beside Fizz, only just preventing himself from reaching for her hand. This was neither the time nor the place, and he wasn't all that sure that it would be a good idea either. She might read too much into it, and God only knew where that might end. He might like it.

For quite a few minutes they just sat there and looked at each other, then Buchanan said, 'How did you get here?'

'Rowena drove.' Her eyes glowed with a sort of amused amazement. 'She was magnificent.'

'But you didn't catch up with Simon, I take it?'

'No. I suspect he didn't take the long way round after all.'

The pilot came over with a cup of coffee for each of them and then carried one over to Rowena who was still getting rid of ten pence pieces like they were going out of circulation.

They sipped their drinks without speaking. Buchanan's head hurt and he knew there would be time for talking later. The pilot wandered from the room and Rowena was in listening mode so it was very quiet. In the distance they could hear the PA system gargling intermittently but the only other sound was a slight humming from one of the fluorescent light fittings.

Just as Rowena hung up, Cullen came back into the room and stood looking at them strangely with his hands thrust into the pockets of his raincoat.

'Well, that's Burroughs under lock and key . . . with a little luck and a little bit of help from his friends.'

'Thank God you caught the plane in time.' Buchanan began, at last, to experience a warm glow of satisfaction. 'It must have been touch and go.'

'No,' said Cullen, with a tight and humourless smile. 'It wasn't what you'd call touch and go. In fact, the plane has not yet left the runway. The security services are still checking it over.'

'Don't tell me there was some sort of fault?' Fizz said, with the wide-eyed look that always made Buchanan's heart sink.

'No, just a bomb scare.'

'A *bomb*?' Rowena, this time. Her frown may possibly have fooled the Inspector but it made Buchanan go cold.

'A bomb,' Cullen nodded, his smile turning into a rictus. 'Someone with an Irish accent phoned up the airport about an hour ago claiming there was a bomb aboard the three o'clock flight to Paris. Quite a coincidence, huh?'

Fizz and Rowena exchanged astounded looks and appeared speechless. Buchanan could do nothing with his face. It was rigid with horror, alarm, and almost overpowering rage. If Cullen could read it, that was just too bad.

'However, there's nothing further you can help us with here,' said the policeman. 'I've spoken on the phone to Zander's mother and she is understandably impatient to have her son returned to her. So . . .'

'Does she know about Zander's background?' Fizz demanded.

Cullen nodded. 'I thought it best to tell her straight away.' He cleared his throat a bit and stared at his shiny shoes while he, apparently, debated the wisdom of going on. Eventually, he said, 'I must say, her reaction was not what I expected. It seems that whatever their problems in the past, she would have been willing, in view of their present relationship, to overlook her husband's chicanery and accept Zander for who he is. She loves them both and would take Simon back tomorrow.'

'So, it was all for nothing,' Rowena said softly. 'Two people dead and all this distress . . .'

Cullen cleared his throat again and got back to business. 'Anyway, Mrs Burroughs wishes me to give Zander into your charge, Mrs Crawford, if you are willing to convey him directly back to Am Bealach. He appears to be taking matters very matter-of-factly but I think your company would be less stressful for him, at this point, than sending him in a police car.'

Rowena nodded graciously. She appeared strangely altered in manner, even in the way she stared down the DI, and her voice had lost the faint trace of Irish accent and taken on the muted authority of an MP's wife. 'I'll be delighted to take Zander home, Chief Inspector, but I'll travel with Mr Buchanan. I'm sure you can arrange for my car to be brought back to Am Bealach for me?'

Buchanan had barely followed this conversation. Coming at the end of a traumatic afternoon, the realisation of what Fizz had done, and of the repercussions, had Cullen had any proof against her, had almost plunged him into a state of shock. He blamed himself. He had known from day one that Fizz was dangerously self-willed and that she could seriously damage, not only his own reputation as a solicitor but the reputation of the firm. He had known that when she had talked his father into giving her a job, but he had allowed his father to overrule him. Now he had to clear up the pieces.

'Any further questions can be left till tomorrow,' he heard

DI Cullen saying. 'If you'll just come through to the desk, Mrs Crawford, I'll have Zander transferred to your custody.'

Rowena followed him out and, as the door shut behind them, Fizz looked up at Buchanan with a wary expression and murmured, 'Beam me up, Scottie!'

'Fizz – this is not funny—'

'Before you declare a fatwah on me—'

'No,' Buchanan said, through gritted teeth. 'I don't want to hear your excuses. You've gone too far this time. *Way* too far. Breaking the law is definitely not on.'

'*Moi*? I didn't do a thing – it was Rowena!'

'Fizz, if Rowena did the talking it was you who put the words in her mouth. Bad enough that you should put Rowena *and* yourself at risk of prosecution, you never gave a thought about the repercussions to myself or the firm. Can't you see what this could do to our reputation?'

She puckered her brow, laughing up at him. 'Don't mince words, Buchanan. Let me have it straight. You're a little mad at me, aren't you?'

Buchanan stood up. 'I'm sorry, Fizz, but I've had you up to here. I can't afford to be involved in breaking the law, and that's final. It's not as if you couldn't have had Simon grabbed at Orly airport. There's no excuse for that kind of behaviour and to put it bluntly, there's no place in a law office for a loose cannon. I'd feel a lot happier if you simply looked for another job.'

She stopped trying to laugh him out of it and stuck her hands in her pockets, staring at him expressionlessly. 'You're a thankless bastard, Buchanan, you know that? I could have been saving your life by stopping Simon when I did, and you're quibbling about a sodding phone call. You're pathetic.' She picked up her jacket and walked to the door, adding, 'I don't feel like driving all the way back to Am Bealach. I think I'll just go back to my flat.'

Buchanan took a step towards her, already wondering if his recent ordeal had made him overreact. 'I'll get you a taxi.'

'Don't bother. Christopher will see I get home all right.' The door shut behind her with a firm click that held more finality than if she had slammed it.

When Buchanan and Rowena passed through the vestibule, as they took Zander out to the car, she was standing talking to McLaren – *Christopher* McLaren, probably – and McLaren was smiling down at her in a way Buchanan didn't like at all.

It was a long, miserable journey back to Am Bealach, with Zander sleeping on the back seat and Rowena lost in her own apparently placid thoughts. Buchanan was in a burning rage all the way up the motorway. Angry at himself. Angry at Simon Burroughs. Angry at Christopher bloody McLaren. Angry at Fizz.

They were crawling up the long slope of Glen Ogle towards the Killin turnoff before Rowena roused herself from her reverie.

'What about Selena?' she said, breaking into Buchanan's turbulent train of thought. 'Are you really going to give her a home?'

'Yes,' he said, 'if nobody objects. I think I'd rather like to take her back to Edinburgh with me. I've never been much of a cat person, but I do like Selena, I don't know why.'

Rowena turned her head to look at him and smiled. 'You really don't, do you?'

Buchanan didn't answer, being engaged in overtaking a long vehicle driven by a driver who had evidently passed his test in a dodgem car, but the question started him thinking.

The recollection of Selena's comforting purr and the softness of her frail little body was strangely soothing. Buchanan found himself hoping she'd be there when he got back to the cottage. He knew that if she *had* got in he would find her sleeping in the half-packed suitcase he had left open on the bed and that she would probably have found the bar of chocolate on the coffee table, and that he would be sure to discover the half-eaten remains of a field mouse or a fledgling lying around somewhere, but that didn't matter. In fact, her insouciant self-indulgence was, for Buchanan, part of her charm. She made him laugh at her arrant cheek, she made him marvel at her self-sufficiency, and it took so very little to make her happy.

'Do you think she'll be happy?' he asked Rowena. 'I just hope she'll settle in all right.'

'She'll be fine,' Rowena said, and turned her head to study Buchanan's face with a look he couldn't quite fathom. 'Just give her time, Tam. She's never had a real home before, you know, so it may take a while before she abandons her wandering ways, but I don't think you need to worry about that. She'll keep coming back – you know you couldn't get rid of her if you tried! – and she'll understand eventually that her place is with you.'

Buchanan didn't answer but he found Rowena's remarks disproportionately cheering. As he slowed for the turn at Am Bealach crossroads he discovered he was whistling.

A Word After Dying

Ann Granger

Superintendent Alan Markby and his girlfriend, civil servant Meredith Mitchell, are in need of a holiday – and the Cotswold village of Parsloe St John seems the perfect choice. Their neighbour, retired journalist Wynne Carter, is as convivial as the village itself and, over a glass of blackberry wine, indulges in her latest obsession, Olivia Smeaton, a racy old lady whose life – and death – she is convinced are not all they seem.

Markby is more interested in buying Olivia's house than the circumstances of her vacating it, but Meredith is intrigued: by the old lady, the death of a cherished horse and a dusty junk shop run by a white witch. When another fatality – of a very grisly nature – is discovered, it seems her suspicion is justified. Clearly Olivia isn't the only enigma in Parsloe St John . . .

'Probably the best current example of a crime-writer who has taken the classic English village detective story and brought it up to date' *Birmingham Post*

'Classic tale . . . a good feel for understated humour, a nice ear for dialogue' *The Times*

'Deft plotting and elegant descriptive prose . . . a delicate comic touch and endearing eccentric characters' *Publishers Weekly*

0 7472 5187 8

HEADLINE

Skinner's Round

Quintin Jardine

By the blade, by water, by the fire, by lightning, shall the desecrators perish . . .

A four-day tournament involving the world's leading golfers is being staged to mark the opening of Witches' Hill, a new country club created on his East Lothian estate by the Marquis of Kinture. But on the Sunday afternoon preceding, one of Kinture's business partners is found dead in his private jacuzzi in the clubhouse – with his throat cut.

The next day an anonymous letter is received by the local newspaper, containing a fragment of a legendary witches' curse upon anyone who desecrates their place of worship.

For Assistant Chief Constable Robert Skinner, the key to the murder is surely to be found in the here and now rather than in East Lothian's grisly past as a notorious centre for witchcraft. But then a second murder occurs, this time by water, and soon Skinner is facing the most challenging case of his career.

0 7472 4141 4

HEADLINE

A selection of bestsellers from Headline

ASKING FOR TROUBLE	Ann Granger	£5.99 ☐
FAITHFUL UNTO DEATH	Caroline Graham	£5.99 ☐
THE WICKED WINTER	Kate Sedley	£5.99 ☐
RAINBOW'S END	Martha Grimes	£5.99 ☐
WEIGHED IN THE BALANCE	Anne Perry	£5.99 ☐
THE DEVIL'S HUNT	P C Doherty	£5.99 ☐
EVERY DEADLY SIN	D M Greenwood	£4.99 ☐
SKINNER'S MISSION	Quintin Jardine	£5.99 ☐
HONKY TONK KAT	Karen Kijewski	£5.99 ☐
THE QUICK AND THE DEAD	Alison Joseph	£5.99 ☐

Headline books are available at your local bookshop or newsagent. Alternatively, books can be ordered direct from the publisher. Just tick the titles you want and fill in the form below. Prices and availability subject to change without notice.

Buy four books from the selection above and get free postage and packaging and delivery within 48 hours. Just send a cheque or postal order made payable to Bookpoint Ltd to the value of the total cover price of the four books. Alternatively, if you wish to buy fewer than four books the following postage and packaging applies:

UK and BFPO £4.30 for one book; £6.30 for two books; £8.30 for three books.

Overseas and Eire: £4.80 for one book; £7.10 for 2 or 3 books (surface mail)

Please enclose a cheque or postal order made payable to *Bookpoint Limited*, and send to: Headline Publishing Ltd, 39 Milton Park, Abingdon, OXON OX14 4TD, UK.
Email Address: orders@bookpoint.co.uk

If you would prefer to pay by credit card, our call team would be delighted to take your order by telephone. Our direct line 01235 400 414 (lines open 9.00 am–6.00 pm Monday to Saturday 24 hour message answering service). Alternatively you can send a fax on 01235 400 454.

Name   ....

Address   ....

....

....

If you would prefer to pay by credit card, please complete:
Please debit my Visa/Access/Diner's Card/American Express (delete as applicable) card number:

Signature .... Expiry Date ....